ATTACK ON THE QUEEN

Other Titles by Richard P. Henrick

Crimson Tide
Silent Warriors
The Phoenix Odyssey
Counterforce
Flight of the Condor
When Duty Calls
St. John the Pursuer
Beneath the Silent Sea
Cry of the Deep
Under the Ice
Sea Devil
The Golden U-Boat
Sea of Death
Dive to Oblivion
Ecowar
Ice Wolf

ATTACK
ON THE
QUEEN

RICHARD P. HENRICK

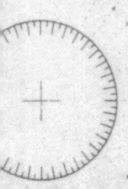AVON BOOKS ◆ NEW YORK

Starboard elevation, deck plans, and information on the *Queen Elizabeth 2* courtesy of Cunard; Schematic, history, and vital statistics of the USS *Polk* courtesy of the U.S. Navy; Schematic and vital statistics of the *HMS Talent* courtesy of the Royal Navy.

This is a work of fiction. Names, characters, places, and incidents either are the product of the author's imagination or are used fictitiously. Any resemblance to actual events, locales, organizations, or persons, living or dead, is entirely coincidental and beyond the intent of either the author or the publisher.

AVON BOOKS
A division of
The Hearst Corporation
1350 Avenue of the Americas
New York, New York 10019

Library of Congress Cataloging in Publication Data:
Henrick, Richard P.
    Attack on the Queen : a novel / by Richard P. Henrick.—1st ed.
        p.   cm.
    I. Title
PS3558.E49673A92 1998   97-42302
813'.54—dc21   CIP

First Avon Books Printing: April 1998

AVON TRADEMARK REG. U.S. PAT. OFF. AND IN OTHER COUNTRIES, MARCA REGISTRADA, HECHO EN U.S.A.

Printed in the U.S.A.

FIRST EDITION

QPM   10   9   8   7   6   5   4   3   2   1

Queen Elizabeth 2
Deck Plans

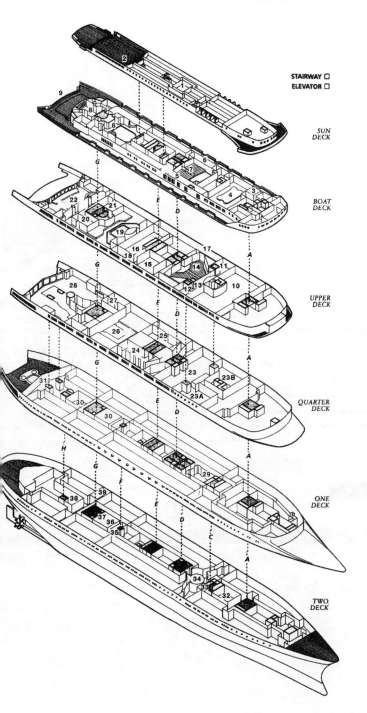

STAIRWAY □
ELEVATOR □

SUN DECK

BOAT DECK

UPPER DECK

QUARTER DECK

ONE DECK

TWO DECK

Key to Location and Facility

Sun Deck
1 Nursery
2 Sun Deck Bar

Boat Deck
3 Radio Room
4 Queen's Grill
5 Queen's Grill Lounge
6 Board Room
7 Theatre Balcony
8 Royal Promenade
9 Sports Facilities

Upper Deck
10 Mauretania Restaurant
11 Entrance to the Princess Grill
12 Entrance to the Britannia Grill
13 The Crystal Bar
14 Theatre
15 The Golden Lion Pub
16 Linn Hi-Fi Demonstration Room
17 The Casino
18 Photoshop
19 Grand Lounge
20 Tours & Travel Office
21 Social Director's Office
22 Yacht Club

Quarter Deck
23 Caronia Restaurant
23ᴀBritannia Grill
23ʙPrincess Grill
24 The Chart Room
25 Library & Bookshop
26 The Queen's Room
27 Club 2000
28 The Lido

One Deck
29 The Cunard Collection Shop
30 Hairdressing & Beauty Salon
31 The Pavilion

Two Deck
32 Epson Computer Learning Centre
33 Lost & Found Office
34 Midships Lobby
35 Bureau de Change
36 Purser's Office
37 Cashier's Office
38 Safe Deposit Centre
39 Doctor's Consulting Room

Three Deck
Synagogue
The Greenery
Launderette

Six Deck
Hospital
Steiner's Health Spa

Seven Deck
Health & Fitness Club

Queen Elizabeth 2
Starboard Elevation

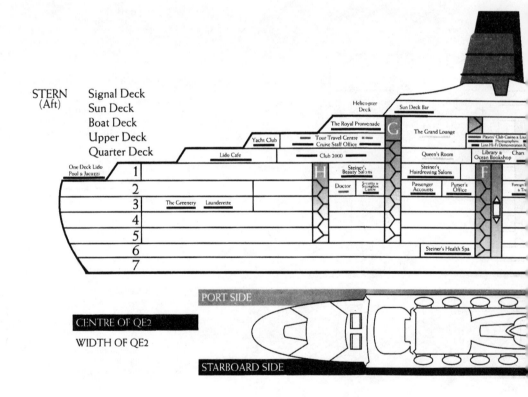

STERN
(Aft)

Signal Deck
Sun Deck
Boat Deck
Upper Deck
Quarter Deck

Helicopter Deck
Sun Deck Bar
The Royal Promenade
G
The Grand Lounge
Yacht Club
Tour Travel Centre
Cruise Staff Office
Players' Club Casino & Lou
Photographers
Linn Hi-Fi Demonstration R
Lido Cafe
Club 2000
Queen's Room
Library &
Ocean Bookshop
Chart
One Deck Lido
Pool & Jacuzzi
1
Steiner's
Beauty Salons
Steiner's
Hairdressing Salons
H
F
2
Doctor
Security &
Information
Centre
Passenger
Accounts
Purser's
Office
Foreign E
& Tra
3
The Greenery   Launderette
4
5
6
Steiner's Health Spa
7

CENTRE OF QE2

WIDTH OF QE2

PORT SIDE

STARBOARD SIDE

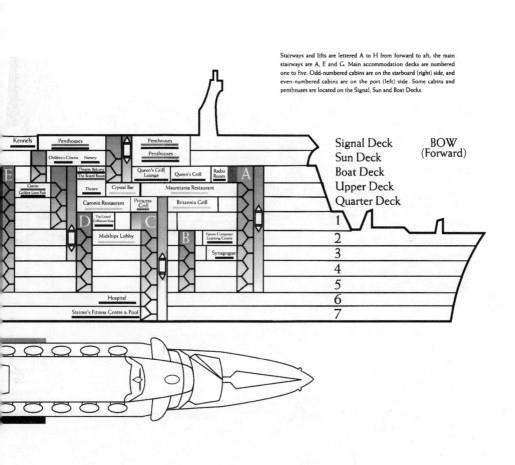

Stairways and lifts are lettered A to H from forward to aft; the main stairways are A, E and G. Main accommodation decks are numbered one to five. Odd-numbered cabins are on the starboard (right) side, and even-numbered cabins are on the port (left) side. Some cabins and penthouses are located on the Signal, Sun and Boat Decks.

Signal Deck   BOW
Sun Deck   (Forward)
Boat Deck
Upper Deck
Quarter Deck
1
2
3
4
5
6
7

Kennels
Penthouses
Penthouses
Penthouses
Children's Cinema   Nursery
Theatre Balcony
The Board Room
Queen's Grill Lounge
Queen's Grill
Radio Room
E
Casino
Golden Lion Pub
Theatre
Crystal Bar
Mauretania Restaurant
A
Caronia Restaurant
Princess Grill
Britannia Grill
The Cunard Collection Shop
D
C
Midships Lobby
B
Epson Computer Learning Centre
Synagogue
Hospital
Steiner's Fitness Centre & Pool

USS James K. Polk

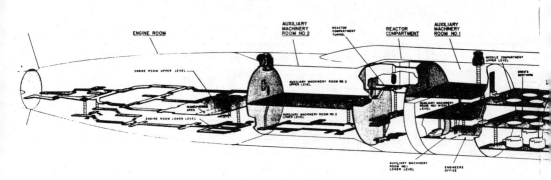

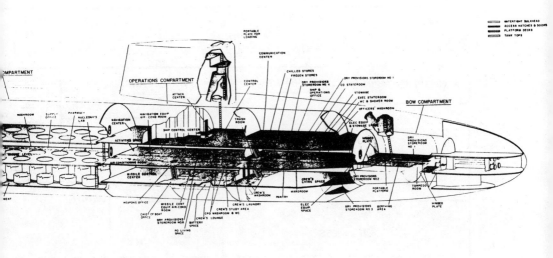

COMPARTMENT

OPERATIONS COMPARTMENT

BOW COMPARTMENT

INTERTIGHT BULKHEAD
ACCESS HATCHES & DOORS
PLATFORM DECKS
TANK TOPS

PORTABLE
PLATE FOR
LOADING

COMMUNICATION
CENTER

ATTACK
CENTER

CONTROL
CENTER

CHILLED STORES
FROZEN STORES

DRY PROVISIONS STOREROOM NO 1

DRY PROVISIONS
STOREROOM NO 4

CO STATEROOM

STOWAGE
EXEC STATEROOM
WC & SHOWER ROOM

OFFICERS' WASHROOM

SHIP &
OPERATIONS
OFFICE

NAVIGATION EQUIP
AIR COND ROOM

TRASH
ROOM

ELEC EQUIP
& STOWAGE

WASHROOM

SUPPLY
OFFICE

PHARMACY

NUCLEONIC'S
LAB

NAVIGATION
CENTER

SHIP CONTROL CENTER

HINGED
PLATE

DRY
PROVISIONS
STOREROOM
NO 1

ACTIVITIES

LEVEL

HINGED
PLATE

AIR CONDITIONING ROOM

MISSILE CONTROL
CENTER

CREW'S
LIVING SPACE

DRY PROVISIONS
STOREROOM NO 2

TORPEDO
ROOM

WARDROOM

PANTRY

PORTABLE
PLATFORM

BERTHING
AREA

MENT

WEAPONS OFFICE

CREW'S
WASHROOM

MISSILE CONT
EQUIP AIR-COND
ROOM

CREW'S LAUNDRY

CREW'S STUDY AREA

ELEC
EQUIP
SPACE

DRY PROVISIONS
STOREROOM NO 3

HINGED
PLATE

CHIEF OF BOAT
OFFICE

DRY PROVISIONS
STOREROOM NO 5

CPO WASHROOM & WC

BATTERY
SPACE

CREW'S LOUNGE

PO LIVING
SPACE

HMS Talent
Accommodation Space Layout

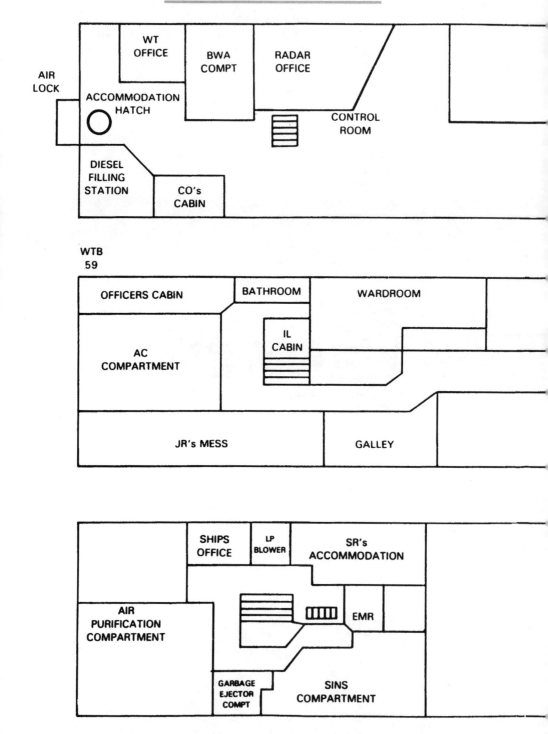

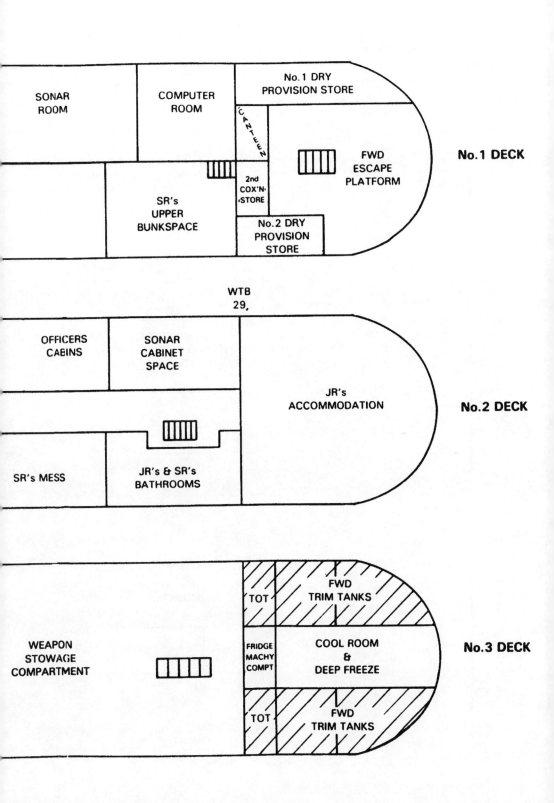

Stand up, all you who refuse to be slaves!
With our blood and flesh, a great wall will be built.
The Chinese nation now faces its greatest danger.
From each comes forth his loudest call:
Stand up! Stand up! Stand up!
Millions as one, braving the enemy's fire, march on.
Braving the enemy's fire;
March on! March on! March on!

—TIAN HAN, *The March of the Volunteers*

BOOK ONE

WAY OF THE WARRIOR

When the situation is serious, the guerrillas must move with the fluidity of water and the ease of the blowing wind. Their tactics must deceive, tempt, and confuse the enemy. They must lead the enemy to believe that they will attack him from the east and north, and they must then strike him from the west and south. They must strike, then rapidly disperse, covered by the black veil of night.

—Mao Tse-Tung
Yu Chi Chan (On Guerrilla Warfare)

"SIR, YOU ASKED TO BE AWAKENED AT SIXTEEN HUNDRED."

"Very well, comrade," answered a soft, scratchy voice from the stateroom's black void.

As the junior ensign who delivered this curt wake-up call stepped back from the doorway to resume his duties, Capt. Shen Fei's eyes popped open. A thin sliver of light emanated from the outside passageway and Shen glanced up at the softly glowing luminescent dials mounted in the partition at the foot of his bunk. A single practiced glance was all that was needed to determine that the *Lijiang* remained on a southwesterly course, at a depth of forty-eight meters, and a forward speed of twenty-three knots.

He was thankful that his two-hour nap had been sound, and he took a second more to continue the pleasant dream he had been enjoying. His lovely Mei-li had prepared a picnic on the banks of the River Li, the same tributary that his current command was named after. A native of nearby Guilin, Mei-li appeared in all her natural beauty, with the limestone hills of her birth, the perfect setting. It was a gorgeous midsummer afternoon, and after a delicious lunch of dumplings, they sat back to watch a passing fisherman work his cormorants. Then, completely out of the blue, Mei-li made the first amorous advance and an incredibly sensuous session of lovemaking followed. Unfortunately, it was just as this

3

act was about to be consummated that the ensign's voice called him to duty.

Shen Fei's heart was heavy with longing as he sat up groggily and swung his bare feet onto his cabin's linoleum deck. Dressed only in his skivvies, he lazily stretched his muscular arms overhead, while wondering how his dream would have ended if it had been allowed to extend to its natural conclusion.

He stood and switched on the stateroom's central light, knowing that such dreams were as close as he'd be able to get to his new bride for the next couple of months. They had only just begun this patrol, and summer would have turned to fall by the time they returned to Chinese soil.

His stomach's protests brought the forty-three-year-old naval officer back to present reality. He was ravenously hungry, having skipped lunch. After completing a hasty toilet routine, he quickly dressed himself in a well-worn pair of blue coveralls and headed for the wardroom.

Shen's comfortable, one-piece garment was known as a poopy suit. It had been given to him by the crew of the USS *Hyman G. Rickover*, an American, *Los Angeles*-class attack submarine. The official seal of this warship, complete with its COMMITTED TO EXCELLENCE logo, was embossed on a colorful patch that was sewn above his left breast pocket. For a Navy officer of the People's Liberation Army, the PLA, to wear such a uniform while on official duty was unheard of. Yet Shen was proud of this practical gift, and he'd never forget the events leading up to the memorable day he actually spent at sea aboard the American warship.

Shortly after graduating at the top of his class at the Dailan Naval Academy, Shen was invited to continue his postgraduate work at the United States Naval Academy at Annapolis, Maryland. This in itself was a great honor, and Shen readily accepted the once-in-a-lifetime opportunity.

The exchange program that allowed his unprecedented visit was brand new, and Shen did his best to be a worthy representative. His fluency in English enabled him to participate in an international forum, whose unclassified focus was naval engineering advances in the Third World.

In the weeks following the forum's conclusion, Shen was given his own dormitory room and free access to the Naval Academy's excellent library. Since his passion was history, he devoured book after book on America's long-standing naval tradition. The exploits of John Paul Jones ignited his imagination, and he spent many a long night discussing the great Revolutionary War hero with his fellow midshipmen.

The father of one of these students happened to be a senior officer in the United States Navy's Office of Public Information. With his invaluable assistance, Shen was invited to visit the Norfolk Naval base in Virginia, where the USS *Hyman G. Rickover* was waiting to take him on a day trip.

One of only a handful of Chinese officials ever allowed to embark on such a sophisticated warship, Shen would never forget the great hospitality that the *Rickover*'s officers and enlisted men graciously extended. Unable to tour the engineering, radio, or sonar spaces because of security limitations, Shen was most satisfied just to get a chance to know this crew of brave Americans, and the proud tradition they represented.

He returned to China an outspoken exponent of closer PRC/American relations. An audience with their new president allowed him to personally describe his enlightening experience aboard the *Rickover*. Li Chen listened intently to each detail, and left Shen with a promise to do his best to champion the cause of peaceful cooperation with the United States.

Now that Shen had become the youngest commanding officer in the PLA Navy's submarine fleet, new realities tempered his once youthful enthusiasm. Security concerns kept him from staying in close contact with his former friends in America. He had new responsibilities, the most important of which was guaranteeing China's sovereignty. Though the Cold War was over, new international battle lines had been drawn in the areas of trade and commerce. Foreign meddling in China's international workings couldn't be tolerated, and even though the United States might have had good intentions, this was an area of control that couldn't be compromised.

The tantalizing aroma of freshly prepared food led Shen down the cable-lined passageway to the nearby wardroom. The soft hum of the ventilation blowers and the muted drone of the nuclear reactor's coolant pump provided the background score for this short transit. These sounds, which disappeared from a submariner's conscious senses through constant exposure, unconsciously soothed Shen and crew. All is right, they reminded them.

An ensign, his white coveralls stained with grease, approached him from the aft hatch. The young sailor alertly bowed his head slightly, and stepped aside so that his captain could pass down the narrow walkway.

The PLA Navy had long ago abandoned the custom of saluting on a vessel as cramped as the *Lijiang*. The warship's eighty-five-man crew coexisted in a relatively informal, classless atmosphere, though the boat's fifteen officers did have separate quarters and their own wardroom. This rather luxurious wood-paneled compartment acted as both a place to eat meals and a meeting room for briefings, studying, or just relaxing.

As Shen approached the wardroom, he could hear the familiar soft strains of an erhu solo coming from the compartment's Japanese stereo. Seated at the far end of the rectangular table, enjoying this melodious music and engrossed in a platter filled with dumplings was Guan Yin, the boat's commissar. A balding, potbellied native of Shanghai, the *Lijiang*'s political officer never skipped a meal, often utilizing the wardroom as his unofficial office. Without missing a bite, the commissar nodded, while Shen took his customary place at the opposite end of the table.

"Good afternoon, comrade," greeted Shen cordially. "What magical dish has our esteemed cook managed to put together today?"

"You won't be disappointed, Captain," Guan Yin answered. "My own mother could take a lesson in cooking dumplings from Comrade Chi."

Almost on cue, a slightly built, bespectacled figure dressed in a spotlessly clean white uniform joined them. An effervescent smile graced the senior cook's smooth-shaven face as he placed a ceramic pot of steaming tea and an empty porcelain cup in front of the newly arrived officer.

"Do I surmise that someone here is hungry?" asked the personable cook with a wink. "And here I just went and prepared a wokful of enchanted shrimp."

"Ah, my very favorite!" exclaimed Shen. "Bring it on, comrade, as well as plenty of rice and some of those delicious-looking dumplings that the commissar is enjoying."

"My, you do have an appetite this afternoon, Captain," noted Chi, who turned and passed through the hatch leading to the adjoining galley.

Shen poured himself a cup of tea and listened as the background music built to a gradual crescendo. It was a haunting tune, evoking visions of home, and perfectly accompanied the cup of flavorful oolong that he thoughtfully sipped.

Noting Shen's apparent interest in the music, Guan Yin washed down his dumplings with a mouthful of tea and asked, "Have you ever visited Xihui Park in Wuxi, comrade?"

Shen shook his head no and the commissar continued. "Too bad. It's one of the most beautiful sites in all the motherland, especially its famous Erquan pool. In fact, it was this pool that inspired the great composer Hua Yanjun to compose this particular piece of music, aptly entitled, 'The Moon Mirrored in the Pool.' "

"This erhu solo has a sad quality to it," observed Shen, refilling his cup.

"What more would you expect from a master musician who spent all of his life poor, and a good part of it blind, as well?" added the commissar.

Shen sipped his tea and listened as the music faded. Another mournful folk song replaced it, this one dominated by an expertly played gaohu, a bowed string instrument much like the erhu.

The song made him think of Mei-li again. His bride had tried to play the gaohu once. Thankfully, only once. By her own admission, she was terrible at it. But she had succeeded in making the instrument a lasting reminder of her modesty and great passion for all aspects of life.

Shen exhaled a long, forlorn sigh as Chi Chiang emerged from the galley, tray in hand. Shen eagerly unwrapped his chopsticks and dug into a platter heaped with large shrimp, bamboo shoots, water chestnuts, diced peppers and onions, all topped with a garlic-flavored sweet-and-sour sauce and served on a thick bed of white rice.

"I'll be right back with your dumplings," promised the cook, who next addressed the commissar. "Anything more for you, sir?"

Guan Yin was watching Shen attack his meal, and he conveyed his response with a wave of his pudgy hand. With Chi's exit the commissar pushed away his now empty plate and picked up a nearby notebook and pen.

"I've been making a list of those officers and enlisted men who have missed two or more Komsomol meetings this week," said Guan. "Your name and that of Senior Chief Wang appear on this list most prominently."

This observation caused Shen to momentarily lower his chopsticks and reply in midbite. "I'm sorry to have disappointed you, Comrade Commissar, but both the senior chief and I have been extremely busy insuring the integrity of this vessel. Must I remind you that we've only just come out of a major refit?"

As if to underscore this comment, a loud electronic ring sounded. Shen reached under the table's lip, pulled out a red telephone handset and put it to his ear.

"Captain here," he said into the transmitter. After a brief pause to listen to his caller, Shen again addressed the handset, this time making sure to meet the commissar's inquisitive stare. "I understand, Chief. When you get a chance, I'd like to see the final readings. And please, pass on a 'job well done' to the maneuvering watch."

Shen hung up the receiver and took the time to fully devour a mouthful of shrimp before explaining the nature of this call. "That was Chief Wang with the latest rad count. The radiation spike we encountered last watch appears to have been an anomaly of some sort. And as for that Party disloyalty that you speak of—here it's the chief's second complete watch in a row and not a word of complaint from him."

"It's not Party disloyalty that I'm concerned with, Captain," returned the political officer, a light sheen of perspiration matting his furrowed forehead. "As senior leaders aboard the *Lijiang*, I'm depending upon your presence at my Komsomol meetings to set an example for the junior crew members."

Shen Fei returned to his food, while Guan Yin dared to add, "And one other area that I'm having problems with is your insistence on wearing that Yankee uniform."

Shen could hardly believe what he was hearing. He disgustedly lowered his chopsticks. "We've been through this before, comrade. The admiralty is aware of my desire to wear this poopy suit while on patrol, and I'll proudly do so until officially notified otherwise."

Guan made a brief note on his pad before replying. "I beg to differ with you, Captain. Admiral Liu's latest directive insists that the proper uniform code be strictly enforced while on naval patrol."

"You know as well as I that this directive isn't meant to be applied to submarine duty," Shen retorted. "The unique nature of our work-space allows us greater freedom of dress than our comrades in the surface fleet."

The commissar realized that it was a waste of breath to further argue this point. He completed yet another entry into his notebook before lightly muttering, "At the very least, your so-called poopy suit displays the patch of one of America's exploited minorities. The great Admiral Rickover was a contemporary of our own Admiral Liu. His birthright as a Jew was condemnation to second-class-rank status, to the waning days of his long U.S. Navy career."

Not willing to give this comment the benefit of a reply, Shen directed his attention back to his meal. He polished off the last of the shrimp, then went to work on the newly arrived dumplings. He tried his best to enjoy them, but found his enraged thoughts focused elsewhere.

How dare the fat political officer question the true degree of Shen's loyalty to the Party! If he weren't one of the faithful, why else would he dedicate the best years of his life protecting the mother-land's maritime interests? To be given command of the PLA Navy's most sophisticated nuclear-powered attack submarine was an honor in itself. Surely it spoke well of the immense trust his superiors placed in him. For this ignorant slob of a man to even hint at any dogmatic impropriety on Shen's part was the ultimate insult, and he winced at the thought of having to be cooped up with such a pomp-ous fool for the rest of their patrol.

As the background music switched to a rousing folk melody enti-tled "Dance of the Yao People," Shen fought to control his rising emotions. The mere idea of having an officer like Guan Yin aboard the *Lijiang* was an anachronism. The rank of commissar belonged to a past decade, when Communism was still in the process of being introduced into the PRC. In the early days of their republic, the political officer was an instrumental part of every military unit. Their vital responsibilities in those exciting days were to teach Socialist principles and policies, and insure Party loyalty. Aboard submarines, they were in charge of chairing the triweekly Komsomol meetings, and helping the senior officers with morale.

But did the commissar have a place in today's navy? Shen Fei thought not, equating such individuals as being totally useless to the operation of the ship. They took up vital living space, and consumed vast quantities of limited foodstuffs. Considerably vast, in Guan's case. Much like the United States Navy, they'd be much better off giving responsibility for the crew's esprit de corps to the executive officer, and retiring the rank of commissar to the realms of history.

The arrival of a junior orderly broke Shen's bitter chain of thought. This newcomer to the *Lijiang* was little more than a skinny teenager. It was obvious that he was nervous as he approached Shen, stood ramrod straight, and loudly cleared his dry throat before speaking.

"Sir, I have a message for you from Lieutenant Commander Deng."

Shen could hear the strained tension in the young sailor's voice. He remembered well his own first visit to the officers' wardroom two decades ago, and tried his best to ease the youngster's anxieties. "At ease, sailor," ordered Shen in his best fatherly tone. "Now, what's this message all about?"

The young man eagerly replied, "Sir, I've been instructed to inform you that we've penetrated the Spratly Island exclusion zone, and that we're proceeding to patrol zone Alpha."

Shen was expecting this and he responded accordingly. "Very well, sailor. Inform the XO that I'll be joining him in the control room as soon as I'm finished here."

"Yes, sir," returned the youngster with a smart nod.

Before he could make good his exit, Shen interceded. "By the way, lad, what's your name and where are you from? I don't believe I've seen you aboard the *Lijiang* previously."

The orderly was surprised at his captain's interest and the tone of his voice relaxed slightly. "I'm Seaman Gui Yongjing, and my hometown is Shaoshan in Hunan Province."

"Shaoshan, you say?" interrupted the sub's commissar. "What an honor it is for you to have been born in our beloved Chairman's hometown, Seaman Gui. Yet I see from my notes that you've failed to attend the last two Komsomol meetings. Surely you realize that you bring disgrace on your family name by missing these all-important sessions."

"I'm sorry, sir," stuttered the embarrassed enlisted man. "This is my first submarine assignment, and it's taking me time to get settled."

"Excuses mean nothing when it comes to one's political enlightenment, comrade," warned Guan Yin.

Shen sensed the lad's discomfort and he quickly chimed in. "Seaman Gui, if you'd be so good as to deliver my message to the XO."

"At once, sir," said the sailor, who looked greatly relieved as he pivoted smartly and exited.

Shen finished the last of his dumplings, and stood up to leave the compartment himself. Yet before he made good his departure, the commissar left him with one last parting shot.

"That young sailor is a perfect example of the *bad* example that you're setting, comrade. How can we expect to get him to attend my Komsomol meetings, if his own captain pays them no heed?"

Shen ignored this comment, ducked out into the adjoining passageway, and proceeded up the amidships stairwell to the deck above. This put him immediately outside the sub's control room. He took a step inside the darkened compartment, and halted momentarily to allow his eyes time to adjust. Lit in red to protect the men's night-vision, the control room was the heart of the *Lijiang*. It was here, inside a space the size of a small apartment's living room, that the sub was driven, its depth controlled, course navigated, and weapons fired.

As his eyes adjusted to the red-tinted blackness, Shen made a brief stop at the helm. Here Senior Chief Wang was perched between the two seated planesmen, their collective glances riveted on the instruments mounted in the bulkhead before them. A hasty glance at these instruments showed Shen that they were now at a depth of fifty-three meters, traveling on a due-southerly course, at a speed of twenty-one knots. The senior chief was in the process of giving the outboard helmsman a lesson in properly catching the bubble. More of an art than a science, the mastering of this difficult technique was instrumental in keeping the sub at its ordered depth.

Shen waited for Wang to conclude his current remarks before interrupting. "Senior Chief, what in the world are you still doing on watch? Don't you ever rest?"

"To tell you the truth, I'm not really tired, Captain. Besides, rest is for the weak," returned the grinning veteran.

Not about to argue otherwise, Shen could only shrug and continue on to his central command position on the periscope pedestal. The boat's twin scopes were situated here, and between them the

Lijiang's officer of the deck kept his watch station. Their current OOD was Lt. Wu Han, their weapons officer. A serious, often glum Beijing native and fellow graduate of the Dailan Naval Academy, Lieutenant Wu greeted Shen with a curt nod.

"We've entered the exclusion zone, sir," he reported matter-of-factly.

"So I understand," said Shen, who examined the sonar repeaters mounted into the cable-lined ceiling in front of them. A slight flutter on the broadband passive monitor caught his attention, and Shen reached overhead for the nearest intercom handset.

"Sonar, control," he spoke into the transmitter. "What are our environmentals?"

"Control, sonar," answered a familiar, high-pitched voice over the intercom. "Isothermal conditions are constant to three hundred meters, where the primary layer is located. We have flat calm conditions prevailing topside, with a pod of porpoises singing up a storm on bearing one-two-zero."

Shen realized that these porpoises were most likely responsible for the sonar flutter he had spotted, and as he hung up the handset, a deep, bass voice broke from the aft portion of the compartment.

"Captain, we've got the expanded navigation chart of patrol zone Alpha ready."

Shen turned and met the glance of his executive officer, Lt. Comdr. Deng Biao. The XO had apparently just arrived in the control room himself, and stood beside the table holding the navigation plotting board.

The plot was located aft of the periscopes. This fully automated table was recently tied into the vessel's new Navstar global positioning system. The GPS produced a three-dimensional navigational fix accurate to within an incredible three meters. Shen joined his XO beside the plot as their navigator was busy placing a piece of tracing paper over the chart displaying their current patrol quadrant.

"Will we be proceeding to Point Luck as planned, sir?" asked the XO.

Although this was Shen's second patrol with Lieutenant Commander Deng, he had yet to break the ice with his second in command, whom he found to be a competent officer, if somewhat cold and impersonal.

"What do you think, XO?" queried Shen, in an effort to build a dialogue with the tall, dark-eyed Hangzhou native.

Deng thought a moment before answering. "Though we can always initiate a random search, I think that we should give Point Luck a try. The Filipinos are a stubborn lot, who never seem to learn a lesson the first time around."

"Then Point Luck it is," agreed Shen. "Draw up the most efficient course to the site of our previous intercept, and make certain to give those uncharted shoals that we chanced upon on the western edge of the quadrant a wide berth."

"Aye, aye, sir." The XO wasted no time in taking up a pencil and ruler to initiate this order.

Shen watched as their navigator assisted the XO with this plot. Two months before, during their previous patrol, the *Lijiang* had chanced upon more than a half-dozen Philippine fishing trawlers working the restricted Spratly waters. They were clearly trespassing inside the PRC's self-declared exclusion zone. When an armed patrol vessel flying the Philippine flag was located in their midst, the matter took on a new degree of seriousness.

It proved to be Adm. Liu Huang-tzu who personally notified the *Lijiang* to surface and directly challenge the trespassers. Shen did as ordered, and a tense, twenty-four-hour standoff ensued.

The crisis further intensified when the Philippine patrol vessel threatened to launch an antisubmarine rocket at the *Lijiang*. International negotiations on the highest levels eventually succeeded in defusing this serious situation that found the *Lijiang* only a scant sixty seconds away from launching a torpedo salvo intended to eliminate the Philippine threat. This was as close to actual combat as Shen had ever come before. And when the trespassers eventually weighed anchor and headed for home, the crew of the *Lijiang* celebrated as if a real war had been won.

China used this incident to show the world how serious they were about defending their territorial claim to the Spratlys. It also caught the attention of Vietnam, Brunei and Malaysia, the other nations, who along with the Philippines, claimed the Spratly Islands for themselves.

The course they finally agreed upon took the *Lijiang* to the mouth of a two-and-a-half-kilometer-wide channel, separating two small, uninhabited islands. A shallow reef lined the western edge of this channel, and to insure that they were properly positioned, Shen ordered the sub to periscope depth.

At a depth of twenty meters, the *Lijiang*'s search periscope broke the water's surface. From the hushed control room, Shen anxiously peered out the eyepiece. A ghostly, fog-shrouded sky veiled a perfectly calm sea. In all directions, the milky twilight prevailed, and Shen was content to order the quartermaster to raise the GPS mast in order to obtain the most accurate fix.

The satellite data placed the submarine exactly in the center of the channel, well away from the projecting reef. Satisfied with the accuracy of this data, Shen ordered maneuvering to proceed at a bare single knot of forward speed. Frequent fathometer readings guaranteed that there was plenty of water beneath their hull, and Shen returned to the periscope for yet another look.

This time, the fog seemed to be lifting slightly. He calculated that the rising sun would soon cause it to dissipate completely. Shen was in the midst of a slow visual sweep of the feared western horizon, when an excited, high-pitched voice broke from the intercom.

"Control, sonar, I've got a contact! Bearing one-nine-five, at a relative rough range of nine thousand meters."

The voice belonged to Chief Tzu, the *Lijiang*'s senior sonar operator. The chief was an expert at his arcane craft, and Shen wasted no time querying him via the intercom.

"Chief, this is the Captain. What have you got?"

"Captain," returned the breathless senior sonar technician. "I'm picking up faint screw sounds in the vicinity of Point Luck."

Shen briefly caught his XO's worried glance before readdressing the intercom. "Could it be our old friends, the Filipinos?"

"It's possible, sir," replied the sonar technician. "But at this range, it's impossible to say for certain."

Shen lowered the handset and addressed Senior Chief Wang, who remained seated behind the helm. "Inform maneuvering to increase our forward speed to three knots."

"Three knots it is, Captain," replied Wang, who leaned forward and manipulated a centrally located console that would relay this request to engineering.

All eyes went to the forward bulkhead's digital knot counter. Slowly it rose two numerals, and Senior Chief Wang called out, "Three knots, Captain."

Once more, Shen's complete attention returned to the scope's eyepiece. He scanned the veiled southwestern horizon, silently willing the fog to thin more quickly.

"Conn, sonar. I've got additional screw sounds, Captain!" Tzu cried over the intercom. "They appear to be coming from various small surface vessels situated in the waters almost directly above us!"

Shen initiated a rapid, 360-degree scan of the surrounding seas, before ordering the periscope to be retracted into its protective well. An unwanted collision could take them to the bottom just as surely as an enemy torpedo could.

"All stop!" Shen ordered.

"All stop," repeated the senior chief.

The *Lijiang* shuddered slightly as the knot indictor dropped to zero. A tense three minutes passed, as sonar began a thorough sweep of the waters above them.

As the control-room crew anxiously awaited the results of this scan, the commissar joined them. Guan Yin positioned himself to the immediate right of the periscope pedestal, beside the fire-control console. From his position on the pedestal next to the captain, the XO acknowledged the political officer's arrival with the barest of nods. No sooner was this gesture reciprocated, than the report they had been awaiting sounded from the overhead intercom speakers.

"Conn, sonar. The overhead contacts are fading. I'm picking up increased screw sounds though, on bearing one-eight-eight, relative rough range down to seven thousand meters, and smack in the middle of Point Luck. From the racket it's making, it could be a Philippine patrol boat!"

Shen digested this information, and instead of conferring with his XO, he turned to the vessel's senior enlisted man. "Chief Wang, do you think we could sneak up on them?"

With more hours spent beneath the seas than any other sailor on board the *Lijiang,* Wang answered confidently. "I don't see why not, Captain. With our new silencing equipment, they'll never tag us."

Shen looked up to the overhead sonar repeater and briefly studied the series of solid white lines that indicated the presence of unknown contacts topside. Also known as a waterfall display, the top of the repeater showed the bearing of the detected frequency, while the vertical lines indicated the particular nature of this frequency over an extended period of time.

Anxious to solve this mystery and identify the largest of these contacts, Shen decided to take a risk and continue their approach. "All ahead slow. Make turns for three knots."

"Three knots it is, Captain," said Wang, as he leaned forward to relay this order to maneuvering.

Shen felt a tightening in the pit of his stomach as his eyes focused on the speed indicator. He planned to wait until they were underway once again before readdressing the periscope. Surely by then the fog would have lifted enough to allow him a visual sighting.

Mentally urging the digital knot indicator forward, Shen was somewhat surprised when a full sixty seconds passed, and the indicator had failed to move off zero. The senior chief also recognized this puzzling fact. It was Wang who spotted the rapidly increasing temperature reading from the instruments monitoring the sub's propeller bearings.

"We've got a main shaft temperature overload!" he warned.

"All stop!" Shen ordered.

"All stop," repeated Wang.

As Shen's directive was carried out, the temperature reading of the suspect gauge slowed its rise, then stopped perilously close to the warning zone.

"What the hell is going on back there?" the captain asked.

"It appears that the shaft was properly answering to three knots, yet the prop was failing to respond," observed Wang.

The senior chief was relieved that the temperature reading was holding constant, but an urgent intercom page from engineering set him to rubbing his forehead. He hung up the handset and turned to face the captain.

"Sir, the engineering officer reports that the shaft bearings came dangerously close to a meltdown. As long as the temperature remains constant, though, he feels that the damages incurred will be minimal."

"And the cause of this unusual problem?" Shen asked.

"As strange as it may sound, it looks like our prop has been somehow snagged," revealed Wang.

"A fishing net no doubt, or some other floating debris," offered the commissar from his position at the weapons console.

"Surely such a net could be responsible for entangling our propeller," added the XO. "Those overhead contacts that we encountered were most likely fishing vessels."

"With the *Lijiang* being the catch of the day!" Guan Yin said with a chuckle.

The joke generated a soft, lighthearted murmur from the controlroom crew, and Shen retook the initiative. "If our prop has indeed been ensnared, the only way to repair it is to go topside. Chief Wang, why don't we head for engineering to see the extent of the damages. If it is a snag, we'll have to surface to clear it. Per standard operating procedure, both the senior chief and I will lead the repair party. XO, I want you to open up the small arms locker. We'll be a sitting duck and I'd rather we not be completely defenseless up there."

It took another forty-five minutes to determine that something had indeed entangled their prop. Before giving the order to blow ballast and ascend to the surface, Shen made certain that sonar showed no threatening surface traffic in the area. Once this was determined to be the case, just enough ballast was released to poke their periscopes out of the water. Both the captain and the XO were relieved to find that most of the fog had lifted at last, and a full golden morning had arrived to this portion of the South China Sea.

With no contacts in sight, Shen ordered the sub to the surface. To a roiling blast of ballast, the now lightened submarine headed upward, where flat calm conditions continued to prevail.

Senior Chief Wang led the way up the *Lijiang*'s main trunk. Two sentries armed with AK-47s were at his heels, followed closely by Captain Shen and six enlisted men. Included in this latter group was Seaman Gui, who carried several pairs of heavy wire cutters.

To the submariner, the surface of the sea was an alien environment. Shen felt noticeably uneasy as he climbed onto the *Lijiang*'s deck. A soft gust of warm, westerly wind hit him full in the face, and as he anxiously scanned the horizon with his binoculars, the ripe fragrance of the ocean filled his nostrils.

Swirling tendrils of fog still veiled the eastern horizon, and Shen supposed that if a surface threat were close by, then that would be the direction of its approach. Several stories above the deck, in the boat's towering sail, a group of figures were visible, sweeping the horizon with their own binoculars. Shen recognized the tallest of these as his XO, while the stocky, bald-headed officer at his side was the boat's commissar. The sub's radar was operational behind them; it would spot any threat long before their binoculars.

"Will you just look at this mess!" exclaimed Chief Wang from the boat's after fantail.

Shen joined the other members of the repair party in front of the *Lijiang's* rudder. A tangled mass of wet netting completely covered the rudder, extending well into the depths beneath it.

"So now we know what's responsible for snagging our prop," observed Shen. "This section of net must have been immense. How in the world are we ever going to untangle ourselves without outside assistance?"

Chief Wang took one of the wire cutters from Seaman Gui and began the backbreaking chore of cutting them free. "It's nothing that we can't accomplish on our own, Captain," said Wang as he cut loose a large section of net and tossed it into the sea. "Come on, men," he added to the others, "let's get on with it!"

The sailors were soon busy with this task. This left Shen free to supervise, and walk the deck along with the two sentries.

Surprisingly enough, even with the sun's continued ascent, the fog was returning, and quickly. A virtual blanket of wet vapor soon enveloped them, and Shen, from an amidships position beside the sail, could barely see his men at work on the after section.

The *Lijiang* was dangerously exposed now. An enemy shell or an innocent collision with another vessel could prove equally fatal. Circumspection warned him to sound the boat's powerful foghorn. But the ever present threat of the Philippine patrol boat kept him from doing so.

An hour passed, and Shen, impatient, returned to the boat's after end for yet another update. He was relieved to find the entire rudder clear of netting. Chief Wang was busy supervising the progress of four of his enlisted men, who were now in the water supported by foam floats, in the process of removing the remaining net from the propeller.

"Radar contact, Captain!" the deep voice of the XO broke in from the top of the sail.

Shen's stomach tightened with this dreaded warning, and he sprinted to the base of the sail where he joined his sentries.

"It appears to be a single sailing vessel, approaching from the east," added the XO from above. "Sonar reports no trace of an engine signature."

This was certainly encouraging news. Yet Shen still didn't like their exposed position, and he cupped his hands and shouted up a single order.

"XO, sound a warning blast on the boat's whistle!"

Ten seconds later, a deep, resonant tone emanated from the direction of the *Lijiang's* bridge. The gathering fog seemed to swallow this blast instantly, though its reverberation could still be felt in Shen's nervous gut.

Despite the fog, Shen raised his binoculars and intently scanned the waters due east of the sub. Like a ghost materializing out of another dimension, the blunted bow of a ship broke from the veil, a mere one-hundred-meters distant. It was a relatively small vessel, shaped much like one of the native junks that worked the Yangtze. Shen doubted that the blunt hull of this junk could do them much damage, but he was nevertheless relieved when the vessel responded to the *Lijiang* with a meager blast from its own foghorn.

"Ready those rifles," Shen warned the sentries, "just in case we've stumbled upon some Philippine pirates."

The captain unbuckled the safety strap of his own holstered weapon, a .45 caliber Colt pistol his friends in the U.S. Navy had presented him with. He looked on as a figure appeared at the junk's bow.

"Greetings, comrades!" cried this individual in perfect Mandarin. "I do hope that's a PLA Navy warship."

Ever cautious, Shen ordered, "Please identify yourself."

"My name is Lo Jung, and this poor fishing junk is the *Moonfire,* based out of Hainan. May I have the honor of knowing your identity, comrades?"

The junk was less than fifty meters distant now, and Shen could readily see the grizzled face of the supposed fisherman. He looked innocent enough, and Shen decided that it would do no harm to reveal their identity.

"I'm Captain Shen Fei, commander of the PLA Navy submarine, *Lijiang.*"

"Thank the stars that the fates led us to you on this tragic morning," continued the fisherman. "You see, not only are our holds still empty of fish, but my dear wife, who serves as our cook, became deathly ill after last night's meal. I realize it's asking a great deal, but could your medical officer please have a look at her? She's burning up with fever, and I fear that she won't last through the day."

Shen hesitated to respond to this request. But from the top of the sail, the commissar egged him on.

"I certainly don't see how a quick look would hurt, Captain. After all, we don't appear to be going anywhere at the moment, and our sworn duty is to serve the motherland and all her citizens."

A bit surprised by the political officer's degree of compassion, Shen readdressed the fisherman. "Go ahead and bring your vessel alongside, comrade. But be forewarned: I can't allow her below deck for fear of infecting the rest of my crew."

"Bless you, Captain!" exclaimed the relieved fisherman.

While the sub's medical officer was sent for, Shen helped the junk make its approach. A narrow, wooden gangplank was extended from the junk's amidships gunwales, with the two sentries helping to attach it to one of the *Lijiang*'s deck cleats.

Their patient soon appeared. A shawl completely enveloping her head and body, she shakily made her way up the gangplank, with the assistance of her husband and another fisherman. Shen helped her make the final step, before turning to see what was keeping the doctor.

In the corner of his eye he saw the woman suddenly move, her shawl parting to reveal the lean, muscular figure of a young man dressed in a black tunic.

Shen's hand reached for his pistol. However, before he could feel its smooth, plastic grip against his palm, he felt himself filled by a pain so excruciating that it seemed to stretch time; the blow landing but not retreating. Shen didn't perceive the eternal darkness that followed.

From the *Lijiang*'s sail, the sub's XO and the commissar watched as the single, expertly delivered karate blow snapped the captain's neck and sent him flopping to the deck like a fish netted, dumped, and forgotten. Their faces betrayed neither fear nor apprehension. As the fog continued to wrap the deck with swirling tendrils of thick mist, they saw the three figures from the junk proceed to disarm and kill the two surprised sentries with a few choice blows.

The assault, by the XO's count, took twenty seconds. Acceptable, he decided. With the first phase completed, he watched as the attackers made for the sub's after end. As design and luck would have it, Chief Wang wasn't yet aware of his captain's fate. His crew had cut the last piece of netting from the prop, and his attention was focused on helping them out of the water.

The commissar stood close at the XO's side. He took particular delight in watching the attackers cut down this group of sailors. Chief Wang was the last to fall to their blows, and Guan mentally crossed off the list in his notebook the last of the *Lijiang*'s political heretics.

Guan looked back at the gangplank, where a tall, distinguished figure dressed in the formal white uniform of a senior PLA Navy officer calmly left the junk and boarded the *Lijiang*. In spite of the fog, the commissar could see the jagged scar that lined the entire left side of this individual's ruggedly handsome face.

"Captain Lee," the commissar called out. "Welcome aboard the *Lijiang*, sir."

The individual to whom this salutation was directed peered up to the sail and forcefully replied. "This warship has seen enough daylight! Prepare to get underway, as we further deceive our enemy by uproaring in the east, before striking in the west!"

2

THE DAY STARTED WITH A LONG BIKE RIDE, ALL BECAUSE THE SHOWERS predicted to ruin yet another Labor Day in the nation's capital never materialized. Thomas Kellogg allowed himself the rare treat of staying in bed until 8:00 A.M. Work had already caused him to miss celebrating the Fourth of July and Memorial Day that year. Yet even with this justification, he still felt guilty as he sprawled on his king-size mattress, listening to his clock radio.

NPR News revealed that an American national holiday meant absolutely nothing to the embattled peoples of Israel, Korea or Pakistan, where bloody uprisings continued to be headline stories. One grim casualty report after the other had a gradual, numbing effect on Thomas, and he only snapped fully awake with the feature on the G–7 summit.

The comprehensive report gave a behind-the-scenes look at the summit that was to take place later in the week. What made this annual meeting of the Group of Seven nations so unusual was that it was to include both the Russian president and, for the very first time, the new president of the People's Republic of China. And of course, there was this summit's unprecedented venue. It would be taking place totally at sea, during a four-and-a-half-day crossing of the Atlantic from New York to Southampton, aboard the last of the great ocean liners, the *Queen Elizabeth 2.*

As a special agent in the explosives-technology branch of the Bureau of Alcohol, Tobacco and Firearms, Thomas knew all about this summit. He had been working on its security plan for the last two months. Yet it somehow became very real to him, after hearing a newscast discussing it.

Ever thankful that the story didn't delve into the summit's unique security concerns, and with the announcement of the local weather forecast, Thomas found his thoughts abruptly shifting from work. The summer showers that had soaked the Washington, D.C., metro area for the past two days mercifully were moving northward earlier than expected. Labor Day wouldn't be a washout after all!

With this excellent news, Thomas sat up, grabbed the telephone, and speed-dialed Brittany Cooper's home. His spur-of-the-moment call caught her already enjoying the second cup of coffee of the day. Yes, she was aware that a sunny day was forecast. And yes, she was still very much interested in going riding before heading to his brother's house for a barbeque.

Less than an hour later, he was pulling his dark green Ford Explorer up to her Georgetown town house. As Thomas unloaded his mountain bike from its exterior rack, Brittany emerged from her garage, pushing her ten-speed and looking incredibly fresh and ready to meet the day head on. Her spandex biker shorts emphasized her long brown legs, while a tight, yellow jersey perfectly highlighted her ample bust.

Weatherwise, it was turning out to be a spectacular morning for a ride. The storm front that had passed in the night took with it the stifling humidity and ninety-degree temperatures of a typical D.C. summer. In its place was a brilliant blue sky and a very comfortable midseventies temperature.

After a warm greeting they set off for a nearby bike path, and followed it over the Potomac, then south toward Mount Vernon. Because it was still relatively early, they encountered a minimum of traffic, and it was easy riding through National Airport and on into Alexandria. Since Thomas hadn't taken time for breakfast, they briefly stopped at an outdoor cafe near the Torpedo Factory Mall, then, fortified, they sprinted through the lush swamps and rolling foothills bordering the western banks of the Potomac.

They arrived at Mount Vernon National Park just as the first tourist bus of the day was pulling into the spacious lot. Quickly locking up their bikes, they were able to make it through the park's turnstile well before the curious hordes exited their bus. This gave them a good quarter of an hour to explore the beautiful, history-filled grounds of George Washington's estate, before the inevitable holiday crowds arrived to spoil the view.

They hadn't spoken much that morning, but Thomas discovered this didn't make him uncomfortable, as it might have had he been with someone else. As they crossed the estate's wide lawn, he realized he enjoyed just being quiet with Brittany.

The ride back to Alexandria was equally uneventful and no less enjoyable. The sun was well overhead by the time they reached King Street. They left the bike path there and turned inland, away from the Potomac. Another seven blocks took them to the quiet, cobblestone lane where his brother's home was located. Vince and his wife Kelly had graciously invited them to stop by for a barbeque. And since they were the two who were initially responsible for getting Thomas and Brittany together barely a month before, they weren't about to disappoint them.

Vince was eight years older than Thomas, and had made a career in law enforcement. He was currently working as a special agent for the U.S. Secret Service, assigned to the White House presidential security detail. It was here that Vince first met Brittany, who was the junior U.S. Naval attaché to the President.

A little less than two months earlier, Vince had introduced Brittany to his wife at the White House reception. Kelly liked her instantly, and upon learning that Brittany was single, immediately thought of fixing her up with her brother-in-law.

It took a full week for Thomas to get up the nerve to call her. They made a date for coffee, and when they finally met, Thomas realized he owed his sister-in-law a special thank-you. Brittany was one of the most naturally beautiful women he had ever laid eyes on, with long, curly black hair, exquisitely formed facial features, and dark, mesmerizing eyes. She had a fantastic mind as well, displaying a sharp wit and a caustic sense of humor. Thomas knew he was hooked from the very start.

For the past month, they had spent practically every spare moment together. Both were on the rebound from long-term relationships that had soured, and decided that it was vitally important to first build a strong friendship before getting romantically involved.

This was a refreshing change of pace for Thomas, whose past relationships were primarily physical.

Her love of bicycling was another plus, and now their first ride together showed that neither one would hold the other back. Instead she enjoyed challenging him, and he enjoyed the challenge. Thomas had ridden hard enough to get his endorphins pumping—he could feel an alien tightness forming in the back of his legs as they pulled into Vince's driveway.

Together, they locked their bikes and ambled up the narrow, brick walkway, whose sides were lined with full beds of blue and yellow pansies. The front door was painted a glossy, bright red. Beside it, a brass plaque was mounted in the brick wall. It indicated that this brownstone was registered as a historic landmark, having been originally built in 1778.

After a brief round of greetings, Kelly and Brittany went to the kitchen to prepare the food, while Thomas and Vince were tasked with the all-important job of getting the outdoor grill prepped. Nine-year-old Joshua Kellogg had yet to get out of the small in-ground pool Vince had installed that year. As his cherished summer was about to come to an end with the resumption of the next day's classes, he was not about to waste his last vacation day and engrossed himself in the summer's two current favorite toys—a remote-control submarine and a slingshot-borne parachutist.

Thomas had given his only nephew this submarine for his recent birthday, and looked on as Josh demonstrated its many features. Four padded, wrought-iron rockers had been set up beside the pool. The grill was close by. Thomas was content to sit in his rocker with a frosty lemonade in hand, listening to his nephew extol the sub's amazing capabilities, and watching Vince double-check the condition of the red-hot charcoals.

"A fire's not ready for cooking until those coals are pure white," Vince said. He took his outdoor cooking most seriously. "That was another thing Pop was always harping on. Like he always used to say, good grilling starts with the fire."

"Uncle Thomas!" cried Joshua from the pool's shallow end. "I can get my submarine to travel underwater to the deep end, then get it to return right between my legs."

"Betcha a quarter you can't," dared Thomas.

"A dollar and you're on," Joshua answered.

Thomas agreed with a thumbs-up. As Josh manipulated the battery-powered controls to initiate this intricate underwater maneuver, Vince flattened out the smoking gray charcoal briquets with a pair of tongs, then sat down beside his brother. He took an appreciative sip of his longneck Rolling Rock, then peered up into a clear, blue sky.

"I tell you, little brother, it doesn't get much better than this."

Thomas nodded affirmatively. "You won't be getting any arguments from me."

A low-flying 727 that had just taken off from National Airport screamed overhead. Thomas waited for the throaty roar of the plane's engines to fade before adding, "I wonder what it's going to be like three days from now?"

Vince looked at his watch and grunted. "Let's see: If we're able to keep on schedule, three days from now, we should be somewhere in the mid-Atlantic, decked out in our tuxedos and getting ready for another calorie-rich, five-star gourmet dinner aboard the QE2."

"This morning on NPR, I heard a feature story on the summit," revealed Thomas. "They made it a point to really emphasize President Li's difficult decision to accept the G-7's invitation."

"That guy sure has guts," observed Vince. "The buzz at the White House is optimistic as all get-out. Just think of it, the People's Republic of China, the most populous nation on earth, finally taking its rightful place at the table."

"Dad!" interrupted Joshua from the pool. "My sub's sunk!"

The large Plexiglas submarine lay immobile on the bottom of the deep end. Vince shouted back, "It's probably just the batteries, son. Put on your goggles. Show your uncle how I taught you to be a frogman, and go rescue your sub."

Joshua grabbed his yellow rubber face mask, which had been sitting on the pool's coping. Like a professional, he spat on the inside lens, to keep it from fogging, donned the mask and took off like a tadpole toward the deep water.

"Remarkable," observed Joshua's proud uncle. "And to think that last year he couldn't even swim."

"He's sure growing up fast," remarked Vince. "*Too* fast, for this old man."

An introspective moment of silence was broken by the overflight of yet another 727.

"Must be an air-traffic-control glitch at National," offered Vince. "It's highly unusual to route traffic over the city on a weekend."

"National's not one of my favorite airports to fly into," added Thomas. "The runways don't leave room for error, and the noise restriction and security-overflight limitations are a real headache."

"I hear you, little brother. But it sure is convenient as all hell. Will you be taking the first shuttle up to La Guardia tomorrow morning?"

"That's still the plan," said Thomas.

"Did you ever get those seasick patches you wanted?"

"Would you believe the pharmacy doesn't have them in stock?" replied Thomas. "Something about a quality-control problem at the plant."

"Why don't I see if Dr. Patton can get you some? From what I hear, the President's not much of a sailor either, and if those patches are as good as you say, we'll have our fair share available to us."

"Thanks, Vince. I sure wouldn't want to ruin the family name by tossing my cookies in the middle of the most historic summit in modern times."

"Hell, you'll do just fine. And just think, for one whole week, you can kiss D.C. goodbye."

Thomas grinned. "Yeah, it will be nice to finally see what life outside the Beltway looks like. I've been working a desk much too long."

"You did say something about being hungry for adventure," Vince reminded. "It looks like your time is finally here."

"Do we have any more batteries, Dad?" asked Joshua, who had arrived back in the pool's shallow end with the disabled sub in tow.

"That's a negative, son," retorted Vince. "Why don't you show Uncle Thomas your new parachute launcher?"

Dropping the sub, Joshua climbed up to the top step of the pool and grabbed a large wooden slingshot that lay on the dry concrete. Tucked in the thick elastic band was a hand-sized, plastic soldier with a parachute draped over its back.

"Wait till you get a look at this, Uncle Thomas!"

Joshua aimed the slingshot skyward and launched the toy paratrooper. The figure shot thirty feet into the air, before gravity took over and the parachute deployed. Because of the lack of wind, the toy floated almost straight downward, into the deep end of the pool.

While Joshua went to retrieve it, his father turned to Thomas.

"The boy loves that toy almost as much as his sub. I think we might have a potential airborne candidate."

Thomas winced. "I'm sure Kelly would love that."

"He could do worse," countered Vince. "And besides, you can't tell me that you don't miss jumping yourself. I know that I do."

Thomas replied while watching his nephew prepare the wet paratrooper for another launch, "As far as I'm concerned, that toy is as close to a parachute as I ever want to get."

The sound of a sliding door opening behind them signaled the return of Kelly, Brittany, and Max, the family's standard poodle. While Max made a mad dash to the water's edge, Kelly set the platter of raw chicken breasts that she was carrying on the redwood picnic table beside the grill. She was noticeably pregnant, yet that didn't stop her from being her usual animated self.

"Brittany was telling me about last night's play at the Kennedy Center, Thomas. How do you compare it to the original?"

Brittany took a seat beside Thomas as he answered. "It was interesting. *West Side Story* has always been one of my favorite musicals. But a modern version featuring the Crips and Bloods—it's topical, but it's stretching the envelope a bit too far for my conservative tastes."

"I understand that you managed to get tickets to next month's visit by the Bolshoi Ballet," Kelly added. "Don't tell me that you're turning cultural on us, Thomas."

Vince looked at his brother in astonishment, then addressed Brittany with an all-knowing grin. "You actually got him to commit to taking you to the ballet? My, my, the relationship is turning serious."

Their laughs were broken by the arrival of a dripping-wet Joshua and an excited Max.

"Hey, Uncle Thomas. Since you used to be a real live paratrooper, why don't you give my toy a try?"

Before Thomas could respond, Joshua jammed the loaded slingshot into his free hand. Thomas put down his drink and examined the manner in which the parachute was draped over the toy soldier's back.

"You've jumped before?" quizzed Brittany, surprised by this revelation.

Thomas humbly answered. "During my stint in the Air Force, I gave it a try a time or two."

"Gave it a try a time or two?" repeated Vince in utter disbelief. "I'm not in the habit of tooting your horn, little brother. But sometimes your humility annoys the hell out of me."

Vince looked at Brittany and added, "Even though he should be proud as all get-out, Thomas has logged well over five hundred jumps. Most of them took place during his years with Air Force Special Operations."

"You never told me that you were an Air Commando," said Brittany to Thomas.

"There goes another skeleton out of the closet," Thomas said lightly, but his serious countenance betrayed that he would like nothing better than to change the subject.

He stood and launched the paratrooper into the cloudless sky. It flew more than three times higher than Joshua's previous shot, and was soon barreling back to earth but without the benefit of the parachute. Somehow it had become tangled around the soldier and failed to open.

The plastic toy plummeted into the pool and disappeared into the shallow end. Joshua was off in a flash to retrieve it, with a barking Max on his heels.

"If I remember from my own abbreviated jump training back in basic," offered Brittany, "I believe you'd call that malfunction a snivel."

Thomas appeared oddly affected by the parachute's failure to open. Vince noticed his brother's posture suddenly stiffen, and his facial features tighten.

"Hey, Thomas, we'd better get those chicken breasts on the fire," he said in an effort to divert his brother's attention.

"And we'd better get back to work on our salad," Kelly said to Brittany.

As the women returned to the kitchen, Vince walked over to the grill to recheck the coals. Thomas remained where he was, his gaze locked on Joshua's efforts at retrieving the submerged toy soldier.

Vince knew what was bothering him, and he decided it would be best not to say anything about it.

"How about getting that platter of chicken, little brother? After that bike ride of yours, you must be famished."

The roar of another low-flying 727 appeared to break his morose spell. Thomas headed for the picnic table, picked up the platter, and joined his brother at the grill.

"Can you imagine a beautiful fire like this one, wasted on chicken?" observed Vince as he picked up the tongs. "Pop wouldn't believe it. The way I remember it, his pit cooked nothing but spareribs and pork steaks."

This innocent comment hit home, and Thomas sighed. "It's times like these when I really miss him, Vince."

A rapturous sizzle arose as Vince laid the first of the butterflied, boneless chicken breasts on the red-hot grill. No sooner did he lay out the next breast, than his beeper began buzzing incessantly.

"Never fails," said Vince.

Just as Vince was in the process of putting on his bifocals to read his pager's digital display, Thomas's beeper activated. Without bothering to empty the rest of the platter, Thomas reached into the back pocket of his cycling jersey. He didn't need glasses to see the flashing message that simply read, CODE NINE.

"Damn!" he softly cursed.

"I'll double that," said Vince. "I knew this day off was too good to be true. There goes yet another holiday barbeque down the drain."

Because their pagers directed them to the same location, they decided to travel together. Without taking the time to change their clothes, and leaving the women with the hastiest of goodbyes, they piled into Vince's Jeep Cherokee and drove off toward D.C. The holiday traffic was light, so they sped past National Airport and crossed the Potomac via the Arlington Memorial Bridge. Here they encountered a brief backup of cars, most of them filled with families headed toward the flag-draped Capitol Mall.

A turn northward onto the George Washington Parkway allowed them to bypass this jam. They passed Georgetown on their right, with the boat-filled Potomac flowing lazily to their left. Four-and-a-half miles later, they turned right onto I–270 north, and exited soon afterward at Burning Tree Estates.

They were in the Maryland countryside now, and Thomas had no trouble finding the two-lane highway that led to their destination. The Federal Executive Branch mail-sorting facility was purposely situated in this relatively isolated location, to insure its anonymity. This little-known installation was responsible for presorting all letters and parcels addressed to either the White House or the adjoining Executive Office Building.

An unmarked driveway conveyed them to the facility's security gate. This was the sole entryway. Completely encircling the thirty-acre site was an eight-foot-high fence of chain-link, topped with razor-wire.

Vince brought his vehicle to a stop in front of a remote-controlled barricade. A uniformed security guard with a pistol and a no-nonsense demeanor approached them and demanded their identification cards. After checking their names off a computerized list of approved visitors, the guard handed each of them a plastic visitors badge to clip to their T-shirts.

The barricade was raised, and once past the checkpoint, a two-lane, concrete driveway led them through a dense forest of mature oaks. At the far end of these woods was their goal—an immense, 100,000-square-foot warehouse, set in the middle of a spacious clearing.

A half dozen large loading docks were set into the one-story, concrete structure's western side. Only two of the bays were currently filled, one with a brightly colored semi-trailer belonging to the United States Postal Service, and the other holding a smaller Federal Express van.

They parked in the visitors lot, and made their way on foot to the main entrance. A few puffy clouds drifted overhead, with the late afternoon sun having pushed the temperature to a delightful seventy-eight, humidity-free degrees.

Another security checkpoint greeted them inside. A female guard took their names, and instructed them to be seated in the waiting area while she called the watch supervisor.

The waiting room was little more than a cramped, carpetless cubbyhole, filled with a half dozen government-issue, light blue, plastic molded chairs. If the decor had a name, it would be early DMV. A soda machine was jammed into the corner, and while Thomas took a seat, Vince walked over to the machine to check out the selection.

"How does an ice-cold Dr. Pepper sound?" Vince asked as he reached into his pocket and pulled out his billfold.

Much to his disappointment, the machine refused to accept any of the three one-dollar bills he was carrying. Even smoothing them out and feeding them in upside down failed to do the trick, prompting Vince to turn away in frustration.

"I don't suppose you have any money on you, Thomas?"

Thomas double-checked the contents of his jersey. "Come to think of it, Brittany's got my money clip."

"So, now you're even letting her carry your cash," teased Vince as he sat down opposite his brother. "Musicals and ballets at the Kennedy Center, bike rides to Mount Vernon, long lunches at the White House commissary . . ."

Any further ribbing was interrupted by the arrival of a short, barrel-chested man in his mid forties. Senior Postal Inspector Mike Galloway knew both Kellogg brothers equally well, and his curt greeting was that of a tired, old friend.

"Sorry about ruining your holiday, guys."

"It's all part of the job, Mike," replied Vince. "Weren't you supposed to be taking those vacation days this week?"

Mike shrugged his broad shoulders. "Hell, I never even got a chance to use up last year's days. And now the First Kid goes and turns sixteen, and this year's vacation's down the tube too."

Mike had been postponing the same vacation for as long as the brothers had known him.

"What have you got for us?" Thomas asked.

"Come on back, and I'll show you," Galloway replied cryptically.

They followed their escort down a tiled hallway that held a series of small, vacant offices. At the far end of this corridor, Galloway pushed open a pair of large swinging doors and led them into a cavernous room that comprised most of the warehouse.

Overhead racks of powerful mercury-vapor lights illuminated an entire mail-sorting facility, currently staffed by a crew of some two dozen individuals. Galloway proceeded to one of the active loading docks. The large U.S. Postal Service semi that they had seen outside was backed up to this bay, and a trio of workers were in the process of loading it with dozens of parcel-filled, cloth carts. Upon closer examination, the brothers could see that the majority of these parcels appeared to be colorfully wrapped gifts.

"This truck they're loading," Galloway explained, "is the sixth similarly packed load we've filled this week. Believe it or not, each of those parcels is a birthday gift that's been sent to the First Kid.

They've originated from every corner of the planet, and so far, we've counted over ten thousand of them."

Without waiting for a response, Galloway took them over to the adjoining bay, where the Federal Express van was being unloaded. The cargo was a combination of letters, boxes, and tubes. Upon entering the warehouse, each item was placed on a conveyor belt, where it was routed to a manned X-ray machine, much like one would see at an airport security checkpoint.

"Of course, just like every other letter and package addressed to either the White House or Executive Office Building, we have to carefully scrutinize each of these gifts."

They watched as a particularly large box passed through the X-ray machine. The conveyor belt briefly stopped, and while the staff checked its contents on the monitor screen, Vince vented his curiosity.

"Once they pass inspection, do the gifts ever make it to the House?"

Galloway was quick to answer. "The only ones that make it inside are legitimate parcels from the First Family's friends and relatives. Protocol sent us a comprehensive list of acceptable return addresses, and so far, this has amounted to less than ten percent of all items received here."

"What happens to the other ninety percent?" Thomas asked.

"A volunteer group of White House staffers are responsible for opening each and every one of them. They're taken over to an empty warehouse on G Street. Toys, clothing, and other appropriate items are being donated to the homeless, with almost ten thousand thank-you cards having been sent out so far."

"Talk about a serious case of writer's cramp," returned Vince.

Their escort ignored this remark, and led them to a large office located at the very back of the facility. Two clerks were at work here, busy checking items off a computerized manifest list. This conscientious duo didn't even bother looking up from their screens as Galloway picked up a large, flat envelope that lay on the table between them.

Thomas and Vince viewed the envelope's contents simultaneously. It was a twelve-by-fourteen-inch photographic negative. Clearly visible on the flimsy plate were the outlines of a pair of nine-volt batteries, placed side by side on the far right-hand side of the negative. The outlines of what appeared to be several twisted wires could be seen stretching from the four battery terminals to the muddled, unidentifiable contents of the rest of the picture.

"The suspect package was addressed to the White House. It was unloaded off the morning USPS truck, approximately two hours ago," revealed Galloway. "Our scanner team tagged it on the first X-ray pass. This is the plate that triggered our code nine."

The negative looked disturbingly familiar. Vince traded an anxious glance with his brother before asking the next question. "Where is it now?"

"We've just finished securing it in isolation." Galloway gestured toward a rear door. "If you'll follow me, I'm sure you'll find the parcel itself most interesting."

They exited the warehouse and found themselves on the back portion of the compound. A two-and-a-half-acre plot of woodland had been completely cleared there, leaving a flat, grass-filled lot, dominated by a single, squat concrete-block structure set in the clearing's center.

An asphalt walkway connected this structure to the warehouse. A helmeted technician, in full protective bomb gear, was in the process of utilizing a remote-control device to steer a four-foot-tall, child-sized robot down this pathway. Nicknamed Freddie, the robot traveled on tractor-tread wheels as it headed back to its storage shed inside the mail-sorting facility.

Thomas and Vince received a nod from the technician as they passed him and continued on to the blockhouse. Their escort opened the structure's heavy steel, blast-proof door, and led the way inside.

The twelve-by-twelve-foot room was cool and dark. Its thick, concrete-block walls absorbed sound like a sponge. There was a certain unearthly quality to the atmosphere as Mike Galloway switched on a bank of red-tinted lights. This ghostly illumination revealed a concrete bench set in the cell's exact center. A single red, white, and blue USPS Priority Mail box sat on this bench. The unopened parcel was 15½ inches long, 12½ inches wide, and had a depth of 3¼ inches.

Thomas fought a subconscious urge to hold his breath as he cautiously approached the bench. With Vince close at his side, Thomas bent over and quickly scanned the hand-printed, Priority

Mail address label. There was no ignoring the sender's distinctive cramped penmanship. Thomas wasn't all that surprised upon noting the familiar return address.

"Do you believe the audacity of this sick bastard, giving it another try like this?" Vince whispered, disgusted.

Thomas had seen enough. He stood up straight and backed away from the bench.

"I told you you'd find it interesting," reminded Galloway.

Thomas was already thinking ahead to how the investigation should proceed. "I hope this time they'll let us disarm it. It will just happen all over again, if they go and blow the device and destroy all the evidence in the process."

"If this IED"—Improvised Explosive Device—"is packed with C-4, instead of a mere blasting cap, I sure wouldn't want to be the one tasked with disarming it," said Vince.

Thomas looked at his brother and countered, "Someone's going to have to take a look inside without blowing it to shreds. Otherwise, one of these devices is eventually going to slip through the system, and take out an entire wing of the White House."

As if to emphasize this statement, his beeper began buzzing. A quick check of the pager's digital display identified the caller, and Thomas reached for the door handle.

"I'm going to need a secure line, Mike."

"You've got it," Galloway replied, before leading the way back to his office in the main building.

While his brother made his phone call, Vince was able to get his longed-for Dr. Pepper with some help from Galloway's wallet. With an extra can for Thomas, they returned to Galloway's office in time to intercept Thomas in the hallway.

"That was short and sweet," said Vince, handing his brother the soda. "What did he want?"

Thomas popped the can's aluminum tab and took an appreciative sip before answering. "The director was calling from the seventh hole of a charity golf tournament in Fairfax. It seems he's already been briefed on the nature of our code nine."

He halted a moment to take another sip before adding, "So, you can forget about getting me those seasick patches, Vince. Because, as of this moment, I've been pulled off the crossing."

3

THE NARROW, EARTHEN FOOTPATH BEGAN AT THE NORTHERNMOST OUTSKIRTS OF the village. Though he hadn't walked its length for almost a decade, the thick jungle he was soon passing through still felt familiar. It had been much too long since he'd taken the time to hike such a wild, desolate spot, and Adm. Liu Huang-tzu realized how much he missed these beloved woods of his birth.

The harsh cry of a bird drew his line of sight to the stand of massive coconut palms lining the western edge of the trail. It took him only seconds to spot the brilliant crimson plumage of the large parrot responsible for this outburst of guttural song. Twisting green vines surrounded the colorful bird. Liu gratefully inhaled a deep lungful of air heavy with the scent of wet wood and dark earth. The mad screech of a howler monkey sounded in the distance, and Liu turned his attention back to the path.

With ever lengthening strides, he penetrated deeper into the ancient jungle, the sky above all but blotted out by an interlocking canopy of thick tree limbs. The trail now followed the meander of a cascading brook, making Liu aware of the path's slight uphill slope. This change in gradient didn't phase the seventy-nine-year-old career soldier in the least, and he quickened his stride in anticipation of what lay beyond.

There was a noticeable band of sweat on his forehead by the

time he reached the terraced stairway that he remembered from his last visit. Without taking the time to wipe his brow dry, he initiated the rather steep climb, whose individual steps were cut from the exposed roots of the nearby trees.

At the top, a wide, dry mud walkway led him out of the humid jungle and up into a new zone of vegetation. The increased altitude here had allowed the canopy of dripping palms to give way to a gnarled forest of dwarfed oaks. A fresh gust of cool wind hit him full in the face. Liu was momentarily startled when he surprised a covey of quail. Like grapeshot, the fat, yellow-feathered birds burst from the underbrush directly in front of him, wasting no time in disappearing into the stunted trees that lay on the opposite side of the trail.

Liu cursed himself for not bringing a shotgun. Fresh mountain quail were a delicacy not to be missed!

The first of several switchbacks conveyed him farther up the mountain. Liu was beginning to feel his walk in the back of his calves—he was thankful he had taken the time for breakfast earlier in the day.

It was hard to believe this meal had taken place barely three hours ago, while he was still at sea, aboard his flagship the *Zhanjiang*. As was his habit, he had awakened well before dawn. The seas had remained blessedly calm, and Liu headed topside to the destroyer's fantail, where he greeted the new day with a full regimen of t'ai chi.

Breakfast awaited back in his cabin. After a glass of fresh orange juice, a slice of sugar-sweet cantaloupe, and a bowl of rice porridge, he took his tea in the warship's bridge, while the destroyer began its cautious approach into Yulin harbor.

Waiting for them pierside was a small welcoming committee of local dignitaries. Liu immediately recognized the portly, gray-haired figure of Hainan's senior Party commissar. Seven decades ago, they had gone to elementary school together. Now, at the end of the gangway, he accepted his old friend's enthusiastic greeting.

His schoolmate appeared to have had his feelings hurt when Liu rather abruptly excused himself to begin his current hike. But one of the benefits of his advancing years was the right to spend his time the way he wished, without feeling guilty for doing so. Besides, there would be time for gossip later in the day. Right now, it was time to get his land legs back and initiate a long-anticipated climb that could well be his last.

The moment he left the harbor area behind and crossed Yulin's ever-expanding streets to the wilderness at its outskirts, Liu knew that he had made the right decision. This hike was a rare chance to rediscover his youth, and in the process, channel his energies on the great challenge that awaited in the days to come.

A hand-sized, gray lizard scampered across the dusty trail ahead of him, as he started around the steepest switchback he'd yet encountered. It was a bit more difficult to catch his breath here, reminding Liu of days long ago, when he had sprinted up this same trail, hardly breaking a sweat.

It was in 1934 that Liu was called to Kiangsi from his island birthplace to continue his education. It didn't take long for the impressionable teenager to fall in with a young group of political idealists, led by a fiery Hunanese visionary named Mao Tse-tung. Mao's passionate socialist teachings made complete sense to Liu, who joined the newly formed Chinese Communist Party less than a week after arriving on the mainland. Barely a year later, he was a grizzled Party veteran, running for his life along with Mao and a hundred thousand loyal cohorts on the infamous Long March.

Across the length and breadth of their homeland, they were constantly pursued by Chiang Kai-shek and his bloodthirsty Kuomintang forces, the ever-encroaching Japanese invaders, and the harsh hand of Mother Nature, but still they persevered. For his loyalty, Liu was appointed to a prominent position in the newly formed People's Republic government that was to emerge from the feudal ashes of post–World-War-II China.

With his youthful friend Deng Xiaoping at his side, Liu's first position of real power was as a senior commissar in the People's Liberation Army, the PLA. In 1952, he was transferred to the newly formed PLA Navy. This feeble force was composed of a handful of obsolete warships, barely capable of patrolling the new country's sprawling coastline. Liu was a major force in the unparalleled era of naval growth that was to follow. By 1955, he had attained the rank of rear admiral.

Liu got his first real view of the vast world beyond while attending the prestigious Voroshilov Naval Institute in the U.S.S.R. He returned to China anxious to apply the same naval doctrines that provided the foundation for the modern Soviet Navy.

Liu spent the sixties and seventies building the PLA Navy's infrastructure, and in 1982, he was honored to become its supreme commander. Six years later, he was named ranking Vice Chairman of the Central Military and the senior serving officer in the Politburo Standing Committee. This made him the only military man among the top leadership of the entire country.

Never one to take his responsibilities lightly, Liu had dedicated his best years to the PRC. He never married; his spouse was his beloved motherland.

Much like the perennial bachelor who didn't have children to mark the years' passing, Liu was barely aware that most of his life was over. There was no denying that the majority of his old friends were long in their graves. Deng's recent passing served as an abrupt wake-up call—Liu now faced the waning years of life with only a handful of old comrades left to share war stories with.

A sharp cry from above broke Liu from the thoughts of his past. He looked up in time to see an immense golden hawk circling effortlessly. A cloudless, powdery blue sky provided a fitting backdrop for the hawk, and Liu marveled at the size of this proud creature. From its lofty vantage point, it could see most of Wuzhi Mountain's 1,900-meter-high summit. Surely the bird of prey was aware of Liu's presence the moment he broke from the cover of the jungle.

Suddenly feeling alone and exposed, the old soldier humped up a final series of twisting switchbacks. His lungs were heaving as he rounded the last turn. A sudden breath of cool, ocean-scented wind engulfed him. A small clearing had been dug into the summit's southern edge. It was to this spot that Liu proceeded.

Once the site of a Taoist shrine, the clearing had long since been abandoned. An intact limestone bench remained, a solid perch on which Liu came to rest. His breathing slowly steadied as a magnificent vista revealed itself before him.

The sparkling blue waters of the South China Sea stretched to the horizon. On the coast sat the city of Yulin. What only ten years before had been a sleepy fishing village was now a bustling community of over ten thousand souls. The region's primary employer was the new naval base that Liu had helped establish. Its main docks were clearly visible, and Liu proudly studied the half dozen ships currently moored there.

Four of these vessels were guided-missile patrol boats. Each of these 185-foot, 530-ton, thirty-eight-knot combatants had just been fitted out with four MM 40 Exocet Block 2 antiship missiles; a 30mm Goalkeeper self-contained close-in weapons system; a sextuple Su-dral launch system for Mistral infrared-homing surface-to-air missiles, and a dual-purpose 75mm gun mount.

A *Ling*-class marine salvage ship was berthed beside the patrol boats. This unique, 255-foot-long vessel was designed to support diver operations to a depth of 850 feet, and could lift submerged objects weighing up to 300 tons from a depth of 800 feet. A massive crane was mounted aft of the bridge, where a group of sailors could be seen preparing the ship to get underway.

Yet the warship that caught Liu's complete attention was berthed immediately forward of the salvage ship—the *Zhanjiang*. This sleek, heavily armed destroyer was the first of two Project 053HT destroyers that were launched from Shanghai in February 1993.

A thin stream of white smoke rose from the *Zhanjiang*'s single amidship stack. At a length of 492 feet, the 5,300-ton ship was fitted with a mix of Chinese-developed and European-supplied combat systems. Much like the varied mix of armaments on the four patrol boats, the destroyer was a hybrid, combining the best of the East and the West. Liu had lobbied strongly to get his obdurate comrades in naval development to expend hard currency and buy these systems. Continued double-digit economic growth helped ease their conservative fears, and the *Zhanjiang* was proof they had made the proper choice.

The sharp cry of the hawk diverted Liu's glance back to the southern horizon, where the sparkling waters of the South China Sea beckoned. It was in those open seas that China's destiny awaited.

For over three decades Liu had been a tireless proponent of an expanded fleet. His cautious transformation of the navy from a meager, coastal-enforcement force to a service with worldwide blue-water capabilities took many frustrating years to initiate, and Liu was well aware that the benefits were already apparent.

In March 1988, a PLA Navy frigate sank three Vietnamese warships off the distant Spratly Island group. For the first time ever, PRC warships had made port visits to Honolulu, Vladivostok, Pakistan, Sri

Lanka and Bangladesh. A pair of ships provided full-time communications and telemetry support for the PRC's Pacific missile test range, while a PLA Navy icebreaker supported China's two research stations in far-off Antarctica.

Liu was particularly pleased with the advancements in their all-important submarine fleet. The modern, nuclear-powered submarine was a force multiplier that couldn't be ignored. When Capt. Lee Shao-chi and his *Han*-class sub successfully penetrated America's *Kitty Hawk* carrier battle group off the coast of Taiwan in October 1994, the PLA Navy showed the world that foreign fleets could no longer patrol Chinese waters without suffering the consequences.

Establishing control of the waters well away from China's coastline became an accepted doctrine as a result of the Persian Gulf war. At this time, sea-launched cruise missiles, aircraft-carrier battle groups, and other over-the-horizon weapons systems demonstrated the vital need to extend the PRC's area of influence as far out to sea as possible.

As Liu guided the navy's difficult transformation from coastal defense (*jinhai fangyu*), to offshore defense (*jinyang fangyu*) to full blue-water (*yuanyang haijun*) operations, he envisioned a series of protective island barriers. The first segment of the Pacific that the PLA Navy had to be capable of patrolling extended from the Kuriles to Japan, the Ryukyus, Taiwan, the Philippines, and the Greater Sundas. A second barrier reached all the way out to the Bonins, the Marianas, Guam, and the Carolines. Only when these vast seas were protected by China's sphere of influence could the PRC control its own destiny.

As the mainland's natural resources continued to be rapidly depleted, the world's most populous nation was facing uncertain times ahead. In 1993 China became a net importer of oil for the first time. And within a few years, the PRC would be needing over seven million barrels of oil a day to satisfy its industrial needs—the same amount that the gluttonous Americans currently imported. With precious hard currency already being stretched thin to import food and to purchase badly needed Western technology, where was this oil to come from? Liu knew that the answer to this question lay beneath the waters of the sea he currently faced.

Approximately one thousand kilometers due south of Hainan Island, in a portion of the South China Sea surrounded by the Philippines to the east, Vietnam to the west, and Malaysia and Brunei to the south, lay the Spratly Islands. Inconsequential as to landmass, the Spratlys' wealth lay submerged beneath their shallow shoals, where oil fields easily rivaling those of the Persian Gulf were located. Claimed by each of the aforementioned nations, as well as the People's Republic of China, the Spratlys were without doubt the most important island chain in all of Asia. For whoever controlled their resources, controlled the destiny of the earth in the twenty-first century.

Liu had no doubt that China could prevail in this struggle—the alternative was unthinkable. The PRC had made control of the Spratlys a foreign-policy priority.

Just as the return of Hong Kong was bringing badly needed financial expertise to the motherland, control of the Spratly oil fields would seal China's ascendence as the world's mightiest nation. With the end of the Cold War and the breakup of the Soviet Union, it was time for a new hierarchy of nations. The once all-powerful Japanese economy was showing signs of serious strain, while the European community remained weakened by a seemingly endless series of petty squabbles.

This left the United States as China's sole competitor. There could be no ignoring the fact that the awesome American military machine had seen its best days. Huge budget deficits, and a weakening of the wills of its citizens, were forcing the Pentagon to cut large chunks out of its defense appropriations. Even the mighty U.S. Navy was feeling the crunch, as a Cold War fleet of more than 500 warships had been cut to nearly half that number.

The timing was thus ideal for the PRC to expand its territorial ambitions in order to incorporate the natural resources needed to feed its future growth. Yet China's current top leadership—a group of untried young fools who'd risen to power following the death of Deng Xiaoping—were failing to act on this once-in-a-lifetime opportunity. Try as he could to awaken them to this fact, Liu was met with a frustratingly polite "not interested." Instead, politicians such as Li Chen, their current president, had decided on a dangerous course of appeasement with the West. This could bring only tragedy, and Liu cursed their inexperienced president's lack of courage and foresight.

Li Chen's rash decision to join the G-7 leaders aboard the luxury ocean liner *QE2* signaled the true degree of his ignorance. But could

Liu expect any better from one who had lived a pampered life, never knowing the Great Leader, or the immense sacrifices they had made to free China from centuries of slavery?

By threatening to join the Group of Seven nations, the president was undermining the foundations of Mao's China. Expanded trade with the West would flood the motherland with decadent, wasteful consumer items. Rock and roll, television, and violent Hollywood movies would destroy China's youth, as it already had America's and was rapidly corrupting Japan's. Indeed drugs, moral corruption, and blind materialism were already on the rise in China's larger cities. With additional exposure, this incurable blight would all too soon reach the countryside. Once the country's greatest asset, its rural population, was infected, China's doom would be sealed.

Now was the time for strength, not weakness! Decades of sacrifice had made this day possible, and Liu was not about to just sit back and watch his beloved country destroy itself.

Satisfied that he had done his best to set a plan into motion that would yet save the People's Republic, Liu's glance returned to the harbor, where the salvage ship was preparing to get underway. Liu himself had written this vessel's new orders, directing it southward to the Spratlys, where the operation's all-important first phase had already been implemented.

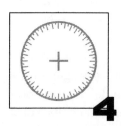

4

VINCE KELLOGG MANAGED TO GET HOME SHORTLY AFTER SUNSET, JUST IN TIME
to pick up Kelly and Josh and head for National. Kelly's sister Julie
was arriving at 8:30 P.M. from St. Louis, and they arrived at the gate
just as she was deplaning. The youngest of three sisters, Julie would
be staying with them for several weeks, while she worked on her
doctoral thesis in economics at the Library of Congress.

As it turned out, the timing of this visit couldn't have been better.
Vince was scheduled to leave early the next morning for New York
City, where he'd be boarding the *QE2* for a planned midnight sailing.
Four and a half days at sea would follow, and he had a six-day stay
in the United Kingdom to look forward to, before he'd be returning
home on Air Force One. He'd feel more comfortable on the trip
knowing his wife and son weren't alone.

As usual, Vince was unable to share the nature of his afternoon
visit to the Federal Executive Branch mail-sorting facility with his
family. They had learned long ago not to ask questions, and he was
content to go about his business as if nothing out of the ordinary
had occurred. He wolfed down a cold, barbequed chicken breast,
spent a half hour with Kelly and Julie getting caught up on family
gossip, then excused himself to tuck in Joshua and complete his
packing. His wife and sister-in-law were still gabbing away on the
patio when he slipped into bed shortly after 10:00 P.M.

The next thing he knew, the 5:00 A.M. news was whispering from the clock radio. The lead story was about the summit, and before getting up, he listened to a group of reporters discuss the virtues of this history-making meeting of the world's top leaders.

As soon as the report ended, he switched off the radio so that the second alarm buzzer wouldn't awaken Kelly, and rose to get on with his morning routine. A half hour later he was stretched, showered, shaved, and fortified by a mug of black coffee, ready to hit the road.

Though he had intended to leave his car at the airport and have one of his associates drive it back home, he was surprised to find Kelly dressed and waiting for him at the front door. Not even morning sickness would keep her from personally delivering him to the terminal.

One of the benefits of living in Alexandria was its proximity to National. The traffic was still light, and they arrived with plenty of time for Vince to leave Kelly with a proper hug. Next year would be their twentieth wedding anniversary, and during that time, they had certainly experienced their fair share of airport goodbyes. Yet perhaps because of her pregnancy—a surprise, to be sure, but a wonderful one—this goodbye lingered much longer than usual, and Vince had to reluctantly break their embrace to make the 6:30 shuttle.

He made it to the gate with a whole two minutes to spare. This gave him just enough time to grab a copy of *USA Today* before boarding. The plane took off soon afterwards, and it seemed that he barely had time to eat a standard airline box breakfast and read the newspaper before the pilot announced they were initiating their descent into New York.

He had saved the top news story of the morning, the summit, for last. It was supplemented by a four-page special section that documented the upcoming summit, and included a full-color picture of the *QE2* and a detailed map showing the transatlantic route the ocean liner would be taking.

Although he had previously read a detailed, thirty-six-page briefing paper about the G-7 that had been circulated within the Treasury Department, Vince nevertheless found the newspaper feature extremely interesting. He particularly enjoyed the story on the G-7's history.

A fairly modern event, the first G-7 summit was born as a result of the monetary crisis of the early 1970s. In the summer of 1971 the United States recorded its first trade deficit. Growing economies in Japan and Europe caused this deficit to continue to deteriorate, and President Nixon vainly attempted to control it with a series of drastic monetary devaluations.

The outbreak of the Yom Kippur war in 1973 led to the first serious Arab oil embargo—within three months the price of petroleum quadrupled, while the supply was cut by 20 percent. Unable to react with a united response, the Western nations found themselves at the mercy of economic conditions over which they had little control.

To address this dangerous situation, France's Giscard d'Estaing and Helmut Schmidt of Germany proposed the creation of a flexible, unstructured economic summit of the Western leaders. Informality, and the need to promote a totally free exchange of ideas, was the key, and the American President, Gerald Ford, somewhat reluctantly accepted an invitation to travel to Château de Rambouillet, deep in the French countryside.

The first G-7 summit was thus convened on November 15, 1975. Though hampered by large staffs, the secluded location and excellent fall weather created the perfect ambiance. Many of the informal meetings took place around the fireplace. They touched upon a wide range of topics including monetary policy, international trade, relations with developing countries, and the continued energy crisis.

The final results were encouraging, and a decision was made to hold another summit in June of 1976, in Puerto Rico. Held in an isolated resort outside of San Juan, this meeting led to a joint trade agreement designed to avoid uncontrollable economic expansion and stem the creation of additional trade barriers.

Yearly gatherings of the Group of Seven had continued ever since. They took place in a wide variety of locations, and were dedicated to such difficult subjects as nuclear arms control, international terrorism, and a desire for continued monetary and trade regulation.

Only recently had Russia joined the United States, Britain, Canada, France, Germany, Italy, and Japan as a full-time summit participant. And with the additional presence of the People's Republic of China, the summit was continuing to evolve as an economic and political institution.

Vince was well aware that what made these annual meetings unique were the personal interactions that took place. Where else could the world's top leaders hold personal discussions on a broad spectrum of concerns, all in a relaxed, trusting environment? And although the most recent summits displayed an increasing tendency to have large personal staffs present, there was a move underfoot to halt this trend.

The upcoming summit at sea aboard the *QE2* was the perfect way to return to the isolated, idealistic setting first envisioned in 1974. Only a single personal representative would be allowed on each leader's staff, with the sessions themselves structured to be as informal as possible.

Of course, the mere fact that the nine heads of state had committed themselves to spending four and a half days together at sea was promising in itself. Surely this would lead to resolutions of problems once deemed unsolvable.

A primary topic of discussion was to be the creation of an expanded Law of the Sea treaty. This new agreement would address the controversial subjects of international maritime boundaries, oil and mineral rights, and establish freedom of passage zones in strategic choke points.

Yet another vital area of discussion was the formalization of a forward-thinking nuclear-arms-control agreement, first proposed by the new Russian president. Labeled Global Zero Alert, this unique proposal signaled the next generation in arms control. To further defuse the nuclear hair trigger, and make an accidental nuclear exchange impossible, the Russians desired to actually remove all nuclear warheads from their delivery vehicles. These warheads would be subsequently stored nearby, close enough to act as a deterrent if a crisis should develop, yet far enough away to make an unwanted exchange unlikely.

Vince could only imagine the spirited discussions that this unprecedented proposal would generate. And he could think of no more-perfect setting to initiate these groundbreaking talks, than the isolated, luxurious confines of the *QE2*.

The one logistical area that was proving extremely controversial, and that the *USA Today* article only touched upon, was the summit's security arrangements. The idea of having the world's leaders afloat in the Atlantic for four and a half days was enough to give any security official nightmares. Vince knew that they had met this challenge head-on, and that a viable, multifaceted plan had been put into operation that would all but guarantee the summit's safe conclusion. For the past two months, Vince had worked with an international cast of security experts and become an instrumental part of this effort. In seventeen hours, this tireless, often frustrating effort would be put to the ultimate test—the moment when the last world leader boarded the ocean liner and the *QE2* set sail.

Anxious to get on with it, Vince listened absently as the flight attendant instructed them to prepare for landing. Minutes later, the 727 hit the runway at La Guardia with barely a jolt. Once they reached the gate area, he was able to exit hastily via the rear rampway. With baggage in hand, he made his way into the terminal and proceeded at once to an adjoining gate, where his next mode of transport awaited him.

He had discovered the water shuttle on a previous visit, and now used it whenever possible. The boat provided a convenient, comfortable way to commute into Manhattan. As an additional bonus, not only was one spared the indignity of having to attempt entering the city by its perpetually packed surface streets, but traveling by water offered a magnificent view of Manhattan's majestic skyline.

Vince was all too soon enjoying this vista, as the water shuttle left La Guardia's Marine Terminal and sped down Riker's Island channel to the East River. The weather was absolutely gorgeous; a deep blue sky, with an occasional puffy cloud, and a temperature in the mid-seventies.

No matter how many times he entered Manhattan in this manner, he could never grow tired of the city's spectacular presence. Building after magnificent building reached to the sky. He could see the concrete and glass canyons that gave this island the topography that made it unique in all the world. It was a testament to man's commercial and artistic genius, and Vince couldn't help but be emotionally stimulated with each passing block.

They passed beneath the Roosevelt Island aerial tramway, and he caught his first view of the United Nations. Several of the G-7 participants had already arrived in town, and were scheduled to address the Security Council that afternoon.

With that stately old dowager the Empire State Building dominating the surrounding skyline, Vince gathered together his belongings as the shuttle turned for the Thirty-fourth Street pier. The boat would continue on to Wall Street, yet this was as far as he'd be going.

Scarcely thirty minutes had passed since he had left La Guardia. To be so abruptly transferred right into the heart of this great city was a bit traumatic, and as Vince stepped onto dry land, he halted a moment to get his bearings.

The morning rush hour was in full swing, and FDR Drive, which lined the island's eastern shore, was a solid, bumper-to-bumper mass of bright yellow taxis, passenger cars, and trucks of all sizes. The persistent roar of this traffic provided the city's soundtrack, with honking horns and squealing brakes giving additional color to the all-encompassing movement. His quiet home in Alexandria seemed thousands of miles distant, and Vince realized that the nation's capital was nothing but a sleepy, Southern town compared to New York.

He had to walk up to the corner of Second Avenue and Thirty-fourth Street before finding a cab, leaping in the second the previous passenger got out. You could never be too slow in staking your claim to a cab in New York. He then directed the driver to take him to the Passenger Ship Terminal.

"QE2?" queried the driver, his English tinged with Pakistani.

Vince caught the driver's dark-eyed glance in the rearview mirror and nodded. "She's the one."

With that, the cab headed west on Thirty-seventh Street, and then proceeded north on Eleventh Avenue through heavy traffic. As they slowly inched their way uptown, Vince made a mental note to give his brother a call. Vince was worried about his stubborn insistence on getting a chance to defuse the IED (Improvised Explosive Device), to derive concrete evidence of its creator.

His brother's safety wasn't his only concern. Thomas was the victim of a traumatic past. His reaction to something as insignificant as the malfunction of Joshua's parachute toy was a prime example that his wounds had yet to heal completely.

Tragedy first touched down in his brother's life on the opening night of Operation Urgent Fury. In a manner of speaking, Thomas lost his innocence off the shores of Grenada when several members of his commando unit were killed during a nighttime parachute jump at sea.

Much like the biblical trials of Job, the powers that be had yet to finish with Thomas, as he arrived back home haunted by these deaths. Barely a year later, buoyed by the news that his wife was expecting their first child, Thomas was again sent plunging into the abyss when he received news that his beloved Maggie had been killed in an automobile accident. The baby was lost as well, and Thomas had to fight to keep hold of his sanity.

After losing another military buddy to a horrible parachute accident in 1985 while training to infiltrate the hijacked cruise ship *Achille Lauro,* Thomas asked for and received a voluntary discharge from the air force. Vince feared that he'd lose his brother to an alcoholic stupor at that time. He was fortunately able to get Thomas an interview at the Treasury Department. This resulted in a three-year stint with the Secret Service, and his current duty at the Bureau of Alcohol, Tobacco and Firearms. Here his makeup was once more tested on February 28, 1993, in a fire-scarred field outside Waco, Texas. Yet another close friend was to die in his arms on that fated morning, taken down by a mad prophet's bullet.

Thomas somehow persevered, Vince thought, and though any lesser man might have been crushed by these events, his brother bravely pushed onward. Having a strong woman like Brittany Cooper in his life now would hopefully signal a change for the better. Love had a way of transforming past hurt into new purpose, and if anyone deserved a fresh start, it was his brother.

Vince had planned to spend an entire day in England with Thomas, roving the countryside together. Because of the crush of family and work, they rarely spent any free time together. Vince had hoped to begin rectifying this situation upon reaching Southampton. The fates—and duty—had willed otherwise though—Vince would have to wait until this trip was over to spend the time with his brother that he deserved and Vince desired.

Of course, first he'd have to survive this cab ride. Faced with what seemed to be an impenetrable line of traffic on Eleventh Avenue, his driver had somehow managed to weave his way to Fifty-fifth Street. With a defiant blast of the cab's horn, he made a left there, followed by another left onto Twelfth Avenue. A large sign indicated that the PASSENGER SHIP TERMINAL was to the right, and it was at that point that Vince caught his first glimpse of a towering red and black funnel that dominated its Hudson River berth with the same surreal presence of an Empire State Building.

The passenger embark gate was on the terminal's upper ramp,

and there Vince saw the forward position of the immense ship belonging to the distinctive funnel. The sharp, dark blue bow of the vessel was on the same level as the two-story ramp on which the cab was now parked. A bright red pennant flew from its forward jackstaff, with the name QUEEN ELIZABETH 2 embossed in black against the ship's upper hull.

"She's quite the ship," observed the cab driver, noting Vince's preoccupation with the vessel.

This being the first time that Vince had actually seen the *QE2* in person, he concurred. "That she is."

He paid the driver, and was soon standing alone on the concrete upper walkway, with his majestic home for the next week floating before him. The videotape of the ship that he had been studying did little to prepare him for its sheer immensity. At 963 feet in length, over 100 feet wide, with a gross tonnage of almost 70,000 tons, the massive ocean liner had a certain modern elegance to it. She was surely the most beautiful ship that he had ever laid eyes on, and Vince knew that very shortly, he'd be intimately acquainted with her.

A group of white-uniformed sailors were congregated on the spacious bow swabbing down the deck. The ship's crane was lifting a large crate onboard behind them. As this piece of cargo was carefully guided into the ship's hold, Vince spotted a single individual standing on one of the long, protruding exterior observation wings that were positioned on each side of the glassed-in bridge. This bearded figure appeared to be an officer. He had binoculars snug to his brow, and it looked like his line of sight was focused directly on Vince. Fighting the urge to acknowledge him with a wave, Vince's attention was diverted by the approach of a uniformed policeman.

"Excuse me, buddy," greeted the burly, Port Authority patrolman. "But this entire area is currently off-limits to the general public."

"Morning, officer," returned Vince as he matter-of-factly pulled out his plastic, laminated government identification card from his breast pocket.

One look at the card's distinctive gold, five-pointed-star logo was enough to dramatically change the patrolman's attitude. "Good morning to you, Special Agent. I gather from this luggage that you'll be boarding this morning. Do you need a longshoreman to give you a hand with your bags?"

"I can manage," Vince answered.

The cop excused himself to continue his rounds. Vince was anxious to see the ocean liner from inside, and he picked up his two-suiter and small duffel bag, and headed for the nearby elevator.

The terminal's passenger-embarkation area was located on the floor below. It looked much like an airport waiting room, but ten times the size.

Although the first dignitaries weren't due to arrive until later that day, the terminal was already bustling with activity. Porters, longshoremen, crew members, and blue-blazered Cunard Line representatives were busy making final preparations to the passenger-embark area. Brightly colored, red, white, and blue bunting hung from the cavernous terminal's rafters, while various roped-off viewing sections were being set up, apparently for well-wishing VIPs and the press.

One enterprising television news crew had already arrived, and had positioned its cameras beside the covered gangway. A shapely, blonde-haired reporter was in the process of interviewing one of the ship's officers. The blindingly bright light of the video camera was hitting the sailor full in the face. Vince sensed that he was doing his diplomatic best to keep smiling throughout the improvised interview.

Uniformed patrolmen from both the Port Authority and New York Police Department were conspicuously present at the terminal's entryways. Vince was forced to show his identification card to several of these individuals, one of whom escorted him over to a registration desk. Once more his credentials were checked, this time by a Cunard employee, who inputted Vince's name into a laptop. Vince handed over his VISA card to set up an onboard account to cover any incidental charges that he might incur during the crossing, and received a VIP Gold card showing that he had been assigned to cabin 1037. His actual ticket was placed in a blue leather document holder, and with this in hand, he headed for yet another security checkpoint.

His bags were placed on a table, opened up, and carefully inspected by a serious-faced, middle-aged woman, who Vince suspected worked for the U.S. Customs Service. Yet another security official arrived with a golden retriever in tow. The dog deftly jumped up onto the table top, and curiously sniffed the exposed contents of Vince's luggage.

Vince's duffel bag caught the retriever's attention. After the briefest of sniffs, the dog let out a series of high-pitched yelps, prompting its concerned handler to take a closer look at the bag's contents.

"It's my ammo," said Vince, referring to the sealed box of 9mm shells which the security official rummaged around for and extracted.

Vince discreetly opened his jacket to reveal his Glock 17 pistol firmly stowed in a chamois shoulder harness. "And I imagine you'll be interested in taking a look at this as well."

"That won't be necessary," replied a deep male voice from behind him.

Vince turned and set his eyes on a smiling, sandy-haired gentleman, nattily attired in a hand-tailored black suit.

"Just wanted to show you that we're on the job, Vince," added this distinguished newcomer. "Glad you could make it."

"It's good to be here, Doug," said Vince as he accepted his co-worker's firm handshake.

Special Agent Doug Algren was assigned to the Secret Service's New York office. In this respect, one of his prime responsibilities for the summit was insuring the security of the terminal area.

"I see that you're traveling light," said Algren, who signaled the dog handler that it was okay to pull off the retriever.

"Agent Sykes," he added to the woman seated behind the inspection desk. "Would you be so kind as to repack Special Agent Kellogg's bags and give them to a porter to be stowed in his stateroom?"

As she got on with this task, Algren escorted Vince over to the gangway. The news crew was just finishing up its interview here, and while the reporter initiated her on-camera summation, Algren quietly relayed the latest operational update.

"I just got word that the prime ministers of Britain, Japan, Canada, and Italy have arrived at the United Nations. All the rest are due to arrive in town as scheduled, except for President Li of China."

"Hope he didn't get cold feet," remarked Vince.

"It's nothing like that," explained Algren. "Because of unexpected headwinds, his plane is being forced into making an unplanned refueling stop in San Francisco. That will make his ETA at Kennedy sometime around nine P.M."

Vince grimaced. "That's certainly cutting it close to the bone."

"The FAA will do its best to give Li's 747 the quickest route over CONUS"—the continental United States—"and a straight-in approach to Kennedy, where Marine Two will be waiting to whisk him into Manhattan."

"Did you ever clear up that mix-up with the longshoremen?" asked Vince.

This time it was Special Agent Algren who frowned. "I really can't believe those guys. The head of their union was going to try and get a court injunction to keep our men off the docks. Since this whole undercover operation was my initial idea, I had IRS do a quick check on the union's books. Needless to say, once the union got wind of this investigation, they got religion. Now we've got two special tactics teams working the terminal right alongside the regulars."

The television crew was packing up its equipment immediately behind Algren, and the ship's officer who had been interviewed walked over to join the two Secret Service agents. He was a barrel-chested, muscular young man, with short, wavy brown hair and a pleasant reserved manner that he readily displayed.

"Man, I'm sure glad that's over," he said with a strong British accent.

"What's the matter, Tuff, don't you want to be a TV star?" teased Algren, who graciously initiated the introductions. "Tuff, I'd like you to meet a very special friend, Special Agent Vince Kellogg of our Washington, D.C., office."

Vince accepted a vicelike handshake, and listened as Algren added. "Tuff is one of the *QE2*'s security officers, Vince. I imagine that you two will be seeing a lot of each other these next five days."

"Are you certain that you won't change your mind and join us at sea, Special Agent Algren?" asked Tuff in all seriousness.

"You're going to have enough hired guns around as it is," replied Algren. "Besides, I'm quite content to have my responsibility confined to this solid side of the gangway."

Tuff's two-way radio crackled alive, and the thirty-four-year-old Englishman received a page calling him to the *QE2*'s Bridge. Before he could excuse himself, Doug Algren made a single request.

"Would you mind taking Special Agent Kellogg up to the Bridge with you, Tuff? That would be the perfect place for him to begin his orientation."

"I'd be delighted." Tuff gestured politely toward the open gangway.

The short transit brought Vince through a large accessway and directly into the *QE2*'s portside hull. A carpeted walkway led him into a lush compartment dominated by a circular reception area. A panoramic mural depicting Cunard Line's past and present history completely encircled this room. Tuff was quick to identify it.

"This is the Midships Lobby, located on Two Deck. In the majority of ports, this is the first portion of the ship that embarking passengers will see. We'll be heading forward to the A Stairway, as we continue on to the Bridge."

From his previous study of the ship's layout, Vince knew this already. But he also knew not to interrupt a man sharing his pride and joy.

Tuff led the way down another carpeted passageway. Passenger cabins lined the starboard side of this corridor, and Tuff identified the closed doorways located opposite them.

"That first door belongs to the auxiliary Security Office. A member of our staff is on duty there twenty-four hours a day. Beside it is where the first officer works, along with his secretary, Sally. Should you ever need to see the captain or any other of the ship's senior officers, Sally will make the proper arrangements."

At the end of the passageway they turned left, and as they headed toward a central stairway, they passed the ship's Computer Learning Center. A large, glass-enclosed room was filled with over a dozen individual personal computers.

Vince followed Tuff up a steep, twisting stairway. It took a total effort on his part to keep up with his English tour guide, and by the time they reached the top landing, Vince was clearly out of breath. Tuff didn't seem the least bit fazed by this climb, and he took a second to give Vince a brief position update.

"We're currently on the Boat Deck. Our climb took us past One Deck, where I believe your cabin is located. Then we passed Quarter Deck, where you can access the Princess Grill, the Caronia Restaurant, the Chart Room Bar, Library, Bookshop, Queens Room, and the Lido. Next comes the Upper Deck. That's where you'll find the Mauretania Restaurant, the largest theater afloat, the Casino, the Grand Lounge, and my favorite hangout, the Yacht Club Bar."

Vince noted that a bank of elevators were located directly across from the stairway they had just climbed. To their immediate right was an intricately carved wooden figurehead, while the curtained entrance to yet another public room lay beyond.

"That figurehead over there is named after the *Britannia*, Samuel Cunard's first ship. She was a wooden paddle steamer, built in 1840 for the express purpose of carrying the mail between Great Britain and North America."

While Vince took a closer look at it, Tuff added, "I hope that you don't mind a little history with your tour, sir. Because this ship's just filled with it."

"Please go on, Tuff," Vince said sincerely. "History's one of my passions."

"Then you'll be pleased to learn that the *Britannia* figurehead has been carved out of Quebec yellow pine by the Cornish sculptor Charles Moore. It was Lloyd's of London that presented it to the ship."

A crew member emerged from a compartment located to their right and Tuff nodded in greeting. He waited for him to disappear down the stairway before continuing. "That sailor just came from our Radio Room. Like Security, it's manned twenty-four hours a day. We offer the latest in satellite communications, and also keep in touch with the outside world by radio telegraphy, telex, and fax."

"What's behind those curtained double doors at the after end of this passageway?" asked Vince.

"That's the Queen's Grill Restaurant. It's the ship's most exclusive dining area, reserved for 231 of our passengers. Unlike the other restaurants that serve off of traditional menus, one can order almost anything the heart desires, including lobster, prime steaks, or all the caviar you can eat, every single day of the crossing."

Vince patted his stomach temptingly. "Sounds good, Tuff, especially since all I've had to eat today is a rubbery bagel on the airplane."

"Lunch will be served shortly, sir. And even though it's not lobster and caviar, we'll take good care of you."

"I'm sure you will."

Tuff proceeded to his left, through a doorway marked OFFICERS AND CREW ONLY. A short hall led to a closed door that Tuff opened and beckoned Vince to join him inside. The spacious room they now found themselves in had a warm, clublike atmosphere, its walls covered with dozens of plaques, photos, and other nautical memorabilia.

"Since you're a lover of history, I thought you'd enjoy taking a quick peek at our Wardroom, sir."

Vince was speechless as he examined signed prints of Her Majesty

Queen Elizabeth II and the Duke of Edinburgh. A gleaming brass bell that was engraved, R.M.S.AQUITANIA, was positioned close by.

"The *Aquitania* was the sister ship to the *Lusitania* and the *Mauretania.* She was delivered in 1914, and allowed Cunard to maintain the first weekly sailing schedule from both sides of the Atlantic." Tuff next guided Vince past a fully stocked pub. "I do hope you'll join me and the lads down here for a pint once you've gotten settled."

Vince found himself drawn to the forward portion of the Wardroom, where a series of large, rectangular portholes afforded an unobstructed view of the *QE2*'s bow and the majestic skyline of Manhattan beyond. Many of the colorful photos and plaques mounted on the bulkhead were gifts from various military units, ranging from Great Britain's Royal Air Force, to the French foreign legion, NASA, and the U.S. Coast Guard.

"Looks like you've entertained some interesting guests, Tuff."

Tuff grinned fondly. "This ship has a long tradition of cooperating with the military. In fact, it was while in Her Majesty's Service that I first sailed aboard the *Queen.* That was back in 1982, when she was converted into a troopship to convey over three thousand of us down to the Falklands."

"Were you Royal Navy?" questioned Vince.

"Royal Marines Special Boat Service, sir," revealed Tuff proudly, who looked at his watch and added, "Now I'd better get you up to the bridge. The chief must think that I've gone AWOL."

Leaving the Wardroom, they made a sharp right, went up a twisting flight of narrow stairs, past the door to the captain's well-appointed office, to a closed, steel hatch labeled, BRIDGE, AUTHORIZED ADMITTANCE ONLY.

Tuff signaled Vince to join him on the top step, and pointed toward the video camera mounted above the hatch. With his guest close at his side, he twice pushed the metal switch that was recessed into the wall on his left. There was a loud buzzing sound, and several seconds passed before they heard the metallic click of an automatic lock triggering. Vince followed Tuff inside.

The Bridge itself was extremely spacious and well lit. A series of large, rectangular windows encircled the elongated, wood-paneled compartment. Set against the forward bulkhead was the main console. It was painted a dull yellow, and was filled with a wide variety of instruments, gauges, and dials. Directly behind it was a five-foot-high, lime-green, lectern-shaped console onto which the ship's dinner-plate-sized wheel was mounted. A shoulder-high wooden partition was set up behind the wheel, with the navigation plot on the other side.

On each side of the Bridge an open doorway led to a pair of adjoining exterior observation wings. Vince spotted a single, somewhat familiar bearded figure on the port wing. This tall, silver-haired individual was dressed in officer's whites, and was scanning the surrounding terminal area with his binoculars. This was surely the same figure that Vince had first seen from the cab.

Tuff headed out onto the wing and addressed the officer. "Sorry that I took so long, Chief."

The officer responded without lowering his binoculars, his words flavored by a rich Scottish accent. "If we were at sea, I'd have you keelhauled, lad. And since I can't give you fifty lashes, I guess I'm stuck with you. Any problems down below?"

While Tuff related a quick security update, Vince took this opportunity to walk out onto the other wing and examine the ship from a new angle. He'd only been there a moment, though, when a deep Scottish voice broke in behind him.

"So you're Special Agent Vincent Kellogg of the U.S. Secret Service. Welcome aboard the *Queen*."

Vince turned and found himself staring into a piercing blue gaze, that locked into him with an intense inquisitiveness.

"Thank you," replied Vince as he accepted the officer's handshake.

"I'm Robert Hartwell, the *QE2*'s security director," said the Scotsman. "I do hope that Tuff has been taking good care of you. And please feel free to call me Robert."

Vince liked this man's directness, and had been impressed with him since reading a report about Hartwell back in Washington. The *QE2*'s current head of security was a decorated Royal Marine veteran, who like Tuff had also been a member of the elite Special Boat Service. As an SBS commando, Hartwell saw past service in Northern Ireland, Dhofar, and the Falklands, where he was awarded a South Atlantic Medal for bravery. He was made a Member of the British Empire in 1993, though he never rose above the rank of warrant officer. It was shortly thereafter that he left the military to take his current position with Cunard.

"I understand that this is your first visit aboard the *Queen*," added Hartwell. "You certainly brought along spectacular weather."

Vince looked up into the clear, sun-filled sky as a helicopter passed noisily overhead. "I hope it holds until this evening."

Hartwell replied while also watching the helicopter, "The latest meteorological forecast shows that this high-pressure system should stay around long enough to insure a dry send-off."

The helicopter began a sweeping turn, and appeared to drop slightly in altitude as it circled the Passenger Ship Terminal. Hartwell examined it through his binoculars.

"Bloody journalists have a video cameraman hanging out that chopper's fuselage door," Hartwell said. "It looks like they didn't even bother rigging up a safety harness for that poor chap."

The helicopter further tightened its banked turn, prompting Vince to comment disgustedly, "They'd better get all the videotape they need today. Because, as of 1800 tonight, the airspace over the entire West Side of Manhattan will be strictly off-limits."

With the loud clatter of the chopper's rotors making conversation difficult, Hartwell beckoned Vince and Tuff to join him inside, where the ship's in-house, VHF, closed-circuit telephone activated. A concerned female voice broke in from the elevated speaker.

"Bridge, this is Delta. Do you copy?"

Tuff picked up the handset and answered. "I copy that, Delta. How can we be of service?"

"Tuff," returned the caller, "Roz Walters wants to reboard the ship, and the Secret Service won't let her because she's gone and left her special access pass in her stateroom."

"Tell Roz to hold on a sec, Delta. I'm on my way down."

Tuff hung up the handset and addressed Robert Hartwell. "Sir, I can get that updated personnel manifest to you right after I take care of Roz."

"Don't worry about it, Tuff," replied Hartwell. "Take your time, and make sure the Secret Service doesn't go and arrest our accommodations manager. My relief should be popping in any second now. I'll pick up the manifest myself while showing Special Agent Kellogg the way to his cabin."

Tuff exited the Bridge with a crisp salute. Hartwell looked at Vince and smiled. "They don't come much better than that one. We entered Port Stanley together, and he's still packing some Argentine shrapnel that had my name on it."

"I had the honor of serving with men like Tuff back in 'Nam," Vince said. "Special Forces have a way of bringing together the best and brightest. Now, I hope that our agents aren't being too tough on your crew. If they're being a pain, please let me know and I'll see what I can do."

"Nonsense," snapped Hartwell. "Your people are doing a brilliant job, and I wouldn't have it any other way. The tighter they manage things outside this ship the easier my job will be once we put to sea."

"Have any other members of the various international security teams arrived on board as yet?" Vince asked.

"Only a contingent from MI5," answered Hartwell. "Right now, they're with our prime minister at the United Nations."

Vince looked at his watch and commented. "I've tentatively scheduled a prebriefing of all embarking security personnel this afternoon at 1600. Could you find us a place on board where we could meet?"

"I'll see about securing us the Library," said Hartwell, who also glanced at his watch. "I imagine that you'd like to unpack your belongings and get settled in your stateroom."

"Actually, I'm anxious to get in a complete tour of the ship," Vince admitted.

"I'll tell you what, Special Agent Kellogg, once my relief shows up, why not accompany me down to my office? Then I'll give you a chance to unpack your belongings before we have an early lunch, followed by a thorough walk-thru."

Before Vince could answer, a slender, crew-cut officer in his mid-thirties arrived on the Bridge. He wore black trousers, a black tie, and a white, long-sleeve shirt, with three golden stripes bedecking his shoulder epaulets.

"Good day, Chief Hartwell," greeted this newcomer, his dialect thick with England's northern district.

"And a good day to you, Mr. Smith," returned Hartwell, who looked over at Vince. "Special Agent Kellogg, I'd like you to meet Steve Smith, the ship's navigator and my current relief."

Vince traded handshakes with the good-natured navigator, and took this opportunity to ask him a question. "Do you mind if I visit you once I get settled in, Mr. Smith? I'd like to know more about our exact route from a first-hand perspective."

"You're always welcome to join me on the Bridge," returned the navigator. "My watch periods for this crossing will be posted this evening, and all I ask is that you forget about the 'Mr. Smith' part, and call me by my first name."

"Steve, it is."

"Good show," said Hartwell as he gathered together some papers he had been working on, and prepared to pass on the watch to the navigator. "Engineering currently has Charlie down for maintenance, with the fuel barge alongside, preparing to pump diesel. We continue at a level-red security alert, with the captain and the first officer still at headquarters. Tuff's down at Delta if you should need him, don't be shy about asking. Many of the crew should be coming back for lunch shortly, and I'll bet my pension half of them forgot to take along their special passes and will never clear security."

It proved to be the grinding clatter of the helicopter that reminded Hartwell of one other matter. "Oh, and Steve, we've got a film chopper out there that's been circling us for the last five minutes. If they get much closer, they're going to smack right into our funnel, so don't hesitate to contact them on Channel Thirteen. And if that doesn't send them packing, call the blooming Coast Guard emergency response team on Channel Sixteen."

"Aye, aye," said the navigator.

Vince followed the ship's security officer out the same hatch that he and Tuff had originally entered. This time when they reached the Boat Deck's A Stairway, they continued their descent to Two Deck using the elevator. Vince felt a bit more at home as they passed by the Computer Learning Center and continued on through the Midships Lobby.

Beyond the Lobby, they began their way down a passageway that stretched the entire length of the shop, giving Vince a new perspective on the vessel's immense size.

Passenger cabins lined the corridor's port side. They were arranged in an odd-numbered sequence, beginning with room 2063 and continuing aft. The carpeted hall looked like it belonged in a five-star hotel, and Vince was hoping that one of the cabin doors would be open so he could see the interior. Yet in every instance, the doors were shut tight, with a strip of red tape sealed across each portal.

"What's with the tape?" asked Vince as they passed the shut door of room 2077.

"It's all part of my security plan," explained Hartwell without breaking his stride. "Because of the light passenger load of our up-coming crossing, we're able to temporarily seal off over seven hundred of our seven hundred seventy-nine available cabins. This means Two, Three, Four and Five Decks will be completely unoccupied. We'll only have to concern ourselves with patrolling One Deck, where the security teams and advisors will be staying, and the smaller Boat, Sun and Signal Decks, where the heads of state will have their quarters."

"I imagine that this lighter passenger load means a reduced staff," Vince offered.

"That it does," answered Hartwell as they passed the Purser's Office on their right. "Over four hundred chambermaids, waiters, cooks, stewards, beauticians, and other utility staff members have been placed on temporary leave. This leaves us with a crew of fewer than six hundred individuals—another plus when it comes down to insuring interior security."

They were near the end of the main passageway now. Vince followed Hartwell down a narrow corridor that wound its way behind the Safe-Deposit Center. They halted in front of a closed, unmarked door, situated beside the H Stairway. The ship's security director reached into his pocket and removed a clip-style key ring. He isolated the first of many keys, and used it to unlock the door.

"This is home for me. Come on in and I'll show you around before taking you up to your cabin."

Vince entered, and found himself inside a small office, dominated by a huge world map that was tacked to the wall behind the sole desk. Several framed photographs of golf courses hung beside the map. The holes pictured were definitely Scottish in design, with huge circular bunkers and tight, treeless fairways. A putting machine, complete with an Astroturf fringe, was set up in front of the book-case. Plenty of golf balls and three different styles of putters were close by. Vince didn't have to see any more to figure out Hartwell's favorite hobby.

"Are you by any chance a golfer, Special Agent?"

"As a matter of fact, I am," replied Vince, who took a closer look at the series of golf-course photos. "St. Andrews?"

"Gleneagles, actually," said Hartwell. "I was born nearby in Sterling, and consider these links my home course."

Vince studied the deep, unforgiving sand traps and commented. "Sure wouldn't want to get stuck in one of those suckers. I'd need a mortar to get out of there."

"I've considered carrying one in my bag for that very purpose," returned Hartwell with a laugh. "Say, is your President really the avid golfer that the press makes him out to be?"

Vince turned away from the photos to face his host. "The man's a golf nut, so much so that his unofficial Secret Service code name is Two-Putt. Even with his crazed schedule, he still manages to squeeze out a couple quick rounds every week. Since I was captain of my college golf team, I often get picked to accompany him."

"Sounds like you must get to play some superb courses."

"That's definitely one of the better perks of my job," Vince returned.

"If you ever want to practice your putting stroke while we're out at sea, please don't hesitate to come down and make yourself at home. I've even got the new *PGA Tour '98* CD loaded into my laptop, and you're always welcome to give it a go."

"I appreciate the offer. But I'm afraid I'm not going to have much free time these next five days."

Hartwell nodded thoughtfully in agreement. "I want you to rest assured that my team is doing everything we can do to make this upcoming crossing as incident-free as possible. One very positive benefit of holding this summit at sea is our ability to control complete access to this platform. With the assistance of your people inside the terminal, we're able to monitor every individual or piece of cargo brought on board. For all effective purposes, the *QE2* is a secured island, and we hold the only entry key."

"I'm certain that you've done a thorough job insuring the *QE2*'s integrity," said Vince. "But I'm still going to feel better once I've completed that walk-thru of the ship to see what we're dealing with."

"That's only understandable. A vessel this size creates a unique security challenge. The below-deck spaces alone offer an almost infinite amount of locations in which to hide a stowaway or explosive device. Because of this ship's high international profile, we constantly drill to address this problem. Our current reduced crew and passenger load makes this difficult task much easier. Since arriving in port yesterday, the ship has already undergone three complete security sweeps. One of your special-tactics teams and its dogs accompanied us in each instance, as we scoured the ship from bow to stern.

"As you very well know," Hartwell continued, "we even have a group of U.S. Navy divers inspecting our exterior hull for limpet mines. And once the various security teams arrive, we plan yet another intensive sweep of the ship, with representatives of each of these groups present."

"The idea of mixing together fifty agents from nine different countries is a challenge all its own," Vince interjected.

Hartwell pointed to the three-inch-thick pile of documents that completely filled his desk's In basket, and added, "Tell me about it. This stack of correspondence arrived only this morning, and was generated solely by the Japanese security service. It covers everything from the amount of ammunition their agents are allowed to bring along with them, to the selection and quality of food being served."

Vince shook his head in amazement. "I'll never forget the struggle we had fighting to get them to agree to the six-agent limit. The Japanese wanted to bring along forty agents all on their own, with the Russians originally proposing to take along twice as many."

"Your six-man limit was an excellent choice," complimented Hartwell. "It allows each head of state a continuous two-man security presence, with individual eight-hour increments. And even then, most of this active duty will be spent idly waiting outside the meeting rooms. Because as you'll soon see, my team is well prepared to handle the monitoring of the rest of the *Queen*."

With this remark, Hartwell led his guest over to the wall beside the bookshelf. A door conveyed them into a dimly lit room about the size of a large, walk-in closet. It held a ceiling-to-floor wall unit packed with a dozen, eighteen-inch video monitors. The Scot gestured Vince to join him in one of the high-backed leather chairs positioned directly in front of the blackened monitors. As Vince did so, Hartwell pulled out a computer keyboard from beneath the console's desktop.

He inputted a series of commands, and one by one, the video screens activated. The crystal-clear, black-and-white pictures that soon filled all dozen screens provided real-time video from twelve different locations inside the *QE2*. Vince scanned the flickering monitors and identified the ship's navigator calmly sipping a cup of tea on the Bridge. Yet another screen was filled with a wide-angle shot of the Midships Lobby, where a uniformed steward was in the process of vacuuming the carpet. Other screens showed various crew members at work inside the vessel's Kitchen and Engine Room, while adjoining monitors displayed multiangled shots of the ship's above-deck spaces, including the exterior Pool, dual Hot Tubs, and Paddleboard Courts.

"Here's the real force multiplier," said Hartwell as he expertly readdressed the keyboard.

Vince watched as the picture on the top, left-hand monitor suddenly split into four different video images. In this instance, the cameras displayed long shots of four different interior passageways.

"That scan covers the Signal Deck, where the VIP Penthouses are located, and also includes a view of the walkway outside the Sports Deck suites, as well as two different angles of the One Deck passenger cabin passageway. When fully utilized, I can monitor forty-eight separate locations at one time, guaranteeing an almost constant surveillance presence from one of the two-hundred-plus video cameras hidden throughout the ship."

Vince was impressed by this sophisticated system, and he watched as the central monitor showing the Midships Lobby filled with two new arrivals. One of these figures was a familiar, barrel-chested officer, the other a shapely, civilian female, with a full head of curly, shoulder-length hair.

"I see Tuff's just entered the Midships Lobby," observed Vince.

"And it appears that he's managed to get your people to allow Roz Walters, our accommodations manager, back onboard," Hartwell added.

With a quick sweep of his hand, Hartwell manipulated a joy stick that sat next to the keyboard. This caused the magnification of the video image they had been watching to greatly increase so they could actually see Tuff's lips moving as he escorted his fellow crewmate out the forward accessway.

"One accessory that's not been fitted is an audio feed," Hartwell remarked.

"I don't suppose that you've got coverage inside the individual staterooms?" asked Vince.

A playful grin crossed Hartwell's bearded face as he answered. "Though that capability is readily available, company policy strictly forbids it. You can rest peacefully tonight, knowing that whatever you choose to do within the confines of your cabin will remain completely private."

Vince watched as Hartwell used the keyboard to isolate one of the four bottom monitors. In quick succession, the screen filled with a scan of the ship's vacant, well-stocked Infirmary and luxurious Spa. The video image abruptly switched to an empty indoor Swimming Pool. Hartwell readjusted the angle of the camera lens, and Vince got his first look at the *QE2*'s renowned Gymnasium. It was known as the most complete workout facility afloat, with a wide assortment of exercise machines, a spacious aerobics area, and a full Nautilus circuit.

Several workmen could be seen removing one of the StairMasters and loading it onto a two-wheeler, prompting the Scotsman to comment matter-of-factly, "Looks like we'll be getting that replacement equipment after all."

"Replacement equipment?"

"Electrical short last crossing took out a StairMaster, rowing machine, and all three of the bicycles. Since I'm a bike rider myself, and constantly fighting to keep my weight under control, those replacements will be greatly appreciated."

"I just enrolled in a YMCA aerobics class to address my own battle of the bulge," admitted Vince. "I must really be starting to feel my age, because those workouts seem just as tough as the ones we went through in army basic training."

"Aerobics, you say? Well you're in luck, Special Agent. Because this crossing, we've got none other than Monica Chang leading our workouts."

"Monica Chang, the actress?" queried the disbelieving Treasury agent. "I'm sure I didn't see her name on the crew manifest."

"That's because it wasn't on the original," revealed Hartwell. "Two days ago, as we were completing the last crossing from Southampton, our entire Gym staff fell victim to a nasty intestinal bug. Ms. Chang is part owner of the firm that runs the Gym for Cunard, along with Dennis Liu, the action-film star. Fortunately for us, they've both just finished their most recent pictures, and offered to personally accompany a hand-picked replacement staff. Between you and me, it may also have to do with getting free publicity for a new workout video I understand they are about to put out. But I'm just happy that all our amenities will be available during the summit. That's good publicity for us."

"This is all news to me," said Vince, suddenly concerned. "Have they traced down the origins of that intestinal virus? If it's salmonella, we're going to have to go through the entire Kitchen with a fine-tooth comb. Hell, it could even mean the canceling of this whole crossing!"

Hartwell sensed the seriousness of Vince's reaction and isolated various shots of the *QE2*'s spotlessly clean Kitchen on four of the screens before attempting damage control. "Easy does it, Special Agent. I'm personally working with the ship's doctor to determine the exact source of the outbreak. We're almost certain that the virus was caused by a meal that the Gym staff cooked for themselves, two nights after leaving Southampton."

"I'm still going to need a detailed report of this entire incident to give to Dr. Patton, the President's physician," said Vince. "And then I'd like to personally speak to the ship's executive chef and the head storekeeper." Almost as an afterthought, he added, "Are there any other last-minute crew replacements who weren't on the original manifest?"

"There are thirteen in all," Hartwell revealed. "I've already faxed the list to the head of your New York office, and there's a copy for you on my desk. As for talking with the chef, he's supposed to be joining us for lunch. Let's get you settled in your cabin first. Then after lunch, you'll be free to explore the ship and initiate any further investigative work."

5

THE MUCH ANTICIPATED PHONE CALL FROM THE BATF'S DIRECTOR, LAWRENCE McShane, found Thomas Kellogg seated alongside Mike Galloway, inside the senior postal inspector's office. Army M. Sgt. Danny Lane had just arrived from Fort Meade, and the explosives-ordnance expert was showing them the latest in bomb-disposal fashions.

The director relayed his decision in his usual clipped fashion. "You've got a green light to defuse, Thomas. So get on with it, work safely, and find something we can use to catch this guy."

Thomas had to hurry his thanks before the line went dead. Then he flashed a triumphant thumbs-up to his associates.

Sergeant Lane seemed particularly delighted with the news, and he addressed Mike Galloway sarcastically. "I sure hope your insurance is paid up on that holding structure, Mike."

Galloway didn't laugh. "Though I still think you guys are crazy for risking your lives, you've got my full cooperation."

"That's much appreciated, Mike," replied Thomas. "Since the Sarge here brought along all the latest gear, all we're going to need from you is to evacuate the facility."

Galloway looked at his wristwatch, then reached out to pick up the phone and notify his workers of this shortened workday. "If my folks hurry, looks like we can get off one last truckload of gifts for the White House before closing up the place."

Less than an hour later, the mood of those left at the mail-sorting facility was noticeably more tense. The time for humor and excitement was over, as Thomas, Sergeant Lane, and his two assistants made the final adjustments to their gear. With Mike Galloway manning the phones inside the warehouse, the quartet of explosives experts waddled out to the isolated, concrete block holding structure, looking like astronauts in their bulky, fireproof jumpsuits.

The game plan for the operation was relatively simple despite the danger. Since the goal was to reap the benefit of a complete set of evidence, the objective was to render the IED harmless. The easiest way to accomplish this feat was to disconnect the device's power source. Without its two nine-volt batteries, the photoelectric circuit they expected to find based on the design of the bomber's first package could not generate the spark needed to trigger the primer, and in turn, ignite the main charge.

Since X-rays of the IED had already determined the exact position of these batteries, all that remained for them to do was to open the Priority Mail box and disconnect the fusing wires from the battery terminals. However, a life-or-death question remained: how could they penetrate the parcel without activating the light-sensitive photocell and triggering an explosion themselves?

Both Thomas and Danny Lane had worked together on several previous occasions, and they decided on a two-prong attack. Their first priority was to complete the installation of a portable, red-tinted safelight. This allowed them to illuminate the interior of the holding cell with the same setup a photographer used to develop film inside a darkroom.

Danny Lane was fearful that the photocell could be sensitive enough to trigger regardless of this safelight array, and he brought along what he fondly called their "supplementary insurance policy." This novel technique, developed by Lane himself, involved using liquid nitrogen to freeze the unopened box and drain the charge from the batteries, thus deadening them permanently.

The final adjustments to the safelight were completed with the invaluable help of Lane's two assistants. The specially designed, pressurized canister holding the liquid nitrogen was then carried inside the holding structure. Meanwhile Thomas readied the instruments for actually cutting into the box.

Completely lit in dim red light now, the interior of the concrete blockhouse took on a sinister appearance. The thick, protective suits were making the men extremely hot, and they decided to start without further delay. The two assistants were excused, and with the room's sole doorway securely sealed, they went to work in earnest.

His hands protected by heavily quilted asbestos mittens, Danny Lane carefully picked up the liquid nitrogen canister, unsealed its pressurized lid, and completely saturated the Priority Mail package with a frigid stream of supercooled vapor. Swirling white fingers of −320° liquid nitrogen enveloped the cardboard parcel, and for a confusing moment, Thomas feared that it had disintegrated. Only when the icy cloud finally evaporated, revealing the now frozen package, did Thomas exhale a long breath of relief.

It was now Thomas's turn to pick up one of the finely honed, scalpel-like instruments and begin the nerve-racking job of slicing into the frigid cardboard. Mike Galloway had previously made a hand-drawn duplicate of the parcel's X-ray negative. This tracing was laid out on the top surface of the package, enabling them to determine that the batteries were located in the right-hand portion of the box, corresponding to a spot beside the outer edge of the address label.

His intention was to make a long incision in the cardboard, alongside the address label. This cut was to be deep enough to pierce the outer layer of cardboard, but shallow enough not to penetrate the layer of protective wrapping they expected to find inside.

To accomplish this delicate task, Thomas had to remove one of his bulky mittens, and make the cut with his hand unprotected. He seriously doubted that the glove would offer much protection should one of the blasting caps detonate; nevertheless he was careful not to allow the bare skin of his hand to touch the package. The frozen cardboard was itself dangerous, able to induce instant frostbite.

Before making the initial incision, Thomas took a second to catch the gaze of his coworker. Danny Lane had just grabbed a pair of slender, needle-nose wire cutters, and the Army EOD technician silently conveyed his own concern with a supportive wink.

The Sarge, as he was better known around the Metro area, was one of the best bomb men in the country. Career military, he learned his arcane craft in Vietnam, where his initial interest was in disarming minefields. He soon enough found that he had an almost inborn knack for this glamourless, all-important work that was responsible for saving untold lives.

Thomas first met Danny three years previously, during a car comb investigation at a Falls Church abortion clinic. The Sarge had only recently transferred to Fort Meade. He showed his valor by crawling under the suspect vehicle, and removing a live pipe bomb from its muffler.

In the years since, Lane had proved himself to be an invaluable associate in the dozens of bomb and arson investigations that followed. He always seemed to be available to help, offering his services not only to the BATF, but to any civilian or federal law enforcement agency that needed him.

His mere presence was a stabilizing factor, his calm professional manner exuding confidence, a commodity that no explosives technician could get enough of. M. Sgt. Danny Lane wasn't about to allow anything to go wrong on his watch. With this hope in mind, Thomas positioned the razor-sharp tip of the scalpel alongside the right edge of the parcel's address label.

"I don't know about you, Kellogg," said Lane, "but the sooner we get this job done the better. This new monkey suit is causing me to sweat up a storm."

Thomas nodded somberly. His body had long since been soaked in perspiration, and he was thankful for the bandanna that he remembered to tie around his forehead.

He applied just enough downward pressure to break through the frozen cardboard liner's stiff outer skin. Holding the sharply honed tip of the scalpel steady with his right index finger, Thomas began a quick, four-inch downward cut. This incision compromised the parcel's seal, allowing them to quickly learn if the IED's suspected photocell triggering mechanism remained active or not.

To determine this, Thomas made two more incisions. These were two-inch cuts, extending from the right-hand upper and bottom edges of the label, continuing on to the side of the box itself. This created a neat, three-sided flap in the cardboard's outer skin that Danny Lane cautiously probed with a slender forceps.

"Excellent job, Thomas," whispered Lane. "Now, if you'll just hold down the cardboard at the upper edge of your incision, we'll see if our suspicions hold true."

Thomas did as instructed, watching breathlessly as the Sarge proceeded to peel back the brittle edges of the cardboard flap. There could be no worse time for his soaked bandanna to fail him. Thomas found his vision momentarily clouded by a torrent of stinging sweat. He wiped his brow impatiently with the back of his forehead, and as he reopened his eyes, he immediately spotted an uncut, inner layer of familiar black, wax-based paper.

"You've got to admit that the bastard's persistent," offered Lane, his suspicions of a photocell trigger apparently confirmed. "Are you ready to go?"

With one more layer of light-absorbing paper left to penetrate before reaching the actual device, Thomas knew that the moment of truth was upon them. They'd learn all too soon whether their precautions were sufficient. His pulse quickened and his mouth was unnaturally dry. He had to clear his throat to speak.

"Let's do it, Sarge."

Danny Lane didn't appear to be the least bit flustered as he picked up the needle-nosed pliers and calmly addressed Thomas. "On the count of three, you'll make the cut and I'll go in."

"Hold on a minute, Sarge," interrupted Thomas, his vision once more clouded by dripping sweat.

Lane watched his coworker impatiently wipe his soaked brow with the back of his hand. Fearful that this moisture would interfere with his grip, Lane alertly handed Thomas a handkerchief.

"Take your time, Kellogg. This baby's not going anywhere."

Thomas used the handkerchief to pat dry his forehead and wipe the moisture off his glistening palm. He took a deep breath before meeting Lane's steady gaze and nodding that he was ready to proceed.

"We'll soon enough be out of these damn space suits and sipping a tall frosty one, Thomas."

"Sounds good to me, Sarge."

Thomas regripped the scalpel and once more placed its tip up against the right edge of the address label. It wouldn't take much pressure to slice into the remaining layer of wrapping, and he listened as Lane began the countdown.

"One . . . two . . . three!"

Thomas made a quick downward cut. Danny Lane plunged the pliers into the parcel's now exposed interior. Without hesitation, he securely grasped the wires that were attached to the battery terminals and yanked them free with a swift, fluid motion. It was all over in a matter of seconds, with the two explosives technicians wasting no time on celebrations.

"Thomas, why don't you cut away that entire upper layer of cardboard, and let's see what makes this baby tick."

Even though the heart of the IED had been removed, Thomas was still apprehensive as he sliced into the upper lid, and following its edges, cut free the remaining cardboard. He used his hand to tear away the inner layer of black wrapping paper, at long last exposing the parcel's contents.

"Will you just look at that," said Lane, in reference to the two twelve-by-four-inch blocks of white, puttylike material clearly visible before them. "If that turns out to be C-4, there's enough explosive power in this IED to have incinerated the entire mail-sorting facility. Our boy's getting more ambitious."

Lane used the tapered nose of the pliers to outline the main body of the device, an 8½-by-11-inch piece of fiberboard. Firmly attached to this base was a maze of wires and an odd assortment of hardware that he was quick to identify.

"The fusing system looks basic enough—our photocell, two transistors, two rheostats, and a relay."

"Why the dual rheostats?" asked Thomas.

"I'd say it's to adjust the sensitivity of the circuit," Lane answered. "All the wiring connections appear to be soldered, and the workmanship looks pretty decent."

Thomas used a compact Maglite to point out the IED's explosive charge. "How do you think it's primed, #8s or J-2s?"

"My money's on dual #8 commercial blasting caps, Thomas. If we find a J-2 military cap in there, I'd be genuinely surprised."

Thomas closely examined all the individual pieces of hardware with his Maglite. The device would be conveyed to the lab now. There each part would be carefully scrutinized, and the results fed into the BATF's Explosives Incidents System, or EXIS for short. This computerized program contained a record of every single explosives incident reported to or investigated by the Bureau. It currently held over 40,000 individual investigations, and a detailed accounting of more than 150,000 pieces of individual evidence. They hadn't been able to connect the previous bomb with any known bomb or bombmaker. With luck, there was something different about this one besides the size of the charge that would let EXIS catch him in its sights.

It took a full hour to prepare the IED for transfer back to the Bureau's laboratory. A specially designed armored van was driven up to the entrance of the isolated blockhouse, with the device itself loaded into a heavy, fire-proof vault, before being carefully carried into the vehicle's rear holding bed.

Although Thomas had planned to drive his own car directly to the lab to continue the intricate task of dissecting the IED, a phone call redirected him. Samuel Morrison was the Special Agent in Charge (SAIC) of the President's White House Secret Service detail. He was well aware that the device they had just defused had been originally addressed to 1600 Pennsylvania Avenue. Morrison politely asked Thomas to proceed to the White House at once to personally brief him on their findings.

It was still much too early in the investigation to come up with any concrete conclusions as to the identity of their suspects. The real police work was only beginning, yet Thomas dared not disappoint the powerful Morrison.

George Washington Memorial Parkway was heavy with late afternoon traffic by the time he was finally free to leave the mail-sorting facility and return to the city. As Thomas bided his time in the bumper-to-bumper traffic jam, he mentally walked through the bomb's disarming. One mere slip of the hand or miscalculation could have meant instant death, so he wanted to analyze every step they had taken to prepare him for future work.

In a macabre way, the realization that he'd been so close to dying was stimulating. He had experienced this sensation before, especially in the military on the eve of battle. By voluntarily putting one's mortality on the line, an individual could get a rare opportunity to savor the real essence of life.

Thomas wondered how many of the frustrated, honking drivers around him realized what a petty and insignificant event a mere traffic tie-up was in the total scheme of things. Obsessed with small, meaningless activities and details, engrossed in purposeless employment and unsatisfying relationships, they wasted their years, totally unaware of how precious each second of their existence was.

When he reached the White House, he circled behind the Executive Office Building, entering the grounds via the South Lawn gate. He personally knew the guards here, so was able to park in one of the spaces reserved for visiting Treasury Department officials.

This was the same lot where Vince normally parked. As Thomas exited his vehicle, he wondered how his brother was doing. He was most likely somewhere on the QE2 right now, in the process of attending to that growing list of last-minute details that always seemed to pop up. Once he completed his business with the SAIC, Thomas intended to find a secure phone and call Vince.

A uniformed Secret Service agent stationed outside the West Portico informed Thomas that the SAIC was last seen headed toward the South Lawn. In little less than an hour, Marine One would be landing here, to whisk the President off to Andrews and a New York-bound flight aboard Air Force One. Before boarding the helicopter, the President would make a brief statement to the American people from the South Lawn's terraced rose garden. The President considered this address so important that even the likes of Samuel Morrison had been called out to insure it went off without a hitch.

At least the weather would cooperate, Thomas thought, enjoying the fresh air. He decided to access the South Lawn by taking the exterior, west walkway. A bed of red geraniums lined this concrete path, passing directly in front of the West Portico's side doorway.

The loud, frightened wail of a cat caused Thomas to stop momentarily. The incessant mewing continued, drawing his attention to the line of ancient oaks that lay on the opposite side of the flower bed. A quarter of the way up the smallest of the trees, stranded on a swaying branch, was a tiny black cat with a white spot on its nose. The poor feline had apparently allowed its curiosity to get the better of it. Thomas could see that it didn't have the nerve to jump to the solid earth below, even though this fall was seven feet at most.

With no groundskeeper in sight, the cat would have been in for a long stay had Thomas not made the spur-of-the-moment decision to be its savior. He crossed the flower bed, careful not to step on the geraniums, and positioned himself at the side of the tree, immediately below the stranded kitten.

"Easy does it, fella," said Thomas, while lifting his arms overhead to see if he could reach the bouncing limb. Two inches remained between his outstretched fingers and the branch. Thomas looked up at the cat and said, "Okay, Kitty. If you really want to get down from there, you're going to have to compromise a bit. Come on, fella, you can do it."

Once again he lifted his right arm overhead, this time cupping his hand directly below the kitten. The cat looked down at this offered perch, initially wanting nothing to do with it, but when no alternatives were subsequently offered, it wisely decided it was now or never. Gauging the distance with a tentative swipe of its paw, the cat gathered its nerve and plopped down onto Thomas's hand. It barely fit, and Thomas wasted no time in gently conveying it to the ground below.

"Bravo!" said a female voice from behind him. Thomas turned to find Brittany Cooper standing alone on the walkway. The Naval attaché was dressed in a crisp white uniform and held a flat map case at her side.

Thomas, suddenly realizing how ridiculous he must look, carefully jumped the flower bed and returned to the walkway. Just as his foot hit the concrete path, the kitten shot past him like a bullet, on the trail of a squirrel.

"I didn't realize that saving stranded White House pets was part of your official BATF responsibilities," Brittany teased.

"I'm just a humble public servant here to serve my government in whatever capacity it might ask of me," returned Thomas, with the slightest of playful bows. "Actually, cat rescue is only my secondary duty at the White House. I'm here at the behest of our esteemed SAIC."

Thomas reached Brittany's side, and though he would have loved to hug her, he reluctantly held back for a more appropriate time. Brittany felt likewise, and reacted to the awkwardness of the moment by trying her best to keep the conversation focused on business.

"Something tells me that your presence here has some connection with yesterday's crisis," Brittany said. Thomas nodded, and Brittany added, "I hope all went well. Can you tell me about it yet?"

"Let's just say we successfully concluded the preliminary stage of an ongoing investigation, and now the real detective work begins," answered Thomas carefully. "I'm sorry that I can't give you more details right now."

"Apologies aren't necessary, Thomas. I'm happy to see you. When you and your brother ran off like that yesterday afternoon, I didn't know what to expect."

"Sorry I didn't call last night. It was getting pretty late by the time I finally got home. And thanks for being such a good sport."

"There you go with your apologies again, Special Agent. I understand the sensitive nature of your business, even though I never realized it included rescuing pets in distress. Once you guys took off yesterday, Kelly and I finished up the barbeque and had a delicious dinner together. She's great company. We even took a walk over to King Street for ice cream, with Joshua and Max in tow. Afterwards, we loaded my bike into her van and she drove me home. So even though the day didn't exactly end the way I hoped it would, I enjoyed it all the same."

Thomas smiled at the innuendo. "I'm glad you understood. So what brings you here?"

"I just finished my final presummit briefing with the President and his national security advisors. We went over the location of the nearest U.S. Navy assets during the crossing, and then I showed them some very interesting satellite reconnaissance photos recently shot over the South China Sea."

"Are Taiwan and China at it again?"

"We can't really say for sure, Thomas. And since the story's going to break on tonight's evening news, I guess I can share it with you.

"Yesterday, during a routine pass over southeastern Asia, one of our Big Birds picked up an unusual flurry of activity taking place at the PLA Navy installation at Yulin. Four surface vessels, including a *Ling*-class salvage ship, were monitored surging into the South China Sea and headed directly toward the Spratlys. These vessels appear to be participating in some sort of underwater search-and-rescue mission."

"Is one of their submarines missing?"

Brittany paused a moment before answering. "This is totally on the hush, but my intel sources tell me that this flotilla is indeed searching for one of their submarines. We believe it's the *Lijiang*, China's newest nuclear-powered attack sub. The vessel was apparently on patrol in the region, and never responded to a prescheduled communications linkup with command. As far as we can tell, the *Lijiang* has yet to show itself, and is suspected to have been lost at sea with all hands."

Thomas grimaced. "Sounds bad. If I remember correctly, the Spratlys was where the PLA Navy tangled with that Philippine frigate several months ago. Who knows, maybe the *Lijiang* was the victim of hostilities."

"That's our greatest fear, with the Philippine Navy not the only possible aggressor. The Chinese claim on the Spratlys remains contested by a number of nations including the Philippines, Vietnam, Malaysia, Brunei, as well as Taiwan and even Japan."

"What a mess."

"You don't know the half of it. Because if it does turn out that the *Lijiang* was deliberately sunk by one of these countries, the entire region could be engulfed in a full-scale war."

"That would be a great way to start off the G-7 summit," said Thomas. "Sounds like my brother is in for an interesting crossing."

"Speaking of which," Brittany checked her wristwatch. "I've got to get back to the Pentagon. We're setting up an op center in the CNO's situation room, to monitor the *QE2*'s progress from the moment she leaves New York until she ties up in Southampton. If you can spare the time, you're more than welcome to come by and have a look."

"I'd enjoy that," said Thomas, who realized that he'd have to be on his way as well. "It was a pleasure seeing you, Commander."

"Special Agent Kellogg," said Brittany in her most official tone. "Speaking for the First Cat, keep up the excellent work!"

She left with a warm smile and a crisp salute. Thomas watched her shapely figure disappear up the walkway, headed toward the North Gate parking lot. Trying his best to refocus on his own duty, he turned in the opposite direction and continued on through a grove of majestic elms originally planted by Theodore Roosevelt and his family.

Upon emerging from the tree line, he found the South Lawn bustling with activity. Nearest to the White House itself, a group of temporary tents were still set up. They had sheltered the First Kid's gala birthday party on the previous evening. Now, the caterers could be seen at work preparing for a much more intimate affair, comprised of the birthday girl and a select group of schoolmates and friends. Unlike the previous party, adults and members of the press weren't invited, with the First Lady promising to make only a brief visit, and the President totally absent of course.

Thomas could see that the afternoon's festivities included a rock band. An elevated stage with a wall of amplifiers had been set up near the tents, with a temporary dance floor in front of it. A roadie was in the midst of a sound check. His drone: "Testing, one, two, three, four," echoed over the grounds.

Approximately three hundred yards due south of the tents, another group of individuals were busy making last-minute preparations for an upcoming event of their own. A small reception area was being prepared near the South Lawn's central fountain. Several lines of folding chairs had been set up, all facing a portable lectern whose microphone and attached PA system were also being sound-checked.

Directly behind this makeshift podium was a wide, circular clearing. Several permanent landing lights were set into the ground here, as well as a limp wind sock, all belonging to the President's personal White House helipad.

Thomas spotted a tall, broad-shouldered black man, dressed in a well-fitting, dark gray suit, standing at the extreme southern edge of the helipad. A good three inches taller than the trio of similarly dressed men who stood at his side, this individual was in the process of studying the large group of tourists who were gathered on the sidewalk behind the South Lawn's seven-foot-high, wrought-iron security fence.

Samuel Forest Morrison II was Special Agent in Charge of the presidential protection detail. A legendary character, with over two decades of Treasury Department service behind him, Morrison achieved heroic stature long before he signed on with the Secret Service.

Cut from the same mold as Danny Lane and Thomas's own brother, Morrison initially showed what he was made of as a devil with a painted face, a Green Beret, in the jungle hell of Vietnam. He was assigned primarily to the Mekong Delta, where he earned a chestful of decorations in the early seventies, for operations that remained classified to the present day.

At the end of the war, no hero's welcome awaited him as he came home to a divided country. He left the Army and decided to continue fighting for the America too many brave men had sacrificed their lives for, by dedicating his remaining years to law enforcement. Much like Vince, he went from a local police beat to the highway patrol before finally finding his true vocation as a U.S. Treasury Department agent.

Morrison earned his reputation as a solid, no-nonsense, dependable agent, through hard work and countless hours of dedication. He was an agent's agent, the type of leader who got results by first earning the trust of his subordinates. In such a manner, he rose through the ranks, with his attainment of the position of SAIC the pinnacle of his long career.

Because Vince worked directly for Morrison, Thomas knew him better than most outside agents did. He had even gotten a chance to party with the man last summer, during one of Vince's infamous backyard barbeques. Thomas thus felt at ease as he made his way down to the southern edge of the helipad and greeted the SAIC.

"Good afternoon, sir."

"Glad that you could make it, Special Agent Kellogg," returned Morrison, his practiced gaze still scanning the South Lawn's expansive grounds, his voice a deep bass James Earl Jones would envy.

The deafening strains of an overamplified rock power chord reverberated around them. Morrison quickly turned toward the stage and addressed one of his three associates angrily.

"Damn those freaks! Moreno, get your keister up there and get that sound man to cut that PA feed. For Christ's sake, this is the White House, not Woodstock!"

One of the agents who had been standing beside the SAIC nodded alertly, then took off for the party site. His two associates looked on as Morrison next vented his wrath on them.

"This whole frigging thing is going to fall apart if we don't get cracking. You guys better get up to groundskeeping and find out why they haven't roped off the helipad. And then get me that list of every soul that's going to be down here for the send-off."

Thomas knew both of these agents personally, and he watched as they flashed him the slightest of "business-as-usual" looks before excusing themselves. This left Thomas alone with their boss.

"See what your brother missed out on by being the first one on the QE2?" said Morrison, who in reality thrived on such pressure. "I bet he's sitting on board right now, sipping champagne and wondering which condiments he's going to pick to accompany his caviar."

"If I know my brother, he'll go for the works—sour cream, onions, as well as the chopped egg," Thomas quipped.

"You Kelloggs certainly know how to live," offered Morrison, who abruptly turned serious. "Now tell me all about this latest IED addressed to the House. When Mike Galloway first called me yesterday, he seemed almost certain that it was a twin of last month's device."

"For the most part, Mike was right," Thomas replied. "It indeed appears to have been sent by the same suspect. Once again, the device was placed inside a Priority Mail box and designed to be triggered by photocell. Even the handwriting on the address label looks to be an exact match, with the same fictitious Winchester, Virginia, post office box listed as the return address.

"There were two major differences, the most significant of which being that this latest device was armed with a good deal more than a blasting cap. We're still waiting for lab confirmation, but the package appears to contain enough plastic explosive to create an incredibly powerful blast. And instead of the President, the package was addressed to his daughter."

"I bet the bastard was hoping to sneak it through with her birthday presents," Morrison said.

Thomas somberly nodded. "At least this time we've got a complete set of evidence to work with."

"How did you keep the photocell from activating?" Morrison asked.

"Danny Lane gets the credit. We illuminated the holding cell with safelights. Then, as an additional backup, before opening the box, Danny froze it with liquid nitrogen, to deaden the batteries."

The SAIC smiled. "I'm sure glad the Sarge is on our side. What's next for the IED?"

"It should be arriving shortly at BATF headquarters, where Les Stanley and his team will be picking it apart piece by piece."

"I imagine that you're anxious to join this effort, Thomas. I realize that you were looking forward to going to sea with Vince, but it was my call to Director McShane that got you pulled off the crossing. Right now, I need you here, on the trail of that frigging madman."

"I appreciate your confidence, sir. And to tell you the truth, I'm not the best of sailors anyway. Hell, that's why I joined the air force."

Morrison laughed and turned his steely gaze directly on Thomas. "Have you talked with your brother since he left for New York this morning?"

"I was going to try to reach him right after seeing you, sir."

"Well I just got off the horn with him, and that bit about champagne and caviar was all in jest. He's up to his thick neck in work, coordinating the arrival of the various security teams, verifying the identities of a group of last-minute crew replacements, and even trying to track down the source of a suspected onboard case of salmonella poisoning. And Vince will really start earning his pay when the heads of state start arriving."

Morrison redirected his line of sight to the opposite side of the helipad and proceeded to change the subject. "Now where in the hell are those frigging groundskeepers with the security fence? I've got Marine One landing here in a little less than ninety minutes, and a President who's just decided to say his goodbyes to the entire country from right out here on the South Lawn."

The amplified crash of a cymbal seemed to underscore Morrison's passionate rantings. Yet before the SAIC could respond to this unwanted noise, he received a call on his two-way radio's clip-on earpiece.

Thomas watched as he pressed the miniature transmitter closer to his ear. Whatever he was hearing caused a look of serious surprise to fill his face, and Morrison peered up anxiously into the sky.

As Thomas followed his gaze, it didn't take him long to spot the object responsible for Morrison's anxiety. Circling directly above them, smack in the middle of one of the most restricted air corridors in the country, was a sole red and white, single-engine Cessna. Thomas guessed its altitude to be about 5,000 feet, and he wasn't all that shocked when Samuel Morrison cried out to him.

"Lord almighty, this is all I need! Come on, Thomas. Let's get up to the White House roof. If this gets dicey, I'm going to need to call on that air force air-traffic-control expertise of yours."

Though Thomas was a good ten years younger than Morrison, when the ex-Green Beret took off running toward the White House, it took a full effort on his part to keep up with him. They sprinted across the South Lawn at full stride, taking the stairs leading up to the South Portico two steps at a time.

Morrison didn't seem the least bit winded as he halted briefly on the exterior porch and took yet another scan of the sky. Thomas found himself gasping for breath as he stopped alongside Morrison. He looked skyward himself. The plane was still there, turning lazily in a tight circle, and if anything, its altitude appeared to have further dropped another 500 feet or so.

"Damn!" cursed Morrison. "You think our bomber has a pilot's license, Thomas? I just hope to God it's some idiotic sightseer because there's no way I want to get Two-Putt down in the box for this."

Morrison was referring to the President's subterranean fallout shelter. Rarely used now except for infrequent exercises, the box was one of the few areas of the White House that Thomas had yet to visit.

The roof of the Chief Executive's mansion was another story, Thomas having visited it in the past month during a routine inspection. The only difference was that then he was able to access it via the elevator, and not the steep enclosed stairway he soon found himself climbing.

At the top a short accessway led out onto the roof. It was cooler there in the open air. Thomas was able to regain his breath while they made their way over to the steel-and-glass guardhouse. This structure served as the roof's operations center and, depending on the level of alert, a pair of uniformed Secret Service personnel were always stationed there.

This standard watch had already been reinforced by another nine agents of a special-response team. Having just arrived on the roof themselves, they were hard at work setting up their equipment. This gear included a suitcase-sized SATCOM uplink, various visual amplification devices, and a variety of weapons.

Amongst this latter group, Thomas identified one of the weapons being hurriedly assembled as a Heckler and Koch PSG–1 sniper rifle. At the sniper's side, a trio of agents were preparing their dark green Stinger missile canisters for launch.

The aircraft responsible for all this frantic activity was still clearly visible in the blue sky above them. To examine it in greater detail, Thomas accepted a pair of Zeiss binoculars from Matt Durham, the special agent in charge of the rooftop operations center. Thomas had served in the air force with Matt, and with the powerful binoculars now nestled up to his brow, Thomas focused on the airplane, all the while listening to Matt's running commentary.

"So far we've been unable to either ID the aircraft or spot its serial number. The local airports have no record of it, and whoever's flying that sucker is either deaf, experiencing radio problems, or is purposely refusing to answer us."

Thomas estimated that the plane was somewhere between 4,500

and 5,000 feet. From what he could see of its fuselage, it looked ordinary enough, no different from the thousands of similar Cessnas that flew out of airports throughout America.

"Hasn't National been able to make contact with them?" asked Morrison, binoculars glued to his own brow.

"That's a negative, sir," Durham answered. "National, Andrews, and Dulles have all had the plane on radar for the last fifteen minutes. But all of them are still experiencing tower communications problems as a result of the unusual sunspot activity that NASA warned us about last week."

"Sunspot activity?" Thomas repeated, his line of sight still riveted on the circling Cessna.

"That's affirmative," said Matt. "It seems we're entering the next eleven-year, active-sunspot cycle with a wicked geomagnetic storm that's wreaking havoc in our atmosphere."

Thomas now knew the most probable reason for the uncommon air-traffic pattern over his brother's house the day before, and he listened to Samuel Morrison's skeptical reply.

"Sunspots aren't the reason for that Cessna's presence up there. Even without a radio warning, every licensed pilot in America knows that buzzing the White House is strictly verboten. My gut tells me that the occupants of that plane have a surprise in store for us, and I want to be ready for it. What are our options, Durham?"

The forty-two-year-old Indiana native lowered his binoculars before answering. "We can continue closely monitoring the Cessna, with the hope that this is all nothing but an innocent sightseeing flight, and that they'll soon lose interest and leave the area. Or, in our next level of response, we launch our F–16s, and escort them out of the zone in that manner. And then I can always deal with the matter on my own, by having one of my men take out the Cessna with a Stinger."

"Damn!" cursed Morrison. "I've got Marine One due here shortly, a presidential press conference on the South Lawn, and the First Kid's birthday celebration to consider. If it were any other time, I might suspect tourists, but not today. Durham, call Andrews and get those F-16s in the air."

Before Matt could carry out this directive, Thomas informed him that the tense situation was about to take an unexpected twist. His binoculars still trained on the Cessna, his words of warning were prompted by the sudden opening of the plane's fuselage door, and the appearance inside of a fully equipped parachutist.

"We've got a jumper!" he shouted.

No sooner were these words spoken than the figure leaped out of the airplane. Thomas followed this descent, looking on as the free-faller's body rushed toward terminal velocity. Just when it looked like the jumper wouldn't have enough time to safely engage the chute, it popped open with a long snaking coil of line. A bare 3,500 feet above the South Lawn, the chute finally inflated. Thomas identified the rectangular canopy as being an MC–4 ram-air model.

"The Cessna's veering off and hightailing it for Maryland!" informed Matt Durham.

"The hell with that frigging plane!" yelled Morrison, whose own glance remained locked on the descending parachutist. "Come on, Thomas. If that fool thinks he's going to get away with crashing our party, we're going to have to show him differently."

They rushed back down the stairs to the South Portico. As they reached the mansion's exterior terrace, Thomas spotted their airborne trespasser. The parachutist was somewhat awkwardly manipulating the canopy's steering risers to fly the chute to a South Lawn touchdown. With another 1,000 feet to go before hitting solid earth, Thomas estimated that the jumper would land somewhere near the helipad. A small army of over three dozen uniformed and plain-clothes Secret Service agents were also headed toward this portion of the South Lawn, and Thomas sprinted past the tent area to join them.

The caterers, band members, and roadies who were congregated beneath the tents, were getting an excellent view of the entire incident. Several of them were capturing this spectacle on their video cameras. As Thomas ran past them, one of the long-haired onlookers shouted out in encouragement.

"Go get 'em, man!"

Thomas reached the helipad area just as the jumper was about to touch down. Thomas didn't bother drawing his pistol, his associates already displaying more than enough firepower to put down a riot. A wide assortment of pistols and revolvers, along with several Uzis, and an Ingram MAC 10, were aimed skyward, and one formidable-looking uniformed agent intently followed the parachutist's final few feet of descent with the glistening barrel of an Ithaca Model 37 pump-action shotgun.

Seemingly oblivious to this awesome arsenal, the jumper aimed himself at the helipad's center. A bare fifty feet from touchdown, Thomas could tell that the jumper would never make it. He showed his inexperience when he failed to compensate for what little wind was blowing, trying vainly to correct this miscalculation by pulling down on the wrong steering riser.

As it turned out, the parachutist was able to make a standing, yet somewhat rough, flared landing on the helipad's southeastern corner. In a matter of seconds, he was completely surrounded, with Samuel Morrison catching the billowing chute and collapsing it in his arms.

Thomas made his way to the outer circle of agents, and watched as Morrison disgustedly handed the chute to an associate. Then, with his own Smith and Wesson .44 Magnum Model 29 drawn, the SAIC moved in for the interrogation.

"Hands up, you idiot!" he commanded.

Their prisoner timidly did as ordered. Yet the jumper's face remained masked by a large pair of goggles. With the addition of a bright yellow, Pro-tech helmet and a green flightsuit, there was no telling who they had captured.

This changed as soon as Morrison positioned himself directly in front of the trespasser, aimed the intimidating barrel of his Smith and Wesson at the jumper's forehead, and pulled back the revolver's hammer, saying, "You'd better have one hell of an excuse, pal."

"Hey, dude, chill out!" the jumper broke out in a rather high-pitched male voice. "I surrender, dude! I surrender!"

Thomas watched as a pair of agents moved in to frisk their intruder. No weapons were found, and they had to remove the jumper's harness before they could handcuff him. It was while doing so that a pink, stuffed teddy bear fell out onto the lawn from the prisoner's backpack. Morrison bent over to grab this toy, and proceeded to roughly probe its stuffed body for any signs of hidden weapons.

This generated a passionate complaint from their trespasser. "Hey, dude, easy does it, big guy. That's my birthday gift for the First Kid. We're schoolmates, and I told her that I might be dropping in like this!"

The same two agents who frisked him were responsible for pulling off his helmet. This revealed the determined, smooth-skinned, adolescent face of a teenager. Thomas guessed his age to be about sixteen. He had longish blond hair, defiant hazel eyes, and in the best Generation X tradition, a golden earring piercing his left earlobe.

"Jesus, kid," managed Morrison as he lowered the barrel of his pistol. "Do you have any idea of what a shit-load of trouble you caused here today?"

The SAIC didn't bother to wait for a response. He holstered his weapon, his coworkers doing likewise. Morrison then turned his back on their youthful intruder, and beckoned two of his senior agents to join him at the southern edge of the helipad beside Thomas.

"Get the kid inside, check out his story, and get his parents on the line," instructed Morrison. "Then find out who the hell was flying that frigging plane. I want that bastard's license. And I want this entire incident played down to the press. All we need in tomorrow's papers is to read how the Secret Service almost blew away a teddy-bear-armed, teenybopper sky diver!"

Looking at Thomas, the SAIC facetiously added. "And here you thought that you had an exciting morning, Kellogg. Still sorry that you won't be joining us at sea? Because if this little incident is any indication of what the future holds, Lord only knows what's going to be waiting for us in the middle of the frigging Atlantic."

6

AFTER UNPACKING HIS TWO-SUITER—WHICH INCLUDED STASHING A SPARE BOX OF 9mm rounds in his stateroom's wall safe and sending his shirts out to be laundered with a deeply attentive Filipino steward named Nelson—Vince wound his way through the ship to the Queens Grill for lunch. He walked through a small intimate lounge area and was greeted by a smiling, tuxedo-clad maître d'. "Ah, Special Agent Kellogg, I presume. Good afternoon, sir, and welcome to the Queens Grill. My name is André, and it will be my pleasure to serve you. This is your first crossing with us?"

Vince nodded that it was. André's smile further widened. "Ah, excellent, sir. I see that you've been preassigned to balcony table Three-C, where Melanie and Neil will be taking excellent care of you. If you'll follow me, your party is waiting inside."

The restaurant was as intimate and reserved as its exterior lounge. Small by the *QE2*'s standards, the Grill was designed to hold 231 passengers. A central dining area held a dozen circular tables, several of which were set for six, with a number of smaller tables set up on a surrounding balcony. The furnishings were elegant and subdued: White leather chairs trimmed in black, fine crystal and silver table settings, fresh flower centerpieces, all illuminated by three large windows on each side of the room. Fewer than a dozen tables were currently occupied. As Vince followed André across the central seating area, he spotted evidence of the Grill's namesake mounted on the after bulkhead—an intricately carved wooden crest of Her Majesty Queen Elizabeth II.

"Special Agent Kellogg."

Robert Hartwell was seated beside two fellow officers. They were already eating their appetizers, and Vince beckoned them not to stand as Hartwell initiated the introductions.

"Special Agent, I'd like you to meet the ship's executive chef, Bernhard Langer, and our esteemed physician, Dr. Andrew Benedict."

Vince exchanged handshakes and took the vacant seat to the security officer's right. No sooner had he done so, than a pair of crew members materialized at his side. The first of these white-uniformed figures was a vivacious, green-eyed blonde, who introduced herself as Melanie and handed Vince a menu. Her bespectacled associate sported clipped brown hair and a serious manner. He efficiently unfolded Vince's napkin and handed it to him, at the same time identifying himself as Neil.

"I hope that you don't mind, but we've already ordered," informed Hartwell. "Please have a look, and do so yourself."

"With pleasure," Vince replied, opening the menu. It had a rendering of the QE2's predecessor on its cover—the long-retired, dual-funneled ocean liner, Queen Elizabeth.

The menu itself offered Vince a wide selection to choose from. It started off with appetizers that included a seafood salad, sliced fruit platter, a cheese soufflé, and tossed pasta salad. He decided to skip this course and begin his meal with Italian bean soup. The entrées ranged from green and white fettuccine in saffron-mushroom sauce, to braised veal chops, grilled paillard of beef, and Maryland crab cakes; Southern fried chicken, too, complete with corn popovers, broiled tomatoes, onion rings, and fried potatoes. Also available was Oriental stir-fry and short-grain brown rice, the QE2 Spa selection for the calorie-conscious diner.

Vince was unable to resist ordering the fried chicken. He picked iced tea to drink, and chocolate mousse with caramelized bananas for dessert. "Selecting lunch has definitely been the biggest decision of my day," Vince said. "What an incredible selection."

"We try our best to satisfy patrons who come to us from every corner of the globe," said Executive Chef Langer, between sips of his consommé.

"And that they do only too well," Hartwell concurred as he finished his gumbo.

The ship's doctor patted his bulging stomach and added, "Though my last cholesterol count showed that I should have ordered the stir-fry, here I went for the fried chicken instead. You'd think as a physician I'd know better."

"Like I was telling you, Doc, it's all a matter of self-control," said Hartwell before downing a last spoonful of soup and wiping his beard with his napkin.

Vince's soup arrived seconds later, and by the time their entrées were served, Vince had caught up with them. Everyday small talk prevailed as they dug into their lunches. While devouring his perfectly cooked fried chicken breast, Vince learned from Langer that the QE2 served over 500 pounds of chicken a day while at sea. Added to this was an average daily consumption of 3,200 eggs, 230 gallons of milk, 200 bottles of vintage champagne, and most interesting, 116 pounds of lobster and 6.6 pounds of premium caviar.

The executive chef was in the midst of describing how important it was to properly account for these stores, when a steward arrived at their table with a document for the doctor. Benedict pushed away his empty plate and hastily skimmed this sheet of paper before dismissing the courier.

"Is that the report, Doc?" Hartwell asked hopefully.

"Aye," replied Benedict after readjusting the fit of his wire-rim glasses, then handing the document to Bernhard Langer.

"Well?" persisted the curious security officer.

Langer held back his reply until reading the report thoroughly. "I told you this would be the result," he said, the barest of German accents flavoring his tone. "My kitchens are the cleanest on all the seas!"

With this haughty outburst, he handed the document to Hartwell. By this time, Vince had pretty well figured out what this exchange was all about. Yet it wasn't until the Scotsman completed his examination of the document and voiced his own opinion, that Vince's suspicions were confirmed.

"Then that's it," said Hartwell, an air of finality to his words. "If the New York public health authorities can find our food storage and preparation areas completely free from contamination, then we can be one-hundred-percent certain that the bacteria originated someplace other than in our Kitchens."

"I presume that you're referring to that case of salmonella poisoning that sickened members of your Spa staff," remarked Vince.

"Make that a *suspected* case, Special Agent," interjected the ship's physician. "We still have no evidence that salmonella was the culprit."

When Vince finally got the opportunity to read the report himself, he skimmed its contents but most of this numeric data meant little to him. He lowered the document and addressed Hartwell.

"I'm certain that Dr. Patton, the President's physician, is going to want to see a copy of this."

"Isn't my kitchen good enough for the President of the United States?" the executive chef said.

"That's not what I was implying," Vince replied. "Whenever the President is traveling, his physician is personally responsible for insuring the safety of all food and drink. This is especially relevant when a kitchen that will be serving our President is being investigated for a possible case of food poisoning."

"But that report proves that my kitchen is safe!" protested Langer. "Come see for yourself, Special Agent Kellogg. Even my floors are so spotless that you could eat a meal right off of them."

"Easy now, Bernhard," Hartwell interceded. "If I can be so bold as to speak for the special agent here, he's not doubting the truth of your words. This is nothing but a routine security matter. Now that we have official documentation of the state of our kitchens, it's only logical that the President's physician should know that he has nothing to fear from your meals."

"Except indigestion from overeating," interjected Andrew Benedict.

This comment caused a wave of shared laughter to envelop the table, and with the tension now broken, Dr. Benedict rose to excuse himself.

"I'm afraid that I have an open clinic to attend to," said Benedict as he reached into his wallet, pulled out a business card and handed it to Vince. "Don't hesitate to call. And please, come down to Six Deck and visit our Hospital. As you'll soon enough see, we're fully equipped to handle not only emergencies, but a wide spectrum of preventative medicine as well."

Vince pocketed the card and replied. "I'd most enjoy seeing your facility, Doctor."

Langer also rose, handing Vince a card of his own. "It was a pleasure making your acquaintance, Special Agent Kellogg. Dr. Benedict's Hospital is not the only facility onboard ship that eagerly awaits your presence. The *Queen*'s Kitchen is always open to you. Just call me first, and I'd be honored to personally show you why our food-preparation areas are second to none."

"If that excellent meal I just consumed is any example of the quality of chow served aboard this vessel, I can understand the reason for your pride," Vince offered.

Benedict and Langer exited the Grill together. This left Vince alone at the table with the ship's security officer.

While Neil cleared the table, Melanie refilled their coffee cups. A thoughtful moment of silence followed, which Hartwell finally broke.

"I'm afraid that our esteemed executive chef is a bit on the emotional side."

"I've never met a good cook who wasn't," observed Vince as he sipped his coffee.

"You know we'd be lying to you if we said that there was never a recorded case of food poisoning aboard the *QE2*," Hartwell remarked carefully. "After all, as Chef Langer was explaining, the volume of food we serve is absolutely astronomical. But when combined with the millions of passengers we've fed over the years, I'd say that the chances of getting sick in such a manner are statistically nonexistent."

"Then how do you explain the nature of the illness that struck down select members of the ship's Gym staff recently?" asked Vince.

Hartwell hesitated a moment before answering. "I still say that it originated from food that was prepared elsewhere."

"I didn't think that you had staterooms with kitchen facilities in them," Vince replied.

"We don't," retorted Hartwell. "In fact, the only place other than our kitchens where preparation over an open flame takes place, is Chinatown."

"Chinatown?"

Hartwell smiled. "Since you haven't had your complete tour of the *Queen* as yet, you haven't had a chance to visit the ship's Laundry down on Seven Deck. That's where you'll find Chinatown, home to seventeen of the hardest working Chinese laundrymen this side of Shanghai."

"I imagine that's where my steward sent the shirts that I asked him to launder?" Vince supposed.

"That's the place. It remains operational twenty-four hours a day, seven days a week, and is responsible for cleaning every piece of dirty linen generated by our dining rooms and passenger cabins, as well as the crew's uniforms, and those personal items of clothing that our passengers might want laundered.

"A character by the name of Ping is the head man down there. He's a fairly new arrival on the ship, and treats the Laundry like his personal fiefdom. The majority of his workers will never even see the light of day during an entire crossing. I believe they're paid by the piece, and being the industrious folks they are, leisure time is kept to a bare minimum. Hell, they won't even sleep with the rest of the crew, let alone eat with them. And that's why we allow them to have their own domain, where all their needs, including food preparation, can be met with a minimum of fuss."

"Did the recent visit by the New York Public Health Department include an inspection of Chinatown's kitchen?" Vince asked.

Hartwell's voice lowered to a conspiratorial whisper. "Actually, as far as the outside world knows, Chinatown's food preparation area doesn't even exist. This is one of those delicate cases where we tolerate a certain behavior for expediency's sake, without sanctioning it officially."

Vince was surprised by this revelation, and he replied accordingly. "Then, who's responsible for insuring that proper safety and sanitary conditions prevail down there?"

"My staff's charged with insuring that all fire and safety codes are strictly enforced in Chinatown," Hartwell revealed. "Yet as far as the sanitation of the food-preparation area is concerned, I believe that's the Doc's area of responsibility."

"So food prepared in Chinatown could have caused the crew members' illness?"

"Doc's questioning of the patients afterwards makes no mention of such a thing," said Hartwell. "My suspicion is that it was something they consumed during a cocktail party the assistant manager of the Gym threw in his stateroom shortly after leaving Southampton."

Vince followed up on this train of thought. "Maybe this party included appetizers prepared in Chinatown?"

Hartwell's brow knitted in thought. "Though they made no mention of any such appetizers existing, I do suppose that it's a possibility. Shall we go down to Seven Deck and find out for ourselves? Besides, this will be the perfect opportunity for you to begin your tour."

They started on Two Deck, where they headed forward past the Computer Learning Center and the A Stairwell. It was at the forwardmost end of the passageway that Hartwell led the way through a hatch that read: NO ADMITTANCE: CREW ONLY. This brought them into a portion of the ship that few passengers were ever allowed to see, the living and work spaces of the QE2's crew.

Vince felt much like Alice after she stepped through the looking glass, finding himself in a whole other world. Gone were the carpeted hallways, the boutiques, and lush furnishings. In their place was a maze of bare, concrete passageways, looking much like those of an industrial plant.

This impression was further intensified as they climbed down a twisting, lattice-steel stairwell, deep into the bowels of the QE2. Vince lost count of the descending decks, concentrating instead on keeping up with his fast-moving guide.

They finally halted on what proved to be Six Deck. A fairly wide passageway led aft here, and Hartwell began a running commentary as they followed this long corridor toward the ship's stern.

"We call this passageway the working alleyway. Crew quarters are located on the port side, along with the Administration Office, ship's Print Shop, and the first of several large storerooms dedicated to the stowage of various food items."

Vince got a chance to peek inside a large deep freeze, about the size of a three-car garage, reserved solely for the storing of ice cream. An adjoining locker held hundreds of cases of every type of alcoholic beverage imaginable, while beside it was a good-sized vault dedicated exclusively to caviar.

Continuing aft, Hartwell showed Vince the ship's main Food Pantry. It occupied an immense compartment, and was filled with shelf after shelf of canned and package goods. It reminded Vince of his local grocery store, though this supermarket could only get its vendors' deliveries while the *QE2* was in port.

After passing a hatch that led into the Hospital, Hartwell guided Vince down another narrow stairway. This conveyed them to Seven Deck and the large room where the vessel's Laundry was located.

The air was hot and humid as they stepped inside. Banks of industrial-sized washers and dryers dominated this equipment-packed compartment. To the steady roar of machinery, Vince watched as two men fed sheets into the jaws of a massive flat ironer that automatically pressed and folded clean linens. Four other men were absorbed in transferring a heavy load of white terry-cloth towels into one of the dryers.

All of the workers were Asian males. They wore T-shirts, shorts, and open-toed thongs, with several of them sporting red bandannas tied around their foreheads.

"Those dryers that they're loading can hold up to two hundred-forty pounds each," explained Hartwell, who had to speak loudly to be heard. "When the ship's fully occupied, it takes a constant twenty-four-hour shift to keep up with the volume, with things getting a bit interesting upon hitting rough seas."

Vince followed his guide past the first churning washing machine. The air temperature seemed to increase further and he felt the first rivulet of sweat roll down the back of his neck.

"Ping must be in the other room," Hartwell surmised after scanning the faces of the workers. "And that's where we'll find Chinatown's food-preparation area."

It was indeed in the adjoining compartment that they found Ping. The short, wiry Asian was supervising the unloading of a pallet packed with fifty-pound sacks of detergent.

"Mr. Robert," greeted Ping, a surprised grin turning the corners of his wrinkled face. "To what do we owe the honor of your presence?"

"Ping, I'd like you to meet Special Agent Vince Kellogg of the U.S. Secret Service," said Hartwell. "Special Agent Kellogg will be joining us for the upcoming crossing, and expressed an interest in seeing your operation."

There was a shy inquisitiveness to Ping's glance as he looked at

Vince and bowed slightly. "It's an honor to meet you, sir. I'm flattered that you've taken the time to visit our humble work space."

Vince returned this gracious greeting with a slight bow of his own and listened as Hartwell continued.

"I see that our reduced crew certainly hasn't affected your workload. If anything, you folks seem busier than ever."

"That we are, Mr. Robert. Right now, we're in the midst of a thorough inspection of the ship's bath linens. Every single towel is being checked for wear and then relaundered."

Vince surveyed the tall stacks of white terry-cloth towels that lay neatly folded on the counters lining much of the room. A long, rectangular table holding piles of hand towels stood in the compartment's center, but Vince failed to spot any sort of kitchen facilities.

"I thought this was where the laundry's food-preparation area was located," he said.

This off-the-wall comment appeared to catch Ping by surprise. He accepted a supportive nod from Hartwell before replying. "Space constraints force us to use this compartment for dual purposes. As mealtime approaches, the counters are removed, and that's where you'll find our sink and stove."

"And where's the food itself stored?" Vince continued.

Ping's expression further tightened with suspicion, prompting Hartwell to intercede. "It's all right, Ping. We're investigating a possible case of food contamination. You're free to answer all of Special Agent Kellogg's questions."

With a confused shrug of his narrow shoulders, Ping opened a nearby doorway and revealed a dimly lit storeroom. Alongside a wall lined with chemical drums, sat a wizened Asian man, innocently peeling vegetables. A large bucket filled with scraps lay between his bare feet, with a stainless-steel refrigerator close by.

"You'll find all perishable items such as fish, chicken, and pork properly stored inside the refrigerator," revealed Ping. "These items are drawn from the ship's larder when needed. You can rest assured that we make every effort to follow Chef Langer's strict sanitation guidelines."

"May I have a look?" Vince asked as he walked over to the refrigerator and opened it without waiting for a reply.

He found the chilled interior to be spotlessly clean. A large covered platter of cut-up chicken sat on the center shelf, along with several plastic tubs filled with an assortment of raw vegetables.

"To my knowledge, not a single one of my workers has ever gotten ill from one of our meals," Ping said as Vince gestured Hartwell to have a look inside.

The Scotsman initiated a cursory inspection of the refrigerator's contents before shutting the door and querying, "Ping, during our last crossing from Southampton, did any members of the crew other than your men use this facility for food preparation?"

"Absolutely not," Ping answered.

"Then is it possible that one of your men could have prepared a dish for an outsider, something as simple as an appetizer for a party?" probed Vince.

Ping responded thoughtfully. "The only time that food cooked here leaves these walls is on very special occasions. From time to time, we prepare a meal for the captain, or one of the other senior officers."

"I understand these special meals are much anticipated and most appreciated," said Hartwell. "Scuttlebutt even has it that upon tasting one of your dishes, Chef Langer requested the recipe."

"Indeed." As Ping went on to describe the details of this fondly remembered incident, Vince explored the storeroom further. He spotted a large steel grille cut into the bulkhead behind a waist-high stack of bagged white rice. A steady, pulsating drone could be heard emanating from this opening. Hartwell revealed its source.

"That grille is a free-flood hole that opens up directly into the Engine Room."

Any further elaboration on his part was cut short by the sudden activation of his two-way radio. With both Vince and Ping looking on, he pulled out the compact device and spoke into the transmitter.

"Hartwell, here."

"Chief," said Tuff's amplified voice. "The Secret Service has just informed me that the first motorcade has left the United Nations. They should be arriving here in another fifteen minutes."

"Roger that, Tuff. I'm on my way up to join you pierside. Over."

Hartwell pocketed the radio and addressed Vince. "I don't know about you, Special Agent, but I'd say that we can cross Chinatown off the list of possible sources of contamination."

"By all means," Vince concurred.

"Thanks for your cooperation, Ping," said Hartwell as he led the way out of the storeroom. "I imagine that you and your lads are excited by the prospect of sailing with President Li this crossing. Did you ever dream this day would come?"

Ping halted beside the partially unloaded pallet of detergent and answered matter-of-factly. "I left China many years ago, and know little of such matters. As far as I'm concerned, all politicians are cut from the same bolt of cloth, with the youngster Li Chen no different from the other world leaders." Then he bowed at the waist and added politely. "It was an honor to be of service, gentlemen."

Vince said his own goodbyes, and as he followed Hartwell out of the Laundry, he accepted his guide's offer to accompany him topside by way of the Engine Room.

A narrow hatch secured by dog-clips conveyed them to an elevated, latticed-steel platform overlooking one of the largest interior compartments on the ship. From this lofty vantage point Vince enjoyed an unobstructed view of the cavernous hold's five immense diesel engines, only one of which was currently operational.

"It was in 1986 that the *QE2*'s engines were converted from steam to diesel power," explained Hartwell, who had to practically scream to be heard over the constant guttural roar. "The ship is presently equipped with nine MAN turbocharged engines. Each of these one hundred-twenty-ton giants are the approximate size of a London double-decker bus, with four fitted forward, and five aft.

"In addition to producing enough electrical power to light a city the size of Southampton, the engines drive two main propulsion motors that in turn spin the vessel's twin propeller shafts. Our top speed is thirty-two knots, with only seven of the engines needed to produce a standard service speed of twenty-eight and one-half knots."

Vince watched as a group of crewmen gathered around the open manifold of one of the engines that wasn't operational. They appeared to be servicing its massive cylinder heads. Even from this distance Vince could clearly see the black grease that stained their white coveralls.

"Why not place all nine engines in one compartment?" Vince asked. "Wouldn't that facilitate maintenance?"

"Aye," said Hartwell. "But our engineers put up with this minor inconvenience, knowing that in the event of an accident, a series of watertight doors separates the two rooms, allowing autonomous operations."

A steep ladder brought them down to the compartment's main deck. Careful not to slide on the slippery catwalk, Vince followed Hartwell aft. Twisting pipe and thick, insulated ducts hugged the bulkheads, with the distinctive stench of fuel oil almost overpowering.

As they climbed over the bottom lip of a massive watertight door, Hartwell pointed to the right. Several oddly shaped, sealed vats were positioned against the far bulkhead, with a number of thick, grease-stained pipes snaking in and out of them. The smell of oil was particularly strong here. Vince soon learned why.

"That's where the fuel is heated," Hartwell revealed. "In its natural state, the oil we use has a consistency much like road tar, and needs to be subsequently thinned. Note the heavy concentration of halon fire extinguishers mounted into the ceiling. The fuel-storage bunkers are positioned directly below us, making this one of the most volatile areas on the entire ship."

"What kind of gas mileage do you get?" Vince asked.

"At service speed, the engines require about 380 tons per day. The ship can hold 4,578 tons, giving us a range of twelve days without having to refuel."

They passed through yet another watertight door, with Hartwell directing Vince's attention to a thick, circular steel manifold that extended all the way up to the ceiling and had numerous pipes connected to it. "Those ventilation shafts go straight up to the funnel. Exhaust gasses from the engines are routed up this trunking. Once they reach the funnel the heat is captured in specially designed boilers. The resulting steam is redirected for a variety of diverse purposes, including heating the fuel and the water you'll be using in your shower."

"Sounds like you're no stranger to this portion of the ship, Robert."

The retired commando smiled proudly. "When I first went in the service, I trained to be a Royal Navy engineer. But being an outdoors sort, it didn't take long for the Royal Marines to get my attention."

The main catwalk continued aft. Hartwell pointed in this direction, and added, "The ship's four vacuum evaporators for the production of fresh water, and her bilge and ballast pumping station are located back there. Perhaps you'll get a chance to visit these spaces during the next bomb sweep, but right now, we'd better head topside."

An adjoining accessway brought them to a closed hatch set into the starboard bulkhead. Hartwell had to use both hands to open this heavy fire door, and Vince wasted no time passing through it. This brought them smack into one of the QE2's carpet-lined passenger passageways. Once more, Vince felt like he had passed into another dimension—from the greasy, noise-filled, mechanical abyss of the vessel's Engine Room, to a plush, luxurious world, where the sounds of a Beethoven symphony emanated softly from the PA system.

Vince felt dirty and hot. He carefully wiped the soles of his shoes on the rubber doormat that sat outside the fire exit. Once Hartwell shut the hatch behind them, there was no evidence that the Engine Room even existed.

"Thanks for the abbreviated tour," offered Vince.

Hartwell took his place on the doormat. While wiping off his own shoes, he responded, "It's my pleasure, though there's still a lot more to see. Don't forget that you've got ten more decks to explore."

Although he'd studied pictures, schematics and cutaways for a month, Vince was just now getting a true feel for the immensity of this vessel, and he knew that he had his work cut out for him. With barely eight hours to go until the ship set sail, it was imperative that he have a personal knowledge of its layout before the heads of state arrived and the summit began. He seriously doubted that he'd be able to master the crew spaces in the limited time remaining, so he decided that his main focus would be on the public areas.

Vince followed Hartwell over to an elevator that whisked them up to Two Deck and the nearby Midships Lobby. A female harpist in a flowing white gown was set up in the Lobby's recessed center well, a strange counterpoint to the two somber, powerfully built black-suited Asians, who suddenly appeared in the starboard passageway following a steward.

Vince knew the lead figure to be Yushio Tanaka, special agent in charge of the Japanese prime minister's security team. They had met previously during the prime minister's last trip to Washington. Vince acknowledged his presence with a polite bow. The two agents returned this gesture before disappearing through the aft accessway, no doubt on the way to their cabins.

Their recent arrival on board ship was further proof of the late hour, and Vince anxiously followed Hartwell over the gangway. As they emerged onto the dock, they were engulfed by a crowd of scurrying porters, Cunard representatives, and smartly uniformed stewards. Nearby, a line of passengers patiently waited their turns at the security checkpoint. Through the din they made, Vince could hear the bouncy show tunes being played by a combo comprised of select members of the ship's orchestra.

On the other side of the security fence, Vince also counted seven separate television news crews, either setting up or actually shooting footage. They were working under the watchful eye of dozens of blue-uniformed policemen, many escorting police dogs. The tension and excitement on the dock was palpable.

Hartwell was apparently no stranger to such glamorous send-offs, and after checking in with one of his female associates, he nonchalantly addressed Vince. "Looks like it's getting close to show-time. The motorcades carrying the prime ministers of Italy and Japan should be arriving any minute now, with the Canadians and Brits preparing to leave the United Nations within the half hour.

"The plane carrying the chancellor of Germany has just touched down at Kennedy. The aircraft carrying the presidents of Russia and France are on their final approach."

"Any word on the Chinese president?" asked Vince.

Hartwell answered as he checked the digital display of his ringing pager. "As far as I know, he's still due in sometime around nine."

Turning toward the terminal's freight entrance, he added, "It appears that Tuff's got some newly arrived cargo that's not on the original manifest. Shall we have a look?"

Vince beckoned Hartwell to lead the way, and together they proceeded to the barricaded section of the terminal reserved for cargo. This portion of the facility was connected to the street by way of a loading dock, with the QE2's majestic hull forming a solid blue wall on the southern perimeter.

They passed a group of longshoremen, busy preparing a crate-laden pallet for transfer onto the ship. This process was facilitated by use of the vessel's own bow-mounted loading crane that would lift the pallet up into the forward cargo hold.

Vince had seen a part of this hold during his trip down to the ship's Laundry. It adjoined the working alleyway off Six Deck and was strategically placed to allow easy access to the rest of the vessel. Already looking forward to continuing on with the rest of his tour, Vince spotted a group of individuals huddled on the loading dock. One of these figures was Special Agent Doug Algren, with Tuff, two Port Authority patrolmen, and the *QE2*'s cargomaster close by.

A short stairway conveyed Vince and Hartwell up onto the dock, where they got a close-up view of the collection of suspect cargo. Placed on the concrete landing were five pieces of gym equipment. There were three exercise bikes, a rowing machine, and a Stair-Master. The equipment was partially covered in protective bubble wrap, and appeared to be brand-new, sporting the latest in high-tech digital displays and biofeedback readouts.

The apparent owners of this machinery stood nearby. Vince's glance was drawn to the only female in this foursome, a gorgeous Asian woman in her early twenties. Her short black hair was cut in bangs that perfectly framed a pair of coal-black, almond-shaped eyes, button nose, and a wide, sensuous mouth. A leotard and tight-fitting jeans displayed the perfect figure that Vince associated with a world-class athlete.

Standing close at her side was a handsome Asian man, who could easily have been her father. He looked oddly familiar to Vince—his solid, five-foot-nine-inch frame dressed immaculately in a long-sleeve, light-blue Oxford shirt and freshly pressed khakis. He wore brown leather loafers and was sockless.

The two men beside him were a study in opposites, even though both were also Asians and wore matching white coveralls with a patch sewn on their chests reading: LIU'S GYM. The taller of the pair towered a good eight inches above his five-foot-six-inch associate. Built much like Tuff, with an expansive chest, wide shoulders, and thick neck, this crew-cut, sad-eyed giant seemed oblivious to all the excitement going on around him.

His wide-eyed coworker appeared enthralled with the milling crowds visible in the terminal beyond. Unlike his bored comrade, he didn't want to miss a thing, his beady eyes and curious stare sweeping the facility in search of the least hint of activity.

"Hello, Vince," said Algren, who appeared surprised to see him. "Once I saw you disappear up that gangway, I thought that would be the last I'd see of you until you got home from England."

"You won't be getting rid of me so easily, Doug."

"The chief was just telling me that my page caught you down in Chinatown, on the trail of the contaminated food that could have been responsible for taking out our gym staff," said Tuff.

"I'm afraid that we hit a dead end, Tuff," Vince said. He looked over to the nearby pallet and added, "I see that the replacement gym equipment has finally arrived."

"I must be the only guy on this dock who knew absolutely nothing about this replacement gear," said Algren, his frustration obvious. "My most recent cargo manifest shows no mention of any such machinery."

Robert Hartwell overheard this comment while talking with the ship's cargomaster and was quick to offer his apologies. "It looks like we're going to have to take the blame for not getting you a copy of the last update, Special Agent. If you'd like, I can have one brought down from the ship's security office, though you can rest assured that this equipment is fully authorized."

"That's all I need to know," returned Algren, immediately beckoning the group of four Asians to join them.

"Good afternoon, Mr. Liu," Hartwell said to the khaki-clad male. "It's good to see you again. I'd like you to meet Special Agent Vince Kellogg of the U.S. Secret Service."

Vince noted the way the Asian's eyes lit up with sudden interest upon learning his title, and a broad smile turned Liu's mouth as they shook hands.

"As I said earlier, Mr. Liu is a part owner of the firm that runs our gym facilities on both the QE2 and three of our other cruise ships," Hartwell said.

"Only on a contract basis," Liu interjected humbly, in perfect English. "And please, I'd be much more comfortable if all of you would call me by my first name, Dennis. Will you be joining us on the crossing, Special Agent Kellogg?"

Vince nodded that he would, knowing full well that Liu was once known as the most promising heir to Bruce Lee's throne. He was now the so-called prince of chop-sockey, the unique, low-budget martial-arts films that were heavy in action but light in substance. Vince's son had enrolled in his first karate class earlier in the year, and it was here that Joshua had discovered Liu's films, which Vince had secretly come to enjoy himself. If he knew Joshua, he'd be much more impressed with a Dennis Liu autograph than those of all of the G-7 leaders combined!

"You must come and visit us down in the Gym," Liu offered. "I can personally guarantee that you'll get a full workout, with my daughter Kristin here leading our aerobics classes."

Liu suddenly realized that he had yet to introduce her. As he did so, Kristin's shy smile melted Vince's heart, and his thoughts remained centered on this ravishing, exotic young beauty as Dennis Liu went on to introduce his two coverall-clad associates. The tallest of the two was appropriately nicknamed Bear, while his wide-eyed associate answered to the name of Sunny.

While Sunny and Bear helped two cargo handlers with the back-breaking task of loading the gym equipment onto an empty pallet, Kristin proceeded through the loading dock's metal detector and joined Vince, Hartwell, Tuff, and Doug Algren on the other side of the security checkpoint.

"I thought that Ms. Chang was supposed to be accompanying you?" offered a somewhat disappointed Hartwell.

"You need not worry, my friend," Liu replied. "Much like myself, Monica wouldn't miss this very special crossing for all the world. Thank heavens that both of us weren't busy filming, and were available as substitutes when we learned that our associates had fallen ill. Have you discovered the source of this sickness as yet?"

"We believe that the illness was caused by something they either ate or drank," observed Hartwell. "Yet so far, we've been unable to determine exactly what it was."

"Nor have I nor my coworkers' doctors," Liu said. Then he related the facts of his visit to the hospital where his coworkers were being treated.

"A longshoreman in a forklift drove up to the loading dock at this point and lifted the equipment-filled pallet. Yet before it could be conveyed into the ship's hold, its contents had to pass their own security check. This arrived in the form of a uniformed Customs official and her good-natured black Labrador named Montana.

The Lab curiously sniffed the wooden-slat base of the pallet before climbing up onto it. The gym equipment was anchored with bands of canvas strapping, and Montana had to awkwardly climb over this obstacle course to begin her work in earnest.

The first piece to pass Montana's inspection was the rowing machine. The StairMaster and the bicycles proved to be a bit more of a challenge. After sniffing the bases, Montana had to stand on her hind legs to inspect this gear's upper portion.

It was while bracing her forepaws against the frame of one of the bikes that Montana scratched the handle's black, glossy finish. This accident generated a passionate protest from Sunny.

"Hey, watch it! That equipment's brand-new and costs a fortune."

Montana instinctively sensed that she was the cause of these angry words, and as her handler pulled her away to inspect the damages, the wail of sirens sounded from the street. Doug Algren's two-way activated. After the briefest of conversations, the special agent readily explained what the outside commotion was all about.

"The Italian motorcade has arrived."

A group of burly cargo handlers emerged from the street entrance of the loading dock pushing carts filled with personal luggage. As the sirens finally faded, several news crews could be seen rushing toward the terminal's main entryway.

Vince and his associates had a new situation on their hands when an overeager cameraman fell headfirst over one of the blue-and-white police sawhorses. Seconds later, the Italian prime minister's party made its grand entrance to a blinding wall of flashing strobes.

The fallen cameraman remained on the ground unmoving, his prone body blocking the confused Italians' progress. As the first Port Authority patrolman arrived to assist the unconscious journalist, the timid voice of the Customs inspector said, "I'm sorry about the scratches. Montana was just doing her job."

"Don't worry about it, miss," advised Dennis Liu, who, along with his daughter, had been riveted on the chaotic scene unfolding at the terminal's entrance.

"It appears that those scratches are the least of our problem," added Robert Hartwell, who momentarily glanced away from the entryway and addressed the Customs agent. "I'll take full responsibility for any damages. So, if it's all right with you, we'd better allow our esteemed cargomaster to get this equipment aboard. Besides, it appears that you and Montana have your work cut out with all that newly arrived baggage."

As the frazzled Customs agent gratefully scrawled her initials on the pallet's clearance form, all eyes returned to the terminal. One of the Italians had managed to get into some sort of verbal altercation with a Port Authority official.

"Oh, hell!" cursed Algren. "I'd better get over there before we have a major international incident on our hands. If I don't see you later, have a safe crossing, folks."

"Thanks, Doug," said Vince. "Good luck yourself."

"And now the fun really begins," offered Hartwell, who, along with Vince and Tuff, watched as Special Agent Algren rushed over to the crowd of onlookers that continued to gather at the terminal's entrance.

7

IT WAS LATE AFTERNOON BY THE TIME THOMAS KELLOGG FINALLY RETURNED TO his office at BATF headquarters on Massachusetts Avenue. The day had already been a full one, yet Thomas knew that his real work was only just beginning.

As expected, he found his desk filled with unopened mail, memos, and phone messages. Though he'd have to attend to these eventually, right now he had other priorities, and his first stop after the short visit to his desk was the explosives technology lab.

The facility contained the latest in scientific equipment. It was located on the floor below and had recently undergone a major refit. Thomas was confident that it ranked among the country's best.

Of course, any forensic laboratory was only as good as its people. The BATF was fortunate to have recruited the finest personnel available—many of these technicians had come from the ranks of the military, where they received their initial training in the arcane business of explosives ordnance technology.

Thomas wasn't surprised to find the agency's seniormost EOD technician hard at work inside the lab as he entered. Les Stanley had once served in the same outfit as M. Sgt. Danny Lane, making him the perfect person to be carrying on Lane's work here at BATF headquarters.

The Priority Mail IED they had defused earlier in the day had preceded Thomas to the lab. It was now Stanley's job to further disassemble the device. Much like a coroner dissecting a corpse to uncover evidence of a homicide, Stanley was picking apart the remains of the bomb searching for clues.

He did so on a well-lit, oblong worktable, with a jeweler's loupe strapped to his eye. Stanley had already cut away most of the cardboard box, and was concentrating his efforts on the bomb's fiberboard base and the various fusing mechanisms that were still attached to it.

"It's all so damn elementary," observed Stanley, while carefully cutting the wire leads attached to the photocell.

Thomas had pulled over a stool alongside the technician, as Stanley continued his remarks without looking up. "On exposure to light, the photocell's resistance decreases, causing the transistors to conduct. Then, when the battery current flowing through the transistors reaches a sufficient level, the relay is activated, the contact closes, and the circuit is completed, firing the detonators."

"Did the liquid nitrogen do much damage to the components?" asked Thomas as Stanley began scraping a sample of soldering into a small vial.

"The only problem it's caused so far is with the outer carton," returned Stanley, who next turned his attention to the device's twin transistors. "The quick-freeze burnt the cardboard surface, and if there were any fingerprints on there, we're going to have a hell of a time finding them."

"At least we've got the rest of it to work with," said Thomas.

He watched as Stanley placed one of the transistors in a plastic evidence bag. Over a dozen similar bags had already been filled, a careful analysis of their contents being the next step in the investigation.

"Anything out of the ordinary so far, Les?"

Stanley somberly shook his head. "There's nothing here that couldn't be purchased in your local hardware store, except for those two blocks of C-4, that is. I've already had Mitchell run a preliminary analysis on it, and the results are sobering. The blend appears to be 91.8 percent RDX and 8.2 percent inert plasticizer, giving it an approximate detonating velocity of some 26,400 fps." RDX, Thomas knew, was a high explosive made from nitric acid and hexamethylenetetramine.

"I was afraid that it would be military grade." Thomas said with a sigh. "I think I'll give Ted Callahan a call over at the Pentagon, and see if the Army's experienced any unexplained shortages lately, especially in the Virginia area."

With this comment, Les Stanley deliberately put down his tweezers. He pushed aside his loupe, sat up straight, and turned his gaze on Thomas. "Hell, last I heard, Callahan and his cronies couldn't even find a pair of M-1 battle tanks and a trio of Humvees that mysteriously disappeared out of their Texas-based inventory. And you think they can help you find out if a couple of pounds of C-4 have been stolen? The damn Secretary of the Army could go missing for an entire week, and they'd never even miss him!"

Thomas didn't doubt there were some thefts his friend couldn't solve, but he decided nevertheless to follow up this avenue of investigation. Col. Theodore Callahan could tell him about every Department of Defense facility in which C-4 was stored, and inform him where these potent plastic explosives were produced, and how they were accounted for afterwards. He excused himself and returned to his office, where a phone call found Callahan at his Pentagon office.

Thomas had served with Callahan in Grenada. They were to go their separate ways afterwards, only to be reunited in the past two years when Callahan was transferred to the Pentagon where he was serving as one of the Army's top cops. It was in this official capacity that they were to work together again when Thomas was sent undercover to investigate an ongoing case involving racial tensions inside Army Special Forces.

Upon learning of Thomas's current case, Callahan immediately offered his services. He also expressed a desire to help them with their bombmaker's psychological profile. And when Callahan subsequently invited him to come right over to the Pentagon to continue the conversation, Thomas found himself unwilling to refuse his gracious offer.

Only after he hung up the phone did Thomas realize the late hour. It was rapidly approaching 5:00 P.M., which meant that rush hour would be in full swing by the time he left his office. Not looking forward to fighting the traffic on Washington's gridlocked surface streets, he decided instead to take the Metro.

His commute was a speedy one. An escalator at the Metro platform carried him right up into the Pentagon's interior entryway.

Looking from the top back down the tunnel from which he had just emerged, Thomas could see why the deeply buried Metro served a secondary function as a bomb shelter.

A tiled corridor led to the building's main reception area and a security checkpoint. Even though he didn't have a military ID, his BATF credential allowed him special access. One of the uniformed guards escorted him around the metal detector, and he was able to enter the Pentagon without having to remove his pistol from its shoulder-harnessed holster.

While in the Air Force, Thomas spent nine months stationed at the Pentagon, so he was no stranger to its miles of mazelike hallways. The office he was presently bound for was on the third floor, located in the five-sided structure's outer section, the E-ring.

It had been many months since he had last visited the Pentagon. As Thomas followed a long, sloping ramp up into its interior, a flood of memories engulfed him. Only yesterday, it seemed, had he been a bright-eyed young officer, fresh out of the Air Force Academy and ready to set the world on fire. What great dreams and lofty goals had guided him as he walked these same hallowed halls. He was going to single-handedly leave his mark on the military, feeling there was nothing he couldn't accomplish if he put his mind to it.

As he was to learn all too soon, his ideals were as clichéd as the phrases he'd felt described them and the system that he once had admired so was to have vastly different ideas as to how he could best serve it. Conformity was the order of the day, with individual initiative definitely frowned upon. Time-consuming, bureaucratic procedures would try his patience, while any suggestions to address these inefficiencies were looked at with scorn. The successful officer learned these lessons early in his career, as the path to promotion was clearly trod by those who had figured out how best to play the game.

A passing group of smooth-faced, ROTC cadets reminded Thomas that this same game was going on today. Intelligent, vibrant, and eager to please, these young men were the fodder relied on by the powers that be to keep the system running. In so many ways, these cadets were the best that the country had to offer, and ultimately it was the military's responsibility to use their talents wisely.

It was on a blustery October day in 1983, in the storm-tossed waters off Grenada, that Thomas was to learn the real nature of war and of the system that he had sworn with his life to perpetuate. Thomas was part of a joint Air Force/Navy special-operations team whose task was to secure Salines airfield for the main Army Ranger assault force that would be landing there twenty-four hours later.

The operation itself was a complicated one. It necessitated a dangerous, low-level, night airdrop into the sea, some thirty kilometers off the southwestern tip of Grenada. Once in the water, they were to rendezvous with a number of small boats that were to be launched from the destroyer USS *Clifton Sprague.* These boats would then convey them to the beach, where they'd attempt to locate a suitable landing spot and get ashore undetected. Only then would they be free to continue on to the nearby airfield.

Thomas was a member of the combat-control team whose duty it was to covertly position radio guidance beacons near the airfield's runway. Once this was achieved, they would be responsible for issuing up-to-the-minute weather reports, and effect terminal air-traffic control for the MC-130E Combat Talons making up the main assault force.

This was his first real combat mission, and he was soon to learn things rarely went as planned during war. An unexpected twenty-five-knot crosswind resulted in the loss of four members of the team during the initial parachute jump. One of these men had been his roommate during basic, and Thomas got his first taste of true horror as he sat in one of the *Clifton Sprague*'s Boston Whalers shivering in the blustery wind and searching the dark seas for any signs of the missing jumpers.

None were ever found. Making the situation even more tragic, a mechanical problem with the Boston Whaler caused the mission to be scrubbed. They tried again the next evening, and once more found their best efforts ending in near disaster. And their failure to secure the airfield caused the entire invasion to be delayed another twenty-four hours.

Until this time, he had barely been aware of his own mortality, cocky and filled with false bravado. All that vanished in the black sea off Grenada.

Returning to the Pentagon now was like coming back to a past life. The surroundings were familiar, but the person who walked these hallways was another man. He understood sacrifice, he thought as he turned down a wide corridor lined with dozens of battle flags and a series of engraved names. He understood the courage of those here commemorated, the soldiers awarded the country's highest decoration for valor, the Medal of Honor. He just wondered if the capacity for either was still in him.

He found the door he was looking for beside the name of Sgt. Alvin Cullum York. It was securely locked, with an electronic keypad above the knob. An intercom was mounted in the wall beside the doorframe, and Thomas pressed the button a single time. After passing the scrutiny of an elevated video camera, the tumbler activated with a click, prompting Thomas to grab the knob and turn it until the door swung open.

The office inside was little more than a collection of some dozen individual workcubes. Each of these spaces had room for a single person, a computer, and a pair of two-drawer, legal-sized, fireproof filing cabinets. Only two of the spaces were currently occupied, with Thomas locating the person he was looking for at the far end of the linoleum-tiled corridor.

Callahan was deeply immersed in a computer entry. Thomas spotted his shiny bald scalp as he rounded the side of the cubicle. Since Callahan apparently still didn't know that his visitor had arrived, Thomas took a second to study his old friend's cluttered workspace. Unlike the majority of orderly cubicles he had passed, Thomas found this one to be decorated like a typical teenage boy's bedroom.

Pictures of various war toys took up much of the wall space. Thomas identified an Abrams Main Battle tank, an M113 armored personnel carrier with a TOW launcher attached to its turret, several photos showing an M110 self-propelled howitzer in action, and another series featuring the M2 Bradley infantry fighting vehicle. Interspersed amongst these colored photographs were smaller ones showing several types of mortars, grenade launchers, an M72 light antitank weapon, and a variety of machine guns. Maps and plenty of Post-it Notes filled the remaining wall space. The cubicle's desk was equally crowded with a combination of paperwork, office supplies, and the remnants of a partially eaten lunch.

"Please feel free to help yourself to what's left of that tuna sandwich, Thomas." The BATF agent jumped at the sound of Callahan's voice. He hadn't moved or looked up. "And there's coffee and soda in the copy room. I'll be with you in a second."

Ted's voice was as deep and gravelly as ever, and Thomas was content to watch him furiously attack his keyboard. Thomas was a self-educated graduate of the hunt-and-peck school. It was obvious that Callahan was an experienced touch typist capable of accessing computer functions Thomas didn't even know existed.

"Your call earlier really caught me by surprise," Callahan said as he finished inputting a final command and activated the computer's printer. "The last time we talked, you had just been picked to ride shotgun for the famous summit at sea."

As the printer chattered to life, Callahan finally swiveled around to face his guest. Thomas noted that he could use a shave. The dark circles under his hazel eyes, and the rumpled shirt, indicated he had been at work for some time now.

"Just my rotten luck, they pulled me off the summit yesterday." Thomas said as he slapped Callahan's hand in greeting. "Hell, I even went and had my tux cleaned."

"If my memory serves me right, you never were much for ships," Callahan said. He pulled out a short stool from beneath his desk and gestured to Thomas to take a seat. "So, did you by any chance see the evening news?"

"Hell, I haven't even had the time to read this morning's paper."

"Then you don't know about the remarkable UN speech given by the British prime minister this afternoon. It seems the Brits have given their full blessings to Russia's Global Zero Alert plan. It's hard to believe, but it looks like that treaty actually has a chance of being signed."

"It'll never happen," Thomas retorted. "No matter how much international support it might be able to generate, I can't believe the United States would ever sign such a treaty. I mean, come on, Ted. I realize the dangers of continued nuclear alert. But to go to the extreme of pulling the warheads from the delivery systems is ridiculous. What's the value of a nuclear deterrent, if it's going to take us several hours to prepare our weapons for use?"

"The Brits seemed to be making a big deal about the dangers of our current hair-trigger nuclear-response policy," Callahan returned. "They're agreeing with the Russians, and taking the stand that such a risky alert posture has no place in today's post–Cold War world."

"A Global Zero Alert policy might make good rhetoric, but in reality, it's totally impractical," Thomas continued. "It's been the threat of a nuclear response that's kept the peace for the last fifty years. Take away our nuclear option and you're stripping us of one of our greatest bargaining tools."

"Hey, man, don't forget that you're preaching to the choir," said Callahan, who turned away from Thomas when his printer finally completed its long run. A pile of some fifty sheets of eight-and-one-half-by-eleven white paper lay in the Out tray. Callahan grabbed the stack and handed it to Thomas.

"What's this all about?" asked Thomas, while flipping through the pages.

"That's the data you requested earlier this afternoon, Special Agent."

Thomas pulled out a page at random, and began reading its first three entries out loud. "March 24, 1998; Fort Monroe, Virginia, U.S. Army Training Command—inventory shortfall: six M72A2 Light Anti-tank Weapons. Unsolved. March 25, 1998; Fort Meade, Maryland, First U.S. Army headquarters—inventory shortfall: forty-eight 81mm M29 mortars, 144 M375 white phosphorus rounds, 168 M301 illuminating rounds, sixty M374 high explosive rounds. Unsolved. March 25, 1998; Fort Knox, Kentucky, 194th Armored Brigade—inventory shortfall: one Light Armored Vehicle. Unsolved.

"Good Lord," Thomas managed as he looked up into Callahan's probing glance. "Do you mean to say that this entire printout is filled with similar data?"

Callahan solemnly nodded that it was, adding, "I began the search as of January 1 of this year, and only queried installations in the four-state region that you asked about. The readout includes all military hardware reported missing, either by unknown inventory shortfall, or suspected theft."

"Surely most of the shortages can be explained away as mere accounting errors," offered Thomas while flipping through the rest of the stack.

"We believe that a large percentage of the losses are indeed paperwork screwups, Thomas. But that still leaves too many unsolved cases that aren't. That means it's either accidental loss or intentional theft as the cause, and the latter is starting to scare the piss out of me."

Thomas knew full well that Callahan definitely wasn't the type of man who could be easily frightened, and he sat forward and carefully probed. "Times are tough all around, Ted. You remember what it was like to exist on enlisted man's pay. With today's thriving black market, a GI who gives in to temptation can make a quick bundle, and chances are we'll never catch him. Take that shipment of Colt Commandos that one of our interdiction teams chanced upon last month in San Francisco. It turned out the guy responsible for stealing them was a twenty-year-old Leatherneck from Pendleton, who swears he did it just to buy his wife a car and put a decent down payment on a house."

"I wish that we could attribute the rest of the unaccounted losses to dumb kids like that one," replied Callahan, his gravelly voice hushed. "But I'm starting to recognize a definite pattern in both the type of installations reporting these thefts, and more significantly, the type of items that have been lost."

Thomas sensed where his old friend was headed. He cut him off with a single pertinent word. "Militia?"

Callahan reached for the printout that Thomas had been holding and nodded affirmatively. "Somebody out there is on one hell of a shopping spree, Thomas. Their list runs the gamut of what every well-stocked army needs to fight both a conventional and a nuclear war. When a dozen mortars go mysteriously missing from one base, the exact caliber shell that they fire goes missing from the next. It's been happening time after time, with every weapon system in the inventory, and my gut tells me that this material isn't meant for export."

"How about C-4?" asked Thomas directly.

Callahan had been anticipating this question. He isolated the last two pages of the printout. He hastily scanned their contents before handing them to Thomas.

"I know that it's not much, but this is all we've got on recorded shortages involving military-grade explosives. Take a look at that June robbery of the National Guard Armory in Wheeling, West Virginia."

Thomas found this particular listing on the bottom portion of the top page. A clear case of forceful breaking and entering, the Wheeling robbery involved thirty-nine 1.25-pound blocks of M112-grade C-4 explosives. This had been the full extent of materials taken, and Thomas found his curiosity piqued.

"What exactly is M112-grade C-4?" he asked.

"That grade refers to the age of the production lot. Unlike recent blocks that are pure white and packed in olive-drab containers, the older lots are dull gray and wrapped in clear Mylar film."

"Any way to find out if the explosives that I'm dealing with came from the Army National Guard Armory at Wheeling?" Thomas asked.

Callahan grinned. "If you can spare me a quarter-ounce sample, I believe that with a bit of lab analysis, the U.S. Army can figure that one out for you, Special Agent Kellogg. But I'm going to warn you up front that it's going to cost you in Oriole tickets."

"I believe we can handle that," Thomas replied. "May I use your phone?"

A call to BATF headquarters found Les Stanley still at work in the lab. After asking the EOD technician to coordinate the transfer of the C-4 sample to Callahan's people, Thomas checked his own extension for messages. He was pleasantly surprised to find that one was from Brittany. She'd left it barely ten minutes ago, and, given the return number, had called from the Pentagon.

Hungry, he returned her call with an invitation to dinner. The offer delighted her. Because Thomas hadn't seen the operations center she was working out of, they decided that he would pick her up down by the Pentagon's National Military Command Center, or NMCC, in ten minutes.

When Thomas hung up, Callahan commented on his wide grin. "Hey, Kellogg, it looks like you just won the lottery. I hate to be an eavesdropper, but who's the new flame?"

"Brittany Cooper. She's a commander on the CNO's staff, who's presently . . ."

". . . working as assistant naval attaché to the White House," Callahan finished.

"You know too much, Ted."

"That's why I'm a colonel."

Thomas smiled, and left his friend with a salute, a thank-you, and a promise to get back to him the next day for the results of the lab analysis. He slipped the computer printouts into his brief bag and set off for that portion of the Pentagon holding the NMCC.

Also known as the War Room, the NMCC acted as the U.S. military's central command post. It was manned twenty-four hours a day, seven days a week, and served as a clearinghouse for military activity worldwide. During times of crisis, the secretary of defense and the individual force commanders would rely on the NMCC for the latest situational updates. Actual field orders would be broadcast from the NMCC by means of a wide variety of secure communications systems, and it was here that the nuclear unlock codes would be first released.

The NMCC was semihardened to withstand an indirect nuclear strike and was located several hundred feet beneath the Pentagon's ground floor. To reach this heavily secured area of the building, Thomas had to descend a series of ramps and stairwells. Since he had stood many an extended watch in the command post while on active duty, he easily navigated the maze of twisting hallways that too often proved a nightmare for the uninitiated.

He soon found himself standing in front of the NMCC's reception desk. A smartly attired MP intently studied his credentials. To gain further access, the MP first had to call Brittany to get her approval. Once this had been achieved, Thomas had to sign an official log and surrender his BATF identification card. Only then was he given a clip-on visitor's tag and allowed to continue farther down the tiled hallway.

As Thomas approached yet another security checkpoint, he returned the curt greeting of a stone-faced MP who was seated behind a tall counter with the emblem of the Joint Chiefs of Staff displayed on its side. He signed another log here and while the guard called the NMCC's watch commander for final clearance, he looked up to examine the digital-display screen mounted on the wall behind the counter.

The screen was comprised of four separate panels, with only one panel lit in red. It read, CLASSIFIED LEVEL ONE MATERIALS PRESENT. Thomas knew that this referred to the nature of the data currently displayed on the NMCC's overhead monitors. Because his current security clearance didn't allow him to see such classified information, he would have to wait until the relevant material was deleted before they'd allow him inside.

A full minute passed before the lit screen deactivated and one reading UNCLASSIFIED took its place. Seconds later, the heavy bank-vault-type door set into the wall next to the counter automatically opened. The guard signaled that he was free to proceed and Thomas wasted no time doing so.

This put him in the NMCC's anteroom. Yet another MP watched

his entrance from behind the bulletproof glass of the final security checkpoint.

"Special Agent Kellogg," the sentry greeted, with a slight Southern accent. "Your escort is on the way."

No sooner were these words spoken than a slightly built, khaki-clad lieutenant emerged from the opposite doorway. This bespectacled young officer had already lost most of his hair, and he welcomed Thomas with high-powered enthusiasm.

"Good evening, sir. I'm Lt. Warren Tolliver, and I'll be escorting you to Op Center Bravo. Commander Cooper says that you once worked the NMCC yourself, while you were in the Air Force. I don't know how long it's been since you've last visited the command post, but we're currently in the midst of a complete face-lift. If you'll follow me closely, I'll try to get you to our destination in one piece."

Thomas soon saw for himself the extent of this remodeling job. The walls and ceiling of the corridor they were soon passing through were totally torn apart. Even at this late hour a group of contractors were at work. Thomas caught a glimpse of a snaking mass of newly installed fiber-optic cable visible inside the partially open wallboard.

The Pentagon was originally designed around the technology of a now long-gone era, and was constantly being updated. It was no different during his tenure, though the computer revolution was just in its infancy then.

On their left, they passed the cavernous confines of the NMCC. Thomas could see the six giant video screens that comprised the command post's main wall. Dozens of individual computer consoles were set up in front of the screens, manned by uniformed personnel from every branch of the military.

It turned out Operations Bravo occupied the same space that once housed the chief of naval operation's personal briefing room. It was located on the far side of the NMCC, its privacy protected by a pair of heavy steel doors that Lieutenant Tolliver opened for Thomas.

Thomas found the room's interior was vastly different since his last visit. It wasn't the room's dimensions that had changed, but rather its contents. In a space the size of a large garage a fully staffed, high-tech operations center had been set up.

To his immediate left was the op center's dominant feature. Three immense video screens were mounted into the wall here. Only the screen on the far right was currently active, with a live CNN broadcast displayed on it. A blonde newscaster was interviewing the prime minister of Canada beneath the brightly lit bow of the *QE2*.

Since Thomas was unable to hear this interview, he turned his attention to the six individual workstations set up in front of the screen. They were positioned in two parallel rows of three each, with only the front tier presently occupied. The two operatives closest to Thomas were women. All were dressed in U.S. Navy khakis and appeared to be petty officers.

A glass partition cut the room in half, with a separate conference room occupying the rest of the operations center. Brittany could be seen seated at the room's large, rectangular table, in the midst of a telephone conversation. Because her back was turned toward Thomas, she apparently hadn't seen him arrive. Lieutenant Tolliver also noticed this and promptly chimed in.

"Sir, why don't I inform the commander that you're here?"

"I'll take care of it, Lieutenant," said Thomas as he walked over to the glass partition and rapped on it three times with his right knuckle.

This impromptu page served its purpose, and Brittany smiled upon spotting Thomas. She signaled that she'd be done with her call shortly. Thomas turned his attention back to his bespectacled escort.

"How long have you had this op center up and running, Lieutenant?"

"Bravo's been functional for over a month now, sir. But the summit watch will be its first real operational test."

"The last time I was in this room, the entire space was the exclusive realm of the CNO. It was basically used for internal briefings, with its cork-lined walls usually filled with charts and maps of all kinds."

"Bravo still belongs to the CNO, sir. After the Korean incident it was decided to create this specialized op center within the NMCC, dedicated solely to naval matters. That way, when the President wants to know where the carriers are, we can show him anytime, day or night, right up there on one of those projection screens."

"Hello, Special Agent Kellogg," a female voice called from behind him.

Brittany looked remarkably fresh, her eyes bright, her starched uniform as impeccably creased as it had appeared earlier in the day.

Tolliver took her arrival as a sign that he wasn't needed anymore, and he excused himself to return to his computer console.

"This certainly is a pleasant surprise," added Brittany. "When I initially called your office I had no idea that you were right upstairs."

Thomas smiled. "I must be living a righteous life to practically bump into you for the second time today."

"From what I've been hearing, rescuing the First Cat wasn't your only adventure at the White House, Thomas. Scuttlebutt has it that you and Samuel Morrison came close to blowing away one of the birthday guests with a Stinger missile."

"I hope that's not what the morning papers are going to be saying," returned Thomas with a painful wince. "When that Cessna first penetrated restricted airspace, we didn't know what to expect—let alone a teenage parachutist with a crush on the President's daughter."

"Sounds to me like this is definitely movie-of-the-week material," joked Brittany, who intuitively sensed that Thomas was under more pressure than he was outwardly admitting. "Pretty long day at the office, Special Agent?"

"And you still don't know the half of it. How about I brief you over a glass of Chianti and a hot vegetable pie at the California Pizza Kitchens?"

"Sounds like just what the doctor ordered for this starving sailor," Brittany replied while glancing up to the CNN broadcast.

Thomas did likewise. "Looks like the heads of state are finally there."

The CNN reporter was still in the midst of her interview with the Canadian prime minister, and she was signaling another individual to join them. This resulted in the appearance of a tall, dignified, black-suited gentleman, whose trademark black horn-rimmed glasses and full shock of white hair could only belong to the prime minister of Great Britain.

"There's the star of the day," remarked Brittany. "I don't know if you heard about his UN speech, but earlier today the Brits relayed what amounts to be their tacit approval of the Global Zero Alert treaty to the world community. Intelligence is telling us that it looks like the French will be the next ones to get on the nuclear-free bandwagon, with China's Li Chen right behind them. You know, this crossing might turn out to be more historic than any of us ever dreamed."

Thomas held back his own editorial comments regarding the novel arms-control agreement, and instead queried, "Has Two-Putt arrived yet?"

"The last I heard, Eagle One was on its final approach to Kennedy," revealed Brittany. "The motorcades carrying the German chancellor and the presidents of Russia and France have just pulled into the Passenger Ship Terminal. Since the prime ministers of Japan, Italy, Canada, and Britain have already preceded them, that leaves only one more to go to make the party complete."

"Is Li Chen going to make it in time, Brit?"

"I just got off the phone with Secretary Kodlick over at the FAA. She's personally monitoring the situation, and right now, it looks like Li's plane should be touching down at Kennedy around 9:15. I know it's going to be tight for the *Queen*'s midnight departure, but barring any further delays, the Chinese delegation should make it in time."

"By the way, they've done wonders with this room," noted Thomas, whose glance remained locked on the CNN broadcast. "The resolution on that display screen is awesome."

Brittany led Thomas over to one of the vacant workstations and addressed the keyboard. As a result, the center screen filled with a nautical chart of the North Atlantic ocean. The eastern coastline of North America was displayed on the left side of the map, with Western Europe the right boundary. A red digital line linked the two continents. This sea route started at New York City and extended to the northeast, roughly paralleling the coasts of Maine, Nova Scotia and Newfoundland. As it passed over the Grand Banks, south of St. John's, Newfoundland, the line made a wide arcing turn to the east, terminating on the southern tip of Great Britain, at the port of Southampton.

"As I'm sure you've surmised, that's the *QE2*'s intended route. At an average speed of twenty-eight and one-half knots, the crossing is scheduled to take four and a half days. Of course, this is subject to change as weather, the possible presence of icebergs in the region of the Grand Banks, and mechanical integrity are factored in."

"Icebergs?" Thomas muttered.

"It's not something that we're losing any sleep over, Thomas. Iceberg activity is heaviest in the spring. But to be on the safe side, the Canadians are closely monitoring the Grand Banks with both surface-ship observations and constant air patrols.

"The same aircraft that will be on the lookout for this ice, will also be responsible for providing air support all the way out to the mid-Atlantic ridge, where British Nimrods will take over. The commanding officer of the Canadian 404 Maritime Patrol Squadron, 14 Wing, paid us a visit last week. They're based out of Greenwood, Nova Scotia, and fly CP-140 Aurora aircraft that are basically heavily modified P3-C Orions. Though their specialty is ASW, the Fighting Buffaloes, as they're called, will also be on the lookout for any air threats, and be available for ocean SAR as well."

"Too bad you can't send along a carrier battle group," remarked Thomas.

"Tell me about it, Thomas. When we first learned about the possibility of this summit at sea, our original security plan centered around the close presence of just such a carrier battle group. I was with the CNO when he showed the President the plan. It was shot down in the first five minutes of our briefing. The President was afraid that the presence of an armed task force in the immediate vicinity of the QE2 would give the world the wrong impression, and he left us with a long list of restrictions. With a bit of arm twisting, we were able to negotiate an arrangement that suits both the President's public relations needs, and more importantly, our own security concerns."

Brittany readdressed the keyboard and a blue star began flashing in the waters directly north of Bermuda. "That's the location of our nearest task force. At no time are we allowed to get within a hundred nautical miles of the QE2. The amphibious assault carrier USS *Iwo Jima* is the lead combatant. She's carrying a full load of helicopters, and a specially trained counterterrorist unit comprised of members of SEAL Team Six and Delta Force."

"There sure is a lot of open water between Nova Scotia and England," said Thomas, who remembered well the strict internal-security constraints that he and his brother had to work within.

"We practically begged the President to cut the hundred-mile limit in half, but he wouldn't budge. So, at the very least, we've got the Canadians and Brits providing constant air patrol, and our task force less than an hour's helicopter flight away," said Brittany, who added, "Of course, satellite coverage is still our ace in the hole. Our eyes in the sky will be closely watching the *QE2* throughout the crossing. And though they can only warn us of an approaching threat, we've been able to incorporate yet another unique reaction force. Unfortunately, *that* I can't discuss with you at the moment."

"Commander Cooper, I've got that met report you've been waiting for," interrupted Lieutenant Tolliver.

"Let's see it," ordered Brittany.

Thomas followed her glance as it returned to the three elevated screens. He watched as the map segment displayed on the middle monitor suddenly shifted its focus southward. The eastern coast of Florida filled the far-left portion of the screen now, with the majority of the map's coverage extending further east to include the northern section of the Bahamas island chain.

Tolliver was able to interface a satellite-relayed weather scan directly over this map segment. He then used a digital cursor to outline the heaviest area of cloud cover that lay to the northeast of the largest of the islands.

"This is the latest NOAA satellite picture taken less than a half hour ago," informed Tolliver. "The area of suspect cloud cover that they're focusing on is approximately one hundred eighty-five miles east-northeast of Great Abaco Island. It's still showing minimum rotation, though they've officially upgraded the formation to a tropical depression. A NOAA Lockheed Electra has been scrambled out of MacDill and will notify us the moment additional data is available."

"Do you believe it, Thomas? As if we don't have enough to worry about, now we've got a possible tropical storm brewing."

"I'm afraid when Mr. Murphy wrote his infamous law, this was just the type of situation he had in mind," Thomas reflected. "So enough of this worrying. Let's go grab some chow. I've got a feeling you're going to see nothing but this op center these next four and a half days, and that we'd better take full advantage of this lull before the storm. Because once that ship sets sail, our personal life is history."

B O O K   T W O

WEST WIND FIERCE

West wind fierce, immense sky, wild geese honking. Frosty morning moon, horse hooves clanging, bugles sobbing.

Tough Pass, long trail like iron.
Yet with strong steps we climbed that peak; green mountains like oceans, setting sun like blood.

—MAO TSE-TUNG
"West Wind Fierce"
Lu Mountain Pass
February 1935

8

"THICK ICE . . . THICK ICE . . . THICK ICE," REPORTED THE ROTE, FLAT VOICE
of the navigator.

For an entire hour now, these monotonous words were the only
ones to escape his lips. The occupants of the *Lijiang*'s control room
anxiously anticipated the moment when the sub's upward scanning
Fathometer would finally report a change in the treacherous conditions topside. Until then, their fates were entirely in the hands of
the navigator.

Of all those gathered inside the cramped, red-tinted compartment, the sub's commissar was growing the most impatient. To have
traveled this incredibly far distance through waters that no PLA Navy
submarine had ever dreamed of penetrating, and be unable to
broadcast a simple, yet all-important, prescheduled radio message,
was extremely frustrating. Such were the humbling circumstances
they currently found themselves in.

From his normal watch position beside the vacant fire-control
console, Guan Yin nervously scanned the nearest bulkhead-mounted
clock. The digital timepiece was rapidly approaching 2400 hours: this
gave them a bare thirty-three-minute envelope in which to find a
clear lead, surface, raise their antennae, and broadcast the message
that Command was awaiting.

This radio broadcast had been originally scheduled to take place twelve hours ago. Still well within the impenetrable confines of the polar icepack at this time, they had been forced to abandon their efforts and continue southward. Time was of the essence now, and with almost two thousand nautical miles still to travel, and a scant sixty hours left to reach their goal, the *Lijiang* could not tarry.

Admiral Liu had fortunately considered the possibility of just such a communication problem when drafting their orders. In case thick ice, mechanical difficulties, or the presence of a threatening contact in the area kept them from fulfilling their original broadcast, they were free to continue on with their mission, and attempt recontacting Command every twelve hours.

Guan could imagine how tense things must be at Naval headquarters at Tsingtao. It had been seventy-one and a quarter hours since the *Lijiang*'s last transmission reached them. They had only just completed their nerve-racking transit of the Bering Strait; they were in the process of penetrating the Chukchi Sea; and the frozen Arctic Ocean and its foreboding polar ice cap still awaited them. So when the clock hit midnight, they cautiously surfaced to broadcast a tightly compressed, heavily coded, high-frequency satellite transmission.

Guan had been one of the fortunate few allowed up into the boat's sail during this all too brief visit to the surface. After spending days on end trapped inside the stuffy, claustrophobic confines of the submerged submarine, he all but ignored the frigid temperatures topside. The fresh air was like a tonic, and bundled up in almost every available piece of clothing he had brought along, Guan got his first view of a desolate frozen wasteland few Chinese had ever seen before.

As luck would have it, the moonless night was crystal-clear. A brisk, icy breeze was blowing in from the west. Guan pulled tight his greatcoat's woolen collar and turned his back to the howling, breathtaking gusts. This allowed him to see the sub's long whip antenna rise from its protective well in the sail. As his eyes followed this device projecting up into the heavens, he saw a magnificent sight that at first startled him. His initial impression was that the night sky had somehow caught on fire! From horizon to horizon, the northern lights illuminated the heavens with ghostly bands of intense, pulsating color.

Fiery reddish orange tendrils of light shot through the skies, looking much like the effluence of an erupting, cosmic volcano. Interspersed amongst these fiery fingers were bands glowing in a full spectrum of colors ranging from golden yellow, bright swirling green, deep indigo blue, and rich violet. All told, it was a humbling, awe-inspiring sight that was to deeply touch each of the sailors who were blessed with the opportunity to view it.

It took several attempts before the message informing Command of their successful transit of the Bering Strait reached Tsingtao. Their radio officer attributed this delay to the disrupting effects of the intense solar storm that was so visible in the heavens. Guan had no doubt that this was the cause of their radio difficulties, and he was pleasantly surprised when a brief, static-filled response from Command reached them a few seconds later.

The receipt of this curt transmission signaled the end of their brief surface transit. As the *Lijiang* was prepared to return to the protective depths, Guan took one last appreciative glimpse at the glowing, ethereal heavens before reluctantly joining his comrades below.

What took place next was no less astounding. For the past three days, the *Lijiang* had crossed beneath the entire frozen breadth of the Arctic Ocean, passing only a few nautical miles from that geographical point known as the North Pole. They hadn't even stopped to pay homage to the fact that they were the first PLA Navy submarine to visit these distant, inaccessible waters but had continued on with their historic mission at flank speed, drawn by an ever approaching deadline.

Barring unexpected mechanical difficulties, it appeared that they had a decent chance of reaching their goal on time. This in itself was an incredible achievement, and Guan's heart swelled with pride every time he contemplated the amazing platform that had safely carried them these many thousands of kilometers beneath the silent sea.

The *Lijiang* was surely the PRC's greatest technological accomplishment to date. With the majority of its operational systems indigenously designed and produced inside the motherland, the fact that they were able to safely get this far without incident was certain proof that their engineers easily rivaled those of the West.

Of equal importance to this technology were the fine men who operated it. Throughout the entire passage, Guan was continuously impressed with the actions of his fellow sailors. Professionals to the core, they worked many a double watch without relief, and not a word of complaint amongst the lot of them.

In addition to their superb work values, Komsomol attendance had never been so high. Since getting rid of the troublemakers back at the Spratlys, a new spirit of comradeship could be sensed inside the *Lijiang*'s passageways. Guan attributed this exciting turn of events to the depth and quality of the remaining crew's ideological values and the leadership so aptly demonstrated by their new commanding officer.

Capt. Lee Shao-chi was everything Guan had hoped for and then some. From the moment he stepped aboard his new command, Lee took over with an iron fist and a will seemingly forged of steel. Within hours he had gained the respect of officers and enlisted men alike.

Though Guan had feared that there would be some on board who would question their former captain's abrupt exit, Lee readily filled the void by instilling a genuine sense of excitement and mystery. A previously agreed upon story was circulated amongst the crew, explaining away Capt. Shen Fei's unexpected departure as all part of an intentional move by Command to guarantee their current mission's secrecy. As far as they knew, Shen, Chief Wong, and the other dissidents had been removed from the *Lijiang* on orders from Admiral Liu. Since none of these unsuspecting sailors knew their real fate, the sham tale had succeeded in putting their minds at ease, with the incident involving the snagged rudder all part of a realistic exercise.

Now it was up to Guan and Lee Shao-chi to keep their suspicions to a minimum. They were able to do so with a demanding work schedule that didn't give the men a chance to have second thoughts. Lee led the way by example, and he worked tirelessly right alongside his crewmates.

Never before had Guan seen a man so driven as their new captain. He hardly ever seemed to rest, his unlimited energy and boundless enthusiasm the by-product of daily periods of t'ai chi and deep meditation.

Lee preferred a vegetarian diet, and when he did eat, it was always in moderation. Though his stays in the wardroom were generally short ones, on those rare occasions when Guan had a meal with him, he was an agreeable dining partner. Like Guan, he enjoyed classical music with his food and was prone to focus wardroom

conversation on either operational concerns or ideological philosophies that he found interesting.

Lee's reputation as a closet philosopher had preceded him. Guan
found their discussions in this field most invigorating. There was no
doubting that Lee admired the Chairman almost as much as Guan
did. He was particularly well versed in Mao's poetry, and could quote
most of his poems by memory. Lee was also an avowed student of
Sun Tzu, the fourth century B.C. master military strategist. He fre-
quently repeated Sun Tzu's doctrines verbatim and was particularly
fond of applying them to the art of modern submarine warfare.

When it came to general philosophies of life, Guan sensed that
Lee was something of a Taoist. He liked to break things down to
their most basic level. He could relate his relatively simple view of
life to both officers and enlisted men. In this respect, he made
Guan's job all the easier. For wherever Lee went, he brought with
him a deeper insight that constantly challenged the men to think
out a problem.

Only the day before, while they were deep beneath the Arctic ice
pack, Guan had come across two young sailors engrossed in the
midst of a philosophical discussion. This spirited conversation concerned the value of getting to know one's true inner self before
taking on an enemy. The two lads were but junior seamen assigned
to the reactor compartment, and Guan realized that the subject of
their discussion was right out of the pages of Sun Tzu. For such
sailors to have lofty thoughts like these was most refreshing. Guan
sensed the great influence that their new captain was exerting on
them.

"Thick ice . . . thick ice . . . thick ice," broke in the monotonous
voice of the navigator for the dozenth time that watch.

Guan was abruptly called back to thoughts of duty. He dared to
once more check the bulkhead clock. Four precious minutes had
passed since his last inspection—the outlook for surfacing further
dimmed.

"I thought that once we passed eighty degrees latitude, it would
be easy for us to surface and get off our transmission," remarked
Guan as he impatiently joined the navigator beside the plotting table.
"The way it looks now, we're soon going to miss this opportunity,
with the next window another twelve hours distant. Admiral Liu will
surely think us long sunk; perhaps he'll cancel the entire operation."

"So I understand, Comrade Commissar. But what else can I do?" returned the perplexed navigator. "As you can see for yourself, these charts the admiralty gave me show that the pack ice should have ended hours ago. Yet here we are already passing by the western shores of Spitsbergen, and look at the pattern our ice machine's continuously sketching."

The device the navigator was referring to was set into the bulkhead beside the plotting table. Designed much like a seismograph, the so-called ice machine was in reality an upward-scanning Fathometer that printed out its findings on a spool of paper, mounted on a rotating, cylindrical drum.

For almost seventy-two hours, the pattern had been the same: jagged lines and sharp inverted spikes, indicating a solid sheet of ice above, with the spikes showing the positions of dangerous, inverted pressure ridges.

Guan knew that this predicament wasn't their navigator's fault, and he softened his tone. "I'm sorry for taking my frustrations out on you, comrade. Everything until this point has gone so splendidly. I can't wait to share our progress with the admiral."

The navigator accepted this apology. "It's hard to believe the unknown seas we've already sailed and the great distances we've traveled. Never in my wildest dreams did I ever think that I'd be called upon to be part of such an historic operation."

"It's a great honor all right," returned Guan. Sailors as honorable as the navigator tempted him to reveal the true reason behind this history-making voyage; it would be their due.

"Depth one hundred and ten meters, course one-eight-zero true, speed three-two knots," reported the steady voice of the diving officer from his position behind the helm.

In the background the current OOD could be heard repeating this operational update. Guan absorbed this rote chatter and focused his attention on the bathymetric chart that was spread out on the plot. A red pinprick of light that was being projected from the interior of the automated table showed their current position to be in the Greenland Sea, halfway between the western shore of Spitsbergen and Greenland's northeastern coast.

"Comrade navigator," said Guan curiously. "I know nothing about our upcoming route. To get to our destination in the most direct manner, what course are you planning to steer?"

"That depends on a variety of factors yet to be determined. The most direct route would continue to take us almost due south. At our current speed, that should bring us to Jan Mayen ridge in approximately twenty-four hours. This is where our transit of the Greenland–Iceland–United Kingdom gap begins."

"Ah, the much vaunted GIUK gap," Guan observed. "While studying in Leningrad, I read an excellent Soviet Naval Institute white paper on the West's SOSUS line, a permanent line of moored hydrophones. Its original purpose was to monitor the former Soviet Union's submarines before they reached the open Atlantic, but from what I understand, the GIUK gap's underwater microphones were shut off years ago, shortly after the breakup of the USSR."

The navigator reached beneath the plotting table and pulled out a large scale chart showing the islands of Greenland and Iceland, and the western shores of the United Kingdom and Norway. He then pointed to the two strategic channels of water that lay on either side of Iceland, and responded to Guan's comments.

"We still have no concrete proof that the hydrophones have been deactivated, Comrade Commissar. My guess is that the paranoid U.S. Navy wouldn't dare shut off the entire array. And that means we'll have to initiate our course change to the southwest with the utmost circumspection."

"You mentioned previously that our exact course depends upon a variety of factors yet to be determined," reminded Guan. "Perchance, could one of these factors be on which side of Iceland we'll be making our transit?"

The navigator highlighted the two channels of water while answering. "Excellent observation, comrade. The safest route is the eastern channel, between Iceland and the Faeroe Islands. Here the deep waters surrounding the southern extension of Jan Mayen ridge should protect us from any elements of SOSUS that might be operational."

Guan picked up a clear-plastic ruler and positioned it on top of this chart. He carefully laid the ruler's top edge on their current position, then aligned it with a distant point in the mid-Atlantic. The most direct course to this spot, halfway between Nova Scotia and the United Kingdom, extended straight through the tight channel of water flowing past Iceland's western shore, prompting the commissar to question once more.

"What's wrong with the western access channel, comrade? It looks to me that it affords us the most efficient route to our destination."

"There's no doubt that your observation is correct," replied the navigator. "The western channel you're referring to is known as the Denmark Straits. Unfortunately for us, the Greenland ridge divides this shortcut roughly in half. Not only are the waters here dangerously shallow, but it is in this vicinity that SOSUS is suspected to have a major presence."

Guan shifted the ruler in order to sketch out the alternative course extending through the eastern channel. This route necessitated a substantial detour.

"With a little more than sixty hours left to get into the North Atlantic, can we afford such a time-consuming detour?" Guan asked.

"That's going to have to be the captain's ultimate decision, Comrade Commissar. As far as I'm concerned it's a simple choice between the need for speed and the importance of picking a route that will most likely guarantee our nondetection."

Guan shifted the ruler to return to the western channel and pointed toward the waters of the Denmark Straits. "If I know our captain, expediency will be worth the risk. Remember how he took charge of this plotting table when we began our dangerous transit of the Bering Sea? Why, the *Lijiang* sped through those shallow waters like a race horse!"

"Tell me about it," added the navigator. "My heart was beating so fast I feared it would burst. Never have I seen such a remarkable job of navigation. It was almost eerie watching Captain Lee calling out those quick course changes. All I can say is that the man must have the gift of second sight, because he didn't get us safely over those reefs by relying solely on our inaccurate charts."

Guan grunted in response to this strange observation and looked up from the plotting table, his glance halting on the upward-scanning Fathometer. The illuminated drum could be seen slowly rotating, with the stylus in the process of sketching out a flat, constant line, a vast contrast to the irregular, spiky pattern recorded previously.

"The ice machine!" Guan exclaimed.

The navigator wasted no time directing his attention to the Fathometer's rotating drum. He excitedly called out his findings to the rest of the control-room's crew. "Thin ice! We've got thin ice above us!"

"Thin ice, aye!" repeated the OOD from his watch station on the nearby periscope pedestal. "All stop! Quartermaster, inform the captain that I'm preparing the *Lijiang* to surface and initiate our prescheduled radio transmission."

As the quartermaster rushed past the navigation plot to personally carry out this order, Guan intercepted him. "Comrade, I believe that Captain Lee is in his stateroom. If you don't mind, I'd like to be the one to inform him of this much-anticipated news."

The young quartermaster almost looked relieved as he replied. "Of course, sir."

Guan briefly met the expectant glance of the navigator before hurriedly exiting the control room by way of the forward accessway. He passed the shut door of the sonar room on his left. The locked entrance to the radio room lay opposite. He ignored both of these vital compartments, choosing instead to climb the adjoining stairwell to the deck below. This put him immediately outside the wardroom, with the closed door to the captain's cabin across the empty hallway. Guan took a second to catch his breath before squaring back his shoulders and softly knocking on the door three times.

The only noticeable response generated by this knock was the muted sound of music coming from the other side of the doorway. Guan picked out the steady beat of a drum and the barely audible strains of string instruments.

Since the captain had made a habit of listening to cassettes while resting, Guan wasn't the least bit surprised to hear this music. Yet time was wasting and he once more rapped on the door.

When this firm series of knocks failed to generate a response, he could think of no alternative but to try opening the door himself. He slowly eased the door open and peeked inside.

He could see nothing but blackness at first. The music was clearly audible. Guan identified the hypnotizing, rhythmic tune as being some sort of Buddhist chant, complete with a melodious male choir, twanging sitar, and deep, pounding tablas.

The sweet, aromatic scent of sandalwood incense could be discerned, and Guan dared to step inside. It was as he shut the door that he spotted a flickering candle on the far side of the stateroom. The thick, partially consumed white taper sat on top of the cabin's small, fold-down desk, with the flame illuminating the immobile figure of the *Lijiang*'s commanding officer seated contentedly on the nearby mattress.

It was apparent that Guan had caught Lee Shao-chi deep in meditation. His bare feet were folded beneath him in the position known as full lotus—with back perfectly straight, hands palm up on the upper thigh, and closed eyes staring straight ahead to where Guan was standing. His breaths were deep and even. Guan noted that Lee was dressed in a white martial-arts robe. He had a black belt cinched around the waist and a blood-red bandanna, decorated with bright yellow dragons, tied around his forehead. The long jagged scar lining the entire left side of his face looked particularly sinister in the candlelight. Guan had trouble finding his voice as he summoned the nerve to break this trance.

"Captain Lee," he muttered. "Comrade, are you awake?"

Guan took a tentative step forward. His words seemed to have no effect, and he decided he'd try one more time before being forced to actually shake the man awake.

"Captain, the upward-scanning Fathometer shows thin ice above!"

Lee Shao-chi's eyes snapped open, with the abrupt suddenness of an electric-light switch activating. The dark riveting pupils locked themselves on Guan, and for a frightening second, the portly political officer felt as if he had just been hit by a small electric shock.

"Do I sense fear, Comrade Commissar? When you are at one with the Way, make your presence known with true purpose, like the fierce west wind."

"The fierce west wind?" repeated a confused Guan. "As in the Chairman's poem?"

"West wind fierce, immense sky, wild geese honking," recited Lee, with a calm, silken tone. "Yes, comrade."

Guan wasn't certain what Lee was driving at and he attempted to redirect the conversation. "Sir, I saw the ice machine with my own eyes. At long last, we can surface and make contact with Admiral Liu!"

Lee responded with the barest of introspective grins. "Did you know that Admiral Liu fought at Mao's side during the entire Lu Mountain Pass campaign? Chances are good that he was with the

Chairman on the morning when "West Wind Fierce" was penned there."

Guan realized that it was useless to resist this man's will, and he replied respectfully. "I've been fortunate enough to have heard Admiral Liu tell his stories of the Long March. It was truly a defining moment in the PRC's history."

"Do you realize that we are presently in the midst of a journey that could have implications even greater than those of the Long March, Comrade Commissar? Much like the founders of our republic, whose own march for freedom lasted three hundred and sixty-eight days, covering some eight thousand miles at a cost of over seventy thousand men, women, and children, we too are on a mission to save China from destruction."

Lee suddenly fell silent, shifted his weight, and slowly unfolded his long legs from the lotus position. As he stood, he looked at Guan and whispered:

"Tough Pass, long trail like iron. Yet with strong steps we climbed that peak; green mountains like oceans, setting sun like blood!"

"Captain's in the control room," informed the alert quartermaster as Lee Shao-chi briskly strode through the forward accessway.

The captain was still dressed in his martial-arts robes, and he wasted no time climbing up onto the periscope pedestal and calling out forcefully, "I have the conn. Comrade navigator, what are our surface environmentals?"

"It looks like we have a large open lead directly overheard, sir," informed the navigator from the plotting table.

The captain swept his practiced gaze over the dozens of gauges and dials mounted into the bulkhead before the two seated helmsmen. As his glance halted on the numerals displayed on the digital clock, Guan Yin breathlessly ducked through the forward accessway. The boat's commissar proceeded at once to his customary position beside the vacant weapons console where he just had time to grab onto an overhead handhold as the captain's voice rang out.

"Blow forward-and-aft ballast tanks and bring us up to thirty meters."

"Blowing forward-and-aft tanks, at thirty meters, aye, sir," repeated the diving officer.

The boat's ballast pumps activated with a muted, whirring growl.

As tons of seawater were subsequently purged from the ballast tanks, the now lightened vessel began to ascend.

Gradually at first, then with rapid regularity, the digital depth counter dropped from 110 meters. As it flashed by the sixty-meter mark, the diving officer reached forward to address the ballast-control panel. His job was to precisely gauge the amount of ballast needed, so that the *Lijiang* would attain its ordered depth and ascend no further.

All eyes were on the depth gauge as it passed fifty meters. The sound of the ballast pumps could be heard once more in the background, followed by the distinct roar of seawater flowing back into the tanks. This delicate balancing act was intended to trim the boat and control its rate of ascent.

"Thirty-five meters, Captain," reported the diving officer, whose eyes were now glued to the digital numbers of the still-descending depth counter. "Thirty-three, thirty-two, thirty-one . . ."

The depth gauge froze on thirty-one. After the slightest of adjustments to the ballast-control panel, the diving officer coolly observed, "Thirty meters and holding, sir."

"Up scope," ordered Lee.

There was a loud hiss and the hydraulically operated periscope lifted up from its well. Lee crouched down low to keep the scope from fully deploying, and he pulled down the hinged grips and peered through the rubberized eyepiece.

"Activate exterior sail lights," he instructed.

While the quartermaster carried out this order, Guan softly addressed Lt. Wu Han, who, as OOD, remained on the pedestal beside the captain.

"Comrade Wu, what in the world does the captain hope to see down here? We're still a good ten meters away from attaining periscope depth."

"Why don't you come up here and see for yourself," offered Lee Shao-chi, adjusting the hinged grips and continuing to peer out the eyepiece.

Guan somewhat reluctantly released his tight grip on the overhead handhold and climbed up onto the pedestal. He wasn't as limber as the captain, and was forced to squat down awkwardly beside the scope.

Only after Lee completed a hasty 360-degree scan did he back away from the scope and beckon Guan to take his place. The commissar did his best to nestle up against the eyepiece. After taking some time to focus the lens, he was rewarded with a totally unexpected sight. Filling the entire lens was a glittering, crystalline wonderland, the nature of which the captain described to the control room's hushed occupants.

"Comrade navigator, I thought you said that we had a clear lead topside. Unless I'm hallucinating, or our scope's malfunctioning, I'd say that there's a good thirty centimeters of solid ice above us. Do you concur, Comrade Commissar?"

Guan replied while pulling back from the eyepiece and stiffly standing. "Though I can't estimate the thickness of that ice floe above us, I can definitely attest to its translucent beauty."

"I'm sorry for misinterpreting the ice machine, captain," apologized the navigator.

"No matter," said Lee, his mind already made up on how they would proceed. "Down scope. Sound the collision alarm. Prepare planes for surfacing in ice conditions."

A steady electronic alarm began ringing in the background and Guan took this opportunity to return to the weapons console. It was apparent that even with the presence of ice, the captain was intending to use the *Lijiang*'s sail like a battering ram. This unorthodox maneuver was a dangerous one. Pack ice is a very unforgiving medium. If they were to misgauge its thickness, the resulting concussion could damage their vulnerable sail-mounted hydroplanes, or worse, split open their hull.

To protect the sub's all-important diving planes, the diving officer was in the process of having the planesman hydraulically rotate them so that they were positioned straight up. In this manner they would hopefully slice through the ice like a knife, though there was always the risk that they could end up permanently jammed in this useless vertical position.

"Let's get on with it, comrades! If we wish to contact Command, we've got a mere ten minutes to get topside and meet the current broadcast window," reminded Lee, his deep voice oozing with confidence.

Guan had all but forgotten about the reason for this risky ascent. Well aware that their mission's success depended upon the *Lijiang* reaching the North Atlantic without serious damage, Guan was set to voice his concerns, when Lee interceded, convincing him to hold his tongue.

"Vent ballast and take us up!" he ordered.

With the collision alarm blaring in the background, the control room filled with the gurgling sound of venting seawater. The *Lijiang* began drifting upward.

"Twenty-eight meters," reported the diving officer, an anxious strain in his voice. "Twenty-seven . . . twenty-six . . ."

Guan braced himself for impact—his legs spread, his hands tightly gripping the overhead handhold. On the adjoining periscope pedestal, the captain calmly stood beside the forward rail, stabilizing himself with a single hand, his eyes glued to the dropping depth gauge.

"Twenty-four meters . . . twenty-three . . . twenty-two . . ."

They were rapidly approaching periscope depth. Guan figured that it was only a matter of a few more meters before the sail made contact. A bead of perspiration rolled down his forehead in anticipation of this collision, as the diving officer informed them that they had just passed twenty meters.

"Brace yourselves, comrades," Lee warned.

A second later, the *Lijiang*'s sail crashed into the ice with a gut-wrenching crunch. The deck vibrated wildly, and Guan's knees buckled while his palms painfully bit into their handhold.

"Depth gauge indicates that we failed to break through the ice," revealed the disappointed diving officer.

"Then we'll just have to take her down and have another crack at it," Lee impassively ordered. "Chief, flood her down to fifty meters."

Guan could hardly believe the captain's obstinacy. The compartment once more filled with the gurgling roar of seawater. Oddly enough, none of the other officers present had spoken out in protest, and Guan feared that he'd be labeled a coward if he did so. As it was, the line officers doubted his operational competency, being a commissar, but he dared not show the least hint of anxiety.

He did his best to take a step back into the corner, where he removed a handkerchief to pat dry his soaked forehead and neck. There could be no ignoring the tight knot that had gathered in his stomach. His throat was so dry he would have given a day's pay for a single sip of tea.

"Forty-five meters and continuing to descend," reported the diving officer.

"That's deep enough, comrade," Lee replied. "Lighten our tanks to surface."

It only took a single turn of the wrist for the diving officer to send tons of seawater ballast back into the depths. Guan grasped for an overhead handhold, his eyes locked on the rapidly descending depth gauge. The thirty-meter mark passed in a heartbeat, and Guan flinched as the counter whisked past twenty meters.

Another bone-jarring collision followed, this time causing the compartment's lights to flicker momentarily. The terrifying sound of rushing water drew Guan's frightened glance to the periscope well, where a good-sized stream of liquid was pouring from the ceiling. Lee took this flood in stride and calmly reached up into the well with a wrench, as the diving officer informed them that they still hadn't made it to the surface.

"It's most obvious that the ice is thicker than we anticipated," dared Guan. "Since the time left for us to broadcast is rapidly dwindling, I say let's postpone the transmission for another twelve hours."

"Nonsense!" retorted the captain, his white martial-arts robe completely soaked by the seawater leak he had just managed to stem. "There's a good five minutes left to get off the signal, and I say let's give it another go. Take us back down, Chief. And this time, blow the main ballast to give us an additional hundred tons of positive buoyancy."

The *Lijiang* sank once more into the silent depths, much like a repeating nightmare. Guan had all but given up hope by this point, with his worst fear being that the captain's stubborn persistence would lead to the death of every one of them. Concerned more by the fear of dying than a loss of face, Guan did his best to prepare himself to meet his fate. It was not the way he ever imagined sacrificing himself for the motherland.

On the adjoining periscope pedestal, Lee responded to the tense atmosphere with an outburst of positive energy. As the *Lijiang* settled in at a depth of sixty-seven meters and the driving officer primed the emergency blow valves, the vessel's commanding officer shared his inner thoughts with his fellow shipmates.

"Only the weak fear death, comrades. It is all part of the Way of the Warrior, and as such, it must be respected and revered. So momentarily close your eyes and breathe deeply with me. Fill your lungs with the life-giving essence, banish thoughts of defeat to the deserts of doubt, and focus your mind's eye on that brightest of suns known as the Tao!''

Lee shut his eyes, squared back his shoulders, and began a series of deep, even breaths. From the compartment's shadows, Guan could clearly recognize the same absent expression that he had first seen on Lee's face while he was meditating back in his cabin. Guan wondered if any of his fellow shipmates found their captain's behavior to be strange, and he turned to the nearby navigator. Remarkably enough, this very individual was wrapped up in the same weird trance that possessed Lee Shao-chi! Several others of the control-room crew had also closed their eyes, their deep full breaths seemingly synchronized.

"For the sake of the motherland, blow emergency ballast!" Lee exclaimed.

The roar of venting seawater rose to an almost deafening crescendo, the *Lijiang* hurtled upward out of the black depths, and Guan found himself tightly shutting his own eyes. When they finally made contact with the ice, this time the concussion was followed by a horrible crack, as if the entire hull had been ripped open.

The morning broke dull and gray, as Admiral Liu Huang-tzu awoke from yet another restless night's slumber. No matter how hard he tried, sleep escaped him, and he found himself tossing and turning, his mind racing with endless worry.

Sleep was usually never a problem for the veteran mariner while at sea. In fact, the fresh ocean air and constant throbbing of the ship's engines had previously been most conducive to a sound night's rest. Yet this wasn't the case on his current patrol—a week had gone by with hardly a dream to remember.

Liu couldn't blame his insomnia on his present means of transport. His flagship, the *Zhanjiang*, had provided a comfortable, inviting home for the past two weeks. The weather had also cooperated, with only two days of rough seas so far experienced.

Most of the time, Liu was barely aware of the seas on which they traveled, so smooth was their transit. Such was the case on this particular morning, as he shuffled around his spacious stateroom completing his daily routine, with the deck hardly rocking.

He could tell by the change in pitch of the background engine noise that the throttles had been recently cut back. This was in preparation for their upcoming return to Tsingtao. They should be in the coastal transit channel by now, and Liu made the final adjustments to his white formal uniform before heading outdoors to check this fact.

A chilling gust of cold air greeted him as he walked out onto his cabin's exterior veranda. The railed observation terrace was situated directly on top of the destroyer's bridge and offered a spectacular view of both the ship's bow and the seas beyond.

The overcast skies were as gray as his worried thoughts. Liu walked over to the forward rail and allowed his glance to wander. As he expected, the low, rugged hills of Shandong Province could be seen to port. Several small fishing junks were visible working the waters between the *Zhanjiang* and shore, and Liu presumed that they were homeported at nearby Jiaonan. Without the assistance of binoculars, he was able to view the motley collection of ramshackled structures that made up this small village. Jiaonan was situated at the base of Shandong's coastal foothills, and sighting it indicated that their final destination was rapidly approaching.

Liu had mixed feelings about returning to Tsingtao. Though it would be good to get back to fleet headquarters, he sincerely enjoyed his time spent at sea. It reminded him of the vibrant days of youth, and he knew that future seagoing opportunities would be extremely rare.

While casting his forlorn glance to starboard, as they passed tiny Lingshan Island, Liu pondered the cause of his mental unrest. It had been more than seventy hours since the *Lijiang* had contacted them. The submarine had already missed one of the prescheduled radio transmissions and they would soon miss the second twelve-hour window. This was a most disturbing turn of events for a mission that, until now, had gone off splendidly.

Their charade in the Spratlys was a complete success. They had easily removed Capt. Shen Fei and his gang of dissidents, and the entire world subsequently bought the story that the *Lijiang* had sunk. Even the foolhardy Filipinos had unknowingly assisted them when they boldly announced that it could have been one of their depth rockets that was the cause of the *Lijiang*'s demise.

Of course, Liu knew that this was a complete lie. Three long days ago, the *Lijiang* was alive and well, their position update putting them in the far-off Chukchi Sea.

But had the legendary Captain Lee been able to make good their submerged crossing of the frozen Arctic Ocean?

His greatest fear was that the submarine had collided with an inverted ice ridge. Then there was always the possibility that an unexpected mechanical problem had caused a loss of power, and unable to surface because of the ice pack above, the *Lijiang* was currently entombed in a frozen grave.

Liu tried to remind himself that these were worst-case scenarios only, that there could be any number of other causes behind the *Lijiang*'s failure to communicate with them. He had personally written the sub's operational orders, and had made certain to allow for a wide variety of possible communications glitches.

The first of these concerned the frozen medium in which they traveled. There was no telling what the ice conditions would be like once they completed their circumnavigation of the North Pole. The position of the pack ice was constantly changing and chances were good that as the *Lijiang* reached the northern reaches of the Greenland Sea, they might have found themselves unable to surface safely.

Yet another possible cause of the delay were the solar storms that were presently ravaging the earth's atmosphere. One of the most active periods of sun-spot activity in recent memory, the electromagnetic storms were playing havoc with all manner of communications worldwide. Only the night before, the *Zhanjiang* had experienced problems reaching Shanghai by radio. And now the *Lijiang* was that much closer to the North Pole where the electromagnetic interference was even greater.

As Liu peered over his destroyer's heavily armed bow, he knew that there was one more plausible factor that could be responsible for the delayed radio broadcast. The cold depths of the Arctic Ocean were home to a variety of warships other than the *Lijiang*. Russian, Canadian, and American icebreakers regularly patrolled its icy surface.

Because of geographical constraints, the Arctic Ocean was also the place Russian submarines called home. Their mammoth *Typhoon*- and *Delta*-class submarines were designed with the ice pack in mind. They were based in nearby Murmansk, a short, submerged transit to the protective shelter of the polar cap. Here they could safely loiter and await the doomsday orders that would direct them to smash through the ice and launch their arsenals of nuclear-tipped, ballistic missiles.

This northern bastion was also protected by a fleet of sophisticated, nuclear-powered attack subs. Code-named Akula, Sierra, and Alfa, these extremely capable submarines were incorporated with the latest in weapons-control systems and sound-silencing technology. This advanced design made them more than a match for the American, British, and French attack subs that also patrolled these frozen seas.

Had the *Lijiang* encountered one of these warships? And was it detected attempting to stalk them? If this was the case, there was no way that Captain Lee would needlessly compromise his command to broadcast a radio report.

A fresh gust of cold wind hit him in the face, and Liu looked to the western horizon from where this breeze blew. They were passing Jia Point now and a small red launch carrying the harbor pilot could be seen approaching them.

The great port city of Tsingtao came into view as they rounded the point. Its modern skyscrapers and dozens of commercial structures extended down to the crowded docks, with the air itself heavily polluted by thick, yellow loess conveyed all the way from the interior by the incessant western winds.

This was the face of modern China. Cities such as Tsingtao were playing an all-important role as the ports where the motherland's abundant exports and vital imports were handled. Since a good majority of this trade was by sea, warships such as the *Zhanjiang,* and the dozens of PLA Navy vessels that soon came into view anchored at their docks, were instrumental in protecting this maritime activity.

With the transfer of the harbor pilot, the *Zhanjiang* slowed further, its bow swinging toward the half dozen piers reserved for the PLA Navy. Liu spotted a trio of formidable-looking *Luda*-class destroyers, with five T-43 minesweepers tied up alongside. These were the same vessels that had recently participated in the successful East China Sea Red Flag exercises. Used to screen the impact area of their ground-launched ballistic missiles, this capable flotilla had helped them send a strict warning to both Taiwan and the other countries who dared support the outlaw nation.

Red Flag was planned before the ascendancy of their new president, and was Liu's creation. It was originally formulated to intimidate the Taiwanese government, which was getting much too cocky of late for China's good.

Deng Xiaoping's passing had left a power void, and Liu and his conservative supporters foresaw a dangerous turn of events if Taiwan were to be allowed to continue flaunting its unlawful powers. A group of liberal politicians that Li Chen was rumored to be part of was said to be advocating an actual splitting of the People's Republic. It was to be patterned after the breakup of the old Soviet Union, and would find the rich provinces of the southeast forming their own independent nation, under the guidance of the commercial powerhouses of Hong Kong, Shanghai, and Taiwan. This would leave the poorer, industrial north alone to fend for itself, and effectively put an end to Mao's dream of a united motherland.

Liu shuddered to think how such a frightening scenario would affect the great navy that he had sacrificed the best years of his life to build. At 260,000 men and 1,150 vessels strong, this fleet was the world's largest.

Not about to give up his life's work without a fight, Liu looked out at the approaching docks. Tied to the end of the pier here, with quick access to the channel if needed, was one of the very vessels that he was depending upon to protect the integrity of his great dream.

She was known by her crew as the *Yellow Dragon*. A byproduct of the same modern, high-tech engineering skills that produced such warships as the *Zhanjiang* and the *Lijiang*, the *Yellow Dragon* was a *Xia*-class, nuclear-powered, ballistic-missile submarine. As such, only the upper portion of her sleek black hull was currently visible.

It was evident from the activity visible on this end of the dock that the *Yellow Dragon* was getting ready to put to sea. This particular patrol could very well be the missile sub's most important ever, and Liu was relieved to find that they would be heading to sea on schedule.

The *Yellow Dragon* was a huge vessel, 160 meters long and displacing over 13,000 tons. It sported a teardrop-shaped hull and a rather squat, streamlined sail, from which the hydroplanes extended.

Most of her length was aft of the sail, where a humped casing held sixteen SS-N-18 missiles. Stored in two parallel rows of eight missiles each, the SS-N-18 was an awesome offensive weapon. It was the first PRC submarine-launched ballistic missile to carry multiple independent reentry vehicles. Each of these MIRVs carried three 200-kiloton warheads. The solid-fuel missiles had a range of over 4,000 nautical miles and could be delivered with an amazing degree of accuracy. This gave the *Yellow Dragon* the ability to hit a wide variety of targets. The sub didn't even have to leave the pier to effectively wipe out such diverse cities as Taipei, Manila, Tokyo, Seoul, Vladivostok, Calcutta, Singapore, Sydney, or Honolulu.

By moving farther east into its normal patrol zone in the North Pacific, the *Xia*-class submarine could hit targets up and down America's West Coast, including Seattle, Portland, San Francisco, Los Angeles, and San Diego. When properly positioned, there was hardly a city on earth that it couldn't destroy, making the *Yellow Dragon* one of the most potent warships ever to sail the seas.

The boat's current commanding officer was Capt. Ma Zhu-lin. Ma was a PLA Navy veteran. At fifty years of age, he was a tried-and-true old-timer, whose reputation as a strict disciplinarian was something of a legend. There was no better man to have at the helm if missile-release codes were to be received, for Ma would carry out any legitimate order without question.

The ranks of armed PLA soldiers standing on the pier beside the *Yellow Dragon* were further proof that she was equipped with a full load of warheads. As with most nations that deployed nuclear weapons, China had a strict command and control policy in place. The PLA's nuclear forces had their own chain of command, separate from the rest of the military, in which Liu was but a single link.

China's president had the ultimate responsibility for ordering the release of nuclear weapons and Li Chen had sole possession of the warhead-release codes. This top-secret, numeric sequence was always kept within close reach of the president in a briefcase carried by a trusted military aide and called the Cobra. In the event of hostilities, this code would be transmitted to the commander of China's nuclear forces, who would in turn broadcast it to the desired units. Then it would be up to the individual field commanders to utilize the unlock codes to arm the warheads and deliver them. Altogether it was a rather foolproof process. Liu was aware that he who controlled these nuclear codes controlled China's destiny.

"Admiral Liu, sir," an unexpected voice broke in from behind him.

Liu turned around and couldn't help but find his expectations rising upon spotting the thin figure of the *Zhanjiang*'s radio officer. He stood somewhat timidly beside the veranda's open hatchway and Liu anxiously beckoned the young officer to join him beside the railing.

"Yes, comrade," said Liu eagerly.

"Admiral, you need not worry any longer. Headquarters has just informed us that less than five minutes ago, they received a brief, high-speed radio transmission from the *Lijiang*. Though heavy static masked a good portion of the message, the course coordinates that they were able to relay put them in the northern reaches of the Greenland Sea, off the Norwegian island of Spitsbergen."

Liu fought the urge to hug the bearer of this fantastic news, and the dark, sullen mood that had possessed him for the past few days suddenly lifted.

"That's wonderful news, comrade," managed the smiling veteran, who noted that the radio officer apparently had something else to tell him. "Yes, comrade, there's more to the message?"

"Not exactly, sir. It's just that moments after I received the coded dispatch from Command telling us of the *Lijiang*'s successful transit, a cellular phone call from Beijing arrived for you. The caller was from the Bureau of Foreign Affairs, and he instructed me to inform you that the president has safely arrived in New York and is presently in the process of boarding the *QE2*."

Liu's mood abruptly soured, and after dismissing the radio officer, he returned to the railing. Below, the deck crew was readying the mooring lines, and he absently watched their efforts, his inner thoughts a world away.

The young fool: so anxious to become an accepted world player, he was now on the verge of wasting the sacrifices of so many thousands who had died to unite the motherland. Sickened by this thought, Liu found his optimism clouded by a single doubt: despite all their recent successes, what if the operation wasn't successful? So much effort had already been expended to put this complicated plan into action that failure could mean the end of the People's Republic of China, with a lifetime of selfless toil on his part all in vain.

9

MIDNIGHT FOUND VINCE KELLOGG STANDING ON THE *QE2*'S BRIDGE. WITH EX-
acting precision, the last mooring lines were cast off, and with the
assistance of a trio of powerful tugs, the immense ocean liner cautiously inched its way into the Hudson stern first.

A bare thirty minutes earlier, the Chinese president and his party
had finally arrived at the ship terminal. As they passed through security and hurried aboard, the ship was cleared to set sail.

To give the heads of state the best vantage point for this rare
midnight departure, the captain had invited them to join him on the
Bridge. The presidents of the United States, France, and Russia, and
the British and Canadian prime ministers had already taken up this
offer. Much like a group of enthusiastic schoolboys, the five statesmen were currently in the midst of a tour of the central enclosed
wheelhouse. This left Vince free to take up a position on the Bridge's
starboard exterior wing.

Securitywise, he had little to be concerned with for the moment.
The Bridge was a sealed, self-contained space, and since each of the
leaders had at least one personal guard present, they were more
than adequately protected.

Thus, he was able to watch the crew at work, as they backed the
963-foot-long, 69,000-ton vessel out into the river. Most of the actual
maneuvering was being controlled from the wing's auxiliary console

situated on a slightly elevated platform at the far end of the wing. Gathered around its rudder, speed, and bow-thruster controls were the ship's first officer, the navigator, and a civilian river and docking pilot. All of these individuals held portable two-way radio handsets, their attentions focused on safely conveying the *QE2* away from the pier.

This was a complicated operation, made all the more difficult by the Hudson's swift current. Here the pilots proved invaluable. The nattily dressed civilians knew these waters intimately and were able to call out suggested course and speed changes with rote precision, all the while coordinating the efforts of the tugs.

It was hard not to feel the excitement generated by this departure. Taking advantage of the magnificent late-summer night, tens of thousands of New Yorkers had come to see the great ship off.

Vince got a bird's-eye view of this crowd that packed all three levels of the passenger terminal. From this structure's interior departure lounge, the spirited strains of a band could be heard playing a seemingly endless rendition of "New York, New York." Confetti danced through the air, with the crowds gaily singing along with the music and wildly cheering.

The departure also brought out an abundance of television-news crews. Dozens of blinding camera lights illuminated the pier, while in the starry sky above flew the single news helicopter allowed to film the event.

To the east, the skyscrapers themselves looked on, seeming to stand a bit taller out of respect for a ship that was their peer in both length and majesty.

A resonant, five-second-long blast from the *QE2*'s air horn heralded its arrival into the Hudson River. They were well away from the pier now, and with another mighty blast of the ship's whistle, the *Queen* was maneuvered into the center of the channel, its bow turned downstream. They passed the collection of superbly restored warships and aircraft belonging to the Intrepid Sea, Air, Space Museum to their left, and Vince got an excellent view of Forty-second Street's wide, well-lit expanse.

The last of the tugs pulled away, prompting a spirited exchange of whistle salutes. The *QE2* easily won this battle of the air horns, culminating in a final, ear-shattering blast that could surely be heard from the Battery to Harlem.

Under its own power now, the ship steadily picked up speed. The Empire State Building's lofty spire was soon behind them, and Vince listened as the river pilot spoke into his radio's transmitter.

"Coast Guard traffic control, this is the *QE2* bound for Southampton, over."

"*QE2*, this is Coast Guard traffic control," replied a crisp female voice from the radio. "We have you in the system headed southbound downriver."

"Aye, Coast Guard," returned the pilot. "*QE2* is currently passing the Holland Tunnel ventilators."

"Roger that, *QE2*. We've got normal ferry traffic westbound," reported the Coast Guard operator.

While this routine exchange continued, Vince spotted the distinctive twin towers of the World Trade Center up ahead on his left. To get a better view of this portion of downtown Manhattan, he crossed through the wheelhouse and stepped out onto the port wing. He found the five heads of state gathered on the wing's elevated platform, their rapt gazes locked on the passing skyline.

"Two-Putt sure seems to be enjoying himself," whispered Samuel Morrison, who had been standing beside the forward portion of the wing, immediately outside the wheelhouse doorway. "I haven't seen him so excited since election night."

"Seeing Manhattan from this perspective is enough to excite anyone," Vince added, joining the SAIC.

Morrison grunted. "I'm glad you're a part of the team, Vince. I gather that all went well today?"

Vince filled him in with regards to the suspected case of food poisoning as they watched a pair of fireboats anchored off Battery Park shoot thin, arcing columns of water high into the night sky.

"Salmonella?" Morrison guessed.

"The New York Public Health authorities are still trying to determine the exact nature of the virus and its source. They did complete an intensive inspection of the vessel's food preparation and storage facilities, and the ship passed with flying colors."

"Make certain that Doc Patton gets a copy of that inspection report," instructed the SAIC. "If it turns out to be salmonella and it's still around, we could have a real problem on our hands. Is there any sort of internal follow-up underway?"

"I believe the ship's physician is handling it," said Vince. "I've already initiated an investigation of my own, with Robert Hartwell's assistance."

"Stay on it and keep me informed," said Morrison as he refocused his gaze on the fading skyline. "I know it's asking a lot of you, Vince, but I trust you can coordinate such investigations and still remain focused on protecting Two-Putt."

"*Mon Dieu!*" an excited voice called out from behind them. "*C'est magnifique, mes amis!*"

As Vince turned to see what had prompted this emotional outburst, the French president rushed past him and ducked into the wheelhouse. He was followed by the diminutive figure of the Russian president, with the prime ministers of Canada and Britain close on their heels. Behind them, their respective bodyguards jostled one another, trying to keep up.

This left the American President as the only head of state left on the port wing. He was in the midst of an animated conversation with the QE2's bearded captain as they slowly made their way together toward the wheelhouse. As he passed Vince and Samuel, he explained what all the excitement was about.

"It seems that President Lenclud just got his first good look at the Statue of Liberty. If you gentlemen would like to join us, the captain here says that the view of Lady Liberty from the starboard wing is not to be missed."

Without waiting for a response to this offer, the President and the ship's captain disappeared inside. Samuel Morrison wasted no time ducking into the wheelhouse himself, and as Vince pivoted to join him, his cellular phone began ringing. Remaining alone on the port wing, he pulled it from his jacket's breast pocket and said curtly, "Kellogg."

"Hey, big brother."

"Your timing's impeccable, Thomas. You'll never believe where your call caught me."

"I'd say that you're just about to pass Ellis Island and the Statue of Liberty. Brittany and I are watching the send-off on television. It looks like quite the event."

Vince looked up at the circling helicopter. "It's even better live. Any news on our pen pal?"

"I'd love to give you all the dirty details, but let's just say that we're a little farther along the pike than our last conversation."

"One step at a time," advised Vince.

"Will do. If I get any hard news, I'll contact you at sea via SAT-COM. So until then, bon voyage and enjoy that caviar!"

Vince rang off and entered the wheelhouse to join the others.

Inside he noted that yet another head of state had just arrived. With Tuff leading the way, President Li Chen and two hefty bodyguards made their way out onto the starboard observation wing.

Vince followed them outside. There was a flurry of excited greetings as the Chinese leader joined his five colleagues. Li Chen spoke excellent English, and after a warm exchange of greetings, a moment of contemplative silence followed. This hushed lapse was prompted by the breathtaking sight they were passing to starboard. Illuminated by a powerful bank of mercury-vapor lights, the Statue of Liberty looked out from her lofty vantage point, her torch of liberty glowing alive with a flickering red flame.

This was the first time that Vince had ever viewed the monument from the waters of New York Bay, and he found himself welling with emotion. He could think of no more fitting image than this one to accompany them these next four and a half days. For if the upcoming summit was to be successful, it was imperative that the heads of state shared the same spirit of freedom engraved on the tablets held at Lady Liberty's side.

As they sailed beneath the arched buttresses of the Verrazano Narrows Bridge the VIPs excused themselves. A late champagne supper for the summiteers was being served in the Queens Grill. Since Vince's official shift ended at this point, he left the ship's Bridge himself with the full intention of retiring to his stateroom. The next day's shift was to begin at 0800 sharp, with the first official summit session scheduled to take place in the Boardroom at 0830.

Even though he had been going steadily now for over seventeen hours, Vince found himself wide awake and not the least bit tired. As he headed down to One Deck, he decided to use this free time to check out the ship's Gym, one of the few public spaces he had yet to visit.

Deep in the bowels of the ship on Seven Deck, the first thing he saw as he entered the Gym was a large, rectangular swimming pool. To the right of the pool was a good-sized carpeted room surrounded by mirrors and noticeably empty. Vince assumed that this was where the aerobics and dance classes were held.

In the left portion of the compartment stood the exercise machines. There was a full Nautilus circuit, four StairMasters, three rowing machines, and four bicycles. A wraparound video screen was set up in front of the bikes, one of which still had protective bubble wrap covering it.

The screen itself allowed the bikers to choose from various courses where they could race against their fellow workout partners. It was a sophisticated piece of hardware and Vince wasn't all that surprised to find a pair of legs clad in blue jeans extending from beneath its video projector. An open tool box was beside them.

"Excuse me," he said loudly. "Problems with the video screen?"

"These damn high-tech toys are all alike," responded a male voice with a slight Southern accent to it.

Moments later, the speaker crawled out from beneath the projector. Whoever he was, Vince had yet to meet this middle-aged, rail-thin character, with slicked-back, dark brown hair, and narrow, green eyes. He wore a gray sweatshirt with the words LIU'S GYM stenciled on the chest and had an unlit cigarette dangling from his thin lips.

"Good evening. Sorry to bother you, but when I saw the lights on, I couldn't resist coming in and having a look around. Vince Kellogg's the name."

A sardonic grin painted the stranger's narrow face as he stood. "Kellogg, like the cereal?"

Vince nodded.

"No kidding. Your pappy didn't invent corn flakes, did he?"

"I'm afraid he didn't," replied Vince. He sensed something about this man that made him uneasy.

Before he could question him further, a female voice rose from behind Vince. "Is something wrong out there, Max?"

Vince looked up into the mirrored wall set before him and caught sight of the reflection of a gorgeous woman standing in the doorway of the Gym's office. She was dressed in tight, flesh-colored leotards that showed every inch of her shapely, lean body. Yet it was her face that drew his full attention. She had a wild mane of long, curly, red hair, exquisitely framing her sharp cheekbones and almond-shaped eyes. She appeared to be Eurasian. As Vince turned around to introduce himself, he remembered the film in which he had seen her.

"I bet you're Monica Chang," he offered.

She stepped out into the room to offer him her hand, saying, "Guilty as charged. And my accuser is?"

Vince took her soft hand. He found himself swallowed by her fathomless, catlike eyes. An awkward period of silence followed when he suddenly realized that he had yet to answer her.

"I'm sorry, Ms. Chang. Vince Kellogg at your service, ma'am."

The actress was well aware of her effect on members of the opposite sex, even married ones, and she took his flustered reply in stride. "I certainly hope you didn't come down here to work out with us this evening, Vince. I'm afraid the facility won't be fully operational until tomorrow."

"That's quite all right," said Vince. "As I told your associate, I was doing some exploring of the ship, and when I saw the lights down here, I decided to take a look."

Monica sauntered over to the exercise bikes to complete the introductions. "I take it that you've yet to meet our resident computer genius, Max Kurtyka. As you might have heard, there were some electrical problems during the previous crossing. It destroyed the components of several of the machines. We most probably would have closed the entire facility during the summit if it wasn't for Max being available to help us install this new equipment."

Max thanked her with a leer aimed squarely at her bust. Vince felt sorry the actress was forced to rely on such a distasteful person.

"Now you'll be certain to give us a try tomorrow, Vince," Monica offered.

"It looks like I've got the early shift, ma'am. But if I can manage to coax some life into these old bones, you can bank on seeing me later in the day."

"I gather that you've got an official function with the summit," she observed. "May I be so bold as to ask what it is?"

"I'm a special agent with the U.S. Secret Service."

This revelation caught her full attention, and she smiled once more. "You don't say. It's an honor to make your acquaintance, Special Agent Kellogg. If there's anything I can do to assist you these next couple of days, please don't hesitate to ask."

"Actually, there is one matter that you could help me with. Does the staff have any cooking or food storage facilities down here?"

Monica hesitated a moment before responding. "As a matter of fact, we do. It's not much, but if you'll accompany me into the office, I'll show you."

The facilities she was referring to turned out to be a small refrigerator and a microwave. As Vince checked the refrigerator's contents of bottled water, Monica voiced her suspicions.

"I bet you're trying to track down the source of the illness that sickened my coworkers."

"You've got it, Ms. Chang."

"Hey, that's Monica to you," she countered.

Vince doubted the bottled water was the culprit, and asked her bluntly, "Do you have any idea what sickened your associates?"

Monica shook her head. "Whatever it was, it sure didn't come from here. We only use this fridge for water, and the microwave for packaged snacks like popcorn."

"Monica," interrupted Max Kurtyka as he poked his head inside. "I'm packing up and hitting the rack. I will deal with that short in the morning."

The actress acknowledged this remark with a nod, and stifled a yawn herself. Vince took this as his cue to leave.

"I'd appreciate any further thoughts you might have as to the source of that food poisoning, Monica," said Vince.

"You've got it, Special Agent," she retorted. "Don't be a stranger."

Vince excused himself and began the long climb up to One Deck. He was winded by the time he reached the proper landing, and was more than ready to call it a day by the time he unlocked his cabin door.

"Mark zero-three-two. Range eight thousand yards."

Comdr. Benjamin Kram listened to his quartermaster while peering out the USS *James K. Polk*'s Mk18 search periscope. Kram was currently using this scope's low-light operating mode to penetrate the moonless night sky and view the object of their search.

Clearly visible in the waters north of them was a single surface ship headed almost due east. Even at this great distance, Kram could tell that the brightly lit vessel was a huge one, well over 900 feet in length. Though he was positive that this was their target, he nevertheless confirmed the fact by picking up the intercom and speaking softly into the transmitter.

"Sonar, conn. Well, Mr. Bodzin, what can you tell me about Sierra Eleven?"

The high-pitched voice of the *Polk*'s senior sonar technician responded over the intercom's speaker. "Conn, sonar. Sir, Sierra Eleven is really churning up a storm. Broadband's picking up a wide-spectrum signature that could only belong to a group of sequenced turbocharged diesel engines, turning dual shafts, with a rev count indicating a good twenty-six knots. She's the *Queen,* all right, and she's heading to England with a bone in her teeth."

Kram couldn't help but grin as he considered the source of this unorthodox report. PO1c Brad Bodzin was one of the best sonar techs he had ever sailed with. The twenty-seven-year-old Houston, Texas, native had demonstrated time and again the rare ability to successfully combine intuition and practical knowledge. As much an artist as a scientist, a good sonar operator often was the difference between a mission's success or failure, and having Bodzin's service on this patrol made Kram's difficult job all the easier.

Kram backed away from the periscope and took a second to massage the cramped muscles at the back of his neck. At forty-five years old, he was easily the oldest member of his crew, and lately he was beginning to feel his age. Extended periods on the periscope had never bothered him before, yet the last couple of months such routine duty never failed to aggravate the muscles in his neck and upper back.

Another sign of his rapidly advancing years were the wire-rim bifocals that he had draped around his neck with a restraining strap. He had been wearing these glasses since Christmas, when his difficulty in reading the fine print pushed him to the extreme of mentioning this problem to his optometrist.

Bifocals and backaches were all signs that the USS *Polk* would be his last operational command. As Kram stared out at the thick black curtains that separated the cramped platform he stood on from the rest of the red-tinted control room, he allowed himself to think about the long career path that had brought him here.

A Vermont native, the son of a career surface-navy officer, Kram enrolled at the Maine Maritime Academy with the express purpose of preparing himself for naval service. NROTC brought him a commission as an ensign in 1972. The Vietnam War was in the process of winding down then, and Kram decided that his best career path would be in submarines. As it turned out, this proved to be a wise choice, for during the Cold War decade that followed, the submarine was the front-line unit.

After graduating nuclear-power school at Orlando, Florida, and the submarine-officer basic course at New London, his first assignment was to the USS *Tullibee*. A *Permit*-class nuclear-powered attack sub, the *Tullibee* was designed to hunt down other submarines, relying not on high speed, but stealth and a sophisticated sonar suite.

The *Tullibee* proved the perfect platform for him to learn his new trade. He remained aboard for two years before attending the submarine officer advanced course in preparation for his next assignment, as engineering officer aboard the USS *Daniel Webster*.

The *Webster* was a boomer, designed to launch ballistic missiles. Since this was the heyday of the Cold War, the six deterrent patrols that he completed were taken most seriously, and it was a definite letdown when the orders arrived directing him to shore duty at Submarine Squadron Two.

A year and a half later he was sent back to sea, this time as executive officer of the USS *Hyman G. Rickover*. Another attack sub, the *Rickover* served as the platform on which he'd prepare himself for command of his very own submarine.

This exciting event occurred two years ago. The USS *James K. Polk* was originally designed as a *Lafayette*-class ballistic-missile submarine. Commissioned as a ship of the U.S. Navy on April 16, 1966, the *Polk* was to successfully complete sixty-six strategic deterrent patrols, armed with both the Polaris and Poseidon missiles, before being converted into her present unique configuration in 1994.

It took a nineteen-month shipyard stay to remove the *Polk*'s launching systems and outfit the sub for its current mission. One of only two such submarines in the U.S. Navy, the *Polk* was fitted with a dual dry-deck shelter. This cylindrical, hangar-shaped structure was fitted to the boat's upper deck, abaft the fin, and was specially designed to support special-warfare operations.

Special Ops, as it was better known, was an important new mission for the current submarine force, and Kram knew that it was a great honor to get such a command. In addition to his sub's normal complement of 130, he was responsible for the vessel's other occupants, the two-dozen members of SEAL Team Two.

To support these SEALs, the *Polk* was also carrying a Swimmer

Delivery Vehicle, or SDV, inside the dry-deck shelter. The SDV was a battery-powered minisub designed to hold up to eight operatives. Such submersibles were favored by the SEALs, who used these stealthy platforms to carry out a variety of clandestine operations.

It was because of the *Polk*'s unique configuration that Command picked them for their present mission. To emphasize the vital importance of this patrol, the chief of naval operations himself called Kram to the Pentagon for the initial briefing. This had taken place almost two months earlier, and shortly afterwards, the *Polk* proceeded to the waters off Andros Island to train for this mission with the help of a chartered cruise ship.

The periscope sighting he had just made proved that the time for training was over. A quick glance at the ceiling-mounted sonar repeater indicated that the surface ship they had been sent to escort wasn't built with acoustic stealth in mind. As the last of the great superliners, the *Queen Elizabeth 2* was designed for speed, safety, and comfort. And as it looked, it was going to take a full effort on the part of the *Polk*'s engineering staff to keep up with this stately greyhound of the Atlantic.

Kram returned his attention to the periscope. As he was bending over to peer out the eyepiece, another individual joined him on the platform, his husky voice wasting no time in getting his attention.

"Skipper, Commander Gilbert just informed me that they're ready for us down in the rec room."

Kram stood up straight and looked over to meet the expectant glance of the *Polk*'s chief of the boat, Mark Inboden. COB, as he was better known, was the sub's senior enlisted man. As such, he held a pivotal position, responsible for being the interface between the *Polk*'s fourteen officers and the rest of its crew.

A gentle, intelligent man who was raised in the hills of Arkansas, COB worked closely with Kram and his XO to maintain a safe, productive working environment. Since the average age of the crew was barely twenty-three, this was often quite a challenge. Officers and enlisted men alike had long ago adopted Inboden as their proverbial father figure, and any problem, big or small, personal or work-related, sooner or later made its way to COB for a solution.

"Would you like to take a peek at the big lady before we take off?" Kram offered.

COB shook his clean-shaven, heavily furrowed face that he

wouldn't. "That's okay, Skipper. It looks like I'll have plenty of opportunities."

"That's if the folks back in *Polk* Power and Light can keep up with her," replied Kram. "Bodzin's already got her going a good twenty-six knots, and she's barely out of New York Harbor."

Kram proceeded to follow COB around the periscope platform's curtained wall and down into the control room. The compact, equipment-packed compartment was dimly lit in red to protect the crew's night vision. Kram passed by the two seated helmsmen, with Chief Stanley Roth, the current diving officer, positioned between them.

"We've sure heard enough of the *Queen* over the sonar feed, Captain," interrupted the amiable Roth, an unlit cigar clenched between his teeth. "But what's she look like on the scope?"

Kram answered without stopping. "Big!"

COB slapped Roth's palm as he passed by. They turned left at the ballast-control panel and headed aft into the next compartment. This elongated, narrow space had two long consoles lining each of its bulkheads. Both were vacant, and it was here that the members of the SEAL team would coordinate the activation of the dry-deck shelter and the launching of the SDV.

A sharp left took them past the space where the SINS, the Ship Inertial Navigation System, was stowed. Against the after bulkhead they stepped through an accessway and entered the former missile magazine.

Kram, leading the way, headed for a nearby stairwell where a tall, muscular SEAL dressed in shorts and a T-shirt almost ran over him. The young, sweat-soaked commando was jogging, and Kram alertly stepped aside to let him pass.

This portion of the *Polk* was the exclusive realm of SEAL Team Two. During the refit, the missiles had been removed, though the tubes remained. There were sixteen in all, located in two parallel rows of eight each. A narrow catwalk encircled the entire magazine. It was this latticed-steel track that the SEAL was running on, with sixteen and one-half laps equaling a mile.

The engineers at the shipyard had ingeniously modified the empty tubes so that they could store extra equipment. The SEALs made good use of this space to stash their weapons, ammo, diving equipment, and assorted combat gear. Tube six was where the access to the dry-deck shelter was located. A ladder extended upward through a pressurized trunk that led to the shelter itself. Cold, wet, and dark, the trunk was a foreboding place to visit, and Kram had a sincere respect for the brave men whose work took them there.

The stairwell they eventually reached took them down to Three Deck, where a short passageway brought them into the relatively spacious compartment normally utilized as the crew's activity space. On this occasion, it was being used as the special operations briefing room.

Twenty-five officers and enlisted men were presently packed into the compartment, with a mix of both *Polk* crew members and SEALs. As usual, the SEALs occupied the right half of the room, where they had set up three tables, one behind the other. Several of the seated SEALs had laptop computers in front of them, with their associates standing beside them or at the back of the room.

Benjamin Kram's arrival generated an immediate response from a wiry, khaki-clad officer, who had been standing beside a large display screen at the front of the compartment. Only a few months younger than Kram, Comdr. Doug Gilbert was SEAL Team Two's commanding officer. Of medium height and build, Gilbert was still in superb physical condition, though he had long since stopped trying to hide the streaks of gray that colored his trim moustache and brown crew cut.

"Captain's here, ladies! Let's get started," informed Gilbert.

By the time Kram reached the vacant chair reserved for him in the front row, the idle chatter that had initially greeted him dissipated. In its place rose Gilbert's firm voice.

"We'll be beginning this briefing with the latest met update. Chief Murray, you're on."

A ruggedly handsome, dark-haired SEAL, who was seated at the front table, alertly stood and turned to address his audience. "Weather topside continues to look good. Air temp is seventy-six degrees, with a light west wind and steady barometer. This quiet pattern extends all the way up to Nova Scotia, where a minor low-pressure front has stalled off the Grand Banks. I don't foresee this front giving us any problems, though I can't say the same for the one I'm about to show you."

The chief picked up a remote-control device beside his open laptop, and pointed it toward the front of the room. The display screen there activated with a click, its flat, black surface filling with a satellite weather map showing the southeastern coastline of the United States and extending well out into the Atlantic to include the Bahama Islands chain. In the waters north of the Bahamas, a circular mass of cloud cover was visible, and this was the feature that Chief Murray highlighted with an electronic cursor.

"As of thirty minutes ago, this gents, is the newest tropical storm of the season. The National Hurricane Center has just labeled it Marti. I've got the latest data on Marti. Just came in within the last couple of minutes from a NOAA overflight. Though she's still rather unorganized, they're picking up increased rotation, with winds up to sixty knots near the center, and the storm moving to the northnortheast. Bermuda has already posted storm warnings as a precautionary measure, yet we still don't know for certain if she'll even get that far north."

"What's the normal course to take for storms forming in that portion of the Atlantic?" asked Benjamin Kram.

Chief Murray addressed the remote control to display a greatly expanded map showing the entire North Atlantic basin. As he initiated his answer, he activated the cursor to highlight corresponding areas of the Atlantic.

"On her current course and speed, Marti should pass well north of Bermuda, skirt the eastern U.S. coastline, and make landfall over the Canadian Maritimes. But this time of the year, the Gulf Stream has a tendency to push storms much farther east. Depending upon what's coming in from the west, I wouldn't be surprised to see her miss land completely, and end up a greatly weakened front somewhere up here in the mid-Atlantic-ridge area."

Kram sat forward with this revelation and once more expressed himself. "But that's smack dab in the middle of the QE2's great circle route."

"I realize that, sir," replied the meteorologist. "But this is all speculation. And even if Marti were to make a beeline for the ridge, she'd have to develop into a major hurricane to keep from breaking up in the cold water up there."

"If my mental calculations are correct," interjected Doug Gilbert, "for the storm to affect this crossing, it would really have to haul ass big-time. Hell, it's a good three thousand miles from the ridge, with an awful lot of water to cover in between."

"Don't forget that we have the *Iwo Jima* battle group cruising north of Bermuda as we speak," reminded Kram. "Marti could sure spoil their day and negate their effectiveness as any kind of quick-response force."

"The hell with the *Iwo Jima* and that group of Leatherneck fags that they're carrying," retorted Gilbert. "Me and my laddies are all the quick-response force that this mission is going to need. And with all due respect, Captain, Chief Murray here is still only a weatherman, and all of us have learned the hard way that when Dave predicts sunny and warm, you'd better bring the rubbers!"

This comment generated a roar of laughter, and Gilbert beckoned the meteorologist to be seated. As he did so, SEAL Team Two's CO looked to his right and addressed the clean-shaven officer seated at Kram's side. "Lt. Comdr. Calhoun will be briefing us on the *Polk*'s operational orders."

Dan Calhoun was the sub's good-natured XO. A Naval Academy graduate, Calhoun was on the fast track to his own command, with his special interest being battle tactics and the history behind them. Like the majority of his crewmates, he was dressed in a dark blue poopy suit, with gold dolphins on his left chest, and the *Polk*'s flying eagle insignia opposite.

"Good evening, or should I say, good morning, gentlemen. I'll try my best to keep this short and sweet, so please bear with me. As all of you know, the *Polk* has been tasked as a National Command Authority asset this patrol, and as such, we're reporting straight to the CNO. A direct SATCOM link has been established between the *Polk* and the CNO's op center in the Pentagon. We're also keeping a radio link open with the *Iwo Jima* battle group, where Admiral Campbell is our NCA contact.

"I appreciate everyone's efforts in getting the *Polk* ready for this mission. The *QE2* left New York right on time, and we made our first contact with her approximately forty-five minutes ago. As planned, she'll be continuing on an easterly heading until she crosses the continental shelf. At her current speed, that will take place sometime in the morning, when she'll be making her first major course change to the northeast. This heading of 060 will convey them due south of Cape Sable, Nova Scotia, where the HMS *Talent* is presently on station.

"Together with the *Talent*, the *Polk* will continue to ride shotgun on the *Queen*, with our next rendezvous point south of Newfoundland's Cape Race. This is where the great circle portion of the crossing begins, and it's here that we'll link up with the Russian *Akula*-class submarine, *Baikal,* and France's *Casabianca.*"

This revelation generated a disgusted grumble from his audience, and the XO was quick with damage control. "Hey, guys, we've gone over this before, and there's nothing we can do about it. Look, I'm no more excited than you about the prospects of working with three other submarines. The *Polk*'s a lone wolf, and even though we're more than capable of protecting the *QE2* on our own, we're just going to have to live with Command's decision, flawed though it may be."

Benjamin Kram was quick to stand and offer his support. "The XO is correct, gentlemen. We've gotten our fair share of unpopular orders before, and the time for whining is over. This is the way the President and the international community wants it, and this is the way it's going to be. Case closed."

This definitive statement served to silence the crowd, and Kram sat back down and gestured his XO to continue.

"Air coverage for the first half of the crossing will be compliments of Canada's 404 Maritime Patrol Squadron. We've worked with the Flying Buffaloes before, off Andros, and for my money, next to the U.S. Navy, these guys are the best.

"East of the mid-Atlantic ridge, Royal Air Force Nimrods will take over, providing air coverage all the way to Southampton. Throughout the crossing, the *QE2* will be under constant satellite surveillance. The National Reconnaissance Office will be coordinating America's space-based assets, including a newly launched Big Bird platform and a U.S. Navy White Cloud unit. The Russians will be providing use of their latest RORSAT radar-scanning satellite, with the French National Space Agency covering the passage with a SPOT recon platform."

"XO," interrupted the sub's COB. "What's the latest on those sunspots? Last time I paid a visit to the radio room, both the VHF and UHF bands were so filled with static that I thought our antennas were malfunctioning."

Dan Calhoun looked to the other side of the room, nodding toward the meteorologist. "Chief Murray, can you help me out with this one?"

SEAL Team Two's weather expert shrugged his broad shoulders

and answered. "The interference that COB is referring to is being caused by the opening shots of what looks to be a very active eleven-year sunspot cycle. Think of it as a period of bad weather in outer space that starts off when plumes of hot, ionized plasma gas are ejected from the sun and directed toward earth via solar winds blowing at over one-million miles per hour. The trouble down here occurs when these gasses slam into the earth's magnetic field at supersonic speeds. And since this is only the beginning of the next active cycle, I'm afraid there's nothing we can do but try our best to work around it."

"Sort of like how the *Polk* is coping with this fucking mission," added Doug Gilbert, to another outburst of laughter, especially from the SEALs gathered on his side of the room.

The *Polk*'s XO got a chuckle out of this as well, and finding himself with nothing else to say, he looked down to Benjamin Kram.

"Commander Gilbert," remarked Kram, after glancing at his watch. "Is there anything else you'd like to add to this brief before we break?"

The moustached commando scanned the familiar faces of his audience and singled out a tall, blond-haired officer standing at the back of the room. This smoothfaced, middle-aged individual wore a dark green woolen sweater over his khakis, and was in the process of calmly sipping a cup of hot tea.

"Lieutenant Colonel Laycob," said Gilbert. "Would you mind joining me up here and saying a few words?"

With a deliberate slowness, the officer this request was directed to put down his mug. As he proceeded to the front of the compartment, Gilbert offered the initial introduction.

"Lieutenant Colonel Laycob of the Royal Marines is the newest member of our team. He joined us two days ago, and many of you haven't had a chance to meet him as yet."

"I'm certain that the pleasure will be all mine," muttered Lawrence Laycob with a clipped English accent. On arriving beside Gilbert, Laycob nodded toward the *Polk*'s CO and added, "Captain Kram, distinguished officers and enlisted men, may I take this opportunity to thank you for your warm hospitality. I realize that I've been sent into your midst by a joint decision of that international community that you mentioned earlier, and I do hope that I don't prove a bother."

Laycob's suave delivery had a slight caustic edge to it, prompting Doug Gilbert to alertly intercede. "Lieutenant Colonel Laycob is a most welcome guest, and I emphasize the welcome. His distinguished career with the Royal Marines Special Boat Service makes him one of our own, and I'll be the first one to say that it's a sincere honor to get this chance to work together."

This unusual emotional outburst on Gilbert's part was met with a hearty round of applause. Throughout it all, Lawrence Laycob hid his embarrassment with a smile, and he bowed at the waist in appreciation of this unexpected welcome.

"Here, here," he humbly replied, as the applause faded. "I didn't mean to insult you with the first words out of my mouth, and I must confess that I understand your predicament. We in SBS know what it means to operate independently. That lone-wolf mentality that you speak of is a vital part of our doctrine. It's what helps make us an effective fighting force.

"As Captain Kram so wisely mentioned, new international realities have led to an unprecedented era of joint military operations. The mere fact of the *Polk*'s existence is proof of this. Though I can't speak for the Russian or French submarines, I can personally attest to the HMS *Talent*'s long record of excellence. Comdr. Mark Eastbrook and his crack gang of pirates are superbly trained submariners, who have gotten me and my lads out of harm's way on a number of occasions. I'm certain that you'll find them a most cooperative, competent group to work with.

"As for the reason behind my presence amongst you, I must admit that as far as I can tell, our navies put their heads together and decided that my services could act as an additional asset for SEAL Team Two. This is especially the case, since one of my previous SBS units was formed with the express purpose of providing security backup aboard the *Queen Elizabeth 2*."

"The lieutenant colonel was one of two SBS commandoes who parachuted onto the *QE2* in the mid-Atlantic, during a terrorist bomb threat in the early seventies," Gilbert added. "He knows the ship from stem to stern, and will be an invaluable asset should we be called upon to render assistance."

"As a sidenote," said Laycob. "The other chap who accompanied me on that mission is currently serving as the *QE2*'s security director. Robert Hartwell is a hero in his own right, who won numerous citations for bravery during the Falklands conflict. Whenever things get cheeky, old Harty's the one you want on your side.

"Also, I brought along a new virtual-reality program of the *QE2*'s interior spaces. All of you are welcome to have a look and see what the Grand Lady looks like on the inside.

"So again, it's indeed a pleasure to be sailing with you, even though I have to admit that there's one naval tradition that you Yanks really should follow up on. How in the world can you even think about putting to sea without a proper pub on board? Why, it's positively uncivilized!"

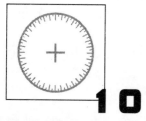

10

By the time Thomas Kellogg reached BATF headquarters the next morning, the return of summer—which in D.C. meant high humidity and an oppressive, saunalike heat—left him in no mood to deal with the mound of paperwork and phone-message sheets that had piled up as he spent a single day in the field. So it was with mixed feelings that he found the petite figure of Ruth Ann Miller, anxiously waiting for him in the lobby. Ruth Ann was the director's personal secretary, and had been working for Lawrence McShane throughout his long career with the Treasury Department. Well into her sixties, but mentally sharp as a tack, Ruth Ann was pacing to and fro, with an uncharacteristic troubled look etched on her wrinkled face.

"Oh, Thomas, thank goodness you're finally here. He's been asking for you all morning."

"What's wrong?"

"It was really quite frightening. The envelope was all part of the morning mail shipment. As usual, after it cleared security, I was the first to open it."

"I hope you didn't discover another IED," interrupted Thomas.

"It was nothing like that. Just a horrible, threatening letter, one of the most repugnant things I've ever read."

As she paused to catch her breath, Thomas decided it was time to see firsthand what had disturbed her so. He excused himself with a comforting hug, and took off for the director's office.

He found three of his associates gathered in the reception area, where Ruth Ann had her desk. They were in the process of carefully placing a United States Postal Service Express Mail envelope into a clear-plastic evidence bag. Two similar pouches had already been sealed and Thomas waited until his gloved colleagues completed their delicate task before greeting them.

"Morning. What's this all about?"

Before anyone could answer him, Lawrence McShane emerged from his inner office. "We've got the bastard now, Thomas! Did you see it?"

Thomas reserved his response until he began his examination of the contents of the first of the evidence bags. Without unsealing it, he held the clear-plastic pouch before the light. A single 8½-by-11-inch piece of white paper lay inside, with the entire front page of the previous day's *New York Times* duplicated on its surface. The reduced headline read: G-7 TO SET SAIL—STORMY ECONOMIC SEAS AHEAD?

Lawrence McShane used the scarred bit of his unlit briar pipe to point to the thin, dark blue cardboard envelope that lay sealed in one of the other bags. The characteristic white-feathered head of a bald eagle graced one of its sides, with the mailing label mounted on the other. There could be no missing the familiar, cramped printing of the person responsible for sending this piece of mail, nor the fictitious Winchester, Virginia, post office box. Yet this time, the addressee wasn't the President of the United States or a member of his family, but Director McShane.

"Well," muttered Thomas. "And there was no hint of an IED inside?"

McShane shook his head no, adding, "The only thing explosive is the letter. But before you read it, check out the top portion of the mailing label.

"As you can see, the envelope was processed at the Winchester postal facility last evening at 4:57. The stamp appears to have originated from that same post office, which means whoever sold it actually saw our suspect or his proxy."

Thomas tried his best to make out the acceptance clerk's initials, his best guess being TWL. Their suspect unfortunately hadn't signed the waiver-of-signature clause, though getting an actual eyewitness to describe this customer would give them just the break they had been waiting for.

"We've got to get Mike Galloway over here," urged Thomas.

"He's on his way," McShane said while taking the envelope from Thomas and handing him the remaining evidence. "Inside this last pouch is the clincher," he added.

Thomas curiously examined the plastic pouch that held another lone 8½-by-11-inch sheet of white paper. It appeared to have originated from the same computer printer that reproduced the front page of the *Times*, though this was as far as the similarities went. A basic word-processing program had been used to print the following:

1. Be it known that from this day onwards, the Sons of the Patriots hereby declare war on the sham organization currently doing business as the government of the United States of America. We recognize this entity for what it truly is, an illegal, immoral body, that has taken advantage of its citizens and broken the trust handed down by the original founding fathers.

2. The opening shots of this war have already been sounded, with our battle cry being; REMEMBER RUBY RIDGE, WACO, AND OKLAHOMA CITY!!!

3. In the second stage of our initial offensive, a sign of our might has already been sent to that BEAST of BEASTS occupying our White House. Know that you have been thusly forewarned, and that the next time we act, it will be with clever subterfuge.

4. The warplan of this offensive has already been put into action. A second Civil War has now begun, and this time we fight to free the WHITE MAN, who has been unjustly enslaved with the responsibility of perpetuating the Jewish created welfare state. No longer will we sacrifice our best years supporting the lazy immigrants and racial minorities, for whom this system was designed to give a free ride.

5. We recognize that the true enemy is International Jewry. Their intention is to create a one-world government, in an attempt to satisfy an insatiable greed. On this very day, the Elders of Zion have called together the world's leaders, for a summit whose purpose is to seal this conspiracy. WE ARE NOT FOOLED!!! And to destroy this Godless cabal once and for all, the Sons of the Patriots intend to strike a blow for liberty. Rejoice you who carry the yoke of oppression. The ATTACK ON THE QUEEN has begun!

Thomas reread this last sentence and only then allowed himself to look up into the worried glance of McShane. The director solemnly nodded and said in a determined whisper.

"We don't know who this group is yet, even if there *is* such an organization. But I'll tell you this: We'll get the sick bastard this time. I just know it."

Though he wished he could share his superior's optimism, Thomas could think of only one selfish thing: Somewhere out on the Atlantic, his own brother was sailing aboard the very ship that this madman had threatened to attack. He needed to reach him immediately.

By 0800 the *QE2* was far out to sea, and Vince Kellogg was off to the Boardroom to begin his first watch of the day. Waiting for him there was a U.S. Customs Service official and Beowulf, her bomb-sniffing German shepherd. A member of the *QE2*'s security staff unlocked the Boardroom for them. Beowulf was then led inside, along with agents representing France, Russia, and Japan.

It took them a quarter of an hour to complete a thorough sweep of the compartment. Even after Beowulf's sensitive nose gave the all clear, the agents still went to their hands and knees to search the bottom of the furniture for anything that didn't belong there. The Russians went to the extreme of using an electronic scanner to check the walls and carpet for possible microphones and other eavesdropping devices. Nothing of the sort was found, and just as the room was about to be resealed, Robert Hartwell's arrival signaled the imminent approach of the heads of state.

The chancellor of Germany and his party of translator and two security guards were the first to show themselves. This group was followed closely by the other statesmen, with the American President escorted solely by Samuel Morrison. The Italian prime minister was the last to arrive, and as the doors to the Boardroom were shut, Vince joined Morrison and Hartwell in the anteroom. Chairs had been set up here for the various security personnel, along with a table holding coffee, tea, and sweet rolls.

This opening session was to be followed by a luncheon in the Queens Grill. Because the Boardroom was effectively sealed off from the rest of the ship, the security staffs had little to do but patiently bide their time, all the while being available for an unexpected break or other disturbance.

"Well, gents," said Hartwell, after pouring himself a cup of tea. "I'm sure you'll be happy to know that our first night at sea was incident-free. The only problem to speak of is in the ship's Radio Room. Unusual atmospheric conditions have caused us to lose the services of the commercial communications satellite that normally handles our telephone calls. VIP transmissions have to be rerouted to military backup platforms, though I'm afraid that telephone calls of a personal nature are no longer possible."

Vince had positioned himself so that he had a clear view of the Boardroom's closed doors and the various agents milling in front of them. "So much for calling my wife."

"Yes, but look at all the money you'll save," Hartwell said. "I believe it's fifty dollars for a three-minute call to the States. By the way, I do hope that your quarters are sufficient, and that you slept well," asked Hartwell.

The SAIC replied, stifling a yawn. "My stateroom's fine, though it looks like I'm going to need some time to adjust to the roll of the ship."

"I slept great," Vince admitted. "Before hitting the sack, I even got a chance to squeeze in a visit to the Gym. Ran into Monica Chang herself. I tell you, she's as pretty in person as she is on the screen."

"I hope that you chaps caught the stunning photo of Miss Chang gracing the front cover of the *Daily Programme*," Hartwell interjected. "Her aerobics classes should be well attended indeed. And I hear the French president would like to engage her as his personal trainer."

Thomas grinned. "While I was with her, I found out that the

Gym has its own refrigerator and microwave. She let me take a peek, and I seriously doubt that's the source of the contamination."

"Late last night, I had a brief meeting with Doc Benedict and your own Dr. Patton," Hartwell added. "Together they plan another inspection of the main Kitchen and food-storage areas. They're also going to circulate an inquiry amongst the stewards, to find out if they can help us."

"I was hoping that we'd finally get some sort of definitive statement from the Hospital," said Morrison. "Back at the loading dock, Dennis Liu said something about having just come back from visiting his coworkers there. Vince, maybe it's worth another trip to the Gym to find out if they said anything to Liu that he forgot to share with us."

Before Vince could reply, the door to the Boardroom swung open from inside. This unexpected disturbance caught the attention of the other security agents as well. Their probing stares locked on the source of this movement, a single uniformed steward pushing an empty food-service cart. The steward froze. For a brief moment, the sounds of a spirited discussion could be heard from inside the room, then he regained his composure and closed the doors behind him.

Vince continued to watch the steward as he headed for the adjoining passageway, where he was forced to brake his cart to a sudden halt again when a young man rounded the corner and almost collided with him. This newcomer was casually dressed in khakis and a black sweater. He stepped aside to let the startled steward pass, and Vince caught a glimpse of the stranger's long, black hair that was tied in a ponytail. It was obvious that he didn't belong to any of the security teams, who had also noted his presence and collectively watched his approach suspiciously.

Samuel Morrison, of all people, greeted this handsome, smooth-shaven young man. "Hello, Ricky. What brings you up here?"

There was a noticeable limp to the newcomer's step as he crossed the room and joined them. "Good morning, sir," he replied sheepishly, well aware of the intense stares his arrival had generated.

The SAIC put him at ease by patting him warmly on the back, and after introducing his coworkers, said, "Ricky is Dr. Patton's son," while the youngster exchanged handshakes.

"I bet you've come for that list of stewards that I promised to deliver to your father right after breakfast," presumed Hartwell.

Ricky nodded affirmatively. Hartwell glanced down at his watch. "Please convey my apologies to him, and let him know that I'll have it to him by lunch."

"Ricky, here, is coming off quite a summer," said Samuel Morrison as he put his hand on the young man's shoulder. "Son, why don't you tell them what you've been going through?"

Ricky shyly replied. "It wasn't all that much, sir. I just went and broke my leg a week before school let out."

"Broken leg, hell," retorted Morrison. "From what I understand, it was more like a severely fractured hip, a spiral break of the femur, and a dislocated shoulder, for good measure. Why, Ricky's still packing so much iron, he's got to carry a doctor's prescription to get through the White House metal detector."

"My goodness, lad," said Hartwell. "How in the world did you manage to do all that damage?"

"Bicycle accident," Ricky revealed. "Hit a patch of green moss on my mountain bike while crossing a creek in Big Sur State Park."

"If it wasn't for a curious park ranger, there's a good chance that Ricky wouldn't be with us today," said Morrison. "The way your father tells it, you were riding alone in some pretty desolate terrain, and by the time the paramedics arrived, you were in shock and close to succumbing to hyperthermia."

Vince looked at the young man with newfound respect. "Considering the damages, I'd say you're doing remarkably well."

"I was lucky to get through surgery in one piece," Ricky returned. "And it doesn't hurt to have a father who's chief of staff at Bethesda Naval hospital. For two months, I wasn't allowed to put any weight on my leg, which left me a virtual cripple. I had to move out of my San Francisco apartment and move in with my folks back in D.C., where they fed and dressed me just like I was an infant again."

"What kind of rehab program are you on?" asked Vince.

"My father's got me walking a full hour everyday, and I'm allowed to do basic aerobics. I've also started working out on an exercise bike, though all in moderation."

"Have you checked out the ship's Gym?" Vince questioned.

Ricky's eyes widened. "That's where I was headed next."

Samuel Morrison looked over at the closed doors of the Boardroom and then back to Vince. "There's no reason for both of us to have to cool our heels out here, Kellogg. If you'd like, why don't you accompany Ricky down to the Gym? Then you can ask Liu all about that hospital visit."

This offer sounded fine with Vince, who readily left the crowded anteroom with Ricky at his side. The youngster's limp was more apparent as they headed for the Quarter Deck and the elevator that would take them down into the ship's interior.

Much to their disappointment, they found the Gym locked. Vince knocked on the frosted glass door. It was finally opened by Dennis Liu's daughter Kristin.

Vince noted how Ricky's interest seemed to perk up the moment he set his eyes on Kristin. She looked as cute as she had back on the pier, though now her fit figure was further accentuated by a flesh-colored spandex bodysuit.

A bit hesitantly, Kristin invited them inside and apologized for her father's reluctant decision to temporarily close the facility until all the exercise machines were up and running. It seemed that the compartment was still experiencing electrical difficulties and that their computer expert was having problems addressing them.

A quick scan of the facility on Vince's part found no evidence of this repair effort, or the individual responsible for it. Max Kurtyka was nowhere to be found.

Dennis Liu was all smiles as he emerged from the Gym's office and walked over to the doorway. He too apologized for the unex-pected problems they were having. Vince was surprised when Ricky spoke up and offered his assistance. Ricky's college major was in computer sciences and he was most familiar with the design of the software utilized in their equipment.

Even though Dennis Liu graciously refused this offer, Ricky in-formed him that if he should change his mind, they could always reach him in the ship's Medical Office. Vince suspected that Ricky's ulterior motive was to get a chance to know Kristin better. They were the same age, and as it turned out after Ricky mentioned the origin of his limp, had shared similar experiences.

Only the year before, Kristin had fallen off a balance beam and broken her ankle so badly, a steel implant was necessary to correct it. She too had to surrender to the care of her father. From Ricky's eyes, Vince knew the boy had found a potential confidante.

They agreed to meet later during the captain's cocktail party. Vince chanced to see the strange look Liu gave his daughter as she accepted the date. Was this glance simply that of an overprotective father, or did it have an ulterior meaning? Vince supposed that he'd have to be a father himself to know the answer, and he decided this would be an opportune moment to ask Liu about his recent hospital visit.

Before he could do so, Tuff stormed into the room. The broad-shouldered security man looked relieved upon spotting Vince.

"Excuse me, Special Agent Kellogg. But could I have a word with you, sir?"

Vince followed Tuff out into the Lobby. "Sir, the ship has just received a Level-Two security alert. The warning was issued from Washington, and includes a fax sent to your attention. I was up in Radio when it arrived. It looks like we're the object of a legitimate bomb threat!"

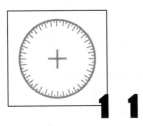

11

THE VIEW FROM THE REAR CABIN OF THE BELL UH-1F HUEY HELICOPTER WAS A magnificent one, Thomas Kellogg thought as he peered out the open hatchway. Five-thousand feet below, a seemingly endless expanse of thick pine forest hugged this portion of the Allegheny foothills. An occasional river could be seen snaking its way through the sparsely populated woods, the sparkling waters illuminated by the late summer sun.

Thomas shifted his line of sight to refocus on the two-lane highway they had been following ever since leaving Winchester, Virginia, a half hour before. Traffic was light, and as they continued following the road westward, he doubted that he had counted more than a dozen vehicles traveling this twisting, concrete artery.

Behind him Mike Galloway was perched beside the opposite hatch. Both of them were outfitted in black coveralls, with BATF emblems on the chest. They also wore black flight helmets fitted with speakers and clip-on chin microphones. An umbilical cord connected them to the Huey's intercom, where a channel had been reserved for their use.

"I imagine there's some excellent fishing down there," observed Galloway, whose amplified voice rose over the constant clattering roar of the Huey's rotors.

Thomas repositioned his microphone in front of his lips and

replied. "I bet the hunting's good, as well. Too bad we can't give it a try."

"Thanks again for taking me along, Thomas. It's refreshing to finally escape the office."

"I'm the one who should be thanking you, Mike. I doubt that the postmaster of Winchester would have been so quick to divulge the location of our clerk's cabin, if you weren't there."

"I still can't believe that our man picks today to start his vacation," Galloway reflected.

"I just hope it's worth all this trouble tracking him down. Maybe he doesn't even remember our suspect."

"Have faith in your U.S. Postal Service, Thomas."

"Special Agent Kellogg," interrupted the voice of the pilot. "It looks like we've spotted the first turnoff up ahead."

Thomas backed away from the hatch and headed forward to a position immediately behind the open flight deck. The Huey's pilot was seated in the right-hand position. The former Army warrant officer wore a green flight suit, with an AIR ATF patch on it. His copilot was similarly attired, and had a map spread out on her lap.

"I'm going to take us down to four thousand feet before beginning this next course change," informed the pilot.

Thomas watched as he pushed down on the collective pitch stick with his left hand. The Huey descended. Thomas looked out the cockpit's wraparound windshield. Ahead of them the highway crossed over a swift-moving river which the copilot identified.

"That should be the South Fork of the Potomac. Our cutoff is a mile and a half due west of the bridge."

The Huey dropped another 500 feet, and it was Thomas who first spotted the narrow, dirt road they were looking for. With a slight adjustment to the cyclic, the pilot turned the helicopter in a southerly direction, expertly keeping the tree-lined road in sight.

Thomas reached into his zippered pocket and removed the directions he had scrawled back in Winchester. "Our next landmark is an abandoned logging camp that's approximately three miles south of the highway cutoff."

Thick stands of pine forced them to descend even more. They were practically skimming the tops of the trees, and even then the dirt road was proving difficult to follow.

Thomas found it hard to believe that only a few hours ago he was back in the familiar confines of BATF headquarters. The utter importance of their case was emphasized when McShane ordered Thomas to personally conduct the interview at the Winchester Post Office. In no way did he want to risk a leak by bringing in any more people than was necessary. Unfortunately the investigation took a frustrating turn when he learned that the clerk they were seeking was off duty for the rest of the week, thus necessitating this flight into the Alleghenys.

"I believe we just passed over a structure of some sort," observed the copilot.

Thomas reached out to steady himself as the Huey initiated a tight, banked turn. It took a low-level hover to spot the collection of ramshackle buildings that had caught the copilot's attention.

At the western edge of the compound, barely visible through the swaying treetops, another dirt road was spotted. This one extended straight up into the foothills. Because of a recent logging operation, it proved a bit easier to follow. They roared over a sharp ridge, and it was on the slopes of the next valley that a rising column of smoke was sighted.

"That should be the place!" exclaimed the pilot.

The log cabin from whose stone chimney the smoke poured, turned out to be a solid, well-built structure, constructed primarily of native timber. A nearby clearing provided just enough space for the Huey to land. As the helicopter's rotors ground to a halt, the sounds of the surrounding forest gradually replaced its racket.

Thomas and Galloway hurried over to the cabin, but their knocks went unanswered, and as they swung open the unlocked door, it was obvious the resident was not there. The furnishings were spartan and for the most part hand-carved out of pine. What few personal belongings that were present were neatly displayed with exact precision.

A clean setting of aluminum flatware was arranged on the kitchen table. The remnants of a charred log smoldered in the fireplace. On the flagstone hearth sat a chipped, enameled coffee pot.

A workbench held a steel vise. Mounted in its grasp was a partially crafted dry fly. Yet more fishing gear was stored on an adjoining shelf, where Galloway discovered a worn, brown leather U.S. Postal Service pouch.

"This is the place all right," he commented while holding up the pouch for Thomas to see. "Now the million-dollar question is, where the hell is he?"

"My money says that he's out catching dinner," offered Thomas. "As we were touching down, I noticed a stream to the north of us. If it's big enough to hold fish, that's where we'll find him."

A ten-minute hike through the woods took them to the banks of the stream. The distinctive bubbling surge of white water rose to an almost deafening intensity, all but swallowing the other sounds of the forest.

Thomas had to practically shout to direct the flight crew down-stream by radio, while Mike and he began their search in the opposite direction. It was rough going at first, though Thomas took heart when he glimpsed a dragon fly disappear into the mouth of a fish occupying the depths of a pool they were passing.

A terraced set of rapids led them to a wide, slower-moving portion of the stream. It was here they spotted a single fisherman in waders, standing in the midst of the channel. His back was turned to them, his attention locked on one particular pool that he was working with his fly rod.

Thomas watched as he swung his long, flexible rod overhead, then snapped it forward with a smooth sweep of his arm. A snaking coil of light green, floating line shot through the air, with his dry fly landing in the center of the pool a good twenty yards distant.

"Hello!" cried Thomas as the fisherman prepared for another cast.

He had to repeat this greeting three more times with ever in-creasing volume, before finally getting the fisherman's attention. Needless to say, the poor fellow looked startled as he turned around and saw the two coverall-clad strangers.

"Mr. Lion?" questioned Galloway while groping in his pocket for his identification card.

"That's me," answered the fisherman. "Now who the hell wants to know?"

"We're federal agents, sir," Thomas replied.

"Postmaster Leachman told us where to find you," added Galloway.

This revelation helped ease the fisherman's apprehensions. Any further doubts were dashed the moment he stepped out of the water and examined their laminated credentials.

"Sorry to bother you like this," said Thomas.

"Don't worry about it, Special Agent," returned the postal clerk. "You guys just gave me a start. I don't get many visitors up here."

Thomas smiled. "I can imagine. It sure is beautiful in these hills."

The clerk all but ignored this remark, his expression tightening with concern. "For you to come all this way, it really must be serious. Am I in some kind of trouble?"

"It's nothing like that," returned Galloway. "We need your help with an investigation that we're conducting. It has nothing to do with any wrongdoing on your part."

The clerk exhaled a relieved sigh, and reached into the stream to pull out a creel holding three fat brook trout. "I've just about got my limit. If you don't mind, how about discussing this matter of yours over some hot joe back at the cabin?"

Thomas waited until they were settled in front of the blazing fireplace with mugs of coffee in hand, before pulling out the Express Mail address label. The clerk examined it, then spoke confidently.

"Not only are those my initials, but I remember clear as day processing that particular parcel. It was right at closing, and I was already totaling up my cash drawer, when in walked that inevitable last-minute customer. I intended to get rid of whoever it was with all due haste. But two things about this piece of mail gave me reason to pause.

"First off, intrastate Express Mail packages are rare, especially in places like Winchester. I mean, why spend the big bucks, when a couple of First Class stamps will get your envelope to D.C. in about the same time?

"Then there was the address. We had just been briefed to be on the lookout for any suspicious mail being directed to the White House. Then again, the director of the ATF isn't quite the President, and my initial impression was that she was an ATF agent herself."

"She?" repeated Thomas, who had mentally pictured their suspect to be a male.

"You bet," said the clerk with a nod. "She gave me a twenty, and while I counted back the change, I made it a point to check her out. She was about five-feet, six-inches tall, one hundred and twenty pounds, and looked to be in her mid-thirties. It was hard to tell because of the wire-rim sunglasses that covered a good part of her face. Her hair was the color of sun-bleached straw, and she wore it in a long braid that extended to the waist of her camouflage BDU jacket.

"It was as she was leaving that I saw she was wearing matching pants, with the cuffs tucked into shiny black paratrooper boots. That's when I figured that she was retired military. If you don't mind me asking, what did she do?"

Mike Galloway answered carefully. "We believe she might be using the U.S. mail to send threatening letters."

While Galloway had the clerk repeat the story so that he could copy down the details, Thomas excused himself. He used the radio in the helicopter to contact BATF headquarters.

Ruth Ann wasted little time getting the director on the line. McShane listened to Thomas's findings, then passed on some pertinent information of his own.

A call from Ted Callahan indicated there was a 97 percent probability that the C4 sample they had given him to analyze had been stolen from the National Guard Armory at Wheeling, West Virginia. With this in mind, McShane accessed the bureau's extensive computer files to track down a suspect militia group, based deep in the Allegheny Mountains, approximately halfway between Wheeling and Winchester.

He made it a point to remind Thomas that the group that had initially threatened them went by the name of Sons of the Patriots. The militia organization the director subsequently chanced upon called itself the Holly River Patriots.

As if that weren't enough to grab his attention, McShane's next revelation was the clincher—the Holly River Patriots were led by a certain Capt. Lee Pierce, U.S. Army, Ret. And what made this fact particularly intriguing was that Captain Pierce was a woman, who was on record as expressing definite antigovernment doctrine to her devoted followers.

12

THEIR SECOND DAY AT SEA SAW THE *QE2* PASS SOUTH OF NEWFOUNDLAND'S Cape Race and turn eastward over the open Atlantic. This portion of the crossing was known as the great circle route, and the ship would encounter no land of any sort until it reached England's southern shores, in eighty-some hours.

Nor would they encounter, if all went right, the four submarines that had formed ranks below them to provide the superliner with a clandestine escort. Led by the USS *James K. Polk*, this lethal quartet wouldn't make themselves known until their charge was safely at harbor in Southampton.

As was normally the case by the second day at sea, the ship's passengers had begun to settle in. Most of those who were first-time sailors had adjusted to the hull's gentle rocking motion. Newcomers to the *QE2* were most likely familiar enough with the giant ocean liner's internal layout to get themselves to their desired destinations without asking directions, or having to refer to their foldout maps.

Included in this latter group was Vince Kellogg, who was making his way through the ship's maze of passageways and decks like a longtime crew member. His expanded knowledge of these interior spaces was an indirect result of the warning they had received the previous morning.

Shortly after his brother's fax arrived, an emergency meeting of the ship's security personnel and the senior agents from each of the G-7 nations was convened. Robert Hartwell chaired this session.

Vince presented the initial briefing. He started by telling them about the two package bombs, then he read the venomous letter from the Sons of the Patriots. Both the BATF and the Secret Service, he said, considered it to be a legitimate threat to the QE2. Since the investigation was still in progress back in the States, Vince couldn't give them any additional information about this heretofore unknown group.

The head of the French contingent was particularly interested in learning more about the Sons of the Patriots. Samuel Morrison promised him that he'd share all intelligence about the group, as soon as it was available. The SAIC then went on to stand before his assembled colleagues, and in his best diplomatic manner, ask them if they considered this new threat serious enough to warrant aborting the crossing. The Canadian port of Halifax was nearby, and the heads of state could be evacuated there, with the summit continuing on land.

Vince was surprised by the passionate response this suggestion generated. A collective "No!" escaped from the lips of the security chiefs. The Frenchman spoke for the group as a whole, and demanded more concrete evidence before even considering terminating the summit in such a manner. Again he asked about the Sons of the Patriots. Were they a legitimate terrorist group whose threats were to be taken seriously? And why hadn't they included any specific details as to exactly what manner their so-called attack was to take?

Great Britain's representative agreed. He also felt that the threat was much too general, and revealed the numerous crank letters he had been receiving for the last month. Many of these letters threatened similar attacks on the QE2 should the summit be convened, and they all turned out to be hoaxes.

The German in their midst shifted the focus back to the QE2's own security force. Even if a terrorist group did desire to interrupt the summit, wouldn't the iron-tight security effort that he had witnessed back in New York keep them from doing so?

Robert Hartwell entered the fray and assured them that regardless of this latest threat's substance, he was standing by his guarantee of an incident-free crossing. This was all the others had to hear to prompt a unanimous response—the crossing would continue.

The meeting was adjourned and Samuel Morrison took Vince aside to plot the way in which they would react to the threat. Though it would mean stretching their already depleted resources and making do with extended shifts, Morrison temporarily relieved Vince from Presidential-escort duty.

Vince's new job was to work with Beowulf and his Customs Service handler. They would err on the side of caution, and resweep every square inch of the giant vessel for any sign of an unwanted IED.

They had already begun the mammoth task the previous afternoon. The Purser's Office was their first stop. The Mail Room was searched, ever mindful of the manner in which the Sons of the Patriots had previously made good their threats. Parcels and letters alike underwent the scrutiny of Beowulf's sensitive nostrils, all to no avail.

Tuff was called in to help them coordinate the rest of their sweep. They decided to start on the ship's bottommost deck and work their way topside. This brought Vince back to the Engine Room, Chinatown, the working alleyway, and the food-storage spaces. He also got his first look at the sixteen-car Garage and the well-equipped Hospital.

Their visit to the Gym found the facility closed to the public. Electrical repairs were still underway, and Beowulf's efforts were hampered by snaking coils of conduit that made the mere act of walking a bit hazardous.

They were on their way to visit the Kitchen, when Vince became aware of the late hour. An exhausted Beowulf was led up to the kennels on Signal Deck, and Vince found himself with just enough time to get ready for the captain's cocktail party.

This maritime ritual went back to the days of sail. It was an elegant, black-tie affair, and Vince was impressed that even the President of the United States had to wait in the receiving line. This only went to prove the power of the QE2's bearded captain, who was the ultimate master of his floating domain.

Afterward, Vince helped fill a hole in their coverage schedule by attending a formal dinner in the Queens Grill. The heads of state occupied a large table in the center of the room. Vince sat on the balcony, his charge in clear view.

Samuel Morrison joined him halfway through the meal, and accompanied Vince and the heads of state to the Grand Lounge for the evening's entertainment. An attractive group of long-legged showgirls performed a musical tribute comprised of songs, dances, and costumes from all nine of the summit nations. The English comedian Max Bygraves followed them, with a hilarious routine that poked fun at each of the world leaders.

The show ended at midnight, when Vince's relief finally arrived. It had been a long day, and he headed to his cabin for a sound, dreamless slumber.

Morning found him reunited with Beowulf. They continued their sweep right where they left off, and Vince got his first close-up view of the ship's Kitchen. The facility was much larger than he had expected, and he realized what an important place food had aboard the QE2. Dozens of sous-chefs worked behind row upon row of stainless-steel counters preparing that day's menu. It was difficult to keep Beowulf focused with all the intoxicating scents, and they did their best to cover the Grill, Bakery, and dishwashing area.

It was alongside one of the dishwashers that they chanced upon Bernhard Langer, Dr. Benedict, and Dr. Patton. They were checking the temperature of a recently completed cleaning cycle, and the head chef's eyes opened wide with horror upon spotting Beowulf. Vince revealed the serious nature of their business, and Langer reluctantly allowed them to carry on, although he signaled a busboy to wipe everywhere the dog stepped, sniffed, or brushed against.

It was in the crew's quarters that the first contraband was discovered. Beowulf's furious pawing at a mattress led to the finding of an ounce of marijuana. Tuff was tasked to deal with the miscreant, who turned out to be one of the stewards.

After lunch, they headed topside to inspect the exterior decks. It was a warm, breezy afternoon and the heads of state appeared to be making the most of it.

They encountered the president of France and the Canadian prime minister sprawled out on poolside lounges, chatting away in animated French. The prime ministers of Britain and Japan were discovered inside the netted enclosure that comprised the golf driving range. Both casually dressed statesmen held pitching wedges and appeared deeply immersed in an anecdote-reinforced tip Robert Hartwell was sharing with them.

The German chancellor and the Italian prime minister were playing deck tennis. The German was dominating the game, which turned ugly when a disputed line call turned into a spirited argument, with each player protesting in his native language.

Beowulf answered them with a resounding bark and led the way up the stairway to the Boat Deck. This was where the *QE2*'s lifeboats were located. It was also where they discovered the presidents of China and the United States power-walking on the teak-inlaid track.

The two statesmen passed by as Beowulf began his inspection of the stern boat. Vince had walked with the American President in the past, and knew he took his exercise most seriously.

"Good afternoon, Special Agent," greeted the President without breaking his brisk stride. "This walk sure wins the prize for the most spectacular scenery."

"That it does, sir," Vince replied, while accepting a polite nod from President Li.

Once the lifeboats were given the all clear, they headed inside to work their way forward. As Beowulf checked the ship's extensive Library, Vince spotted Ricky Patton and Kristin Liu browsing in the adjoining Bookstore. Vince didn't have the heart to interrupt them and only waved hello before continuing on to the Bridge.

This was where they chanced upon the final head of state. The Russian president and his translator were gathered around the ship's prototype navigation console. Steve Smith was showing them its many advanced features, and Vince watched as the navigator displayed the low-pressure storm system that lay to the east of them.

Their next visit was to the Radio Room. Vince took advantage of this stop to attempt contacting his brother. While Beowulf sniffed the compartment's equipment, Vince learned that atmospheric problems had now put all calls to the outside world on temporary hold. The French communications satellite that it was hoped would solve this problem was in the process of being repositioned, and the radio officer promised him that once the system was on-line, his call would get priority.

It was both frustrating and frightening to be surrounded by all this sophisticated gear and still be unable to make contact with Washington. For all he knew, Thomas could have information vital to their current search and there was absolutely nothing he could do to access it.

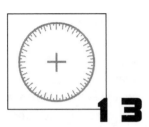

13

Thomas chose the small mining town of Holly, West Virginia, as their base of operations. They arrived with the dawn, in two black Hueys that touched down on an abandoned baseball field. Director McShane had insisted that a six-man special-response team accompany them. This heavily armed unit would provide the necessary firepower should their reception be a hostile one.

Both Thomas and Mike Galloway were decked out in the same camouflage fatigues as their six associates. Each of the men also wore a layer of lightweight body armor, combat boots, and Kevlar-lined helmets.

The U.S. Forestry Service provided ground support. The senior ranger had previously helped the ATF break up a major bootlegging operation in nearby Mill Creek. During the course of this raid, a blazing gun battle had resulted in the wounding of two agents and the death of one of the moonshiners.

Before climbing into the trio of all-terrain vehicles that would be conveying them into the mountains, Thomas gathered together his assault force. He emphasized that gunplay was to be avoided if at all possible. As authorized by a federal search warrant, their sole goal was to determine if the Holly River Patriots were in any way involved with the two IEDs mailed from the Winchester post office.

The Forest Service ranger shared what little he knew about their suspects. They occupied a hundred-acre site that abutted the much larger Holly River wilderness preserve. He had only visited their compound once before, when a forest fire threatened to head their way.

Like most self-styled militia groups, they were tight-lipped, reclusive, and suspicious of the ranger's offer of assistance. The portion of camp he visited was comprised of several wooden A-frames. The structures were set into a grove of old-growth forest, and from what little he saw, they appeared sturdily built and well cared for.

The only complaint that had ever involved the Holly River Patriots took place when a group of Boy Scouts stumbled upon several militia members in the midst of an orienteering exercise. The militiamen were decked out in full battle dress and appeared to be armed with assault rifles. It was later learned that the weapons were harmless replicas carried as realistic props.

So that they'd be prepared for any contingency, the special-response team was outfitted with a variety of very real weapons including M4 assault rifles, Heckler and Koch MP-5 submachine guns, and an assortment of sidearms. Thomas's weapon of choice was a trusty .45 caliber Colt handgun. Mike Galloway was taking along a 9mm Browning, and together they made certain that the safeties were engaged before boarding the dark green Forest Service vehicles.

The roads they traveled got progressively worse, going from asphalt to gravel to a narrow dirt track whose surface was nothing but a pair of deep ruts. Frequent stream crossings made this transit an uncomfortable one, and Thomas was relieved when they finally braked to a halt forty-five minutes after leaving Holly.

They now set off by foot through stands of virgin pine. A thick canopy of limbs all but blotted out the morning sun, and pockets of dense fog were encountered as they crossed through an occasional hollow.

Thomas had taken up a position behind the ranger, who was their point man. Their pace was quick—it took a full effort on his part to keep up. A check of his compass showed that the earthen trail was taking them in a northwesterly direction, and Thomas was grateful for the services of their expert guide.

As they crossed over a brook, a spooked deer bounded out of a thicket. A raven's harsh cry sounded from above, and Thomas marveled at the area's pastoral beauty.

An hour passed, with no sign of any other humans out there.

They heard the Holly River long before they saw it. The roar of its fast-moving waters rose with an all-encompassing clamor. On reaching its rock-strewn bank they halted.

"This is the preserve's northern border," informed the ranger, whose powerful voice was barely audible over the rushing waters. "Militia territory begins on the other side. I'm afraid we're going to get a little wet crossing over there."

The water turned out to be icy cold, and at the deepest portion of the channel, it extended well up to their thighs. Ever cautious of the swift current, Thomas followed the ranger over the slippery footing. The ranger seemed less concerned. "Wouldn't be bad fishing here," he said over his shoulder, "if you didn't mind the risk of getting shot."

Any sort of trail was conspicuously absent on this side of the river, and they passed through a grove of gnarled oaks. A ghostly fog had settled here, yet this didn't stop Thomas from spotting the hand-scrawled sign that had been nailed to one of the tree trunks. It read: WARNING—PRIVATE PROPERTY! NO TRESPASSING! NO HUNTING OR FISHING! VIOLATORS WILL BE SORRY!!!

The fog further thickened as they crossed a scrub-filled hollow. The air temperature had dropped a good ten degrees and an eerie silence prevailed, broken only by the heavy sound of their footsteps.

On the muddy banks of a small stream, the ranger stopped once more. He checked his compass before addressing them in a hushed voice.

"This hollow will lead us to a ridge that partially encircles the compound. We should get rid of this fog up there and get a good look at what we're up against."

"Heads up for snares and booby traps," Thomas added. "Remember, these folks are being led by a professional soldier."

They crossed a stream and began a slight uphill climb. The fog dissipated slightly as they passed through a stand of pines whose lower trunks were still wrapped in thick tendrils of swirling mist.

Thomas, second in line, sensed a sudden tentativeness to their guide's steps. This circumspection proved to be a lifesaver when a hunting arrow struck the tree directly in front of the startled ranger. The razor-sharp, barbed tip penetrated the dense trunk with a resounding thwack. Two steps farther, and it would have impaled his neck.

"Take cover!" warned Thomas as the horrifying reality of this near miss sank in.

"Don't bother!" countered a female voice from the surrounding wood. "If any of you go for your weapons, you'll die!"

This chilling threat took human form as a line of heavily armed figures materialized out of the fog. White camouflage fatigues gave them a phantomlike appearance as they completely surrounded Thomas and his men with an overpowering force that made resistance impossible.

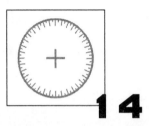

14

"Bond. James Bond," said Ricky in his suavest, mock-English accent, while making the final adjustments to his tuxedo.

Peering into his stateroom's bathroom mirror, he straightened his bow tie and pulled his shirt cuffs beyond the tux jacket's black sleeve. He had to admit, he liked what he saw. And to think he'd fought his mother every inch of the way when she urged him to purchase a tuxedo for the crossing.

He buttoned his double-breasted jacket, and had to reach out and grab onto the marble counter when the deck below began rolling from side to side. This rocking motion had been getting increasingly noticeable, especially within the last hour.

Ricky hoped that the rough seas responsible for this movement weren't the first signs of the tropical storm that everyone had started talking about. The ocean had been almost perfectly calm until now, and the resulting ride was so smooth Ricky had sometimes forgotten he was at sea. But reality struck home when the hull of the giant ocean liner rolled in the grasp of yet another massive swell, throwing Ricky hard against the counter top.

At the same time, his cabin phone rang. Steadying himself, he moved to answer it, hoping the caller was Kristin. He thought they'd been getting along pretty well, and so, earlier in the day, he had invited her to attend this evening's gala dinner. But she immediately turned him down, giving him some lame excuse about having to work then. Maybe she had reconsidered.

His hopes were dashed, though, when he spotted his father seated at the stateroom desk, the telephone to his ear.

"Of course I understand, Sam," he said into the handset. "And, listen, it's nothing to be embarrassed about. Take two right off. I guarantee that in a half hour, you'll be feeling like your old self again."

As he hung up the phone and began scribbling on a notepad, Ricky could see that the call had interrupted his father while he was getting dressed himself. His formal shirt was still partially open at the neck, the studs yet to be buttoned, his bow tie and cuff links still on the dresser.

"Problems, Pop?"

Dr. Jim Patton looked up and smiled as Ricky crossed over to him. "You're looking awfully handsome, son. Your mom would be mighty proud."

The distinguished, silver-haired physician briefly turned his attention back to the notepad before adding, "Appears that these seas have caused my first real case of seasickness. How are you feeling?"

Ricky responded while bracing himself against the dresser as the QE2 rolled into another swell. "Right now, my stomach's fine, but I feel like a punch-drunk sailor. I guess it's going to take a little time for me to get my sea legs."

"Don't forget to watch that hip," warned his father. "If these seas get much rougher, I'd like you to keep off your feet whenever possible."

"I'll be fine, Pop. And besides, when I was watching the sunset earlier with Kristin, the whole western horizon was aglow. You know what they say: Red sky at night, sailor's delight." As if to spite nautical wisdom, the deck rolled over with enough force to cause Jim Patton's jade-Buddha cuff links to slide off the dresser. Ricky picked them up, and looked on as his father pulled a small vial of pills out of his medicine bag.

"I'd better get moving, or I'm going to be late for cocktails," said Jim Patton, placing the vial at his side and reaching for his cuff links. "I've still got to deliver these pills to Sam Morrison."

"I can do it for you, Pop. After all, that's the least I can do to help work off my passage."

Jim Patton took a second to snap his right cuff link in place before picking up the vial and handing it to Ricky. "I appreciate the help. Special Agent Morrison is waiting for these up on Signal Deck, outside the President's Penthouse. And please, watch that leg of yours."

Ricky flashed his father an okay sign, pocketed the plastic vial, and turned to leave the cabin. He had yet to visit that restricted portion of the ship where the heads of state were staying, and he needed to refer to his pocket map to find the way.

Because he had to travel by elevator whenever possible, he chose a somewhat convoluted route. A short detour took him down to Two Deck, where he headed forward to the A-Stairwell and an elevator that whisked him up to the Sports Deck. He turned to his left, passed by the Radio Room, and proceeded through the Queens Grill, as the staff was putting the finishing touches to the decorations for the gala. The aft exit brought him into the Lounge and the Signal Deck's private elevator.

Before he could enter this small lift, he had to pass the scrutiny of a plainclothes security guard. This brawny, no-nonsense individual asked to see Ricky's ID, and after verifying his identity, inquired about the purpose of his visit to the Signal Deck. Ricky explained his mission of mercy and showed him the pills. The guard relayed this information into a miniature, two-way radio transmitter that projected from beneath the collar of his jacket. The response arrived via a compact ear receiver. Only then did the sentry hit the button to summon the elevator and indicate that Ricky was free to continue.

The ride up took twenty seconds at most, and deposited him in a short, carpeted hallway, with the Penthouse Suites situated on each side. A ceiling-mounted security camera watched his every move as he tried to determine which way the President's Penthouse was located.

He looked to his right and spotted a black-suited Asian man standing outside a suite marked, PICCADILLY. He was obviously a member of one of the security teams, and Ricky approached him to ask for help.

"Excuse me," said Ricky. "But could you tell me where the President of the United States is staying?"

The security agent bowed graciously and pointed to the forwardmost cabin saying, "American President-san."

Ricky thanked him and continued forward. A recessed vestibule intersected the right side of the hallway, and here he found Morrison seated on a folding chair with his forehead buried in the palms of his hands. Clearly, he was not on good terms with the sea.

"Good evening, sir. Are you going to live?"

Morrison looked up, sweating. "Young Mr. Patton," he managed as the ship canted over hard on its right side. "How about if I give you my .45 and you put me out of my misery once and for all?"

Ricky reached into his pocket and pulled out the vial. "This might not be as quick as a bullet, but at least the aftereffects are easier to live with."

Morrison gratefully popped open the vial and downed two of the tiny green pills. "So much for a drugfree America," he muttered after swallowing them.

Ricky first met Samuel Morrison shortly after the President's inauguration. He liked the big, amiable man right off, and he sensed that the feeling was mutual.

"I just came from the Queens Grill, and it looks like this dinner will really be a special one. Are you going to be able to join us?"

Morrison held back his answer until the shuddering deck stabilized. "Right now, the mere thought of food is enough to turn my stomach. But unless I roll over and die sometime within the next sixty minutes, I'll be there, sure enough. I drew the night shift this evening."

Ricky pointed toward the closed doorway labeled, QUEEN ELIZABETH SUITE, positioned to Morrison's right. "How's the President doing? Any word on his reaction to the summit?"

"From what I can tell, Two-Putt seems real satisfied with the way things are turning out, Ricky. I haven't seen him this pumped up since the campaign. He's even given up his regular afternoon siesta. In fact, he's in there right now with the British prime minister, and I don't believe they're merely discussing their putting strokes."

A sudden pitching motion of the deck forced Ricky to grab the edge of Morrison's chair to keep from falling over. "Hang on there, Ricky," the SAIC commented, "All you need now is to go and break your good leg."

Ricky held his tongue as he was forced to brace himself awkwardly and a shooting pain coursed up his hip. It was a sobering reminder that he was far from being one hundred percent fit.

"Hey, Ricky, I don't mean to be nosy, but who's the good-looking Asian babe that I saw you hanging with earlier? Man, she's a real looker."

Ricky proudly replied, his pain all but forgotten, "Her name's Kristin Liu. She's the daughter of the man who runs the ship's Gym."

"Is she a movie star like her father?"

Ricky's brow furrowed in thought. "To tell you the truth, I really don't know. We only met yesterday, and we're still getting to know each other."

"Most exciting part of a relationship," offered Morrison with an introspective smile. "Will Miss Liu be joining us at dinner this evening?"

"She said she had to work. But I think I'll go down to the Gym and give it another try."

"That's the spirit. It sure would be a shame to waste those fancy duds being stuck at our table, with us old farts."

Inspired, Ricky excused himself to see if he could convince Kristin to change her mind. But when he reached the Gym he was surprised to find the doors still locked. He knocked on the cloudy glass panels. A full minute passed before a shadowy figure appeared on the other side of the translucent doorway.

"We're closed!" shouted a male voice from inside.

"I need to talk with Kristin." No answer.

"Please, is Kristin there?" persisted Ricky.

Ricky's stubbornness paid off as the lock clicked open, and a man poked his head out.

"So," sneered Max Kurtyka. "And *whom* shall I say is calling?"

Ricky ignored his mocking tone. "Please tell Kristin that Ricky Patton would like to speak with her."

Kurtyka looked at him lustfully and flicked his tongue in and out of his mouth a number of times.

"So you're the young buck who's got the hots for Kristin," he said with a slow drawl. "Watch it, Bubba. You go and touch a hair on that pretty head, and her daddy will snap your scrawny neck like a twig."

Ricky was saved from having to hear more of this when Kristin showed up behind Kurtyka. She pushed her way past him and through the doorway, before giving Ricky a terse smile, and addressing her coworker.

"Beat it, Max. Okay?"

Kurtyka eyed Ricky one more time, and gave him another tongue flick before disappearing back into the Gym. Kristin made certain to shut the doors behind her as she joined Ricky out in the hallway.

"You look wonderful," she observed sincerely. "Do you always dress that way for dinner?"

"Doesn't everyone?" deadpanned Ricky, already losing himself in her dark, almond-shaped eyes.

"From the way you're dressed, I assume that you didn't come down here to work out."

"You assume correctly," Ricky replied while looking at his watch. "Now if you hurry, you've still got a good half hour to get dressed yourself and join me."

"Ricky," she whined. "I told you I simply can't."

"But why not? I thought we had a great time this afternoon."

"Believe me, Ricky. I had a wonderful afternoon, too, and if it were any other evening, I wouldn't hesitate to accept your invitation."

Not about to be denied, Ricky went for the full court press. "What's so important that you can't have dinner with me? Surely it can't be work. The Gym isn't even open."

Kristin hesitated, and just when it seemed her will was weakening, her father burst through the doorway. Dennis Liu was dressed in a white martial-arts robe, with a black belt cinched around his waist, and a crimson red headband embossed with a series of bright yellow dragons. From the sweat that matted his brow, it appeared that he had been working out. Ricky felt a bit uncomfortable dressed in his monkey suit, and looked on as Dennis Liu swallowed him with an intense gaze and bowed.

"Good evening," he said in a dry whisper. "Is everything okay out here?"

"Everything is fine, Father. Ricky was just inquiring if I could join him for dinner this evening."

"It's a special gala banquet, hosted by the captain in honor of the G-7 participants, sir. I'd be honored if Kristin could accompany me. There's an extra place at our table, and I'm sure she'd enjoy meeting my own father and his associates. In fact, I can even introduce her to the President of the United States."

Liu thought a moment before responding. "Your gracious invita-

197

tion is most kind, and speaking for my daughter, you honor her with your offer. But unfortunately, I need Kristin's services this evening. So I'm afraid that this matter is closed. Kristin."

Liu beckoned toward the doorway. His daughter met Ricky's perplexed stare before meekly bowing and leaving without another word spoken. Liu pivoted, then he too was gone, leaving Ricky alone, dejected, and trying his best to figure out where he had gone wrong.

Vince Kellogg's evening started off strangely enough—he almost slept through it. Upon returning to his stateroom to get dressed for the banquet, he lay down for what was to be but a short, fifteen-minute nap. Lulled into a sound sleep by the constant rocking motion of the QE2's hull, Vince was out for a good forty minutes.

He would have most likely continued his slumber, if it hadn't been for a particularly nasty swell that sent a vase crashing to the floor. With groggy, unbelieving eyes, he glanced at the bedside clock and sat up with a start.

Dinner was to begin at eight sharp, which gave him less than thirty minutes to shower and dress. Fighting the rolling deck he accomplished this feat in record time, and jogged into the Queens Lounge with ten whole minutes to spare.

He spotted the ship's security director seated alone at one of the cocktail tables, a well-limed Bloody Mary before him, and made his way over to him.

"Good evening, Special Agent," greeted Hartwell. "Please have a seat and join me for a cocktail."

Vince sat down opposite him, and looked on as a waiter approached. Because he was on duty, Vince couldn't have any alcohol, but he took Hartwell's lead and asked for a Virgin Mary.

"Perhaps you'll be able to join me in the Wardroom after dinner, and we can have a real drink together," offered the Scotsman as Vince's cocktail arrived.

Vince had to reach out and steady his glass when the ship rolled heavily. This prompted Hartwell to lift up his own glass, and toast.

"Here's to following seas and fair winds."

As the QE2's stabilizers bit into the surging swell and evened out the ride, Vince was able to pick up his glass and clink its frosted side up against his tablemate's.

"I do hope you brought along your appetite," commented Hartwell. "These galas are usually quite memorable."

Vince took a sip and replied. "Even with these rough seas, I'm starved. Is all this rocking and rolling being caused by the outer fringes of tropical storm Marti?"

"Actually, she's now been officially upgraded to Hurricane Marti. And no, she isn't responsible for these seas. We're currently passing through the remnants of a low-pressure ridge, and if you think this is rough, wait until you sail through a real storm."

"I hope I can postpone that experience for another time."

Hartwell noticed the strained expression on Vince's face and did his best to ease his guest's anxieties. "You'll be pleased to learn that once we pass through this ridge sometime early tomorrow morning, the weather map looks clear all the way into Southampton. As for Marti, she might have been a factor had we left New York a day or two later. But as it now looks, we'll be well clear of her path, should she decide to pay the North Atlantic a visit sometime later in the week."

Hartwell halted a moment to take another sip of his drink, then added, "I understand from Tuff that you completed your inspection of the ship. I do hope that you're satisfied with the results, and that you have a better understanding of why I was such a strong advocate of continuing the crossing. Any word as to the legitimacy of that supposed terrorist organization that issued the threat?"

"I finally managed to get a clear line to Washington shortly after we completed today's sweep. I'm waiting to get an update from my brother, who's still in the field."

"I do hope you'll let me know the second you hear from him," said Hartwell as he watched the Chinese contingent enter the Lounge.

The party was led by four security agents, each dressed in a similar baggy black suit, white shirt, and bright red tie. President Li Chen could be distinguished from this group by the fashionable, double-breasted tuxedo that he was wearing. Close at his side was his translator, with a short, crew-cut young man on their heels. This last figure carried a black leather attaché case, and as they passed through the Lounge on their way to the main Dining Room, Robert Hartwell discreetly whispered.

"I wonder if President Li has been able to keep in contact with

Beijing? From what I understand, that chap with the briefcase is carrying the unlock codes to China's nuclear arsenal."

"Back home, we call our version of that briefcase the football," informed Vince. "I was shocked when our President made the unprecedented decision to delegate responsibility for America's own unlock codes to the Vice President, for the entire duration of this crossing. This is the first time I've ever been with the President away from the White House, and not had the football close by."

"As it turned out, your President made a wise decision, especially when you factor in the manner in which those sunspots are affecting communications. It appears that my prime minister also delegated the responsibility for Great Britain's war codes to a land-based subordinate, with the French and the Russians doing likewise."

"Who knows?" reflected Vince. "Perhaps after this summit, such things as the football will be anachronisms."

"Here, here," toasted Hartwell.

Quick to follow the Chinese into the Lounge were the German, Italian, Canadian, and Japanese delegations. Unlike President Li, each of these heads of state only brought along a pair of security men, and in each instance, they were dressed immaculately in formal attire.

"Scuttlebutt has it that the Japanese and Chinese got into a bit of a row last night," Hartwell whispered. "What was intended to be an informal nightcap between old adversaries, supposedly turned into a shouting match that could be heard all the way out in the Grand Lounge."

"I can personally attest to hearing a similar disagreement on the Tennis Court yesterday, between the German chancellor and the prime minister of Italy," Vince revealed.

"Boys will be boys," offered the Scotsman with a wink.

It was just as Hartwell was polishing off his drink that the French arrived, looking chic and dapper in their matching black-satin tuxedoes. The Russians followed them in a large, animated group that included the British and the Americans.

Both Vince and Hartwell stood as the prime minister of Great Britain and the President of the United States walked by. The President's physician was positioned between the two heads of state, in the midst of telling a joke. Vince could only overhear the words *nurses* and *breasts,* as they passed, with the apparent punch line delivered seconds later to a laugh-filled reception.

Samuel Morrison was the last member of the President's party to enter the Lounge. He tried to maintain a strong bearing but his stomach was obviously in no mood for being professional.

"Evening, Chief. You feeling all right? You look a little green around the gills, sir."

"I'll survive," said the SAIC who leadenly made his way over to their table, and was forced to grab onto Vince's arm when the deck suddenly dipped downward. "Now I remember why I picked the army over the navy," he added.

"You know, my brother was worried about getting seasick before he was called off the crossing," remarked Vince. "I was going to try and get him some of those patches that Dr. Patton was telling us about."

Morrison replied while trying his best to steady himself on the back of Vince's chair. "Those patches might be effective, but I understand that there are too many friggin' side effects for my likes."

"We called them puss pads back in the Royal Marines," said Hartwell. "And nobody knows about those side effects better than me. On the way down to the Falklands, I stuck one behind my ear to be on the safe side. It worked brilliantly. Only problem was that all I did was sleep for the next two and a half days, until I was finally told that the bloody pads were supposed to be removed after twelve hours."

A soft electronic chime sounded in the background, signaling that the banquet was about to begin. Hartwell signed the bill, and beckoned his guests to lead the way into the adjoining dining room.

Vince was the first inside, and he found the Queens Grill buzzing with activity. The ship's orchestra, set up on the balcony for this special occasion, was playing spiritedly. The flags of all nine attending nations hung from the ceiling, while bunting that matched their colors decorated the room's pillars.

The Grill's focal point was the large table where the nine heads of state were seated. It was positioned in the exact center of the room, with no other tables close by. Lying on its surface was an immense intricately detailed ice sculpture of the *QE2.* The funnel had been dyed red and black to complete the *Queen's* distinctive look, with a column of dry-ice-generated smoke rising from it.

Melanie and Neil escorted the party to their balcony table. Dr. Patton was already there. Two seats remained vacant.

"Looks like my son has yet to make an appearance," said Patton, who had his back to the room's main entrance.

"Last I heard from him, he was off trying to fill that extra seat of ours with the prettiest young woman on this entire ship," Morrison revealed.

Kellogg, Morrison, and Hartwell all made certain that their chairs faced the room's interior and that they had a clear view of the Grill's two entryways. As they seated themselves, the band segued from a Russian folk tune into a German polka and Melanie handed out the menus.

Vince was torn between the pâté de foie gras or the chilled Russian Malossol caviar for an appetizer. Neil put a quick end to his dilemma by suggesting that he order both. Vince readily did so, and completed his order by selecting the cream of sweet potato soup with toasted pine nuts, and a fresh Maine lobster served with green asparagus tips, corn on the cob, and sautéed new potatoes. Robert Hartwell also went for the dual appetizers, picking the chateaubriand for his entrée, while Dr. Patton chose a jumbo shrimp cocktail and paupiettes of sole stuffed with broccoli. Morrison, aghast at the thought of all that food, ordered just a bowl of chicken broth and some white toast. Dr. Patton seemed especially concerned with the SAIC's condition, and began a detailed discussion on the healing effects of chicken soup and other folk remedies.

During this discourse, Dr. Patton's son showed himself. With a plodding heavy step, he limped toward the table. His father was immediately worried.

"Are you okay, son? You didn't fall, did you?"

Ricky seated himself and answered while taking a menu from Neil. "I'm fine, Pop. Just feeling a little queasy from motion sickness, I guess."

"Don't be afraid to order yourself a hearty meal," instructed the physician. "There are several studies that show that a full stomach is better than medication when it comes to treating seasickness."

A better cure for loneliness too, Vince thought. Dr. Patton completed the prescription by looking at Neil and nodding at the extra place setting. Neil removed it, and indeed the boy perceptively brightened.

As the entrées were served, a steward arrived at their table with an envelope for Dr. Patton. Vince watched as the physician opened it, and noted his perplexed expression as he read its contents.

"That certainly is strange," Patton muttered, drawing the attention of his dining companions. "Dr. Benedict got a response from that memo we distributed to the room-service staff. It seems a Filipino steward has come forward to swear he witnessed an attendant from Chinatown deliver a platter of shrimp to the Gym staff, on the day after leaving Southampton. I bet you that's the source of our food poisoning!"

"If that's the case," interjected Hartwell, "surely Ping would have known about it. But as Special Agent Kellogg can attest, the folks down in Chinatown told us that no such delivery ever took place."

"Well, it's obvious that someone's not telling us the truth," offered Vince.

"That's certainly a possibility, though if it's Ping, it's a bit out of character," Hartwell returned. "Why don't we pop down there after dinner, along with the chap who answered Doc Benedict's memo? That should get us to the truth of the matter."

Vince nodded that this was fine with him. As he polished off the last of the lobster, the Grill's forward doorway opened and in walked the *QE2*'s bearded master. Capt. Ronald Prestwick surveyed the dinner's progress, and satisfied that the guests were in the process of completing their entrées, he made his way down to the table of honor. Here he circled the table, making it a point to speak to each head of state.

He ended his rounds at the head of the table, where the British prime minister was seated. There Captain Prestwick accepted a cordless microphone from a steward, and raised it to his lips.

"Mr. Prime Minister, I want to thank you for taking my place at the head of the table, for this distinguished gathering. Presidents, prime ministers, and chancellors all, it is my great pleasure to welcome you on this most special of nights. And to all of you who are also assembled here, know that it is a sincere honor to be of service to each one of you.

"All of us at Cunard are proud of the great tradition of excellence that this wonderful vessel so magnificently represents. The *Queen Elizabeth 2* is much more than a mere technological marvel, for above all, it's her crew who make this ocean liner second to none.

Thank you for honoring us with your presence on this historic crossing. And may we be part of history together."

A polite round of applause caused the captain to briefly lower the microphone. He waited for it to fade completely before addressing them once again, this time with increasing fervor.

"As I speak to you, honored guests, be aware that the QE2 is rapidly approaching the midpoint in our voyage. Here in the mid-Atlantic, there are no geopolitical boundaries to restrain us. In a manner of speaking, we are all citizens of the world out here, stripped of our individual nationalities and united in a common fate.

"May the spirit of concord and union be a part of you for the remainder of this crossing. And even though this gala dinner is usually reserved for the last full day at sea, we thought it appropriate to hold it now. For our arrival in these international waters signals a homecoming of a sort never before experienced by the peoples of the world. May you who hold the destiny of the planet in your hands take this opportunity to come together, and share the spirit of peace with all the earth's inhabitants. For if this great ship could speak, this would be her epitaph—an end to all war, needless suffering, and deprivation."

The room erupted with a rousing chorus of applause that included a good number of spirited "Well dones!" The captain appeared to be taken aback by the intensity and length of this response that rose even louder when the nine heads of state stood in unison. This caused the rest of the Grill's applauding patrons to stand, and the embarrassed captain allowed them to continue for only another fifteen seconds before finally raising his hands overhead and beckoning them to be seated.

"Thank you very much, and I hope you enjoy the rest of the crossing. And to continue on the right foot, let the parade of the baked Alaskas begin!"

The lights snapped off, throwing the room into total darkness. Vince found himself momentarily disoriented. Then he heard the orchestra begin to play Beethoven's "Ode to Joy," and a long line of waiters emerged from the aft entryway. They held aloft silver serving trays, lit sparklers projecting from them, and wove their way around the tables.

He watched the procession encircle the table holding the heads of state, and then suddenly halt as the stirring crescendo reached a pause. The waiters turned in unison to face the summiteers, their fiery sparklers still aglow, while the orchestra segued into a rich version of "Auld Lang Syne."

An impromptu singalong session was initiated by the President of the United States and the prime ministers of Great Britain and Canada, who joined hands and began singing the familiar lyrics. The Grill's other patrons joined in, and soon all nine world leaders had their hands linked together, their bodies swaying to the ageless melody.

This sight alone was a moving one, and Vince realized that this gala banquet had exceeded his every expectation. He felt a tremendous spirit of camaraderie in this room that he hoped would spill over to the summit sessions yet to come.

Even though he himself had never been much of a singer, he couldn't help joining in on the final refrain of "Auld Lang Syne." Hartwell had his glass held high, and Morrison slapped him on the back at the song's conclusion, then the room erupted with another boisterous round of applause.

It was then that the lights snapped back on, and Vince spotted a strong figure standing beside the Grill's main entrance. This individual wore a hooded balaclava, which masked his face; was dressed completely in black; and held what looked to be a Sterling submachine gun firmly in his grasp. Before Vince could react, a trio of similarly attired figures, also holding submachine guns, burst through the entryway and took up positions on the balcony. At the same time, yet another armed threesome entered the Grill by way of its forward door.

By this time instinct took over, and he frantically reached into the folds of his jacket to pull out his pistol. But before he could do so, the first intruder that he had spotted pointed his weapon at the ceiling and let loose a deafening, five-second volley. He then readjusted the aim of his gun squarely on the Grill's central table, and cried out.

"If I see one single weapon exposed, the heads of state will die!"

His six hooded accomplices also aimed their weapons at the nine astounded summiteers, and the shocked waiters who continued to surround them and block any of the guards from reaching them. Vince had no choice but to let go of his pistol's plastic grip. His two armed tablemates did likewise, and Vince briefly met the concerned stares of both Samuel Morrison and Robert Hartwell.

"I'm sorry to have interrupted your dessert," continued the leader. "But this theatrical opportunity couldn't be resisted. Bring in the rest of them!" he added.

Seconds later, a long line of three dozen or so passengers entered the Grill, accompanied by a pair of armed escorts. Several of these sullen figures were dressed in terry-cloth robes, and Vince recognized them as members of the international security teams who weren't on duty. As they were directed to be seated on the carpeted floor of the main dining area, the leader once more addressed them.

"Before any of you decides to be a hero, be aware that my forces have already secured the ship's Bridge, Radio Room, security department, and engineering spaces. My people have also made their presence known to the rest of the vessel's crew, who have been notified that no one will be harmed as long as you obey my rules and instructions.

"I suspect each of you is extremely interested in who we are and what we want. For the time being, though, our identities are unimportant. What's of vital significance is that you abandon all hope of challenging us. We will be making the rounds of this room to confiscate all armaments, which I understand are quite substantial. Know that any attempt at resistance will result in instant death, both for yourselves and for the men you've sworn to protect.

"To further insure your cooperation, be it known that a powerful bomb has been hidden on this ship. The timer of this device has already been activated, and should I fail to show up to deactivate it, the entire vessel will be doomed to destruction."

The leader lifted his right hand and snapped his fingers a single time. This signal caused one of his hooded accomplices, who stood to his right and was obviously a female, to repeat these exact instructions in perfect German, Italian, French, Russian, Japanese and Mandarin.

Once the final translation was completed, the leader snapped his fingers a second time. Without hesitation, two of his masked associates climbed down from the balcony and approached the circular table that was set up against the room's far right wall. Vince knew that this was where the Chinese delegation was seated, and he watched as the gunmen raised their weapons and began speaking in rapid Mandarin.

Whatever they were saying caused one member of the Chinese contingent to stand hesitantly. This crew-cut individual held a briefcase close at his side, and Vince didn't have to see any more to know that this was the fellow responsible for holding the PRC's version of America's nuclear football.

"Oh, shit!" cursed Samuel Morrison.

The gunman reached out for the briefcase. Just as he was about to take possession of it, one of the PRC security agents seated beside the trembling aide lunged forward and attempted to grab the case himself. As he made hand contact with it, his seated associates drew their pistols, while the aide began scuffling with the figure who had tried to take the briefcase from him.

But a mere second before the Chinese agents could put their weapons into play, the other gunman brought his submachine gun to bear. With a quick precise sweep he emptied the Sterling's entire thirty-four-round clip into the torsos of the unfortunate Chinese men. With a deafening extended blast, the 9mm bullets tore into the bodies of the PRC agents, who collapsed onto the floor and across the table, a twitching, bleeding mass of torn flesh.

Sickened by this sight, and by the nauseous scent of cordite, Vince could only mutter, "Oh, sweet Jesus, no!"

The gunman simply replaced his clip with a new one from his belt.

An anxious murmur of shocked chatter escaped the lips of the other captives, who continued looking on as the smoke generated by this gunfire cleared. Standing beside the blood-soaked table, with the briefcase firmly in his grasp, was the lead gunman. His hood had been torn off during the brief scuffle, and Vince gasped upon identifying him. Clearly exposed for all to see was the face of the man that Vince had only briefly met back on the pier in New York, an employee of Dennis Liu, the Asian who went by the name of Bear.

A myriad of thoughts rushed into Vince's mind as he watched Bear return to the balcony and hand the briefcase to his leader. Only when he had this cherished item firmly in his grasp, did this figure bother to reach up and yank off his own hood.

Vince gasped once more as he set his startled eyes on the gloating face of Dennis Liu. One by one, in quick succession, the other gang members also exploded their faces. Vince recognized Max Kurtyka, Monica Chang, and Liu's daughter, Kristin. Vince didn't know the identities of the others, who were all Asian males.

In a disgusted whisper, it was Robert Hartwell who revealed where these others had come from. "Damn it, those bloody bastards are from Chinatown!"

Ricky Patton was beyond shock upon setting his astounded eyes on Kristin. His thoughts still in a frightened haze, he realized that he had most likely interrupted them down in the Gym, as they were making final preparations for this assault.

"I find myself in the midst of a script of my own making," said Dennis Liu to his rapt audience. "You who know my work, only know my shadow. Desperation directs our efforts, and rest assured that we are perfectly willing to sacrifice our own lives for the great cause that we serve. What is the soul of a single individual, when a billion and a half others depend on us to succeed? Our great movement is their last chance, and failure isn't an alternative.

"But cold-blooded murder is not our intention, only a potential means. So follow our rules, and you shall live. Resist, and you will die. It's as simple as that, for the *Queen* and her occupants are now mine!"

B O O K   T H R E E

RETRIBUTION

I heard the voice of the Lord saying, "Whom shall I send, and who will go for us?" Then said I, "Here I am; send me!"

—Isaiah 6:8

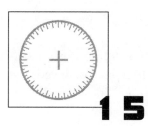

15

THOMAS EXPECTED THE WORST AS THEY WERE DISARMED, GAGGED, HAD THEIR eyes covered and hands restrained with electrical tape. Other than the warning threat from the raspy-voiced woman, their attackers kept silent during this whole process, their faces hidden behind camouflaged hoods. Before his own eyes were masked with tape, he counted at least twelve individuals in the militia party, who now proceeded to prod them forward with the barrels of their weapons.

To keep from straying from the path, Thomas was forced to grab onto the shoulders of the man in front of him. It was disorientating to travel in this manner, and he had to hurry to keep pace as they continued up a steep hill.

As they reached the summit, one of the militia members announced their arrival with a series of bird calls. The path was flat here, and Thomas counted off some two dozen steps before they were led into a structure.

The air inside was heavy with the scent of burning logs. It was the woman with the raspy voice who ordered them to their knees. Thomas did as instructed, and listened as she began a furious, accusation-filled diatribe.

Thomas had heard it all before. She started off declaring that this was yet another instance of the United States government infringing on the rights of its citizens. They had been apparently expecting this incursion for some time, and accused them of illegal trespass and a litany of other crimes that included the tragic deaths at Ruby Ridge, and the slaughter at the Waco Branch Davidian complex.

She went on to declare her belief in the right of all Americans to bear arms. She also revealed her fear of a United Nations-sponsored one-world government that the ATF and the FBI were secretly laying the groundwork for.

With rising frustration, Thomas was forced to listen to these paranoid, unfounded attacks that finally ended when she ordered the leader of her group of captives to stand. Thomas did so, and suddenly felt the tape painfully stripped off his forehead.

His eyes stung as he looked out at a bank of powerful mercury-vapor lights that continued to veil his accusers. A hooded figure dressed in BDUs came forward, frisked him, and pulled the search warrant out of his zippered pocket. This figure disappeared back into the light, and Thomas listened as the woman with the raspy voice read the warrant.

"So, you're looking for an organization responsible for threatening the life of our commander in chief," she repeated with a skeptical laugh. "What a clever cover story to justify this flagrant act of trespassing. From the weapons you were outfitted with, it's obvious that you already considered us guilty as charged, and were on your way to carry out the government's sentence. Before we pass our own judgment, how do you plead?"

This same individual stepped forward and ripped the tape off Thomas's mouth. He cleared his dry throat, and finding himself with nothing to lose, described in detail the two IEDs that had brought about this intrusion.

Thomas tried his best to contain both his anger and his fear as he revealed the nature of the evidence that had brought them to the Holly wilderness area. He decided to include the description of their suspect, as given to them by the Winchester post office clerk, still not certain if this individual and the woman who stood before him, were one and the same.

"Look," he said. "We didn't come out here to attack you. And I don't think you find it strange that government agents are armed. If this is a case of mistaken identity, then I'm sorry to have bothered you this morning.

"But believe me, I personally helped defuse that second IED, and the C-4 it held was very real. Before more bombs are sent and innocent lives endangered, all we want to do is enforce our warrant. If you're not involved, then you have nothing to hide. Let us look around and determine this fact, then I swear that we'll leave you in peace and be gone from here."

A single, BDU-clad figure stepped forward. Short and stocky, this individual halted in front of Thomas and yanked off her hood. The defiant face of a fifty-year-old woman stared back at him. She had penetrating hazel eyes, with cracked skin stretched tight over prominent cheekbones. Her spiky hair was cut short, and Thomas saw that the characteristic straw-colored braids were noticeably absent.

"Your candor is appreciated," she whispered as she took him aside. "And as shocking as this may sound, I believe you. Though I don't always agree with my government, violence isn't the way in which I've chosen to express my displeasure.

"I'm Capt. Lee Pierce, formerly of the U.S. Army's 82nd Airborne Division. I formed the Holly River Patriots in a last-ditch effort to *defend* the Constitution, not destroy it. Senseless bloodshed isn't in our charter, though I'm sorry to say that there could be others in our midst who don't feel likewise. If that description you related is accurate, I believe the suspect you seek could be amongst us. Shall we see for ourselves?"

Pierce ordered Thomas and Galloway's restraints removed, and quickly escorted them back into the woods, the rest of their team still held captive back at the main compound. They soon found themselves on an isolated corner of her property.

"It was my great-great-grandfather who originally settled this land," she explained while leading them up a tree-lined ridge. "The cabin we're headed to was part of his original homestead. My stepson moved up there this past spring, shortly after his father died. We never were close, and after the accident took my husband, he got increasingly extreme in his ideas, so much so that I was forced to castigate him in front of the others. And that's when he moved into the cabin with his girlfriend Emma."

"I realize that this isn't easy for you, Captain," said Thomas as they reached the top of the ridge. They started down into a fog-filled hollow.

"The boy always was too headstrong for his own good," she continued without breaking her stride. "At first I feared that I was the cause of his rebelliousness. But even when I wasn't around, he had a way of alienating those around him. I'm afraid he's just a bad seed who believes that violence is the only way to get his point across."

The air temperature dropped as they climbed down into the valley. A stream could be heard nearby, and it was beside it that a cabin materialized out of the fog. It was an ancient structure, formed out of white stone blocks.

Lee Pierce peered through the cracked window, and seeing no one inside, unlocked the front door with a key she extracted from the top of the wooden door frame. The stench of tanning animal skins was overpowering as they stepped inside. The place was a mess, and it was obvious that its occupants didn't devote much time to housekeeping. Clothing and used supplies littered the floor, with a thick coating of dust covering the furniture.

"If these two are up to no good, we'll find the evidence either up in the attic or down in the root cellar," said Pierce.

Mike Galloway volunteered to check the attic. Thomas and Pierce grabbed a pair of flashlights off the counter and headed down below. The old timbers of the stairway strained under the weight of their steps as they entered the cellar. Their flashlights cut through the blackness, the air thick with swirling dust.

As his feet hit the earthen floor, Thomas scanned the debris-strewn room, his flashlight coming to a halt on a closed door. "What's in there?" he asked.

"That's where my father had his darkroom. He was quite the wildlife photographer in his day."

Thomas found his pulse quickening as his thoughts returned to the IED's photoelectric trigger. "What did he use for light?"

"He rigged up that old generator over there to a red safelight inside the lab."

"I don't suppose that it still works?" he questioned hopefully.

Pierce crossed the cellar, bent over, and pulled the generator's starter. The buzzing growl of a one-stroke engine sounded, and she walked over to the darkroom's shut doorway.

"The light's right inside. Shall we give it a try?"

"I think it's best if we kill these flashlights first," said Thomas as he joined her.

For a second, the room lapsed into total blackness. Pierce opened the creaking door, then reached up and pulled the cord to the safelight.

In the dim red glow of a single bulb, Thomas surveyed the dark-room's interior. He discovered a cracked, white-enamel basin, and a wooden counter filled with an odd assortment of materials. He identified several boxes of electrical components, and a large roll of black, wax-based wrapping paper. It was beside a Scotch tape dispenser that he spotted a shoebox-sized lump of what appeared to be putty. It was wrapped in green Mylar, and upon closer examination, he saw that the plastic had a label on it reading, PROPERTY OF NATIONAL GUARD ARMORY WHEELING, WEST VIRGINIA.

"Special Agent Kellogg, I was afraid of this, but it appears that your visit was justified after all. Take a look at this."

His hands were trembling slightly as he took possession of a partially completed Priority Mail address label. The familiar cramped handwriting revealed the fictitious Winchester, Virginia, post office box of the sender. Yet this time it was the addressee's name that had changed to the Honorable Speaker of the U.S. House of Representatives.

"Do you find that interesting?" inquired a man's voice from behind Thomas.

Thomas pivoted, and found himself looking down the menacing barrel of a twelve-gauge shotgun. A scruffy-looking, long-haired male in his thirties held the weapon, and there could be no missing the long, straw-colored braids of the woman who stood beside him.

"Put down the gun, Andrew," ordered Lee Pierce. "And for once in your life, listen to me! I warned you that violence wasn't the way to get your views across, and now you're going to have to pay the price for your pigheadedness."

"Shut your trap, Captain!" countered the gun-toting extremist, whose eyes opened wide with abhorrence upon viewing the BATF patch that graced his prisoner's coveralls.

"What do we have here?" he added snidely. "Captain, I think you should pay a bit more attention to the friends you're hanging out with. This one's got a stink that could put a stuck pig to shame, and it's going to be a joy to put him out of his misery."

"You're in enough trouble without adding murder to your crimes," replied Pierce. "Put down the gun, and let's talk about it."

"I'm sick of talk!" shouted Andrew as he cocked the shotgun's hammer. "Me and Emma have made our choice, and talk isn't on the agenda. It's apparent that the President won't listen to us, and now we're going to introduce the Sons of the Patriots to our enemies in Congress."

Thomas realized that the two warped souls standing before him were the extent of this organization. There was no way that they could have made good an attack on the QE2. And though he was relieved by this, he now had a much more immediate threat to be concerned with.

"If you've got a favorite prayer, Mr. Jackboot ATF man, now's the time to be saying it," advised Andrew.

Thomas met his crazed glance, doubting that he'd be able to talk his way out of this predicament. This certainly wasn't the place or time where he expected to meet death, and just as he was about to surrender to Andrew's suggestion of prayer, a sudden movement behind Andrew caught his attention; then a voice:

"Drop it, you bastard!" he heard Galloway say.

As Andrew snapped his head around, Thomas threw himself forward to divert the barrel of the shotgun. It discharged with a thunderous blast, the pellets boring harmlessly into the ceiling. While Galloway moved in from the rear, Thomas grabbed Andrew in an armlock. By the time Pierce restrained Emma, Thomas was already calculating how much time it would take to reach a telephone and relay the all clear to his brother somewhere in the mid-Atlantic.

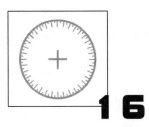

1 6

BRITTANY COOPER WAS CERTAINLY NO STRANGER TO IMPORTANT BRIEFINGS. YET in this instance, she found herself dreading the thought of disclosing the reason behind this hastily convened meeting in the operation center's conference room. Her guests had only just arrived, and as they gathered around the table, she made certain that they had a clear view of the three large projection screens that were set up on the other side of the glass partition.

Adm. Richard Buchanan sat at the head of the table. The youngest chief of naval operations ever, Buchanan was personally responsible for Op Center Bravo's creation. At the former submariner's right sat Gen. William Ridgeway, the medal-bedecked chairman of the Joint Chiefs of Staff. Ridgeway was in every way the consummate veteran in their midst, whose Army service went back to the early days of Vietnam.

As a pair of aides set up their laptops opposite them, Brittany addressed her own keyboard. In response, the projection screen on the left side of the room filled with a large scale chart of the North Atlantic. A red icon flashed in the narrow strait of water separating Greenland and Iceland, and Brittany activated a cursor to highlight this feature.

"It was twenty-three-and-a-half hours ago that the U.S. Navy SOSUS facility at Reykjavik, Iceland, received a report of an anomalous submerged contact beneath the waters of the Denmark Strait," she revealed. "This data was subsequently analyzed, with the results arriving here within the last hour."

"Why the delay?" asked Ridgeway.

It was the CNO who answered. "Since the breakup of the Soviet Union and the end of the Cold War, Russian submarine deployments into the Atlantic have been extremely limited. Because of this, SOSUS monitoring of the GIUK gap has been downgraded to a Level-Two priority."

"You'd have thought that we would have bumped up the alert level for this crossing even though the Russian president is on board," remarked Ridgeway. "But that's water over the dam. Now, what's so important about this particular contact?"

The CNO flashed Brittany a supportive glance, and she swallowed nervously before replying, "Computer analysis of the sound signature shows a 93 percent probability that the vessel responsible is a Chinese *Han*-class, nuclear-powered attack submarine."

"Chinese?" repeated Ridgeway. "What in the hell are they doing way up there?"

"It looks to me that they're trying to clandestinely enter the North Atlantic by way of the Pole," returned the CNO. "This in itself is unprecedented, and I'd sure like to know which one of their boats managed to pull it off."

"If you look to the middle projection screen, I believe I can answer that, sir," said Brittany as she addressed her keyboard.

A black-and-white, overhead reconnaissance photo of a naval installation filled the screen, and Brittany identified it. "That's the PLA Navy berthing facility at Tsingtao. This Big Bird shot is the most recent in a series displaying the base's refit berths. If you'll follow my cursor, you can make out the two other advanced *Han*-class submarines in their fleet. This pair of vacant slips nearby indicates that two of Tsingtao's submarines are currently at sea. One of these vessels is the *Yellow Dragon*, a *Xia*-class ballistic-missile platform that set sail several days ago, for what appeared to be a routine deterrent patrol. The remaining empty slip belongs to the *Lijiang*, and that's the sub that I believe SOSUS tagged."

"Hold it right there, Commander," interrupted Ridgeway. "How can it be the *Lijiang*? Isn't that the sub that reportedly sank off the Spratlys?"

"It's obvious that the entire Chinese search-and-rescue operation in the Spratlys was nothing but an intentional act of deception," she dared. "And what makes this act even more interesting is the possibility that the top leadership in Beijing could know nothing about it."

"What do you mean by that?" quizzed the chairman.

Brittany looked at Ridgeway and answered. "I know it's all speculation at this point, but there's always the possibility that portions of the PLA Navy sincerely believed that the *Lijiang* was missing, and that their SAR effort was a legitimate one."

"I believe what the commander is implying is that outlaw elements inside the Chinese Navy could have succeeded in commandeering their most capable attack sub, without President Li's blessings," interjected the CNO.

General Ridgeway thoughtfully rubbed his furrowed forehead and took this speculative possibility one step further. "It's scary, but it almost makes sense. We all know how the surviving Maoists reacted to Deng's death and Li Chen's amazing rise to power."

"And let's not forget about our old friend Adm. Liu Huang-tzu," reminded the CNO. "As the senior hard-liner, no one was more publicly opposed to Li's participation in the G-7 summit than he. And since Liu continues to hold the seniormost rank in the PLA Navy, what better person to plan and execute such a clever act of subterfuge?"

"But would the old fox really have the cajones to steal one of his own submarines, then send it into the Atlantic where it would be free to cause all sorts of mayhem, including interfering with the *QE2*'s crossing?" asked Ridgeway.

Brittany readdressed her keyboard. The third projection screen filled with an expanded chart of the North Atlantic. Halfway between Newfoundland and the United Kingdom, she highlighted a blue icon and the quartet of flashing red stars that surrounded it in a neat, boxlike formation.

"As you probably suspect, that blue symbol represents the last-known position of the *QE2*," she informed them. "The coordinates were updated less than an hour ago, during the last pass of our White Cloud recon satellite. If an outlaw Chinese submarine is indeed on its way into the mid-Atlantic, we're more than prepared to deal with it."

"Commander, can you break down the individual identities of that escort formation for the chairman?" requested the CNO.

Brittany replied while highlighting the red star at the bottom, left-hand portion of the rectangular box. "This icon represents the approximate position of our wolf pack's command boat, the USS *James K. Polk*. The *Polk* is carrying our SEAL team, and their Mark VIII Swimmer Delivery Vehicle."

She shifted the cursor to the top, left-hand star and continued. "This is the location of the HMS *Talent*. The *Talent* is one of the Brits' newest, *Trafalgar*-class nuclear-powered attack boats. They've been fitted with the latest in quieting measures, and the new Smacks fire-control system. They're also carrying a full load of prototype Spearfish torpedoes. With a closing speed of over sixty knots, the Spearfish is one of the most potent torpedoes ever developed."

Moving the cursor to the star making up the bottom, right-hand portion of the box, she added, "The French *Rubis*-class submarine *Casabianca* is the point boat. She's been tasked with clearing the southern perimeter, and though substantially smaller than either the *Polk* or the *Talent*, she more than makes up for it with a state-of-the-art DUUX 5 Fenelon passive ranging sonar suite. The Marine Nationale's finest is also equipped with the latest DLT D-3 fire-control system, capable of launching the new F-17 acoustic-homing torpedo."

"And finally," said Brittany as she highlighted the upper, right-hand star. "We've got the *Baikal*, a Russian *Akula*-class attack sub. The *Baikal* is without a doubt the fastest sub in our foursome, and represents the best of Russia's long involvement with nuclear-powered-submarine engineering. She's been given the northern sector to patrol, and with a speed of over thirty-five knots, and a diving depth second to none, the *Baikal* should be able to hold her own against our suspected *Han*, or any other threat that she might come up against."

"Thank goodness you managed to talk the President into sending along those subs," remarked Ridgeway. "Do they know about the *Lijiang* as yet?"

Brittany accessed her laptop and held back her reply until the proper data flashed across the monitor. "I'm afraid not, sir. Normal VLF traffic has been disrupted by the same solar storm that's affecting our satellite communications with the *QE2*. We've got a TACAMO on the way to pass on the message via ELF."

"Can the *Iwo Jima* task force help us with ASW?" asked Ridgeway.

"Though their choppers are more than capable of tagging our bogey, the last I heard from Admiral Campbell, they were suspending all air ops to batten down the hatches for the arrival of Marti," informed the CNO.

Brittany alertly accessed the computer, and the main projection screen on the far-left side filled with a satellite weather map showing the eastern coast of the United States and a good portion of the Western Atlantic. The focal point was the tight, spiraling band of clouds north of Bermuda. A time-lapse sequence showed this storm system as it whisked past the island. It was headed to the northeast, its mass continually widening, with a definite eye forming in the center.

"It looks like the *Iwo Jima* battle group is going to take it right on the chin," observed the CNO. "Admiral Campbell mentioned that they're preparing for one-hundred-mile-per-hour gale-force winds, and Force five sea states."

Ridgeway winced. "Sounds like there are going to be some awfully sick Leathernecks out there."

"Not to mention the crews of the five ships accompanying them," added the CNO.

Brittany was in the process of requesting the computer to display the *Iwo Jima*'s last-known position, when Lieutenant Tolliver entered the conference room. The junior officer appeared uneasy, as he stood ramrod-straight and nervously cleared his throat before speaking.

"Excuse me for interrupting, but something's come up that I thought you should know about. I was in the middle of receiving a routine SITREP from the *QE2*, when the signal went dead. My first hunch was that electromagnetic interference was the culprit. Yet I succeeded in establishing a solid uplink with our COMSAT, and when I went to transmit, all I got was a digital message saying that the party I wished to call was off-line."

"Are you positive the problem wasn't with the satellite, Lieutenant?" queried the CNO.

"The problem was definitely with the downlink portion of the transmission, Admiral. Which leads me to believe that either the ship had a major mechanical failure in its radio room, or something else has happened making them unable to respond to our call."

"This is all we need at the moment," remarked Ridgeway with disgust. "Lieutenant, keep trying that COMSAT link, and try alternating those frequencies."

"Yes, sir!" returned Tolliver, smartly saluting before exiting.

"Commander Cooper," continued the chairman. "I want you to personally find out what in the hell that communications snafu is all about. Since we already can't reach our submarines, if we lose contact with the QE2 as well, we could be in one hell of a mess. This is especially the case if your suspicions hold true, and we've got a damned outlaw Chinese submarine headed out into the North Atlantic for God knows what purpose, and the leaders of the free world sitting out there with us unable to warn them!"

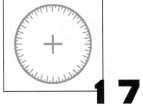

17

THE SUBMARINERS' WORLD IS DIVIDED INTO FOUR, SIX-HOUR INCREMENTS. BE-
cause of the unique medium in which they sail, the crew often has to
depend upon the nature of the meal being served to know whether it
is day or night topside.

Thus, when Benjamin Kram woke up at the start of the USS
Polk's third straight twenty-four patrol segment at flank speed, he
had dinner. It was still only midnight.

He found three of his fellow officers gathered around the wardroom's elongated table. As Kram took his customary seat at the head,
he noticed that his shipmates were almost finished with their meals.

Lt. Michael Ritter, the *Polk*'s radio officer, was seated to Kram's
left, eating a large bowl of chili. Directly across from him, Comdr.
Doug Gilbert, the SEAL team CO, was also eating chili, along with
Lt. Col. Lawrence Laycob of the Royal Marines. The blond-haired
Englishman was wearing his customary green woolen sweater, and
Kram could tell from the way he was devouring his meal that he
was enjoying himself.

"Looks like we all lucked out tonight," remarked the captain as
he pulled his blue napkin out of the thick silver ring that had his
name engraved on it. "I've got to start coming to midrats more
often."

"This dish is truly an extraordinary one," reflected the Englishman after spooning in a final mouthful of the savory concoction. "And to think that it doesn't contain an ounce of red meat."

The SEAL grunted. "Hell, as long as we've been on this pig boat, I can count on one hand the number of times we've been served a decent steak."

"Who needs steak when we've got turkey?" offered CPO Howard Mallott, as he emerged from the serving pantry. The portly head chef was dressed in khakis and a royal blue polo shirt. The crest of this shirt showed a palm tree with a colorful parrot superimposed on top of it, with JIMMY'S BUFFET embossed in gold below. He carried a tray with a large bowl of chili and a platter filled with chopped onion and shredded cheese.

Kram dug into his chili with gusto. It was as delicious as ever, and the only feedback that he needed to give Mallott was a single look of heavenly delight.

Mallott took this as his cue to leave, and he filled his tray with empty bowls before returning to the galley. This left the Polk's captain free to enjoy his meal, while his shipmates sipped their drinks.

"Captain," said the SEAL as he watched Kram spoon on some more onions. "Lieutenant Ritter was telling us about the radio problems that the boat's been experiencing. Do you think this will affect our ability to carry out this mission?"

Kram held back his reply until he swallowed the mouthful of beans that he had been chewing. "As long as conditions don't worsen further, I don't see how our difficulty establishing a clear VLF channel with Command will compromise the Polk's operational status. If they really need to reach us, there's always TACAMO to fall back on."

Kram shifted his focus to his communications officer. "I was planning on doing a complete walk-thru this shift, and the radio room was going to be one of my first stops this morning, Lieutenant. I take it that VLF remains inoperable."

Ritter nodded. "Nothing's changed since your last visit, sir. We get a few teasing seconds of clear channel, followed by long segments of static. Those solar flares are continuing to play havoc with our frequency propagation."

"I imagine that Talent and the other submarines in our flotilla are experiencing similar difficulties," supposed Laycob. "Certainly there must be other frequencies available to contact Command on."

"If the *Polk* really needed to deliver the mail, all we'd need to do is go to PD"—periscope depth—"and pop up our high-frequency antenna," said the SEAL matter of factly. "The trouble is, the *QE2* is moving so fast that if we were to slow down to surface, we'd end up losing the very ship that we've been assigned to ride shotgun on."

"The commander's right," said Kram. "Our main focus is keeping up with the *QE2*. These lousy atmospherics are bound to clear up eventually, and when they do, we'll be getting such an earful from the CNO that we'll be looking back at this radio blackout and praying for those sunspots to return."

As Kram's audience laughed at this remark, the intercom growled loudly. The nearest handset was mounted beneath the lip of the table. Kram reached down with his right hand and grabbed it.

"Captain," he said into the transmitter.

Whatever he was hearing caused a puzzled look to cloud his expression. "Are you absolutely certain?" he asked, as if he weren't hearing properly.

"Well, I'll be," he said with a grunt. "No, there's no need to wake the XO. Just make sure to log the exact time of the course change, and I'll join you in control shortly."

Kram hung up the handset, and met the curious stares of his dining companions. "That was the COB. A couple of minutes ago, sonar picked up an indication that the *QE2* has changed its course. It appears that they've broken off their great circle route, to proceed on a north-northeasterly heading of zero-three-zero."

"Perhaps they've spotted some ice in the area," suggested Lawrence Laycob.

"Or maybe weather has forced them to alter course," offered the SEAL.

"Whatever's happened up there," said Kram, his expression still pursed in thought, "it wasn't part of the original operational orders. I'm going to see about closing the distance between us and the *Queen*. Lieutenant Ritter, I want you to see if you can hail the *Talent* on the underwater telephone. Perhaps the Royal Navy can tell us what the hell is going on up there."

Comdr. Mark Eastbrook was a lucky man, and he knew it. To get command of his very own nuclear-powered attack sub, in these post–Cold War days of rapidly shrinking fleets, was an amazing turn of good fortune. To get this command having barely graduated secondary school, was simply incredible.

As he sat in his cabin, staring at the open pages of his diary, he realized that he must have had a guardian angel looking after him, on that rainy morning in 1975, when he joined the Royal Navy as a junior rate. A mere six years later, he completed initial officer training at Dartmouth's Britannia Naval College, having worked his way up the ranks via the Upper Yardman scheme.

He received his commission in time to see combat in the Falklands, where he was assigned to the destroyer HMS *Sheffield*. An Argentine exocet missile showed him the dangers of duty in the surface fleet. Severely burnt while fighting to save his ship, Eastbrook promised himself that if he survived that fateful day, he'd volunteer to spend the rest of his Royal Navy career as a submariner.

Survive he did, and following a succession of assignments aboard a number of submarines, he was selected for the command course in 1990. Perisher school was almost as tough as real combat. But he persevered, and after spending two years as the XO of the HMS *Trenchant*, and a stint in Groton, Connecticut, on exchange with the U.S. Navy, he was finally promoted to commander in 1995, when he also assumed command of the *Talent*.

This was quite a career path for the son of a Birmingham collier. But it only went to show that any man could work his way to the top, no matter one's social standing at birth, if an individual was willing to work hard, apply oneself, and make the necessary sacrifices.

His country had entrusted him with a warship worth many million pounds, one of the most sophisticated vessels ever to fly the white pennant. As commander of the third Royal Navy submarine to carry the name *Talent*, Eastbrook was also responsible for the lives of 111 officers and enlisted men. Never one to take his duty lightly, he knew that his current assignment was probably the most important of his entire career.

The halfway point of the crossing was rapidly approaching, and Eastbrook was so absorbed in his duty that sleep was all but impossible. To pass the lonely midnight watch, he sequestered himself in his cramped stateroom, one of the few private spaces in the equipment-packed vessel.

Even though his cabin was about the same size as his walk-in closet back home in Yelverton, he was not about to complain. East-brook had done his best to make the stateroom as comfortable as possible, including setting up a small stereo system. Currently playing in the background was a CD that the captain of the *Casabianca* had given him. Saint-Saëns's Symphony no. 3 was a new piece of music for him to enjoy, especially since it was orchestrated for the organ, one of his favorite instruments.

An abrupt knock on his cabin's closed door broke the music's spell and he replied with a curt, "Enter."

Quick to do so was the lean, six-foot figure of his executive officer. "I'm sorry to disturb you, Captain, but something's come up that I thought you should know about."

Eastbrook turned off the stereo and looked up to address his bearded shipmate. "No bother at all, Number One. I couldn't sleep anyway."

"It's the *Queen,* sir. She's broken from her great circle route, on a new course of zero-three-zero."

"Is it ice?" quizzed Eastbrook, thinking out loud.

"It's certainly possible, sir. Though pack ice in this portion of the Atlantic is usually limited to the Grand Banks sector."

Eastbrook glanced at the bulkhead-mounted, framed picture of the *QE2* at sea that the ocean liner's bearded master had given him. "It's most unlike Captain Prestwick to deviate from his planned route," he reflected. "It must be prompted by an environmental factor that we don't know about. Any change in the status of our inability to receive VLF?"

"Negative, sir. The chief RS has tried every filter available, yet the static remains."

"If only we could afford the luxury of going to periscope depth and establishing a high-frequency radio link with the *Queen,*" Eastbrook muttered. "But right now, all we can do is try to further decrease the distance between us. Inform the chief engineer that I'd like to up our speed to thirty knots. And make our new course zero-three-zero. Once this has been attained, I think it's best if we try to contact the *Polk.* Perhaps the Yanks know the reason behind this unexpected detour."

Commissar Guan Yin couldn't have been more satisfied with the *Lijiang*'s continued progress. Ever since successfully penetrating the

GIUK gap, a certain sense of expectation had filled the vessel. After the thousands of kilometers of hazardous underwater travel, they were finally closing in on their mission's ultimate goal. And even though the majority of the crew hadn't been briefed on the exact purpose of their mission, all seemed to be aware that they were approaching some moment of truth.

Morale remained excellent, with not a vacant chair available during his last Komsomol meeting. Above all, the men genuinely appeared to be taken with their new captain, as was Guan.

Several of the crew had recently taken to abandoning their uniforms, and standing their watches clothed in their own martial-arts robes. At first, this upset Guan. But then he realized that the men were only trying to imitate their commanding officer, who continued wearing his own unique outfit of white robe, matching cotton trousers, black belt, and bright red headband.

Unlike their previous captain's American poopy suit, Lee Shao-chi's outfit resembled more the traditional uniforms of China's ancient warriors. It was nothing to be ashamed of, and the commissar decided that he could overlook this minor infraction.

The control-room watch that Guan was presently standing had two members thusly dressed. One was Lt. Comdr. Deng Biao. The XO stood on the adjoining periscope pedestal clothed in his white cotton-twill robe that was closed at the waist with a brown cloth belt. This color indicated the level of his martial-arts skills, one below that of their captain.

It was well after midnight, and the *Lijiang* was headed almost due south, at flank speed. As always, the muted red lights that illuminated this compartment gave the control room a sinister appearance. A hushed quiet prevailed, with the only audible sounds being the soft hum of the ventilation blowers and the distant drone of the sub's single propeller shaft.

Beside him, the boat's navigator was making the latest course update at the plotting table. A recent check of this chart showed that the long-anticipated geological feature known as the Hecate Seamount was well within reach. Named after the Greek goddess of the underworld, the seas above this underwater mountain were a fitting place in which to unfold their mission's next all-important stage.

Guan's calculations indicated that the *Lijiang* should be able to actually hear their quarry. The navigator agreed with him, and together they had discussed the numerous factors that could have delayed their prey.

Patience had never been one of the commissar's virtues, and when the door to the sonar room swung open and out strode the captain, Guan expectantly made his way over to the XO's side. Lee Shao-chi navigated a straight course directly to the periscope pedestal. He climbed up onto the conn and studied the dozens of glowing dials and gauges mounted into the bulkhead above the helm. Apparently satisfied with what he was seeing, Lee shut his eyes and initiated a series of deep, even breaths.

"Comrades!" he shouted, his eyelids tightly sealed. "The time is right for you to return with me on the path homeward. Close your eyes, and empty your cluttered minds by expelling your breath to its limit. Then refill your lungs with the sweet essence of life, and prepare yourself for the strategy of the Way."

Guan decided that it would do no harm to obey their captain's unusual directive. Yet before shutting his eyes, he noticed that his shipmates had already followed Lee's instructions without question.

What a strange sight this would make to an outsider, thought Guan, as he closed his eyes tight and purged the air from his lungs. He forced himself to do this completely, before inhaling the deepest breath possible, and then repeating the process. He did this three complete times, and was in the middle of his fourth inhalation, when the captain's forceful voice boomed forth once again.

"Comrades, above all else, you must know yourself before attempting to know your enemy. Make your body like a rock, and a thousand things can't touch you. By training one's body and spirit, you need never doubt that you will prevail in combat.

"I have just heard with my own ears, the great ship that we have been sent on this long voyage to intercept. Aboard this surface vessel, nine of China's most-feared enemies are hopefully being held captive by fellow followers of the Way. The *Lijiang* shall rendezvous with this ship, and the nine traitors transferred into our hold for safekeeping.

"Yet before this rendezvous can be safely initiated, an unexpected obstacle has been brought to my attention that must be dealt with. Sonar indicates that we share these waters with a Russian *Akula*-class submarine. I fear that our enemy has cleverly assigned this formidable warship with the task of protecting the surface vessel that we seek. I also suspect that there are other submarines that have yet to be detected in these same waters. We must scour these seas clear of every suspected adversary before this most vital of missions can be completed.

"And how will we achieve this difficult task, you might ask? We shall first recognize the enemy's strategy, to determine his weak and strong points. And if we still remain unable to determine his position, we shall feint an attack on the *Akula,* and cause our opponent to ultimately show his hand. And only then will we attack, with lethal force and an unsuspected manner."

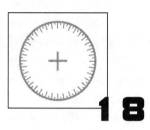

18

I*T WAS A SIMPLE PAPER CUT, OF ALL THINGS, THAT KEPT* T*UFF FROM AT-*
tending the gala banquet. The broad-shouldered security officer had
been on his way to the Queens Grill when he decided to make a
quick stop at the Security Office to see how his replacement was
doing. You can never be too sure, he thought.

He found Annie Cooksey seated behind the camera console in
the midst of an automatic scan of the ship's public spaces. Annie
was a former London bobby, who after a nasty divorce, decided that
a complete change of lifestyles was in order. In the past year, she
was invited by Robert Hartwell to join their staff. She had no ties to
speak of locking her to land, so she readily accepted.

Tuff had the pier watch when Annie arrived in Southampton for
her first day on the job. He liked her straight off. Attractive in a
matronly way, she had a sparkling personality and had been an
important part of their small security staff ever since.

Tuff took a quick look at the security-watch sheet, but when he
handed it back to Annie, the edge sliced open her right index finger.
She tried to stem the sudden flow of blood by sucking on her finger,
but when this tried-and-true method failed, she began a frantic
search for a Kleenex.

The only handkerchief that Tuff could offer was the silken one
that graced his tuxedo's breast pocket. Annie wouldn't hear of such

a thing, and it was then she asked him if he'd mind holding down the fort for her, while she tried to track down a real bandage.

Being a proper gentleman, Tuff assented without hesitation. With Annie's exit, he decided to pass the time manipulating those security cameras placed in and around the Queens Grill.

From a variety of angles he watched the first summiteers arrive, then spied on his boss and some of the other agents. Dinnertime was rapidly approaching, and with no Annie in sight, he checked out the ship's Infirmary. Sure enough, that's where he found his blonde associate. Annie was helping one of the nurses attend to a steward who appeared to have been the recent victim of a twisted ankle. A close-up showed that she already had her Band-Aid in place over her finger, and though Tuff could have called her on the phone to hurry her on, he decided that her efforts at the moment were more important than the high-calorie meal he'd most likely miss.

Annie was all apologies when she arrived back in security a good twenty minutes later. By the monitors Tuff saw that the diners had long since assembled, their appetizers already served. He was still debating whether to join them, when the entire wall of video screens suddenly went black.

He knew that this surely signaled the end of any formal dinner plans that he might have had. With a resolute sigh, he took off his jacket, rolled up his sleeves, and headed for the adjoining electrical panel to check the circuit breaker.

This panel was located in a cramped access space that was set into the bulkhead immediately behind the security room. A key was needed to open the elongated wall panel that lay to the right of the main video console. A wire ventilation grill was mounted in this panel that Tuff pulled open and closed behind him.

The narrow compartment he now found himself in was packed with dozens of snaking cables that led from the back of each monitor and extended into a central conduit. This main trunk eventually found its way to each of the security cameras located throughout the ship.

The electrical panel was locked, and Tuff had to return to Robert Hartwell's office to get the proper key. Along the way, he tripped over an Astroturf putting carpet that the Scotsman had recently set up in the middle of his office. This in turn knocked over a large bucket of golf balls that went rolling in a hundred different directions, as diverted by the constant pitching of the deck.

It took another ten minutes to round up all the balls, and several more to find the right key and return to the monitor room. Annie, turning from the screens, appeared to have been enjoying his trials and tribulations, and he brushed aside her mocking offer to check the circuit breaker in his place.

As he reentered the stowage space, a large swell caused the access panel to slam shut. The overhead light flickered, and finally failed altogether. This forced him to pull out his trusty Maglite, which he always kept clipped to his belt beside his holstered Beretta.

Tuff located the electrical box on the opposite wall. With barely enough space in which to turn around, he inserted the key and opened up the panel, all the while shifting his weight to compensate for the pitching deck.

A cursory inspection found all the circuit breakers open. He double-checked each of them with his hand, and determined that this was going to be a job for the ship's electrician.

It was as he shut the circuit breaker panel that he heard Annie in the adjoining security room arguing with another man.

Tuff didn't like the man's tone of voice. He shut off the Maglite, hunched over, and as quietly as possible, made his way over to the access panel's ventilation grill.

What he saw there both shocked and sickened him. Standing in the middle of the room, in the process of binding Annie's wrists together with electrical tape, were two hooded, black-clad individuals. Both of them were armed with Sterling submachine guns, and Tuff noted that the security monitors were somehow working once more.

His first hope was that this was nothing but a realistic drill, secretly planned and implemented by Robert Hartwell to test their readiness. Unfortunately, the rough manner in which they were treating Annie didn't correspond to a mere drill. This fact was further proved when one of the intruders pulled off his mask.

Tuff took a look at the man's slicked-back brown hair and narrow green eyes, and identified him as a new member of the ship's Gym staff. While his associate taped Annie's mouth shut, the lanky male sat down at the console and expertly addressed the keyboard. Tuff watched as he managed to fill each of the screens with a different view of the Queens Grill. The diners were well into their entrées, and seeing this seemed to spur the intruder into action. He stood and addressed his associate, totally unaware that he was being over-heard by Tuff.

"I'll take care of the bitch. I want you to work the console just like I taught you. Don't be afraid to contact me on the two-way the moment that something doesn't look right. Because like I said before, the first hour will be the most important."

With this, he grabbed Annie roughly by the upper arm, and forc-ibly led her out of the room. Tuff fought the urge to pull out his pistol and go to Annie's rescue, and he let his SBS training take over. He calmed himself with a series of breaths, and carefully weighed his options.

If what he was witnessing was indeed what it seemed, a carefully orchestrated takeover of the ship, he could very well be one of the only crew members in a position to do something about it. This was surely every security man's greatest nightmare.

Tuff realized that it was too late to alert the heads of state. He decided instead to abandon the gun-blazing, lone-hero, Hollywood approach, and do the obvious: get word of this unthinkable event to the outside world.

Since securing the QE2's Radio Room would be one of the hijack-er's primary objectives, Tuff's next best alternative was to get to Doc Benedict's ham radio set. By the good grace of God, and a desire to get better reception, Benedict had recently moved this set up to an auxiliary stowage space, beneath the funnel, up above the Signal Deck. Not a single security camera covered this infrequently visited portion of the ship that many long-time crew members didn't even know existed. Tuff's problem now was to get there without being discovered. From where he was, the storage space with the radio was six decks straight up.

Tuff looked to the ceiling, where another ventilation grill beck-oned invitingly. This opening led into the ship's air-duct system. These shafts extended to almost every portion of the ship, and since they were fully accessible to the maintenance staff, Tuff supposed that the ducts were wide enough to fit his beefy torso.

Tuff could barely reach the square metal grill by standing on his toes. He used a penknife to pry it loose, and as quietly as possible, he yanked the grill free and set it aside. He then reached up, grabbed the edge of the opening, and with a grunt, lifted his body upward.

From the security room he heard the wheels on the chair squeak. Had he been heard? With his feet still dangling down into the storage space he would be readily spotted. Tuff braced himself there, scarcely breathing. After a moment, he didn't hear the chair move again or the hijacker get up to investigate, so he pulled himself the rest of the way up.

The sheet-metal shaft inside which he now found himself proved to be just wide enough to fit his shoulders. It was pitch black, and while a cool gust of air-conditioned air hit him in the face, Tuff stabilized himself on the stirrup-shaped, iron handholds that lined the shaft's square interior. With a bit of difficulty, he worked his hand down to his waistband and pulled out his Maglite. Because he needed both hands free for climbing, he had to put the pencil-thin, compact flashlight in his mouth, and in this manner illuminated the shaft's dark recesses.

He climbed upward for a good five minutes before reaching a portion of the duct system that was intersected by a parallel shaft. This duct appeared to extend into both the forward or aft sections of the ship, and Tuff decided to see if he'd be able to reach the E-elevator shaft by moving forward.

Travel now was by crawling on his hands and knees. The bare metallic surface of the duct was icy cold, and Tuff wished that he had brought along a warm pair of gloves. He supposed that he was somewhere in One Deck's ceiling, verifying this when he crawled over an open ventilation grill and spotted the darkened, vacant interior of the hairdressing salon. Encouraged by this sight, he tried his best to ignore the bitter chill and a rising sensation of claustrophobia.

The rest of his journey in the tight confines of the duct was thankfully short. The beam of his flashlight found a circular, port-hole-shaped accessway, cut into the shaft before him. Tuff squeezed his body through this opening, and allowed himself a relieved sigh only upon viewing the cable-lined interior of the elevator shaft he had been seeking.

A proper iron-rung ladder was mounted into the aft wall of the shaft, and it extended all the way up to the Signal Deck. The steep climb went quickly. When Tuff finally crawled out of the blackened shaft, he found himself in a portion of passageway just aft of the Kennels. The nearest security camera was in the Kennel itself. Tuff headed in the opposite direction, to a closed iron door that had a CREW ACCESS ONLY warning sign on it.

Lady Fortune was again with him upon finding it unlocked. He swung the door open, and a gust of cool, fresh ocean air enveloped him.

The steady, pounding drone of the engines was clearly audible, and a thick cloud of dark smoke could be seen pouring from the funnel. The compartment he wished to reach was situated only a few steps away. He crossed the open deck and anxiously reached for the door latch.

The sound of the lock activating was music to his ears. He ducked inside, flicked on the overhead light, and hastily surveyed the room. Not much bigger than a small cabin, the stowage space was cluttered with painting equipment and all sorts of spare deck gear. He located the object of his search against the far wall. Solidly anchored between two wooden cases of paint was Doc Benedict's blessed ham radio set.

Never again would Tuff complain when the ship's physician cornered him to brag about his latest radio contact. As an avid ham enthusiast, the Doc took advantage of their time at sea to establish a worldwide network of fellow radio enthusiasts. During one crossing, he had even talked with the Space Shuttle. The event was memorialized on Doc's office wall, where a framed photo of the shuttle was hung, complete with a signature from the very astronaut he had spoken to.

As Tuff pulled out the padded leather chair that Doc used during his long radio sessions, he realized that this room would also make an excellent base of operations. It even had its own coffee maker, and a decent supply of tea bags and cocoa. The only real problem he'd have to cope with was the room's lack of direct heat. The North Atlantic could get awfully chilly, even during summer. Yet Tuff hadn't earned his nickname by being a pampered softy. As one who had survived his fair share of exposed bivouacs on Dartmoor and Goose Green, he'd manage to persevere.

Well versed in the operation of several types of military radios, Tuff reached out and flipped on the ham's power switch. A green light activated, and the ex-commando adjusted the frequency dial in anticipation of informing the world of the *Queen*'s dilemma.

*   *   *

"Damn it!" cursed Vince, in a tone expressing more frustration than anger. "And to think I was probably down in the Gym when they were making the final preparations for the takeover."

Still seated at his table in the Queens Grill, Vince's vacant stare surveyed the four, black-clad terrorists patrolling the dining room's balcony, submachine guns at the ready. Both Samuel Morrison and Robert Hartwell were seated beside him. Their pistols had long since been confiscated and removed from the room, and they could only remain there until otherwise ordered.

"I still think you're taking this whole frigging thing much too personally," whispered Morrison to his subordinate. "Believe me, we all share equal responsibility for this nightmare."

On the far side of the room, Dr. Patton and Ricky did their best to attend to the four Chinese agents who had survived the shooting. The lifeless bodies of their two associates had already been removed, and because the terrorists wouldn't let them transfer the badly wounded survivors to the Hospital, it looked like they'd bleed to death unless proper care could be administered.

"At least our honored guests appear to be taking this hijacking all in stride," observed Hartwell, in reference to the nine heads of state, who were still gathered at their table in the center of the room.

"I bet the bastards hid their weapons inside that gym equipment," continued Vince, unable to shift the self-incriminating focus of his thoughts. "I should have ordered New York Customs to unwrap the gear and break it down for closer examination."

"We still don't know that's the way they smuggled in their armaments," remarked Morrison.

"From the looks of things, I'd say that they've been using the ship's laundry to bring their contraband on board," said Hartwell, who waited until one of the sentries strolled by before adding, "Ammunition could have easily been concealed inside the sacks of detergent and other dry-cleaning chemicals that were recently delivered to Chinatown."

"It looks like your old friend Ping really did a number on us," said Vince.

"I'd say that we don't have to look any further to determine the source of that food-poisoning outbreak," Morrison added.

"I still can't get over the way I allowed myself to be snowed by those two actors," said Vince. "I was nothing but a star-struck fool!"

"Easy does it, Vince," Morrison cautioned. "Don't forget that my team was responsible for doing the background checks on Liu and his cronies. If anyone's to blame for this frigging mess, it's me."

Robert Hartwell didn't like the direction in which this whispered, guilt-ridden conversation was headed, and he did his best to change the focus. "All this talk about blame is meaningless at the moment, chaps. Right now, I think it's best if we concentrate our thoughts on how we're going to rectify our mistakes."

"Robert's right," agreed Morrison, who gestured toward an adjoining table where a restless group of French, Italian, and German security agents were seated. "I'm afraid that our colleagues might go and try something desperate."

"I think it's best if we try to circulate a note to the other tables, emphasizing the vital importance of restraint," Hartwell quietly advised. "A coordinated response is our only chance to retake the ship. Any premature move now will only result in more needless death and carnage."

Samuel Morrison nodded in agreement. "The bastards are bound to drop their guard eventually, and that's when we'll strike."

"I wonder where the rest of the crew is being held, and if there have been other casualties?" asked Vince.

"My best guess is that it's merely business as usual for the others," offered the Scotsman. "Don't forget that we're the hostages. All Liu has to do is remind the crew of that fact to keep them in line. I'm hoping that someone has managed to slip away. This is an awfully big ship, and one of my staff could easily be hiding in the shadows, organizing a plan of attack even as we speak."

"And I guess we shouldn't give up on an outside rescue effort just yet," reminded Vince. "Washington's bound to realize that something's wrong next time they attempt calling us, and it's only a matter of time until they send in the cavalry."

"And what cavalry are you referring to, Special Agent?" Hartwell questioned. "You forget that we're in the middle of the bloody Atlantic Ocean."

Vince looked at the QE2's security director and answered resolutely. "I believe that there's a little lady called the USS *Iwo Jima* in the vicinity. And though they won't be arriving by horseback, I sure wouldn't want to be in Dennis Liu's shoes when the guys from Delta Force come dropping in to find out what the hell is going on down here."

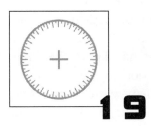

1 9

LITTLE DID VINCE KELLOGG REALIZE, BUT THE ORDERS TO THE USS *IWO JIMA* mobilizing Delta Force had already been issued. This alert was the result of the Pentagon's continued inability to establish radio contact with the *QE2*, and the failure of the National Reconnaissance Office to provide them with an operational reconnaissance satellite. Until a Canadian Aurora patrol aircraft could be flown in from Nova Scotia, or contact finally reestablished with one of their submarine escorts, Command had no alternative but to assume that a worst-case scenario existed.

To address this nightmarish possibility, the NCA was relying on the *Iwo Jima*'s helicopter borne commando units to provide visual proof that the ocean liner was still afloat. Op Center Bravo was the origin of these orders, and the current clearinghouse for all incoming theater updates. As such, it was packed with personnel including General Ridgeway, Admiral Buchanan, Brittany Cooper, their staffs, and a newly arrived Thomas Kellogg, who headed straight for the Pentagon from the hills of West Virginia, after being unable to make contact with the *QE2* himself.

A static-filled radio link with the storm-tossed *Iwo Jima* allowed them to get a real-time report of the rescue force's liftoff. Hurricane Marti's howling winds and pounding seas made the midnight disembarkation an extra hazardous one, with two Marine CH-53E Super

Stallion helicopters used to carry out the mission. Each of these all-weather-capable aircraft was tasked with carrying a different unit that included Delta Force and SEAL Team Six.

As it turned out, the only helicopter that was able to get safely airborne was the one carrying Delta Force. An overheated engine scrubbed the SEAL team's chopper while it was barely in test hover, and the weather kept a replacement helicopter pinned to the rain-soaked deck.

Being a former air force commando, Thomas knew that they were lucky that at least one of the units was good to go. The Super Stallion was an incredibly sophisticated platform, with state-of-the-art avionics. Capable of flying at 196 miles per hour, with a range of 540 nautical miles, one CH-53E would be more than sufficient to do the job at hand. The hope now was that it wouldn't experience mechanical difficulties and be forced to return to the *Iwo Jima.*

Thomas listened to the static-filled voice of Flight Tango Zulu's pilot as it was relayed into the op center. It wasn't all that long ago that he could have been one of those soldiers prepping themselves for action in the back of that chopper. There was nothing that could equal that feeling of anxious anticipation, as the pilot put the helicopter into hover, the rear tail door was lowered, and the fast ropes deployed. He knew that a proficient squad of commandos could clear a helicopter in a couple of minutes. This was the ultimate rush, one that easily rivaled freefall in intensity.

Under ideal conditions, the Super Stallion could have reached the *QE2*'s last-known position in a little more than a half hour. The presence of the hurricane changed all that, the swirling, multidirectional wind gusts making the mere act of flying a challenge.

Confident that the chopper's three General Electric T-64-GE-416 turboshaft engines would get them through the storm, Thomas was somewhat surprised when he was invited to join the chairman of the Joint Chiefs of Staff, the CNO, and Brittany in the conference room. Thomas and General Ridgeway had originally met during Urgent Fury, and it was the chairman who asked Thomas to brief them on his recently concluded investigation.

Though Thomas was still anxious for more information about the *QE2,* he presented the details leading up to the arrest of their two suspects only a few hours earlier. As he was documenting their lead suspect's admission that his threat on the *QE2* had no real substance,

Lieutenant Tolliver entered the room. The junior officer handed Brittany a fax, which she read while Thomas began a hasty summation.

"What's this all about, Lieutenant?" she asked once Thomas had completed his brief.

There was a hopeful gleam in Tolliver's eyes as he replied. "All I can tell you, sir, is that the Coast Guard auxiliary watch center at Bath, Maine, sent us this fax. It was generated by a garbled ham radio transmission that they picked up less than fifteen minutes ago. And what makes it interesting is that those signal letters and official number are assigned to one vessel only, and that's the QE2!"

"Then they're still out there!" exclaimed Brittany, whose remarks were cut short by the loud, crackling voice of Flight Tango Zulu's pilot, from the overhead PA speakers.

"Roger that, mother base. Going down to five hundred and fifty feet, one hundred and thirty knots, approximately twenty miles to target."

A burst of static momentarily interrupted the transmission. When it finally cleared, it was the nasally voice of the Iwo Jima's air-traffic controller that they heard next.

"Aye, Tango Zulu. Target should be in sight, on bearing zero-two-fiver. Over."

"Roger that, mother base. We have a visual on target, bearing zero-two-fiver, range one-niner miles and closing."

This vital information was delivered in such a rote, informal manner, that for the first second or two, not a single occupant of the conference room reacted to it. Only when the reality sank in, did Brittany express the relief that all of them were sharing.

"They found her!" she shouted. "They found the Queen!"

Dennis Liu couldn't believe how smoothly things had gone so far. Like an award-winning movie production, the takeover of the giant ocean liner had proceeded with split-second timing and superb coordination. All of the vital watch stations had been taken, with his people currently placed in strategic areas throughout the ship to guarantee that their captives wouldn't try to challenge them.

Having the nine heads of state as hostages was the ultimate bargaining chip, and Liu doubted that any of the crew would do anything foolish to compromise their safety. Yet as a student of the Way, Liu knew that he had to be prepared for every contingency, no matter how improbable it might seem.

To insure that Sunny had properly secured the Bridge, he decided to pay it a personal visit. As he climbed up its accessway, he visualized his assault force as they climbed these same steps in preparation for their initial takeover. This act was timed to coincide with Liu's own arrival in the Queens Grill.

To get past the security camera monitoring the Bridge's locked doorway, they used one of the Philippine stewards as a decoy. A gun pointed at his back insured his cooperation. Once his identity was confirmed by the Bridge watch, the automatic bolts were triggered, with Sunny and his two-man force now free to burst into the Control Room.

Liu was afforded the luxury of merely having to press the doorbell two times and looking up to the lens of the overhead video camera, to gain entrance. The door lock automatically unbolted itself with a loud buzz, and he entered what was now *his* Bridge.

A gust of whistling wind engulfed him as the air pressure was suddenly equalized. The light was dim here, to protect the watch stander's night vision. As his eyes adjusted, he spotted Sunny standing behind the softly glowing luminescent dials of the center console. His associate was armed with an MP-5 submachine gun that he had casually trained on the two officers seated on tall stools before an auxiliary navigation plot. Liu recognized them as the ship's first officer and his navigator. Both of them were rather calmly sipping their teas, their stares lost in the black seas visible out the forward observation windows.

Liu had to steady himself against the side of one of the navigation consoles when a large swell rocked the ship. By glancing down at the console's display screen, he was able to determine that the *QE2* had broken out of its previous great circle route, and was presently headed on a north-by-northeasterly course, away from the normal transatlantic shipping lanes and the probing eyes of the pre-positioned recon satellites above.

By addressing the console's ball-shaped mouse with the palm of his right hand, Liu was able to determine that at their present speed and course, they'd be passing over the Hecate Seamount shortly after dawn. His old friend Lee Shao-chi and the crew of the *Lijiang* should be waiting for them there, and the next portion of their mission would then be initiated.

Satisfied that all looked well, Liu joined Sunny behind the helm. "Well, comrade," whispered Liu in Mandarin. "I gather that things went smoothly."

Sunny replied without shifting his glance from the two officers. "Incredibly so. The big lady handles like a dream, and so far, I've barely heard a peep out of the officers; no complaints, no questions, nothing."

"Typical stubborn English resolve," observed Liu. "But don't kid yourself. They know that we're their new masters, and they will continue to serve us as long as we can keep the upper hand. But to further eliminate the temptation and insure that they don't attempt to compromise the secrecy of our position, I'm going to make certain that the Bridge's emergency-locator equipment is disconnected. Only then will this ship's destiny truly be ours."

"Per your instructions, I've already cut the power to the VHF and HF radio telephones," revealed Sunny. "I also deactivated the dual GMDSS sets that were mounted behind the navigation plot, right where you said they'd be."

An acronym for Global Maritime Distress and Safety System, the GMDSS was designed to automatically send a long-range distress signal to a series of orbiting satellites.

"And the distress buoys on the Bridge wings?" queried Liu, in reference to the final system that had to be dealt with.

Sunny shamefully shook his head. "I'm afraid that I forgot about them," he admitted.

"No matter. I'll deal with it," offered Liu, who left Sunny with a supportive pat on the back and took off for the starboard wing.

The cool air outside was refreshing. He readily spotted the bright orange buoy that he was looking for, hanging on the aft rail. Known as the Emergency Position Indicator Radio Beacon, or EPIRB for short, this buoy merely had to hit the water to activate and send a satellite-relayed, hourly position update to NOAA headquarters in Washington, D.C.

It was after he ripped out its battery pack and tossed it overboard that he surveyed the cloud-filled night sky. An unexpected flash of lightning momentarily lit up the distant horizon directly astern of them. Liu supposed that this was the first sign of Hurricane Marti's northern fringe.

He looked on mesmerized, as yet more lightning illuminated the heavens—and briefly highlighted an alien black speck high in the sky. Another jagged bolt of lightning lit the skies, and revealed it was steadily increasing in size.

Liu cursed with the realization that this object was a helicopter—bound directly for them! A surge of anger-generated adrenalin coursed through his body, and like the trained warrior he was, his only thought was of countering this potential threat from above.

"Incoming helicopter, directly astern!" he warned Sunny as he rushed inside and headed for the aft doorway. "Inform Monica and Bear to meet me at the helipad, and make certain that they bring along the RPGs!"

Liu mentally calculated the most direct route to the helipad that was located on the aft end of the Sports Deck, and he exited the Bridge and hurried down the stairs. It was his New York-based, black-market arms dealer who had urged him to take along the two RPG-7D, lightweight, portable rocket launchers. They had been previously stolen from an armory in New Jersey, and subsequently hidden away inside the recesses of their rowing machine. Each of the RPGs came complete with a 4.95-pound, HEAT improved, fused warhead that had been smuggled aboard in a sack of detergent bound for the QE2's Laundry. With a range of 328 yards and a muzzle velocity of 984 feet per second, the warhead could play havoc with a helicopter's vulnerable tail rotor, especially when delivered on target via the launcher's NSP-2 infrared-guided night sight.

But all of this would mean little if the airborne intruder beat him to the helipad. Liu sprinted toward the exterior deck accessway adjoining the nearby Radio Room. This route would lead him directly aft, with the helipad only a single deck above.

"One hundred feet. One hundred and eighteen knots. Eight miles out."

A burst of static swallowed the transmission from the Super Stallion, and the occupants of the op center's conference room anxiously stirred. Included in this group was Thomas Kellogg, who traded a concerned glance with Brittany as the interference finally cleared.

"Ninety feet. One hundred and seventeen knots. Seven-point-five miles out."

"Kind of makes you miss the old days, doesn't it, Thomas?" remarked General Ridgeway, an introspective grin on his weather-beaten face.

"That it does, sir," Thomas replied.

His recollections of serving under Ridgeway's command during the Grenada invasion were mixed. The way Thomas saw it, the general failed to make the best use of the Air Commandos' varied skills, and insisted that they operate under Green Beret or SEAL coverage. Of course, this was in the early days of joint operations, and the mere fact of having an Army special forces officer in charge of an Air Force unit, was still something of a novelty.

"Special Agent Kellogg," interjected Admiral Buchanan. "Weren't you involved in a similar helicopter mission back in eighty-five that was tasked to attempt a rescue aboard the *Achille Lauro?*"

"Actually, Admiral, I was part of a special unit that was training to clandestinely board the cruise ship via parachute," Thomas revealed.

"I didn't think that such a thing was even possible," remarked Brittany.

Thomas held back his response until Tango Zulu's pilot reported their latest position.

"Eighty-five feet. One hundred and eighteen knots. Six-point-eight miles out."

"Though I wouldn't want to make it a habit," said Thomas as the garbled transmission faded. "To insure a safe landing at sea, all you really need to do is properly gauge both the crosswinds and the forward speed of your target. In preparation for our aborted attempt, I successfully completed a half dozen HALO jumps onto the deck of the USS *Saratoga.*"

"Seventy-eight feet. One hundred and seventeen knots. Six-point-three miles out," continued the pilot with rote exactness.

Thomas couldn't help but visualize Tango Zulu's Marine pilot. He'd be seated on the right side of the Super Stallion's cockpit. Because the helicopter was steadily losing altitude in preparation for its fast-rope deployment, the pilot would be pushing down on the collective-pitch stick with his left hand. This in turn would cause the throttle to retard and decrease the degree of pitch of the blades, to move the 70,000-pound helicopter downward. He'd also be manipulating the cyclic-pitch stick with his right hand, as well as the dual pedals with his feet, to keep the craft on course by influencing the action of the main and tail rotors.

Altogether, flying a helicopter required excellent physical coordination and superb training. The mere fact that Tango Zulu's pilot was assigned to this crack unit, indicated that he had these qualities and many others. For, as Thomas knew from firsthand experience, Marine chopper pilots were some of the best in the business.

"Seventy feet. One hundred seventeen knots. Five-point-one out," the pilot reported.

"I'm still wondering how those security teams aboard the *QE2* are going to react to the squad's arrival," said General Ridgeway. "I'd feel a lot better if we had been able to get out a clean message, informing them of Tango Zulu's arrival."

"I hope that the reaction of those shipboard security teams is the extent of our problem," returned the CNO.

Both Thomas and Brittany heard the worry in the Admiral's voice. Buchanan had already admitted that he wouldn't be able to rest until he knew for certain the reason behind the *QE2*'s unexplained course change and the complete failure of its communications equipment.

"Sixty-seven feet. One hundred eighteen knots. Four-point-three out."

This latest update indicated that the mystery would soon be solved, and Thomas felt his pulse quicken. He was also aware of a slight anxious knot gathering in the pit of his stomach.

"Sixty feet. One hundred seventeen knots. Two-point-three out. This will be a left-turning approach . . . We're good to go. LZ's on the nose . . . One minute out . . . I've got the spot . . . Stand by for ropes . . . Good hover."

There was an excited tenseness to the pilot's voice, and Thomas could picture the chaotic scene taking place in the helicopter's rear cabin. At the open ramp, the helmeted flight engineer would be preparing to deploy the forty-five-foot-long fast ropes. Behind him, the heavily armed members of Delta Force would be awaiting the order from the pilot that would send them sliding down these ropes in quick succession to the deck of the awaiting ocean liner.

"Stand by for ropes," instructed the pilot. "Forty-seven feet. Good hover . . . Pro—"

A burst of static momentarily cut the pilot off in midsentence, only to be followed by a terrified outburst, that none of the occupants of the op center would soon forget.

"Jesus, RPG at four o'clock! . . . There's a launch . . . We've been hit! . . . We've lost the tail rotor . . . Fuckin' hold on. We're goin' in! We're goin' . . ."

There was another deafening burst of static before all went silent. Stunned and horrified by this unexpected turn of events, the shocked occupants of Op Center Bravo peered up at the ceiling-mounted PA speakers as if willing the next update to come forth. Yet none came, and a wave of alarmed chatter filled the room with a somber resonance.

"I knew this damned crossing was no good from the start," declared the CNO bitterly. "What the hell is going on out there?"

"Easy now, Richard," advised Ridgeway, his own furrowed brow tightly knit with concern. "It's evident that we've got a pack of rats aboard the *Queen,* and now it's up to us to take the situation in hand and figure out another way to address it."

Thomas dared to take the role of devil's advocate. "Perhaps what that pilot saw wasn't an RPG after all. For all we know, it could have been a deflected bolt of lightning that knocked them out of the air."

Before Ridgeway could argue otherwise, Lieutenant Tolliver's booming voice projected from the PA, "We've got an emergency transmission coming in from the *QE2!* Pipe down, people!"

All eyes went to Tolliver's workstation at the front of the room as he addressed his keyboard, and rerouted this transmission through the room's speakers. A momentary flutter of static was followed by the steady, deep voice of a single male. He was apparently caught in midsentence, his words clear and crisply delivered.

"Once more, this is the voice of the legitimate People's Republic of China, calling to you from the ocean liner *QE2* in the mid-Atlantic. Do you acknowledge? Over."

Tolliver looked up from his keyboard, to the knot of senior officers gathered at the back of the room. "Should I acknowledge?" he asked, his strained voice cracking.

"Do it!" ordered Ridgeway.

Without further hesitation, Tolliver addressed his keyboard, and spoke into his throat microphone. "This is the National Military Command Center acknowledging your message. Over."

"I copy that," returned the amplified male voice. "The conditions of this transmission are as follows: No broadcast interruptions, except for technical reasons, will be tolerated. There are to be no questions on your part, and no negotiations. Do you accept these conditions?"

By this time, both General Ridgeway and Admiral Buchanan had arrived at Tolliver's side, and both senior officers nodded affirmatively.

"I accept the conditions. Over," returned Tolliver, who alertly activated the console's digital-tape machine to record the conversation.

"Very well, National Military Command Center, this is our manifesto:

"Number One: Be it known that Li Chen, the current president of the People's Republic of China, has assumed his position of power illegally. As such, he does not represent the will of the Chinese people and is to be returned to the Republic and tried for the crime of treason. All international agreements and treaties made by Li Chen are to be deemed null and void.

"Number Two: The People's Republic is to be granted full and irrevocable geopolitical control of the Spratly Island chain. The governments of the Philippines, Malaysia, Brunei, Vietnam, or any other country laying claim to these islands and their surrounding seas, shall publicly disavow their claims before an international tribunal of our choosing.

"Number Three: The island of Taiwan is to be immediately returned to its rightful place in the People's Republic. Its present illegitimate government is to be given a chance to recant, and admit to the world community the errors of its ways. Then, like Hong Kong, they too will become at one with their motherland.

"All of these demands are nonnegotiable, and are to be drafted in treaty form at United Nations headquarters, and signed by all members of the Security Council no later than three days from now. Until this document is delivered to us, we shall continue to hold the eight heads of state, and the traitor Li Chen, in protective custody.

"Let it be stressed that it is not our intention to indiscriminately kill. We reserve the right to do so only when justly provoked. Any sign of another rescue attempt on your part, like the helicopter assault we have already repelled, shall be considered an act of provocation, and will be responded to accordingly.

"The military forces of the People's Liberation Army have already been placed on alert, and shall be authorized to respond with all offensive systems at their disposal, including nuclear weapons. The release codes of these strategic delivery systems are already in our rightful possession. Any preemptive strike against us shall be deemed an attack against the Republic, and will result in a nuclear strike of global proportions. We also reserve the right to destroy the ship on which we travel, as a further expression of the sincerity of our demands.

"This, then, is the extent of our manifesto. Never doubt our will. Long live the Republic!"

With this, the radio link unceremoniously went dead, and a concerned murmur filled the operations center. Not bothering to silence his staff, the CNO ordered Tolliver to get a copy of this tape to Naval Intelligence with all due haste. Not only did its legitimacy have to be assured, but the voice analyzed in an attempt to identify the caller.

Thomas once more found himself part of a small group of individuals invited back into the conference room by General Ridgeway. As he sat down between Brittany and the CNO, Thomas listened as a spirited discussion of their options ensued.

A terrorist takeover of the *QE2* was one of the worst-case scenarios that Admiral Buchanan had wisely instructed his staff to prepare for. Since Brittany helped draft the report, she offered her initial conclusions.

As far as she was concerned, there was a definite link between the terrorists who had supposedly hijacked the ship, and the mysterious Chinese submarine that had recently penetrated the GIUK gap. Brittany went as far as to theorize that the manifesto's threat to destroy the *QE2* wouldn't take place until a successful rendezvous between the *Lijiang* and the ocean liner was completed. At that time, the hijackers and their nine hostages would most likely be transferred onto the submarine for safekeeping, and only then would they dare destroy the *QE2*.

General Ridgeway's main concern was the nuclear threat that the caller had mentioned. Of all the leaders participating in the summit, only the Chinese president had brought along his version of the "football." This meant that the codes could easily be compromised, making this a global threat, with major cities throughout the world presently at risk of nuclear annihilation.

Since the terrorists' demands were completely unrealistic, and there was no practical way of ever fulfilling them, especially in three days, their only option was to forcefully intercede. Once more it was Brittany who shared an operational plan, one her staff had drawn up to address a variety of worst-case scenarios. Its primary component was the USS *James K. Polk*, and the men of SEAL Team Two. By means of their Swimmer Delivery Vehicle, the team could clandestinely board the ocean liner, eliminate the hijackers, and retake the ship.

Though this plan certainly sounded interesting, General Ridgeway came up with a number of problems that would have to be addressed before it could be implemented. The primary one involved their continued inability to contact the *Polk*, and the fact that the *QE2* was traveling at speeds well beyond the SDV's rather limited, battery-powered propulsion system.

The CNO readily responded to Ridgeway's first concern. In the event that VLF contact with the *Polk* couldn't be reestablished, the Navy had already scrambled an E-6A TACAMO (Take Charge And Move Out) aircraft into the North Atlantic. This plane's primary mission was to communicate with submerged submarines by means of a 5,000-foot-long trailing antenna. By stationing itself well out of visual range of the *QE2*, TACAMO would be in a position to guarantee them reliable communications with the *Polk* and the other three submarines of the escort force, within the next hour.

As promising as this sounded, it still left them with the problem of how to slow down the *QE2*, to allow for the transfer of the SEALs. Because of his previous experience with the *Achille Lauro* hijacking, Thomas dared to speak up at this point. Unbeknownst to the other occupants of the conference room, an SDV-borne SEAL team had been seriously considered as one of the possible rescue contingencies available in the retaking of the Italian cruise ship. At that time they were also faced with the challenge of finding a way to slow down the vessel so that the SDV could reach it, and a plan had been devised to snag the ship's propellers with a cable or net. After the tragic loss of a passenger, events in the Mediterranean eventually led to a peaceful outcome aboard the *Achille Lauro*, without this daring scheme ever having to be attempted.

The CNO appeared to be fascinated by this story, and though he doubted that they could come up with a quick, practical way of snagging the *QE2*, he did ask Thomas for more information about his intended role in the rescue. In particular, he wanted to know what they had hoped to achieve by having Thomas parachute aboard the *Achille Lauro?*

Before Thomas could answer, Brittany sat forward and excitedly proclaimed, "That's the way we can do it; by airdropping an operative onto the *QE2* to disrupt the ship's propulsion system, all timed to coincide with the arrival of SEAL Team Two's SDV!"

"I like it!" snapped General Ridgeway. "I'll give the AFSOC folks down at Hurlburt a call, and get the location of the nearest Combat Talon that's available for the drop. All that leaves is finding someone qualified to actually make the jump."

"Preferably someone who's been previously trained in the art of HALO jumping onto a moving ship on the open sea," added Brittany, while turning to Thomas.

Both Ridgeway and Buchanan did likewise. And Thomas Kellogg, who'd sworn to himself he'd never jump again, swallowed heavily, knowing full well who they hoped this someone would be.

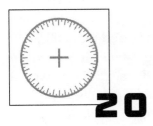

20

THE USS *POLK*'S ALL-OUT FLANK SPRINT BENEATH THE COLD WATERS OF THE North Atlantic ended as the speedy ocean liner it was doing its best to follow neared the mid-Atlantic ridge. It was here that the *QE2* finally cut its forward speed from twenty-eight and one-half knots to twenty-four knots, thus allowing the *Polk*'s engineering watch to throttle back their engines.

With this slowdown came an audible respite from the incessant pounding roar of the *QE2*'s nine powerful diesel engines. Nowhere was this more evident than inside the *Polk*'s sonar room, or sound shack, as it was commonly called. Here senior sonar supervisor Brad "Sup" Bodzin and his two-man watch team were the first to report the ocean liner's change of speed. The data showing this velocity alteration arrived by way of the various passive-hydrophone arrays that were mounted throughout the sub's hull. This sonic evidence was then routed into the sound shack through the technician's sensitive headphones, and was visually projected over the individual waterfall displays mounted above each console.

Bodzin's current watch team had an average age of twenty-three, but what they lacked in experience, they more than made up for in enthusiasm. A spirited twosome, who volunteered for submarine duty for the express purpose of learning sonar, this duo was content to let Bodzin rule their cramped, dimly lit workspace.

Bodzin, a grizzled veteran by comparison at the age of twenty-seven, was known for his hands-on management style. He liked to work standing up, as he was presently doing, positioned directly behind his seated associates.

To his immediate left was the rather antiquated, bulky console belonging to their BQS-4 active-sonar system. Also known as the "space heater" for the warmth it produced, the BQS-4 was not much different from the sonars of the prenuclear navy, and was still powered by old-fashioned tube amplifiers. Since the *Polk* depended on stealth to survive, active sonar was infrequently used. The powerful pulse of sound it projected was mainly utilized for collision avoidance and to determine a target's precise range by calculating the time it took for the deflected sonar signal to return.

To the right of the BQS-4 were the two consoles reserved for passive detection. Far from being the most sophisticated passive sonars in the U.S. Navy, the *Polk*'s BQ-21 was a medium-range broadband unit, while the BQ-7 was a conformal, long-range array that was mounted into the sub's spherical bow. It was the sensitive hydrophones of the BQ-7 that first picked up the change in pitch of the *QE2*'s engines as they were slowed.

S1c. James Echoles was seated at the far-right console. He was the one who originally detected the ocean liner's speed change. An easy-going, solidly built African American from Cahokia, Illinois, Echoles's nickname was Jaffers, and his alert discovery had earned him a Snickers candy bar and a box of Cracker Jack from Bodzin's cherished overhead stash.

"Hey, Sup," mumbled Jaffers while chewing on his candy bar. "That weird flutter is back on narrowband. What do you make of it?"

Bodzin scanned Jaffers's waterfall display, and isolated the suspect frequency on his headphones. "It still doesn't sound much to me, Bubba. I'd say it's an anomalous bathymetric."

"I'll bet you a cool can of Dr. Pepper, otherwise," Jaffers challenged.

"You're on," returned Bodzin, who listened as the young sailor seated to Jaffers's left spoke up.

"I don't know about you guys, but I think something strange is taking place on that ocean liner," offered S2c. Scott Wilford, a blond-haired, St. Petersburg, Florida, native. "Why else would they go and change their course like that? They're headed toward Iceland, not England."

"Maybe they decided to move the summit up to Reykjavik," Jaffers suggested.

Bodzin's tendency was to agree with Wilford's assessment, and he spoke carefully. "Let's not forget about that approaching hurricane topside. There's still a good chance that weather is the cause of that unplanned course change. And if they keep going at their current rate of speed, we'll all know the real cause soon enough."

"How's that, Sup?" asked Wilford.

Bodzin innocently massaged the muscles at the back of the young sailor's neck while answering. "Now that the *Polk*'s able to stand down from flank speed, the skipper's going to have a chance to bring us up to PD and establish a high-frequency SATCOM uplink. Then Command will be able to tell us everything we want to know."

"I want to know why the Brits went and dropped out of the formation like they did," remarked Jaffers as he addressed his console's frequency-select dial. "Do you think that the *Talent* just couldn't keep up with us?"

"Unless they had some sort of engineering casualty that I haven't heard about, scuttlebutt says that it was a tactical decision between the skipper and the Brit CO," revealed Bodzin. "It seems the two had a powwow over the underwater telephone, and the *Talent* fell back shortly afterwards.

"I'll tell you one thing," he added while lowering the volume of his headphones. "You can rest assured that this is one party that the Royal Navy doesn't want to miss. After all, the *QE2* is flying their flag, and from what little I've seen of their operational abilities, you definitely want the Brits on your side."

"Back in sub school, we saw a film on the way they train their submarine officers for command," said Wilford. "Did you know that their COs don't even have to be nuke-qualified to get command?"

"It's called the Perisher course," Bodzin explained. "And you're right, they don't have to pass engineering qualifications to get their dolphins. It seems the Brits are content to allow their engineers to run the reactor spaces, leaving their skippers free to fight the boat."

"Sup," interrupted Jaffers, pointing to a thick white line that was beginning to form on the upper-left-hand portion of his waterfall display. "It looks like you're going to owe me that Dr. Pepper, because that contact at zero-two-eight is back, and it sure doesn't look like any bathymetric anomaly to me."

Bodzin was quick to check the monitor himself, and he spotted the ever-widening white band. In an effort to hear the sound that the display was visually sketching, he addressed the auxiliary console and isolated the hydrophones responsible for picking up this contact. After determining the frequency, he turned up the volume gain of his headphones to its maximum level. Closing his eyes to better focus his concentration, he listened to a barely audible, whining sound, that was repeated with a pulsating, mechanical regularity.

"It's man-made all right," he whispered. "Could it be the Russians?"

"Only if the *Baikal* went and moved out of its patrol sector," Jaffers returned, his own headphones tuned to the same muted signature. "Because this bogey's positioned almost due north of the *QE2*, well within the no-patrol zone."

Bodzin reached up for the overhead intercom handset, and spoke into the transmitter. "Conn, sonar. We have an unidentified submerged contact, bearing zero-two-eight. Maximum range. Designate Sierra Seven, possible hostile."

This chilling report resulted in an almost instantaneous visit to sonar by the *Polk*'s captain. Benjamin Kram had been in the nearby radio room when Bodzin's voice broke from the intercom, and he wasted no time rushing across the passageway to check out this report firsthand.

"What do you have, Mr. Bodzin?" asked Kram breathlessly.

Bodzin answered while plugging in an auxiliary set of headphones and handing them to the captain. "Sir, I realize that it's not much, but there's a barely audible, low-frequency contact, almost due north of the *QE2*. It could be the reactor-coolant pump of another submarine."

Kram put on the headphones and did his best to pick out the noise. For the first couple of seconds, he could hear nothing but a distant crackling sound. Increasing the volume to full amplification, the crackling further intensified, only to be undercut by a faint mechanical whine that faded in and out with a disturbing regularity.

"Is it the *Baikal*?" he queried.

"Not unless they really strayed out of their patrol sector, sir," Bodzin replied.

Kram had heard enough. He removed the headphones, and sig-naled his senior sonarman to do the same. Only then did he beckon to Bodzin to join him at the after end of the compartment beside the room's tape recorder.

"Mr. Bodzin," Kram said in a bare whisper. "The *Polk* was just the recipient of a Priority One TACAMO transmission. Though I'll be briefing the entire crew shortly on its contents, I'd like you to be one of the first to know that there's trouble aboard the *QE2*. I know that it's going to sound farfetched, but it looks like she's been the victim of a hijacking."

"What?"

"My initial reaction exactly. Sometime within the last couple of hours, what appears to be a group of Chinese terrorists seized opera-tional control of the ocean liner. As far as I know, our President and the other heads of state haven't been harmed, though a Marine Super Stallion helicopter carrying a Delta Force interdiction unit was lost effecting a rescue attempt.

"The National Command Authority also believes that the terror-ists have gained control of China's nuclear-warhead unlock codes. The terrorists are threatening to begin launching the PRC's strategic nuclear arsenal if their irrational demands are not met, or another rescue effort is attempted."

"So that's why they broke off their great circle route and turned north," reflected Bodzin. "Surely we're not going to just sit here and let them get away with this."

"As a matter of fact, we're not. Both the *Polk* and SEAL Team Two have been placed on alert, and ordered to stand by to initiate a clandestine rescue attempt sometime within the next four hours."

"But what about the storm that's blowing topside, Captain? And how is our SDV ever going to catch up with them, sir? Unless the *QE2* reduces its speed substantially, the SDV's eight knots is never going to cut it."

Kram was impressed with his senior sonarman's tactical fore-sight, and he answered him directly. "We've only experienced Marti's outer fringe so far, and weather conditions are still within the pa-rameters of a safe SDV launch. As far as the way in which our SDV is going to be able to catch the *Queen*, Command didn't say. We've only been instructed to stand by for additional orders."

Kram paused to shift his glance to the two seated sonar technicians, and added, "There was one additional portion of the TACAMO broadcast that I thought you'd be particularly interested in hearing. We've been informed to be on the alert for a Chinese *Han*-class attack sub that Command believes might have secretly penetrated these waters from the north, and is an integral part of the terrorist conspiracy."

"Sierra Seven!" exclaimed Bodzin.

"It could very well be, Mr. Bodzin. I need you and your boys to do your best to determine that fact for certain. And if Sierra Seven does turn out to be that outlaw sub, I have a feeling that we're soon going to find out what kind of punch those fish we're hauling down in the torpedo room are really carrying."

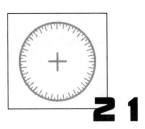

21

A LITTLE LESS THAN TWELVE HOURS AFTER THOMAS KELLOGG MADE THE RASH decision to volunteer his services, he found himself inside the rear cabin of a MC-130H Combat Talon, well on his way to the North Atlantic. From an uncomfortable steel-and-nylon-webbed bench set against the cargo hold's forward bulkhead, he gazed out at the cavernous hold, empty except for the sleeping loadmaster. He was the extent of this aircraft's cargo package, to be delivered to a spot above the ocean, some 3,000 miles to the northeast of Washington's Andrews Air Force Base. The flight had begun there, and Thomas knew that Command had really pulled out all the stops to get this complex operation organized in so little time.

As the MC-130H momentarily shook in a pocket of turbulence, Thomas reached down to brace himself against the steel seat frame. The plane's interior was cold, drafty, and noisy, the four Allison T56-A-15 turboprop engines grinding away with a constant, guttural roar. A partially eaten box lunch sat at his side, along with the detailed schematic diagram of the *QE2* that he had been studying for most of the morning.

This foldout, cross-section guide of the ocean liner had been hand-delivered to Andrews shortly after dawn by a Cunard representative and former staff captain of the *QE2*. This individual flew in on the first shuttle of the morning from New York, and he gave Thomas an extensive briefing on the ship's layout and the best way to carry out his mission.

He started off by recommending that Thomas utilize the Sun Deck's helicopter pad for a landing zone. It was situated immediately abaft the funnel, on the topmost deck—this area being the largest portion of unobstructed open space available to safely accommodate him. It was also encircled on two sides by a six-foot-high Plexiglas windscreen that could help snag the chute in case a violent cross-wind was encountered.

The jump itself was scheduled to take place at dusk, and once on the QE2, Thomas would have until midnight to get into position to implement the rest of the plan. Because the transfer of the SEALs was timed to take place precisely at the stroke of twelve, it was imperative that the QE2 be slowed down to at least eight knots, the SDV's top speed.

To accomplish this feat clandestinely, the Cunard employee suggested that Thomas access the dual pitch-control levers located in the aft portion of the Engine Room on Eight Deck. These levers were mounted onto each of the ship's two drive shafts, and by manipulating them in a manner that he subsequently demonstrated, the pitch of the propellers could be altered and the vessel slowed.

Designed for use in emergency situations only, the levers were totally independent of both the Bridge and the Engine Room. It was impossible to override the system in any other way.

The levers were in an infrequently visited portion of the ship. To get into this isolated compartment without being discovered, Thomas was given a somewhat circuitous route. Once he safely landed on the Sports Deck, he was to proceed forward to the amidships stairwell. By climbing to the deck above, he'd be able to stash his gear in a vacant stowage locker on the Signal Deck, located aft of the ship's Kennels. From there he was to return to the E-elevator shaft, where an access hatch would lead him down to Four Deck. From there he'd head aft. At the sternmost portion of the ship, another emergency-access ladder would take him down into the Engine Room and drop him off directly beside the dual pitch levers.

To allow Thomas to better blend in, should he be discovered transiting one of the public passageways, Cunard had sent along a ship's officer's uniform for his use. This outfit of black trousers, shoes, tie, and a white shirt with gold-and-purple-striped epaulets, identified him as an engineering officer. It was a cursory disguise at best, but certainly better than relying on the olive-drab, thermal jump-suit he was presently wearing over it.

By the time the briefing was ending, his means of transport had finally arrived. With the invaluable assistance of the Air Force Special Operations Command, the nearest available MC-130H had been lo-cated at Dover Air Force Base in Delaware. This aircraft belonged to the 15th Special Operations Squadron. It was normally based at Hurl-burt Field, Florida, and had been visiting Dover on an exercise.

Being a former Air Commando himself, who was once based at AFSOC headquarters at Hurlburt, Thomas felt right at home upon being introduced to the crew. To make their 11:00 A.M. liftoff, little time was wasted prepping the Combat Talon for its long flight, and fitting Thomas with his flight suit, gloves, goggles, helmet, oxygen mask, and of course, his HALO parachute gear.

It wasn't until he signed for the parachute, though, that the reality of the mission he had volunteered for abruptly sank in. His mind still filled with the myriad of details he'd have to remember about the QE2, he knew that they would all be useless if he didn't survive the jump.

As he continued out onto the flight line, Brittany at his side, he began to have second thoughts about his participation in this mis-sion. Regardless of his previous decision never to strap on a para-chute again, it had been much too long since he had completed his last HALO jump.

Gut instinct warned him that this entire effort was totally foolish, and he fought the urge to drop his gear and walk away. Yet Brittany's presence and a stubborn will kept him from doing so.

As the plane's engines were warmed up for takeoff, Brittany es-corted him to the aircraft's hatch. She couldn't help but feel respon-sible for sending him, and tears filled her eyes as she wished him a safe flight. Out on the tarmac, a kiss would have been as inappro-priate as at the White House. They stood a moment facing each other, then Agent Kellogg saluted the Naval attaché. She returned it smartly. He wanted to make her some sort of promise, but as her salute barely quivered as she continued to hold it, Thomas saw he didn't have to. She trusted him. He snapped his hand down and turned away.

Climbing into the Combat Talon was like returning in time. The sights, smells, and sounds were all too familiar, and regathering his nerve, he strapped himself into his current seat and prepared himself for takeoff.

Once they were safely in the air, he got a chance to visit the flight deck. When he was in active duty, this particular model of the Combat Talon was only in the planning stages. First deployed in June 1991, the MC-130H model was one of the most modern platforms in the Air Force inventory.

Thomas was impressed with the manner in which the cockpit's highly automated controls and digital displays were designed to reduce crew size and workload. Unlike the MC-130E Combat Talons on which he flew, the H-model's cockpit was fully compatible with night-vision goggles. Basic aircraft flight, tactical, and mission-sensor data was displayed on a compact video monitor that had its own data-entry keyboard.

The navigator/electronic-warfare-operator console was situated on the aft portion of the spacious flight deck. It too was designed around several mounted video screens filled with a wide assortment of flashing data.

One console here was of special interest to Thomas. This was the display screen on which the Talon's HARP radar system would be projected. Short for High Altitude Release Point, HARP was another one of those high-tech marvels that were only in the planning stage when Thomas saw service. It was used to drop off a HALO jumper at his optimum release point. As the aircraft neared the LZ, it would make a low-altitude pass in order for HARP to gauge the crosswinds. Upon their return to altitude, HARP would assimilate this data to determine the most favorable release point.

By the time Thomas completed his tour of the cockpit, they were well on the way to their objective. For the most part, the Combat Talon would be following the *QE2*'s original route, up America's east coast and continuing over the southern tip of Newfoundland to the seas above the mid-Atlantic ridge.

Since leaving Op Center Bravo much earlier in the morning, Thomas was able to rest a bit easier knowing that Command now had a firm lock on the hijacked ocean liner. A number of space-based reconnaissance satellites were in position to give them a constant update on the *QE2*'s exact location.

Command had also managed to establish communications with

the USS *Polk*. A TACAMO aircraft would be constantly airborne, to guarantee that this radio link wasn't broken.

One peripheral element that was proving a bit more difficult to control was keeping a complete press blackout on the crisis. This was vital to avoid a public panic. By restricting all news access to a need-to-know-basis only, the Pentagon had so far been able to keep a lid on the hijacking. This was in spite of the fact that emergency ham transmissions were continuing to be broadcast from the *QE2*.

All this would have to be addressed in less than two days from now, when the *QE2* was scheduled to arrive at Southampton. Command's hope was that through Thomas's efforts, and those of SEAL Team Two, the terrorist threat would be nullified before they'd have to inform the public that a crisis had ever existed.

Another pocket of turbulence shook the Talon, and Thomas once more grabbed the edge of the bench. The painful knot that had gathered in his stomach earlier further tightened, and he tried his best to ignore the first nauseous hint of airsickness. As his anxious glance strayed to the light gray HALO rig that hung from the bulkhead, he considered the strange sequence of events that had presaged this moment.

He supposed that the first presentiment of this unthinkable duty arrived on Labor Day, as he watched his nephew shoot his parachute toy into the air. This was followed by the arrest of the trespassing teenage parachutist on the South Lawn of the White House.

When seen as a whole, surely these diverse experiences hadn't been mere coincidence. They were rather a sign; a cosmic warning, that another life-and-death struggle with the ageless demons of doubt and fear was about to be reinitiated.

Had it been cowardice on his part that precipitated his traumatic decision to leave the Air Force and never jump again? Try as he could for the last ten years to answer this simple question, Thomas knew that he was still unable to do so.

Courage and bravery had been two all-important qualities instilled in Thomas by his father from early childhood. A retired career Army officer, the elder Kellogg had made certain to leave his sons with one piece of advice above all others—that there could be no greater honor than selflessly sacrificing one's life in defense of country.

On the day that Thomas received his Air Force commission, his father was at his side, beaming with pride. Shortly thereafter, a brief taste of combat in Southeast Asia fooled Thomas into thinking that he was the fearless soldier his father wanted him to be.

The first crack in this false perception became evident in 1983 off the coast of Grenada. Fear, revulsion, horror; these were the real impressions of war that Thomas brought back from the Caribbean, as he found himself struggling with the realization that he'd never be the hero that his father wanted.

Two years later, in October 1985, Thomas was to experience the traumatic event that would lead to his premature retirement from the Air Force, and his decision never to strap on a parachute again. The terrorist hijacking of the cruise ship *Achille Lauro* resulted in a call to duty for his special-tactics unit. They had been temporarily stationed at Comiso Airfield in Sicily when word reached them to begin training for a possible rescue attempt.

The aircraft carrier USS *Saratoga* was made available to practice the difficult task of landing on a ship by parachute. The initial training package was for six HALO jumps. An acronym for High Altitude, Low Opening, a HALO jump guaranteed a covert insertion, as the aircraft responsible for dropping the jumpers couldn't be seen or heard.

His teammate for this final HALO jump of the series was Jack Dempsey Mackey, his closest friend and confidant. They had attended the Air Force Academy together, where they were members of the Wings of Blue parachute team. Their paths parted after graduation, when Thomas picked special operations for his career specialty, and Jack chose to become a fighter pilot.

At about the same time that Urgent Fury was coming down, Jack made an unusual career change and transferred into the special-operations community. After a brief stint flying AC-130 Spectre gunships, he decided to see if he had the right stuff to pass the combat-control/pararescue indoctrination course. Not only did he pass with flying colors, but he sincerely enjoyed himself doing so, and this led to his decision to give up flying and join the elite special-tactics group.

Jack was in turn transferred to Hurlburt, where Thomas was based. The two continued their friendship right where they left off. When Jack married and their first son was born, Thomas became the godfather. They spent weekends together, boating and fishing, and even shared ownership of a battered cabin cruiser that Jack chanced upon while attending air-traffic-control school at Keesler Air Force Base in nearby Biloxi.

When Command assigned them to Sicily, they could hardly believe their good fortune. They looked upon this duty as a Mediterranean vacation at Uncle Sam's expense, and for the first couple weeks, it was everything they had hoped for. They were able to spend several days in Rome, enjoy a weekend in Venice, and travel up to the Italian Riviera, where both of them visited their first nude beach.

The hijacking of the *Achille Lauro* put an end to their sightseeing, and they were soon back to work, practicing for a possible rescue mission. It was a bright, sunny Sicilian morning as they boarded the MC-130E for their final high-altitude airdrop. At 15,000 feet, they began prebreathing oxygen. The jump itself was to take place at 25,000 feet, and it was Jack who signaled Thomas to be the first one out.

According to Air Force statistics, the odds of experiencing a parachute malfunction were one out of every four hundred and fifty jumps. Many jumpers went an entire lifetime without a problem, while others experienced one their first time out.

In this instance, Thomas's problems started shortly after the jump light turned green and the jumpmaster pointed out the Talon's open rear ramp and shouted, "Go!" As he leaped off the ramp, and his freefalling body plunged seaward at a terminal-velocity speed of 120 miles per hour, the strap of his helmet snapped in half, and his helmet, goggles, and oxygen mask were ripped off his head. While jerking back his head in a frantic effort at figuring out what had happened, his rucksack abruptly shifted from its mount on his equipment harness, causing him to begin a terrifying, out-of-control spin. He suddenly found himself tumbling head over heels, and he struggled to attain a stable, spread-eagle position. Yet vertigo ensued, and Thomas momentarily blacked out.

When he eventually came to seconds later, he found that he had rolled on his back and was still in the midst of a disorienting spin. In a desperate attempt to stabilize himself, he arched his back and spread his arms and legs. This allowed him to roll over to a freefall position, and he was able to quickly check his altimeter.

He was still disorientated by the spin, and with his eyesight blurred from the loss of goggles, Thomas let circumspection take over and he pulled the ripcord regardless of the relatively high altitude. He was thankful that his MC-4 ram-air chute was good, and he was able to get a clear view of his floating LZ several thousand feet below.

It was as he looked up to initiate a routine controllability check before beginning to steer his chute in for landing, that he spotted another freefaller. This individual appeared to be headed straight for him, and they only missed colliding when his own chute opened.

Though Thomas never could say exactly what happened next, somehow their lines became entangled. Once again heart-stopping terror possessed him, as his canopy collapsed, and he identified the jumper who had struck him. Jack had apparently seen his previous difficulties, and had risked life and limb to hurtle through space to catch up with him. Now both of them were falling, with their main chutes collapsed and hopelessly entangled.

Because Jack was the top jumper, he had cut away priority. The proper procedure was for him to get rid of his main chute, and deploy the reserve. They were practically freefalling side by side at this point, rapidly approaching 2,000 feet, and Thomas fought to regain his composure.

He watched as Jack gave him a brave thumbs-up before yanking his cutaway ripcord with his right hand and pulling his reserve with the left. Though the cutaway activated, the reserve did not. Jack was doomed unless Thomas could activate his own reserve and somehow bring his best friend down with him.

For the rest of his life he would endlessly replay the horrifying sequence of events that followed. Thomas cut away his main, got a good chute on his reserve, then frantically reached for Jack's outstretched hand. For the briefest of seconds, their fingertips touched. And the last he ever saw of his friend was the terrified look of fear that etched Jack's face as he realized that he was going to die.

They pulled Jack's broken body out of the Mediterranean several hours later. Thomas had been able to make good his landing on the *Saratoga*, and was right there in the small boat as Jack's corpse was retrieved.

The official inquiry cleared Thomas of any direct responsibility for his death. Yet in his own mind, he judged himself guilty—if it had not been for his difficulties during the jump, Jack would have lived.

Thomas was mentally broken by this traumatic experience that in reality had begun two years earlier, off the coast of Grenada. And it was with this heavy baggage to carry that he began his difficult transition back into civilian life.

How very fitting it was that his life should come full circle like this, thought Thomas, as he sat in the wildly shaking rear cabin of the Combat Talon II on his way out to the storm-tossed mid-Atlantic. Just when he thought that he had successfully put one set of demons behind him, they had come back into his life like a returned letter. Running away had given him nothing but a ten-year respite.

Now was his chance to show what he was really made of. Somewhere out there on the cold seas, his own brother's life was at stake, not to mention that of the President of the United States, and eight of the most powerful men in all the world. There could thus be no better time for him to finally face his inner demon, or forever be its slave.

The tension-packed day just passing seemed to be filled with one frustrating delay after the other. As a student of the Way, Dennis Liu knew that he shouldn't allow such trivialities to disturb his inner equilibrium. But they had come so far, and now that their goal was just beyond reach, he couldn't help but find himself overly anxious.

Their primary difficulty had been making contact with PRC's Red Star communications satellite. They had already made two attempts to establish a secure uplink, yet in each instance, severe static kept them from being able to transmit the nuclear unlock codes to Adm. Liu Huang-tzu's forces in Tsingtao. Max Kurtyka blamed this interference on the unusual solar-flare activity. Their computer expert promised that during the next overhead pass of Red Star, later that night, he'd devise a way to deal with the static.

Once the codes were safely sent, their next step would be to signal the *Lijiang* and prepare for the transfer of their prisoners. To hail the *Han*-class submarine, they'd be ordering the QE2's Bridge watch to initiate a three-minute-long, sprint-and-drift process. At thirty-second intervals, the ocean liner's nine engines would be run at flank speed, followed by a thirty-second-long period of silence. This would provide the distinctive audible signal that would bring Capt. Lee Shao-chi and his crack crew out of the black depths.

It appeared that all of this would take place that evening. To bide his time and make certain that none of the prisoners tried to disrupt their plans, Liu spent most of the day making the rounds of the immense vessel.

The tour of inspection began in the below-deck spaces, where his team had done a superb job of intimidating the crew. To get their point across, the senior Filipino steward was led away in handcuffs and sequestered in the ship's Library. This man served as the official leader of the large Philippine community aboard ship, and by threatening to shoot him, they were able to keep the rest of the crew in line with a minimum of supervision.

Liu made several visits to the Queens Grill throughout the day. Almost a hundred prisoners were being held there, including the nine statesmen, who spent a restless night bemoaning their tragic predicament. The Grill's two small bathrooms were the only restrooms made available to them. Meals were limited to sandwiches and water, far from the decadent gourmet fare they were used to.

Only once was he informed of possible trouble inside the Dining Room. This happened when Bear caught the captive security agents trying to circulate a note. Liu's inspection of this document showed that it was advising patience and circumspection. These were qualities that Liu certainly couldn't complain about. Yet since the next note could have been one orchestrating an insurrection, he severely castigated his prisoners for this futile effort, and shot off a few rounds of submachine-gun fire into the ceiling to make his point.

Liu's last stop of the day took him to the security room. He was expecting to find Max Kurtyka here, monitoring the surveillance screens. Instead he found his daughter alone at the console, still doing her best to learn how to operate the complicated system.

This was the first time he had been able to visit with her since the initial takeover. He was pleased to find her adjusting quite well. Liu had feared that she would have trouble coping if things got violent. He made certain to remind her about the reasons behind their actions. Satisfied that she'd hold up under the continued pressure, Liu learned that Max had gone outside to have a smoke.

He left Kristin with a kiss on each cheek, and headed aft to locate Max. A dark gray sky greeted him as he walked out onto One Deck's exterior pool area. The air was brisk, and though he failed to spot Max here, he proceeded to the deck's aft railing, where the vessel's flagless jackstaff was mounted.

The *QE2*'s prop wash could be clearly traced, a thin snaking line of agitated seawater that extended to the lightning-lit southern horizon. Dusk was falling, with not a trace of a sunset in the cloud-filled heavens.

Hoping that the hurricane would stay to the south, Liu turned around. He scanned the series of terraced decks capped by the upper portion of the ship's towering red funnel, from which poured a constant stream of black smoke. It was at the stern rail of the uppermost deck, directly aft of the helipad, that Liu spotted a single, rail-thin figure, thoughtfully scanning the same stormy horizon that he had been inspecting. The bright red glow of a cigarette could be made out between this individual's lips. Liu didn't have to see any more to proceed up to the Sports Deck to join him.

"Hang on, Special Agent," warned an amplified voice from Thomas's headphones. "We're going down on the deck to check the winds for our HARP calculation, and things could get a little rough."

Thomas depressed his intercom button and curtly acknowledged this warning that came to pass all too soon with a violent jolting motion of the MC-130H's fuselage. The Combat Talon rapidly lost altitude, its four turboprop engines whining away in futile protest.

Thomas tried his best to control his rising nausea, aggravated by the rubber oxygen mask tightly strapped around his mouth. In preparation for the HALO jump, he had been prebreathing oxygen for the past hour.

The darkened rear cabin shook wildly, rolling from side to side with such intensity that Thomas feared he'd be torn from his seat belt. This extreme turbulence even managed to get the loadmaster's attention, who finally awoke from his nap and rushed over to strap himself securely to the same bench on which Thomas was seated.

A cursory glance at his watch showed that the moment of truth was almost upon them. In a strange way, he was relieved. The long flight had given him too much time to think about his traumatic past and the great dangers he would soon have to face.

His primary worry was whether he had lost his jump skills. This attempt would be difficult enough during the day, with perfect weather conditions prevailing. It was only too apparent from the Combat Talon's wildly shaking fuselage that severe crosswinds would have to be dealt with. When these winds were factored in with a hostile, untested landing zone, presently cutting through the pitching seas at over twenty knots, all the ingredients for disaster were in place.

Thomas could take small solace in the LPU that he wore beneath his parachute harness. In the event that he missed the *QE2*, he hoped the life preserver unit would keep him afloat. A water-activated radio beacon, which the Combat Talon would be monitoring, was sewn into the preserver's outer seam. The water temperature in this portion of the North Atlantic was in the low forties—he'd have but a few precious minutes to get into the sheltering confines of a life raft, before deadly hypothermia set in.

The pitch of the Talon's turboprops further deepened, and Thomas was aware that his body was no longer being pulled forward. After several minutes of level flight, the MC-130H initiated a steep climb that forcefully pushed Thomas back against the bulkhead, with all the pressure of a prolonged stiff-arm.

His headphones crackled alive. He could hear the copilot calling out their rapidly increasing altitude. As they passed 20,000 feet, the navigator informed him that HARP had calculated that there was a dangerous 170-degree wind shear present, with the winds themselves gusting up to eighteen knots at sea level. These disturbing environmental factors did not bode well for a safe jump, and since they were at the marginal permissible limits, it would ultimately be up to Thomas to make the final decision to go.

His inner debate was a short one. And even though he could have easily scrubbed the mission, he found himself activating the intercom and firmly declaring, "Let's go for it, gentlemen!"

He reached up and further tightened the fit of his parachute's chest harness. The loadmaster unbuckled his seat belt and stood. With careful steps, he continued to the rear of the cabin to prepare the ramp for opening.

"HARP indicates that we've got four minutes to go until we reach our optimal release point," informed the amplified voice of the navigator.

No more notification was needed to get Thomas to unbuckle his own seat belt and stand. He made a final check of his equipment, then began the short transit to join the loadmaster at the back of the cabin.

"Three minutes," informed the navigator, from his console on the flight deck.

While Thomas allowed the loadmaster to double-check the fit of his gear, the intercom crackled alive with the voice of the pilot. "Good luck, Special Agent."

"Thanks, Major," replied Thomas. "Don't forget to give my regards to the folks back at Hurlburt."

"Will do, sir. And enjoy your cruise!"

With the delivery of this optimistic comment, Thomas disconnected the intercom. He tried his best to steady his rapidly beating pulse, and he took a series of deep draws on his oxygen mask, the tank of which was securely strapped to the side of his harness.

The clamshell doors of the Talon's rear ramp parted, and Thomas got his first view of the gray dusk sky. Cloud cover kept him from spotting his target down below. He expectantly looked up to the jump indicator lights that were mounted into the fuselage beside the helmeted loadmaster. Only the bottom, red caution light was illuminated.

Fifteen seconds from green light, the loadmaster flashed him a thumbs-up. This allowed Thomas to make a final adjustment to his goggles before the green light popped on, and the loadmaster pointed outside into the gathering darkness and shouted, "Go!"

Without hesitation, Thomas leaped off the ramp. The first thing he was aware of was the sudden silence, and the incredibly strong, icy cold wind that appeared to be blowing from below. He immediately arched his back and spread out his arms and legs to establish a stable spread-eagle position. Too invigorated to feel fear, he subconsciously found himself counting off ten seconds, the approximate time it would take him to attain terminal velocity. As long as he remained in a Delta position, terminal velocity indicated the maximum speed of his freefall—roughly 120 miles per hour.

Thomas knew that he had attained this speed, when he suddenly felt as if he were no longer falling. This strange sensation was caused by the gravitational pull of his body being equalized by the wind resistance. For all effective purposes, he was now balanced precariously on a huge bubble of air, with the merest abrupt movement on his part able to cause an unwanted spin, backloop, or barrel roll.

Confident of his ability to hold a stable position, Thomas shifted into a compact, frog posture, by slightly bending his arms and legs, and pulling his hands closer to his shoulders. A quick check of his wrist-mounted altimeter showed that he had already broken 15,000 feet. This meant that it was time for him to get a firm visual lock on his intended landing zone.

He angled his line of sight downward, and found his vision blurred by ice crystals that had formed on the inner lenses of his goggles. Try as he could to spot his LZ, the only thing visible was a blurred gray mass of dark clouds.

As he pulled in his wrist for another altimeter check, he shifted his weight, and a heart-stopping flat spin resulted. To counter it, he tried to twist his body in the opposite direction of the spin. When this proved ineffective, desperation led him to sweep his arms to his sides and bend forward at the waist. This caused his entire body to tumble forward in a lightning-quick flipping motion that served to break the flow of air that had been supporting the spin.

To regain control, he arched his back and spread out his arms and legs in time to see a glorious sight, barely visible through the gray muck beneath him. Like a thousand glittering jewels, the sparkling lights of the *QE2* beckoned, approximately 5,000 feet distant. The ocean liner appeared to be well within range. Thomas counted off the seconds before he'd pull the ripcord of his MC-4 ram-air parachute to begin the next stage of this perilous endeavor.

"So you really think that this computer-generated program of yours will filter out any static that we might encounter during Red Star's next overhead pass?" probed Dennis Liu, while casually strolling around the helipad's outer perimeter with Max close at his side.

Max's own steps were tracing the perimeter's white circular border, and he replied without bothering to remove the cigarette from his lips. "Tonight's the night, Chief. I feel it in my bones."

A heavy swell rocked the deck, and Liu alertly shifted his balance to compensate for it. "I certainly hope that your instincts are correct, comrade. As they say, the natives are getting restless, and it's only a matter of time before we start having some serious problems controlling them."

"I understand that you intercepted a note that the fools inside the Grill were attempting to circulate," remarked Max. "Any idea who wrote it?"

"My best guess is that it originated with the Americans," offered Liu as he peered up into the darkening sky.

Max halted and replied forcefully. "We've been tolerant long enough. It's time to set an example and put fear back into the hearts of our captives. Just say the word, and I'll personally blow away those trouble-making Secret Service pigs."

Before Liu could respond, his cranial headset activated. Whatever he was hearing caused his eyes to narrow with concern. He spoke rapidly into the radio's lapel-mounted transmitter. "Monica, keep your cool—don't do anything foolish. I'm on my way with Max!"

Thomas pulled his ripcord seconds after the altimeter showed him passing below 3,000 feet. The parachute opened with a jolting shock, causing Thomas to look up to check for any problems. The rectangular, ram-air canopy appeared to be fully deployed, and with one eye on the rapidly approaching LZ, he began a rushed controllability check.

Two thousand feet was the absolute limit for him to cut away his main chute and open the reserve. Because his flared landing would necessitate pinpoint accuracy, it was absolutely essential that the main canopy was perfect in every way. To guarantee this, he released the brakes, allowing him to use the steering risers to initiate a ninety-degree turn to both left and right. Only after he was satisfied that all looked well, and that his stall point was correct, did he turn his complete attention back to the landing.

He readily spotted the QE2's helipad, directly aft of the vessel's funnel. His intention was to land in the pad's exact center, where a thick white cross bisected its circular perimeter.

Now the trick was to maneuver in such a way that he'd land into the wind. Since it was last reported to be blowing in uneven gusts from the southwest, he would approach from the northeast. This meant he'd have to come in from the bow, on the vessel's starboard side.

His MC-4 parafoil chute was designed to be flown much like an airplane. As air was forced through its square nose, it was channeled back to fill the canopy's cells, creating a winglike airfoil effect that could generate over thirty miles per hour of forward speed.

Thomas tried his best to ignore the roiling seas that surrounded the QE2. He instead focused his attention solely on a fixed spot directly behind the ship's massive funnel. With a series of firm tugs, he manipulated the steering risers, sending the chute downward in a final sweeping turn. The bow of the mighty ship passed on his right, and he feared that if one of the vessel's occupants were to look outside at this moment, they might actually see him as he flew by.

Golden light poured from the windows and portholes as Thomas sped past the long line of bright orange lifeboats. A sudden gust of wind pushed him dangerously close to the smoke-belching funnel, and as he brushed past it, the helipad suddenly loomed before him.

At this rate, Thomas was moving much too swiftly to hit his intended mark. He was forced to pull down firmly on the steering risers. As air was dumped from the canopy, he went into a sudden stall that sent him crashing downward.

His feet cleared the helipad's starboard, Plexiglas windscreen by the barest of inches, and with the white cross of his LZ now in front of him, he yanked down hard on the risers once more. This resulted in an abrupt bleeding off of all forward airspeed, and his feet gently touched down onto the deck, only a few inches from the helipad's exact center.

Before he could settle down completely, a gust of wind caught his partially collapsed canopy. Unable to hit his harness release, Thomas was thrown violently to the deck, with the chute dragging him aft toward the open stern railing. Now he was in danger of being pulled right off the ship, and he managed to yank the cutaway release mechanism, seconds before the billowing canopy was sucked beneath the rail, with his head less than a foot behind.

As the harness was jerked free of his body, the chute filled completely and shot off downwind. The last view Thomas had of the chute was when it was already well on its way out to sea.

His limbs were trembling from both the bitter cold and the pure exhilaration of this wild ride. It was imperative that he get under cover with all due haste, and he grabbed the rail and shakily stood up.

Thomas followed the advice of the QE2's former staff captain—he made for the deck above, headed for the auxiliary stowage room. He found the forward passageway without problem. After making sure that no one was in sight, he sprinted down the carpeted hallway to the stairwell that had a sign marked KENNEL beside it.

These stairs conveyed him to a closed hatchway, set into the port bulkhead. He ignored the CREW ACCESS ONLY sign, and swung open the hatch and stepped outside. This put him in a narrow open accessway, with the QE2's funnel behind him. The air was cool and smelled of

the sea, and Thomas was aware of the deck's constant rocking motion.

Anxious to get out of his jumpsuit and begin his journey deep into the bowels of the Engine Room, he located the closed door of the stowage space. He allowed himself the barest of relieved sighs upon finding the door unlocked, and gratefully pushed it open.

Much to his utter horror, there was another man inside! This stocky individual was dressed in a standard officer's uniform, and was seated in front of what appeared to be a radio transmitter. He had headphones over his ears, and looked just as surprised as Thomas to have a visitor.

Long before Thomas could even think about pulling out his weapon, the stranger grasped a 9mm Beretta handgun and used its barrel to signal Thomas to shut the door. Only then did he remove his headphones, and while curiously studying his visitor's strange garb, pointedly questioned with a distinctive English accent.

"I'm almost afraid to ask, but who in the blue blazes are you?"

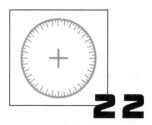

22

VINCE KELLOGG KNEW IT WAS GOING TO BE A DIFFICULT DAY, FROM THE MO-
ment the muted light of dawn became visible outside the Queens
Grill's picture window. It had been a miserable, sleepless night, aggravated by the *QE2*'s constant pitching and their cramped living
quarters. Since the takeover, their captors had confined them to
their tables, and those able to sleep, had to do so right there. The
limited restroom facilities were inadequate; in place of caviar, lobster, and champagne, a platter of tuna fish sandwiches along with
several pitchers of ice water were inelegantly pulled out on a serving cart.

Food was definitely not on Vince's mind, as he spent the early
morning hours contemplating their dilemma. Beyond blaming himself for allowing this hijacking to occur, the central focus of his
thoughts was on figuring out a way to retake the ship.

What little whispered conversation he was able to have with his
equally concerned tablemates, resulted in their writing a message.
The note stressed patience, and was circulated amongst the other
security agents. As it was passed from table to table, an alert sentry
intercepted it. This brought a visit from Dennis Liu, who expressed
his displeasure with a threatening round of submachine-gun fire.

As Liu exited, they realized they'd have to act soon. As both captives and captors continued to tire, it was only a matter of time

before either a minor incident, such as the discovery of their note, or the foolhardy efforts of a hotshot hero, would ignite the volatile atmosphere.

As it turned out, the spark occurred later that afternoon. After spending a frustrating, tense day, with nothing to do but try to catch a few minutes' sleep, or dare trade a whispered secret with one's associates, the Russians attempted a breakout.

It took place near dusk, when two of the Russian agents rose to use the restroom. Since only one individual at a time was allowed in either of the two small bathrooms, their joint efforts drew the immediate attention of the nearest terrorist.

This black-clad figure had long ago removed his hood, and was armed with a Sterling submachine gun. Hartwell had identified him as a member of the ship's Laundry.

Vince could see it coming, as the two Russians approached the men's room, and the guard ran to intercept them. As he shouted for them to stop, one of the Russians, either by accident or plan, collided with the cart holding the sandwiches. The force of the collision was enough to send him crashing down hard on the cart's glass top, instantly shattering it, and sending the water-filled pitchers flying.

The other Russian used this noisy distraction to his advantage, as he reached his fallen associate's side just as the sentry did. Though it initially appeared that he was just bending over to assist his co-worker, the agent instead grabbed one of the partially filled pitchers, and flung its icy contents into the guard's face. Then without hesitation, he sprang up, ripped the submachine gun off the blinded sentry's shoulder, and immobilized him with a painful arm lock. The other Russian retrieved the Sterling and aimed it at their prisoner.

This commotion drew the attention of Monica Chang and Bear, who had been standing watch beside the Grill's aft entryway. Her figure well displayed by the tight black jumpsuit she wore, the actress showed a savage, vicious side that Vince never saw portrayed on the movie screen.

"Let go of him this instant!" she screamed.

Monica addressed her two-way radio, before following Bear to the overturned cart, where the Russians stood with their prisoner.

"I said let go of him!" she ordered, emphasizing her determination by letting loose a deafening round of bullets into the Grill's ceiling.

The Russians didn't budge, and if anything, the fact that a woman had arrived to challenge them, only served to bolster their confidence.

"No, comrade," countered the agent holding the disarmed terrorist. "It's you who will let all of us free."

"Like hell I will," Monica retorted, aiming the barrel of her weapon at the armed Russian's forehead. Bear kept his gun turned on the rest of the room to discourage anyone from joining in.

The tense standoff was broken minutes later by the breathless arrival of Dennis Liu and Max Kurtyka. They hurried over to join Monica.

Liu alertly sized up the situation. With his lungs still heaving for breath, he pulled out his .45 caliber sidearm and also aimed it at the forehead of the Russian holding the prisoner.

"I'll only ask once, comrade. Let him go!" Liu ordered.

The Russians did their best to use their hostage for cover, the one holding him bending his knees slightly, to hide his head behind that of his shorter prisoner. "I'm warning you. I'll kill this man if you don't put down your guns and surrender," instructed the other Russian, who jammed the barrel of his weapon up against the Asian's neck.

Dennis Liu answered with a wicked, devilish laugh, that was all too soon shared by his fellow terrorists. "You really think that this man's life means anything to us?" managed Liu between continued peals of laughter. "Our movement is a billion-and-a-half strong, and one individual's life is insignificant!"

There was gathering madness evident in Liu's glowing eyes, as he clicked off the pistol's safety. Max wasn't about to miss out on all the action, and he lifted his own pistol, which he aimed at the unarmed Russian.

"Just say the word, Chief," offered Max, a sadistic edge to his tone. "And I'll send this Russkie to meet his fucking maker."

Liu added impatiently, "Enough of this foolishness! Release our man, or both of you shall die, along with your cherished president."

This last threat caused the armed Russian to turn the Sterling on the trio facing him and pull the trigger. A blazing gunfight erupted that sent all of the room's other occupants diving to the floor for cover.

By the time Vince and his tablemates looked up, the report of the last round still reverberating in their ears, only devastation remained. The two Russians and their prisoner were crumpled on the carpeted deck, their lifeless, blood-soaked bodies in a tangled heap.

Dennis Liu and Monica Chang miraculously remained standing, completely untouched. Kneeling beside them was a badly bleeding Bear, who had taken a round in the shoulder. Max Kurtyka's bullet-ridden corpse lay sprawled out close by, his body still twitching in the final throes of death.

The scent of cordite hung thick in the air, as Kristin Liu came sprinting through the aft entryway. Her relief was apparent upon seeing her father, then she spotted Bear.

"We need a doctor over here!" she cried while kneeling beside her wounded associate, trying her best to stem the spurting blood with a table napkin.

Her father appeared to be more concerned with Max Kurtyka's lifeless corpse. There was a startled look of disbelief in his dark eyes, as Liu watched his computer expert issue his final breath.

"Oh shit!" he cursed. "Who's going to get the codes off?"

"Father," interrupted Kristin. "We need a doctor, or Bear's going to bleed to death!"

Though his concerns were obviously elsewhere, Dennis Liu managed to tear his glance away from Max's body. With vacant, glassy eyes, he looked out to the opposite balcony, where Vince and his party were seated.

"Dr. Patton!" he summoned urgently.

The silver-haired physician had no choice but to stand. He traded the briefest of concerned glances with Ricky and the rest of his tablemates before crossing the room to attend to the wounded terrorist.

Vince meanwhile found himself anticipating more trouble, as Liu rushed down to the room's main table. Not certain what he would do if Liu isolated his fury on the American President, he watched as the terrorist halted alongside the president of Russia.

Liu was still seething with rage. He grabbed the Russian statesman by the lapels of his tuxedo, and yanked him roughly to his feet. This in turn caused the remaining two Russian security agents, who were seated at an adjoining table, to also stand.

Liu laughed at this futile effort to protect their charge. He appeared to be taking sadistic pleasure from this tense encounter, as he jammed the barrel of his pistol up against the Russian president's graying temple.

"I warned you," he muttered angrily. "And you, my dear pitiful comrade, shall be the first head of state to pay for this act of folly."

Vince feared that the blood would really start to flow now, and he looked on as Monica joined Liu at the center of the room.

"Why waste the bullet?" she commented haughtily. "Besides, the spineless idiot's worth more to us as a living bargaining chip."

"Max's death has changed all that," returned Liu. "Without his computer expertise, we'll never be able to transmit the unlock codes back to Admiral Liu. So to hell with our original plan. I'm going to take great pleasure in blowing away each one of our special guests, before detonating the charge that will take this entire ship to her watery grave."

"But, Father," Kristin countered from the balcony, where she was watching Dr. Patton work on Bear. "How can we abandon our cause so readily?"

"Who said anything about abandoning it?" Liu replied. "Our martyrdom shall ignite the spark of world revolution!"

Kristin was desperate to refocus her father's crazed thoughts. Her anxiety was obvious as she scanned the room. It was as her gaze passed over Vince's table that she spotted a very scared Ricky Patton, and a thought suddenly inspired her.

"Father, we've got Max's replacement seated right there on the balcony! Dr. Patton's son knows computers. He should be able to take Max's place at the console."

This alert observation hit its intended mark, and Dennis Liu relaxed his grasp on the Russian president's tuxedo jacket. Once again he broke into a mad fit of laughter that ended after he disgustedly shoved the sweating Russian statesman back into his chair.

"Ricky!" shouted Kristin, her voice firm and urgent.

The young man didn't really know how to react to the summons. Vince noted his confusion, and realizing that his presence could very well defuse this trying turn of events, nodded supportively.

"For the sake of all of us, Ricky," Vince whispered. "You've got to do what they say. Just buy us some more time, and I promise you that we'll figure a way out of this mess."

Ricky was already traumatized by the events of this tragic day, and he stood tentatively, his injured leg rubbery. One of the onlooking terrorists arrived at the table. Ricky was led at gunpoint over to that section of the balcony where his father continued working on Bear. Dennis Liu and Monica Chang joined him there, and with Kristin close by, Ricky listened to her father's forceful ultimatum.

"Young man, destiny has just selected you to take your place in history. You need only to obey me and apply your unique skills to all that I ask. In return, I promise on my own daughter's life that no harm will come to your father."

Liu halted at this point. He aimed his pistol at the kneeling physician, rammed a bullet into the gun's chamber, and added: "And should you disobey me, or attempt in any way to intentionally sabotage our efforts, know that I won't hesitate to put a bullet into your father's skull. Do you understand me, comrade?"

Ricky nodded meekly.

"Kristin, I want you to escort him down to security," said Dennis Liu in Mandarin as he lowered his pistol and handed it to her. "Have him help you with the operation of the video console. We only have a couple more hours to go until Red Star arrives overhead. I'll be down shortly, to escort Comrade Patton up to the Radio Room, where he can begin getting familiar with the equipment."

"Very well, Father," replied Kristin, who somewhat limply held onto the shiny .45 pistol.

Dennis Liu reached down and tightened her grip on this weapon, saying, "Your vigilance is needed now more than ever before, daughter. Can I count on you to carry out this all-important task?"

"Of course you can," she replied with renewed determination.

"Then get moving," Liu whispered. "With no one down there monitoring the cameras, there's no telling what other conspiracies are being hatched elsewhere in the ship."

High above Liu, inside the auxiliary equipment stowage space on Signal Deck, Tuff listened intently as Thomas explained the exact nature of his mission. Of particular interest was the reason behind having to cut the ship's speed below eight knots precisely at midnight. Just knowing that an organized rescue effort was about to be attempted, lightened Tuff's spirits. He was quick to offer his services, suggesting that before he showed Thomas the best way down to the Engine Room, they make a preliminary stop along the way.

Ever since making good his escape, Tuff had been busy secretly exploring the ship to see what they were up against. He carried out these clandestine recon missions by traveling through the QE2's duct system whenever possible. His intelligence indicated that there were at least two-dozen terrorists, all armed with a variety of sidearms and submachine guns.

Thomas wasn't all that surprised to learn that Dennis Liu was their leader, and that the majority of the weapons were smuggled in via the replacement gym equipment. After Thomas shared the nature of the strategic nuclear threat that the terrorists had conveyed to the Pentagon, Tuff better understood why most of the hijackers were Chinese, with the majority of them having been planted inside the ship's Laundry.

Tuff had already witnessed the ruthless manner in which the terrorists operated, and had no doubt that their threats were to be taken seriously. His excursions had previously taken him up into the ceiling of the Queens Grill, where he was able to peek through a ventilation grating and confirm that both Vince Kellogg and the heads of state were still alive as of late that afternoon. Hunger pangs had directed Tuff past the kitchen, where the presence of several armed guards kept him from accumulating a proper stash of victuals. He instead had to make do with a raid on an adjoining storeroom, where the only available food was caviar and pâté de foie gras.

Tuff pulled out a tin of expropriated pâté that Thomas consumed while the Englishman further plotted out the exact logistics of their upcoming excursion. In order to reach the dual pitch levers and slow the ship without being discovered, Tuff recommended that they first disconnect the security cameras in the aft end of the Engine Room. To accomplish this feat, he suggested that they visit the equipment access space, where he had been working when he first learned of the hijacking.

Kristin abandoned any pretense of toughness the moment they exited the Queens Grill and stepped into the passageway. She made certain that the pistol's safety was engaged before stashing it in the pocket of her coveralls.

"I'm really sorry that you had to experience any of this," she said while leading the way aft. "I know that you must think we're crazy, but there really is a purpose to our madness, Ricky."

Ricky grunted skeptically. "There's no excuse for cold-blooded murder."

Kristin had been expecting this attitude, and she tried her best to plead their case. "What you view as murder, we look upon as unfortunate casualties of war. You see, we're currently in the midst of an armed struggle; a fight for survival, that's as important to us as the Civil War was to your ancestors in preserving your country."

As they reached the landing, Kristin hit a button to summon the elevator. They entered the lift, and as they headed down to Two Deck, she continued.

"Don't get me wrong, Ricky. I'm not trying to justify the bloodshed that you witnessed back there. What I would like to do is give you an inkling of what's motivating us. The cell that's carrying out this operation may be but a few dozen strong, yet the movement we represent counts its loyal members by the hundreds of millions. Do you know much about the history of modern China, Ricky?"

"I know enough," he retorted icily, still hesitant to be drawn into a civil conversation.

"Then I'm sure you know who Chairman Mao was," she said, noting the continued distrust in Ricky's eyes. "No one was more instrumental in the birth of the People's Republic than Mao Tse-tung. Almost by himself, the Chairman single-handedly freed our country from decades of slavery, pestilence, and war.

"I'm proud to say that my paternal grandfather was one of Mao's closest advisors, who personally accompanied the Chairman during the infamous Long March. In fact, it was on October 14, 1934, that grandfather left his childhood home in Kiangsi Province to join Mao and a hundred thousand others on a desperate retreat from encroaching Kuomintang Nationalist forces under Chiang Kai-shek."

Kristin continued her tale as the lift reached Two Deck, where they continued on foot to the Security Room. "In the first three weeks of the Long March, nearly twenty-five thousand would die in combat. Grandfather received a severe wound to his leg at this time, during an attack on a Nationalist blockhouse. From that point on, it was a painful struggle for him to keep up with the rest of the dwindling Red Chinese Army. Grandmother always said that it was the force of his convictions alone that saw him through all three hundred and sixty-eight days of the march. He covered over eight thousand miles altogether, through deserts, swamps, snow-covered mountains, and fast-moving river gorges.

"Mao was forced to abandon three of his children during the course of this epic journey. He also had a brother who was killed and his wife injured, along the way to their final stop in the loess caves of Shensi Province."

They found the door to the Security Room wide open. Kristin led the way inside to the inner room that was dominated by a wall of video monitors. She made certain that Ricky was comfortably seated behind the keyboard of a console before giving him a quick demonstration of the system's capabilities. She was able to isolate one of the cameras in the ship's Bridge. She then used the mouse to pan the lens of the camera from one side of the darkened control room to the other, and even managed to get a close-up of one of the officers updating a navigation chart.

Ricky couldn't help but be impressed with the system, and he voluntarily took hold of the mouse to move the camera himself. "Do you mean to say that you've got video coverage of this entire ship?" he asked while manipulating the mouse to get a close-up of the beard-stubbled face of the navigator.

"I believe so," she answered. "Though I don't think it's possible to spy on individual staterooms. Max was the real expert on this system. He was teaching me how to use it, right before he was killed."

Ricky experimented with the keyboard, and learned that different cameras could be isolated by hitting various combinations of letters and numbers. By depressing the key marked F1, he was able to access a view of the ship's engine control room on the center video monitor. Randomly hitting F8 caused the screen beside it to fill with a shot of the *QE2*'s Bakery. Ricky used the mouse to catch two Chinese sentries helping themselves to a tray filled with chocolate eclairs.

Kristin could see that Ricky was hooked, and as he continued his experimentation, she went on with her story. "In 1949, after twenty-two years on the run in the rural interior, Grandfather was one of the lucky patriots at Mao's side as he triumphantly entered Beijing. As survivors of the Long March, they felt they could meet any challenge, including that of creating a new nation.

"My father came into the world one year later, shortly after Grandfather fell in love with a feisty political writer from Nanjing. The countryside was still filled with roving bands of Nationalist bandits in those early days of the Republic. While on a mission to Lanzhou, Grandfather was captured by such a band. The Kuomintang scum recognized him as one of Mao's advisors, and a mock trial was convened, with Grandfather labeled a traitor. He was beheaded that same evening, his body tossed on the side of the road to be devoured by wild dogs.

"When Grandmother heard of this tragedy, she was forced to make the difficult decision to leave China and move to San Francisco with her brother's family. Even though Father grew up in California, his uncle's household instilled in him the utter importance of an independent, self-sustaining China, free from corrupt Western influences. Frequent trips back to mainland China allowed him to establish relations with a powerful group of Communists who shared his concerns. It was this group of patriots who introduced him to the movement to which we currently belong.

"The reason for our present actions are solely prompted by Li Chen's illegal power grab after Deng Xiaoping's death. Entry into the G-7 would mean the end of China as we now know it, making all of the sacrifices that Grandfather, Mao, and the rest of the Red patriots were forced to make be totally in vain."

"Maybe that wouldn't be such a bad thing," returned Ricky as diplomatically as possible. He didn't want to agree with her actions nor did he want to condemn, either of which might turn her more harshly against him. Still, he couldn't just let all these excuses go unanswered. That wasn't how his father had raised him.

Kristin was relieved to hear that Ricky had been paying attention to her, and she attempted to draw him out further. "What do you mean by that?"

Ricky replied while filling a single screen with a live video shot of the Midships Lobby, the darkened Theater, the Beauty Salon, and a carpeted Penthouse passageway. "What I'm trying to say, Kristin, is that it's time for China to take its rightful place in the twenty-first century. And you're not going to do this by running away like scared children who are afraid to grow up. China has nothing to fear from the world community. Change is frightening by its very nature. And for your country to reach its full potential, you must put your fears aside, and work with the other nations to make this planet a better place for all of us."

This spirited discourse generated a smattering of applause from the room's doorway. This was where Dennis Liu was standing, an amused grin on his face.

"Well said, comrade," reflected Liu, as he stopped clapping. "Though I must admit that your political outlook of the world is naive at best. What do you know of class struggle and a people's desire for real freedom? Your pampered upbringing has limited your sight and clouded your soul that's been stripped of its vibrance by the cancerous sameness of Western consumerism.

"I experienced this same decadence firsthand in Hollywood, and believe me, it will lead to your country's eventual demise, comrade. We Chinese can only pray that we stopped the disease before it reached epidemic proportions. That's what this takeover is all about—a last ditch, desperate effort by a group of dedicated patriots, who can't just sit back and watch their beloved country swallowed by capitalism's insatiable greed!"

Any further comment on Liu's part was interrupted by his sighting of a scene on the screen at the console's top, left-hand corner. It showed Monica in the midst of what appeared to be an angry confrontation with a group of Japanese security agents seated around a table in the Queens Grill.

"Damn!" cursed Liu. "Won't those fools ever learn? Come on, Kristin. We'd better get up there and teach them another lesson."

Before leaving, Liu pulled a pair of handcuffs out of his pocket. He cuffed Ricky's wrist to the solid, tubular-steel edge of the main console.

"And don't even think of participating in any foolhardy antics yourself, comrade," he warned. "Remember that we still have your father."

Ricky nodded that he understood, and accepted the barest of supportive smiles from Kristin. Once he was alone, he was able to use his right hand to address the keyboard, and he watched the encounter in the Queens Grill unfold with as many camera angles as possible.

So focused was his concentration on this effort that he didn't notice the access panel to the room's equipment space suddenly popping open. First to emerge from this entryway was Tuff, followed closely by Thomas Kellogg.

Tuff found himself forcing back a boyish grin as he loudly cleared his throat and greeted, "Evening, lad."

Caught totally by surprise, Ricky spun around, and his eyes opened wide upon spotting the ship's security officer. Standing beside him was a tall, dark-haired stranger. This middle-aged male wore the uniform of a ship's officer, though this was the first that Ricky had seen of him.

"If you don't remember, lad, my name's Tuff and I work with Robert Hartwell. I managed to escape right before the terrorists took over, and I'm most aware of your predicament. My accomplice here is Special Agent Kellogg's younger brother, Thomas."

Ricky appeared confused by this. "I didn't know he had a brother who was a member of the crew."

"He doesn't," replied Thomas. "I'm a federal agent myself, working for the Bureau of Alcohol, Tobacco and Firearms."

Ricky scratched his head. "Then how come you didn't join us earlier?"

"Because, believe it or not, I only arrived on this ship a couple of hours ago," Thomas revealed.

Before Ricky could further express his confusion, Tuff broke in. "Easy does it, lad. Special Agent Kellogg is the first wave of a rescue effort that the military's about to attempt. And by the way, he joined us by parachute."

As Thomas nodded that this was true, his gaze was distracted by the ugly scene continuing to develop on the screen. "Looks like there's serious trouble brewing."

"It's another damn confrontation in the Grill," observed Tuff. "As far as I'm concerned, midnight can't get here fast enough."

Tuff took a closer look at Ricky's handcuffs before reaching into his pocket, pulling out his key chain, and handing one of the keys to Ricky. "You're lucky that the hijackers are using the ship's cuffs. Right now, my best advice is to stay here, lad. Use the key only if you really have to."

"Isn't there anything else that I can do to help you?" offered Ricky.

Thomas gestured toward the console. "Your presence here can make all the difference in assuring our mission's success. Just stay out of trouble, and keep your head down once midnight comes around. That's when things are going to get real interesting."

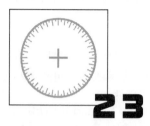

23

Brad Bodzin's second watch of the day called him back to the USS *Polk*'s sonar room at 2100. Together with Jaffers and Seaman Wilford, the team prepared themselves for what could very well be the most important watch of their entire patrol. In three more hours, SEAL Team Two was scheduled to disembark aboard their SDV for the crucial task of retaking the *QE2*. In a sign of supreme confidence in Bodzin's team, Captain Kram had personally asked for them to stand this vital watch, and the Texan proudly accepted this challenge.

To properly motivate his men, Bodzin gave each of them a couple of Kit Kat chocolate bars, as they settled in behind their consoles. A confessed chocoholic himself, Bodzin satisfied his craving with a mug of hot cocoa. With this beverage in hand, he assumed his usual standing position behind his two seated associates.

The first fifteen minutes of the watch were spent reacquainting themselves with the *Polk*'s tactical situation. They were presently monitoring five separate sonar contacts. Their primary target of course was the *QE2*. The ocean liner's distinctive sonar signature was designated Sierra One. The *QE2* was continuing on a north-by-northeasterly course, and had slowed its forward speed to twenty-one knots.

Further TACAMO broadcasts had confirmed the fact that the ship had indeed been hijacked, and that a crisis of international proportions was taking place aboard the superliner. In response, the *Polk* had settled into a position some 10,000 yards to the southwest of the *QE2*, proceeding on the exact same course. This was in anticipation of the transfer of the SEALs, at which time the *Polk* would substantially cut the distance separating the two vessels.

Because it was absolutely vital that no hostile submarines be encountered during the vulnerable SDV launch, Command had also decided to further tighten the positions of two of its submarine escorts. Sierra Two was the designation for the *Baikal*. The Russian *Akula*-class boat was ordered to take up a point position, patrolling the northeastern sector, roughly 20,000 yards off the *QE2*'s port bow.

The French submarine was assigned the southeastern sector, with the *Casabianca* designated Sierra Three and lying some 20,000 yards off the *QE2*'s starboard bow. This left the *Polk* to take up the rear, almost directly behind the *Rubis*-class submarine.

The *Talent* had received permission to drop out of what had been a rectangularly shaped escort formation, with the *QE2* smack in the middle. The Brits were designated Sierra Four, and were last picked up by sonar quietly following in the *Polk*'s baffles.

The fifth and final sonar contact they were aware of belonged to a pod of noisy whales. Designated Sierra Five, the high-pitched squeals and deep-bass bellows of this boisterous bunch emanated from the waters due north of them, a good ten nautical miles distant.

The mysterious sonar contact labeled Sierra Nine had been conspicuously absent from their screens, since last showing itself almost twenty-four hours before. Bodzin knew that this had disturbing implications, especially if this contact turned out to be the suspect Chinese submarine. Tagging this vessel was now their number-one priority.

The *QE2*'s further reduction in speed had given the *Polk* additional options to carry out this search successfully. No longer having to concentrate their efforts solely on keeping up with the ship, they could now initiate a proper sonar sweep in an attempt to locate their elusive quarry. The *Polk*'s two-hundred-and-forty-foot-long towed array was presently deployed, its thirty-seven hydrophones giving them a sonic picture of any potential underwater trespassers to the rear of the formation. They were also in the midst of a sprint-and-drift effort, whereby the *Polk* would travel at set periods of noisy flank speed, only to abruptly slow down to allow their hydrophones noise-free listening conditions.

They were currently in the midst of a sprint leg, with the *Polk* rushing to the northeast to regain the distance it had lost during the last drift. The sound of their own sonic signature was the predominant audible noise, and Bodzin and his team bided their time until the next drift phase began. Content to sip his cocoa while his men nibbled on their candy bars, the *Polk*'s senior sonar technician listened as Jaffers's voice broke the hushed quiet.

"Hey, Wilford, did you catch sight of those SEALs in Jimmy's Buffet tonight?" Jimmy's Buffet was what the sailors had named the galley.

The team's junior member answered while rotely isolating the hydrophones of the medium-range BQ-21 broadband sonar. "You bet I did, Jaffers. Those guys were really wolfing down the chow."

"They looked to me like a bunch of condemned men eating their last meal," remarked Jaffers, who was monitoring the BQ-7 long-range sonar.

Wilford isolated the BQ-21's lowest frequency range and quipped. "Hell, what else do they have to do but eat, sleep, shit, and exercise."

"Those guys are going to be earning their keep soon enough," Bodzin interjected, his eyes scanning Wilford's waterfall display. "Brother, you couldn't pay me enough to crawl into one of those SDVs and attempt what Command is asking of them tonight. As I was on my way up here, I passed through the missile magazine on Two Deck, and the SEALs were already jocking up for their midnight ramble."

"Williams says that he was down there earlier, and saw some of the SEALs working with a virtual-reality helmet," said Jaffers. "He asked what they were looking at, and some English dude explained that the SEALs were touring the interior- and exterior-deck layout of the *QE2*."

"I sure didn't see any high-tech hardware when I passed by," Bodzin observed. "The SEALs I saw were getting ready to tango the old-fashioned way, with grease paint, K-Bar knives, Sig Sauer 9mm pistols, and MP-5 submachine guns. Bubbas, if we ever do get in a position where we'll be able to launch that SDV and get them to the *Queen*, I sure wouldn't want to be one of those unsuspecting terrorists. Hell, I was scared just watching them put on their war paint, and they're on *our* side!"

Almost to underscore this comment, the *Polk*'s captain unexpectedly entered sonar. Benjamin Kram wasted no time joining Bodzin behind the main console.

"Good evening, Mr. Bodzin," he greeted.

"Evening, sir," Bodzin replied, genuinely surprised by this visit. "Welcome to the sound shack. Can I get you a Kit Kat bar or some cocoa, Captain?"

"No thanks, Mr. Bodzin. I wanted to take this opportunity to emphasize the importance of these next couple of hours. The latest TACAMO update informs us that the midnight rescue attempt is still a go."

"So I understand, sir," said Bodzin.

Kram took a minute to scan the various waterfall displays before expressing his number-one concern. "I gather that there's still no sign of that Chinese *Han?*"

"That's affirmative, Captain. But you can rest assured that if he's out there, me and my boys will tag him, especially now that we can use the towed array and cover more water through sprint-and-drift."

Kram continued his examination of the glowing monitor screens, and Bodzin noted the abundance of age lines that creased the captain's face. Kram looked unusually tired, his tension obvious as he worriedly remarked: "What I don't want to face is a situation where we're about to release the SDV, and still have to worry about that *Han* showing up and taking a potshot at us. If they're out there, it's imperative that I know about it long before we ascend to flood the dry-deck shelter."

"I hear you loud and clear, sir. Between our detection capabilities and those of the *Baikal, Casabianca,* and *Talent,* we're bound to tag them if they're still in the area. We were able to get a firm tonal lock on them the last time, and unless the Chinese have been able to correct that sound leak, I don't see how it's possible for them to be close enough to cause us any alarm, and us not be able to hear them."

It was but a short transit that took Comdr. Mark Eastbrook from his cabin into the HMS *Talent*'s control room. As expected, the crowded compartment was dimly lit in red, and Eastbrook halted at the hatchway to let his eyes adjust. As his pupils widened, he spotted the single planesman seated behind the boat's wheel. The diving officer was positioned alongside the massive bank of instruments that controlled the *Talent*'s ballast, with the sub's dual periscopes positioned to his right.

In between the helm and the fire-control and navigation consoles lining the starboard bulkhead, a high-backed leather chair was mounted into the deck. His XO was seated here, with an excellent view of the boat's tactical systems. Robert Lyall was concentrating on a report from the coxswain, and was caught by surprise as Eastbrook joined them.

"How goes it, Number One?"

The XO answered while alertly standing. "We've completed the back-down maneuver as ordered, Captain."

"And the results?" Eastbrook asked.

The XO dejectedly shook his head, prompting Eastbrook to give his second in command a supportive pat on the shoulder. "Hang in there, Robert. In this game, patience is everything."

"Perhaps the *Han* figured out what they were up against and backed off," offered Lyall hopefully.

"They've come much too far for that, Number One. If I know our Chinese friends, they're lurking out there somewhere close by, just waiting for an opportunity to mount an ambush. As we painfully learned during World War II, it will be up to the *Talent* to guard the back door, and insure that the *Han* won't try entering the formation from our baffles. Too many U-boats caught our convoys napping in just such a manner, and if I know the bloody PLA Navy, it would be just like them to apply a tactic taken directly from the pages of history. The only trouble now is trying to figure out which bloody history book they'll be taking that lesson from."

Commissar Guan Yin had little doubt that the moment of truth was almost upon them. Ever since the *Lijiang* had taken up a defensive position directly beneath the *QE2*, an atmosphere of tense expectation had prevailed. All this seemed to come to a head several hours before, when Lee Shao-chi approached Guan in his cabin, and politely asked him to postpone that evening's regular Komsomol meeting. Guan was not about to refuse the request of a man whose tactical brilliance was responsible for maneuvering them into their current position.

Guan was in his stateroom reading a pamphlet written by Chairman Mao entitled, *Yu Chi Chan* (On Guerrilla Warfare), when Lee entered and informed Guan of his unorthodox decision to attempt penetrating the submarine convoy. Lee displayed the same confidence that he showed during their successful transit of the Bering Strait, as he went on to explain how he intended to pull off this daring maneuver.

"He who is shut inside is a pheasant. He who enters to arrest is a hawk."

This was the poetic example Lee offered to justify his dangerous plan. By stealthily scouting the surrounding seas, Lee was able to determine that there was a total of three submarines that had been sent along to secretly escort the *QE2* during her crossing. Regardless of the fact that Dennis Liu and his forces had apparently succeeded in wresting control of the ocean liner and had altered her course, these submarines continued to stubbornly tag along. They would have to be eliminated before the *Lijiang* could even think about surfacing and making good the rendezvous.

Though one against three would make most oddsmakers put their money on the opposition, this wasn't the case with Lee. He merely looked at this tactical disadvantage as an additional challenge that would have to be compensated for with guile and cunning.

His plan was simplicity itself, the first stage of which had already been initiated. To penetrate the convoy, Lee positioned the *Lijaing* in the direct path of the oncoming ocean liner. A Russian *Akula-* and a French *Rubis*-class submarine were the point vessels. By scramming the *Lijiang*'s reactor and enveloping the boat in a state of ultraquiet, they easily escaped detection. Only when the *QE2* was almost right on top of them, did Lee order the reactor back on-line. The roaring noise of the passing ocean liner's nine engines was clearly audible inside the *Lijiang*, with this same racket effectively masking any sound that they were soon making.

Now that the fox was safely inside the hen house, it was time to begin whittling down the opposition. Lee was hesitant to explain the strategy that he planned to employ to achieve this end, and he left Guan with a cryptic invitation to join him in the control room at 2130.

His stomach tight with anticipation, Guan passed up dinner for the first time on this patrol. Endless cups of sweet green tea provided his only sustenance, as he tried his hardest to refocus his thoughts on the guerrilla-war tactics of Mao Tse-tung.

Now that 2130 was almost upon them, Guan found himself reading one of the Chairman's verses over and over again. It had universal application, and could even apply to their current circumstances. It read:

> "When the situation is serious, the guerrillas must move with the fluidity of water and the ease of the blowing wind. Their tactics must deceive, tempt, and confuse the enemy. They must lead the enemy to believe that they will attack him from the east and north, and they must then strike him from the west and south, quick to disperse to fight again where the enemy least anticipates."

At military school, the principles of guerrilla warfare had been continually stressed. Guan had never taken them seriously at the time, and only now realized that this strategic wisdom could be readily applied in today's modern battlefield. The ancient saying, *Sheng Tung, Chi Hsi* (Uproar in the East, Strike in the West), appropriately summed up Mao's teachings in this field, as well as those of Capt. Lee Shao-chi. Anxious now to hear how Lee planned to make good his own deception, Guan arose and took off for the control room.

The *Lijiang's* passageways were vacant as he climbed up the amidships stairwell and made his way to One Deck. He continued forward, and needed barely eight steps to reach the hatchway leading to control.

Little was he prepared for the fat white candle that flickered alive on the floor of the periscope pedestal, or the rich scent of sandalwood incense that filled the compartment with an alien sweetness. The rest of the equipment-packed room was dimly lit in red, and Guan gasped upon noting that almost every sailor present was dressed in a similar white martial-arts uniform. This included their captain, who stood behind the candle, his customary red bandanna tied tightly around his forehead. This hushed assemblage appeared to have been waiting for Guan's presence, for no sooner did he take his place beside the fully manned fire-control console, than Lee Shao-chi addressed them.

"Comrades, it's time to momentarily close our eyes, and unite our spirits in joint purpose. Breathe deeply with me, emptying your lungs completely, before refilling them with the blessed essence of life. This is the secret of the Way; practice it continuously, and no enemy need ever be feared.

"From our position of power, it's time to become one with the enemy. We shall strike where least expected, with the fleeting shadow of our presence, our only weapon. Confusion shall ensue, causing them to blindly strike out in a rage that has no true center.

"Once we see that they are beaten back, we shall quickly separate and attack yet another strong point on the periphery of his force, like a winding mountain path. This fighting strategy is the key for one against many. Strike down the enemies in one quarter, then grasp the initiative and attack further strong points to the left and right, as if on a winding mountain path. For victory is certain when the enemy is caught up in a rhythm that confuses his spirit."

Guan had tightly shut his eyes, and surrendered his breath to a deep, even pace. Yet with the captain's abrupt silence, he couldn't help but open his eyes to see what was taking place around him.

The flickering flame, a terrifying thing in a submarine, created an eerie setting for an even stronger terror, one that caused goose-bumps to form on his flesh. Like a single entity, the compartment's entire complement appeared to be breathing in unison, their eyes closed, their thoughts united in joint purpose.

Guan almost felt like a traitor for opening his eyes and disrupting the spell, and he found his glance drawn to the periscope pedestal. Here the man who orchestrated this odd underwater ritual suddenly opened his own eyes. Lee's scarred face displayed an unearthly determination, as he cried out for all to hear.

"Comrades, it's time to strike down the twin demons of doubt and fear! Become like a rock, and ten thousand enemies can't touch you! So open your eyes, and dare climb this winding mountain together, on a warrior's pilgrimage to save our Republic.

"For the glory of Mother China, all ahead flank speed, on bearing one-two-seven!"

*　　*　　*

The *Polk* was in the drift phase of their scan, and Brad Bodzin took advantage of the excellent acoustic conditions to closely monitor their current sonar contacts. With the assistance of a pair of bulky headphones, he listened to the familiar growling roar of Sierra One's powerful diesel engines. The *QE2* remained on a northeasterly course, continuing to cut through the gathering swells above at a constant twenty-one knots.

To monitor Sierra Two, Bodzin substantially narrowed the frequency range of his scan. The *Akula* lay off the *QE2*'s port bow, easily matching its speed on a similar bearing. Design improvements, such as sophisticated sound insulation, made this Russian warship much more difficult to detect than earlier classes of Soviet submarines that were inherently noisy. It was Jaffers who had originally detected the fault in Sierra Two's acoustic integrity. It was a constant high-pitched hum that was most likely an unwanted byproduct of a faulty propeller. Especially audible at high speed, the singing prop was readily recognizable, and the senior sonar technician turned his attention to the vessel that comprised the point formation's southern perimeter.

The *Casabianca* was the smallest of the escorting submarines. It had been a struggle for the French boat to keep in position, especially when the *QE2* was traveling above twenty-eight knots. Now that the *Queen* had slowed, the *Casabianca* was holding its own, though Bodzin had little trouble detecting the first signs of strain inside the French warship's engine room. The throaty, pulsating rush of a defective reactor-coolant pump proved to be Sierra Three's acoustic weakness, and the pride of the Marine Nationale would need a comprehensive refit to correct this problem.

The one major biological contact that they had to deal with continued singing up a storm in the waters due north of their formation. Bodzin had a great affinity for whales and other marine mammals. They were man's cousins in the seas, and their resonant, bellowing cries had kept him company during many a boring watch. Regardless of the fact that their boisterous presence could make his job that much more difficult, Bodzin always looked at the presence of whales as a sign of good fortune.

Sierra Four proved to be the only contact that the *Polk*'s sensors could no longer detect. The *Talent*'s signature had last been picked up by a towed array sweep. That was over a half hour before, at which time the Royal Navy warship was trailing in the formation's sound-absorbent baffles. Bodzin was well aware that the *Talent* was difficult enough to pick up under near ideal acoustic conditions. When masked by the *QE2*'s roiling wake, she would be almost impossible to find.

The one contact that remained conspicuously absent from their sensors was the Chinese *Han*-class submarine. SEAL Team Two's SDV was still scheduled for launch in a little more than two hours. Bodzin couldn't forget the recent visit by Captain Kram, and the unprecendented manner in which he practically implored them to tag the *Han* before the SEALs were deployed topside.

Patience and perseverance were key ingredients to any successful sonar search. It was usually the slightest sonic deviation, a mere flutter on the waterfall display or muted hiss from the headphones that signaled the presence of an unwanted underwater trespasser in the area. That was the subtle manner in which Bodzin was expecting the *Han* to eventually reveal itself. And that's why he was caught completely off guard when a deafening, freight-train-like roar erupted from his headphones. His eyes instantly went to the flickering repeater screen of the BQ-21 display, as Jaffers verbally revealed the nature of the contact that he too had picked up on his headphones.

"It's another submarine, Sup! It looks to be churning up the water at flank speed beneath the *Queen*'s bow, headed with a bone in its teeth on bearing one-two-seven."

This heading would take the bogey right through the slot of water lying between the *Baikal* and the *Casabianca*. This was the same channel reserved for the *QE2*'s use, and Bodzin was unable to figure out the significance of this unorthodox tactical display. He grabbed for the overhead intercom handset.

"Conn, sonar. We have a new underwater contact, traveling on a bearing of one-two-seven, at a relative rough range of twenty thousand yards. Classify Sierra Six, possible hostile *Han*-class submarine!"

Of no immediate threat to the *Polk*, Bodzin nevertheless intently monitored Sierra Six's progress. It was continuing to make good its sprint for the waters separating the formation's point vessels. This channel was roughly eight thousand-yards wide, and Bodzin wondered if either the *Baikal* or the *Casabianca* had yet picked up this underwater interloper approaching from their rear.

It was as Sierra Six broke the thirty-knot threshold that the *Polk*'s captain returned to the sonar room. Benjamin Kram arrived in time to hear Jaffers excitedly reveal a verbal picture of the latest sonar data.

"It appears that both Sierra Two and Three have tagged Sierra Six. The *Baikal* is turning to starboard, with the *Casabianca* in the process of making a turn to port. Both submarines appear to be preparing to engage Sierra Six!"

"What in the hell is that *Han* trying to pull off?" asked Bodzin, his eyes locked on the collection of thick white lines now visible on the waterfall displays.

As Benjamin Kram grabbed for a set of headphones, his XO also entered the compartment. Lt. Comdr. Dan Calhoun settled in behind the vacant BQS-4 console, as Jaffers's voice loudly cried out,

"Torpedoes in the water! I show various high-pitched tonal aspects, indicating a launch by both the *Baikal* and the *Casabianca*."

"And Sierra Six?" queried Kram, who was unable to sort out the sonic mess being conveyed through his headphones.

"They appear to have disappeared right off the screen, sir!" informed the *Polk*'s perplexed senior sonar technician. "All we're showing is the signature of four torpedoes, and increased screw counts on both the *Baikal* and the *Casabianca*."

"Damn!" cursed the XO. "We've got us a fucking turkey shoot out there."

Benjamin Kram traded the briefest of concerned glances with his second in command, as he removed his headphones and passionately expressed himself. "I told Admiral Buchanan that assigning four submarines for this mission would only confuse matters. And now someone out there's about to pay the ultimate price for a tactical decision made by a bunch of damn politicians!"

Kram's fears were seemingly confirmed by Jaffers's next update. "Oh, sweet Jesus! Those fish appear to be crossing in midchannel. Shit, the Russians and the French are going to end up taking each other out!"

A feeling of powerlessness and frustration possessed Benjamin Kram, as he watched the manner in which the *Baikal* and the *Casabianca* were reacting to this unwarranted attack on each other. Both submarines were pouring on the speed, with a full spread of decoys already launched, all in a desperate attempt to escape the onrushing torpedoes.

It proved to be the slower of the two warships that was the first to succumb to this tragic friendly fire incident. Almost simultaneously, both Bodzin and Jaffers tore off their headphones, as a deafening series of booming blasts was projected into the surrounding waters. Bodzin alertly switched on the compartment's overhead speakers in time to hear yet another pair of sharp, resonant explosions sound outside their hull. This was followed by a distinctive crackling noise that sounded much like popping popcorn.

"Damn, they're imploding!" revealed Bodzin, who had once heard this same sickening signature on a tape back in sonar school. "The *Baikal* and the *Casabianca* are gone!"

The shocking reality of this astounding revelation only sank in as the crackling faded and was replaced by the single, all-encompassing roar of the *QE2*'s engines. Completely oblivious to the underwater battle that had just taken place in the depths below, the ocean liner transited the seas directly above the accident site, its progress unimpeded.

"Where the hell are the bastards responsible for this tragedy?" questioned the XO.

"I've never seen anything quite like it," muttered Bodzin.

There was an air of finality to his movements. He tore off a piece of paper towel and reached out to erase Sierra Two and Three off the sonar update board. Bodzin's hand was shaking slightly as he penciled in Sierra Six, and followed it with a large question mark.

"What scares the hell out of me," he added, his voice strained. "Is not only that they went and disappeared right off our sonar screens like they did, but that Sierra Six actually seems to have planned this whole attack all along."

"I hear you loud and clear, Mr. Bodzin," returned Benjamin Kram. "And now we're going to be even more vigilant, to make sure that the same outcome doesn't befall the *Polk*. Whatever it takes, you've got to track down that *Han* by 2400 hours, or SEAL Team Two is never going to get a chance to equal the score."

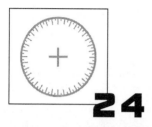

24

VINCE KELLOGG WATCHED AS THE SITUATION INSIDE THE QUEENS GRILL CONTINued to deteriorate. Only minutes after the bodies of the two recently killed Russians were dragged out, the next confrontation took place. This one appeared to have been triggered by an insulting remark that one of the Japanese agents mouthed as Monica Chang passed by their table. Whatever was said caused the actress to go ballistic, and she stormed over to the table, her submachine gun raised and ready for action.

"Stand up, you Japanese dog!" she screamed at the offending agent.

The two tuxedo-clad Japanese security agents who had been seated there rose in unison, defiant smirks on their smooth-shaven faces.

This challenge to her authority only served to aggravate Monica even further, and she let loose yet another volley of submachine-gun fire up into the bullet-ridden ceiling. The Japanese agents reacted to this noisy show of force with barely a flinch. As two armed sentries arrived at the table, Monica confronted the senior member of the Japanese contingent.

Vince knew this individual personally. A former member of Japanese Special Forces, Yushio Tanaka, or Tiger as he was better known, was a decorated veteran, not the type of man who could be easily intimidated. He also wasn't a fool, which led Vince to wonder what he was trying to prove by acting in such an insubordinate manner.

"We warned you what would happen to troublemakers," she reminded, her infuriated glance cast upward to meet the impassive stare of the solidly built, six-foot-four-inch Japanese agent. "And now we'll have to make an example of your beloved prime minister."

Tiger glanced down at Monica as she added scornfully, "You Japanese might have thought that you could get away with raping my ancestors' homeland yet another time in this century, but now the tables have turned. You are nothing but a barbaric, despicable dog, and it will be a pleasure watching your expression as we cut your prime minister's throat."

From his vantage point on the balcony, Vince could see that Tiger looked ready to explode. The senior agent's muscular body was ramrod rigid, his reddened face flushed with anger, as he fought back the suicidal urge to retaliate.

Before he could do so, Dennis Liu and his daughter came storming into the room. The head terrorist appeared furious. His arrival prompted a whispered comment by both of Vince's tablemates.

"And now the shit's really going to hit the fan," observed Samuel Morrison.

"It's not going to be pretty, lads," Robert Hartwell added.

Vince's main concern remained centered on the safety of the American President. The chief executive was still seated at the main table along with his eight colleagues. The Japanese prime minister was positioned directly across from him, and Vince prayed that the terrorists wouldn't lose control and spray the whole table with bullets.

"Now what?" Liu demanded in Mandarin as he approached the table where Monica was in the midst of her standoff.

"This Japanese dog had the nerve to insult me," said the actress, also in Mandarin. "And I was just explaining the nature of the penalty for this offense."

A look of disgust painted Liu's face as he examined the tall security agent who faced Monica. "Your name and position, comrade?" he questioned, resorting to English.

"Yushio Tanaka, and I'm the special agent in charge of the prime minister of Japan's security detail."

This matter-of-fact response was delivered without the least hint of fear, prompting Liu to further test the depth of this man's commitment. "Special Agent in Charge Tanaka, how would you like a chance to substitute your life for that of your prime minister?"

"I would do so without a moment's hesitation," Tiger retorted.

Liu continued to size up his brawny opponent, and finally decided upon the best way to use him as an example to the others. "Your loyalty is most admirable, Special Agent. To test the degree of your convictions, I'll not only allow you to take your prime minister's place on the executioner's block, but I'll also give you a chance to earn your freedom. What I propose is a hand-to-hand fight to the death, with no quarter to be spared the loser."

This offer caused a wide grin to turn the corners of the Japanese agent's mouth, and he readily bowed in acceptance of these terms. A muted murmur filled the room. Included in this concerned group was Kristin Liu, who watched as her father stripped off his radio and handed it to Monica.

"Father, have you gone insane? The risks in such a fight surely outweigh any gains that you might win."

"What risks are you talking about, daughter? I'll snap this Japanese dog's neck like it was an immature bamboo stalk."

"But, Father, the Red Star satellite is due to pass overhead shortly. Have you forgotten already about the rest of our mission?"

Dennis Liu had heard enough. He looked sternly at Kristin, while removing a 9mm Glock from its holster at the small of his back. He handed it to her, saying, "I want you to stand behind the Japanese prime minister, with that pistol aimed at the back of his skull. If any of the other prisoners make the slightest threatening move, you're to shoot him without question. Do you understand?"

Kristin meekly nodded. Trying her best to ignore Monica's gloating sneer, she somewhat reluctantly walked over to the table holding the nine heads of state, and took up a position behind the Japanese prime minister.

This time the stare that met hers belonged to the President of the United States. Kristin was surprised that his expression displayed more compassionate understanding than either fear or anger.

Kristin was afraid to look him full in the face, and she diverted her line of sight back to that portion of the room where her father was preparing to fight. The Japanese agents were in the process of moving their table and chairs out of the way, creating an open space the size of a boxing ring. It was here that her father beckoned to his opponent to join him.

Vince Kellogg was also watching this scene from the opposite balcony. There was a certain absurdity to the mere thought of sitting here on the *Queen*, in the middle of the Atlantic Ocean, watching two men about to fight to the death, in front of an audience that included the nine most powerful men in all the world.

Vince had previously seen Dennis Liu in action in the martial-arts films that he had watched with his son. Of course, these had been carefully staged events, and Vince wondered how the actor would handle himself in this realistic situation.

While Tiger took off his tuxedo jacket and rolled up his sleeves, Liu did a few stretching exercises in the center of the improvised ring. A series of large swells picked this inopportune moment to arrive, and the ocean liner pitched from side to side in a jarring, shuddering motion. Vince didn't know how the combatants could keep on their feet, let alone fight under these conditions. Yet they stubbornly persisted, both men taking up a martial-arts stance in the ring's center.

Tiger was a good four inches taller than Liu, and had a much longer reach. As he swung his muscular arms overhead to loosen up, Liu began a rhythmic sequence of t'ai chi movements. Ignoring another set of rolling swells, the two combatants faced each other and bowed.

Once more they took up martial-arts stances, and the fight commenced as they began slowly circling. Liu's posture appeared to transfer itself into more of a classic Western form, as he lifted his clenched fists to protect his face. Tiger, in contrast, kept his hands open, constantly pawing the air kung fu style. Each of them attempted several minor punches before Tiger initiated the first real combination of blows.

They were delivered by both hand and foot. Liu deflected them with an efficient parry, moving in to strike blows himself. The subsequent vicious exchange was delivered with such lightning-quick rapidity that Vince had trouble seeing the individual blows. From his distant vantage point, all he could make out was a whirlwind of punches and kicks, most of which appeared to be delivered by Dennis Liu.

In comparison to the fleet-footed martial-arts star, Tiger's movements appeared ponderous. His powerful punches too often met only air, and in almost every instance, these miscues cost him badly, as Liu turned every successful parry into an effective attack.

When one of Tiger's roundhouse kicks grazed Liu's chin, the Chinese man let loose a deep, bloodcurdling yell. This signaled the start of a furious sequence of superbly timed blows, delivered by Liu with his fists, elbows, knees, and the sides of his feet. A violent head-butt appeared to stun Tiger. Liu followed it up with a front kick aimed right at his gut. This blow made solid contact, causing Tiger to double over and painfully gasp for air.

Once more Dennis Liu let loose an animalistic cry. Then, in an incredibly swift move that Vince almost missed seeing, Liu initiated a spiraling forward flip that ended with a solid knee to Tiger's forehead.

Liu continued this relentless onslaught without stopping. After leaving Tiger with a sharp elbow to the right temple, he slipped behind his dazed opponent and got him in a firm headlock. Vince knew that this lethal hold could prove to be the *coup de grâce*. With the palm of one hand on Tiger's bruised temple and his other arm securely locked beneath the Japanese agent's jaw, all it would take was a single push on Liu's part to break his opponent's neck.

The crazed Liu demonstrated amazing upper-arm strength. He lifted Tiger and carried the helpless agent over to the table holding the nine statesmen. As he resecured the lock on Tiger's neck, Liu's line of sight swept the table, finally locking itself on the fear-filled face of the Japanese prime minister.

"Comrade," shouted Liu, fighting to calm his heaving breath. "This brave fool willingly put his life on the line in your behalf. He knew the terms of this struggle. Yet before I execute the sentence, I'll give you one chance to take this man's place. It's your decision, Comrade Prime Minister, for your actions will determine who shall live and who shall die."

A look of shocked bewilderment filled the prime minister's pale face. Sweat poured down his forehead with such abundance that the round lenses of his wire-rimmed glasses became drenched. Directly behind him, a stunned Kristin appeared equally affected by this trau-matic standoff, forcing her to use both hands to hold her father's pistol steady.

Dennis Liu's glance swept the terror-filled faces of the other heads of state, his eyes finally locking on the only other Asian seated before him. President Li Chen appeared close to tears, and Liu further tightened his grip on Tiger's neck, all the while addressing China's trembling young leader.

"Comrade Li, to think that all this is a direct result of your cowardly, illegal actions. The tragedy is that this isn't your scrawny neck in my arms. But your time is coming, never fear."

Vince continued watching from the balcony, and his worst nightmare came to pass when the figure seated across from the Japanese prime minister spoke out.

"Stop this madness at once!" ordered the President of the United States.

"Oh, shit," muttered Samuel Morrison, as all heads turned toward his chief executive.

Liu reacted to this unexpected outburst on the part of the President by first snapping Tiger's neck with a single push of his hands, and then dumping the twitching corpse on the floor. There was gathering madness in the terrorist's eyes as he coolly rounded the table, took the Glock pistol from Kristin, and aimed it at the chest of the American President.

"So the leader of this group of buffoons has finally summoned the nerve to speak. Tell me Mr. President, if that was one of your vaunted Secret Service agents, would you have condemned him to death, like the spineless prime minister just did?"

Kellogg and Morrison couldn't believe what they were seeing— The President of the United States defiantly pushed back his chair and stood.

"What in God's name do you hope to achieve with all this bloodshed?" he asked Liu, his tone pleading. "If you've got a legitimate complaint, speak your piece and we'll do our best to deal with it. But this wasteful madness has to stop at once!"

The arrival of a swell forced the President to reach out and steady himself on the edge of the German chancellor's chair. Liu managed to keep his balance without lowering the barrel of his pistol, and he faced the President and smiled.

"So you're willing to step in and mediate my cause," remarked Liu, a sudden calmness to his voice.

The President was hopeful that his plea was getting through, and he readily replied. "I'm willing to offer the full services of the United

States of America to insure that your complaints are fairly dealt with."

This proposition caused a demented peal of laughter to escape Liu's lips. "Wonderful!" he exclaimed. "The very nation that desires to suck the life's blood from my country, now wants to mediate a truce between us. How very fitting!"

Well aware that this dangerous encounter had gone far enough, Vince made the difficult decision to stop it. And the only way he could do so was to directly intercede himself.

"Mr. President!" he shouted, while pushing back his chair and standing erect. "Shut your mouth and sit down at once. Sir!"

Vince could hardly believe it when the President actually obeyed his brash order. Unfortunately, now the spotlight shone in his direction, with Liu's initial reaction quick in coming.

"Ah, and what brave soul do we have up there?"

Before Liu could follow up this question, Kristin checked her watch and broke in. "Father," she pleaded. "The Red Star is approaching!"

Dennis Liu seemed to suddenly forget all about Vince's presence. Even his expression changed, as he lowered the pistol, checked his own wristwatch, and called out to Monica.

"Kristin is right. I have an all-important duty to fulfill before I can return and personally attend to this insurrection. I will leave all this in your capable hands, comrade. Don't hesitate to shoot first and ask questions later. Because the next couple of hours could very well be the most important span of time that this planet has ever known!"

Watching the confrontations on the security monitors, what Ricky had to keep reminding himself was that this wasn't fiction, but reality of the harshest sort.

To calm himself, he also followed Thomas Kellogg and Tuff's progress as they left the Security Room and headed below. He currently had them isolated on Four Deck, where a camera showed them headed aft.

Another video screen displayed a wide-angle view of the Hospital's operating room. His father and Dr. Benedict were in the midst of an operation there, removing a bullet from the shoulder of the terrorist called Bear. Ricky knew that as long as he and his father were needed by the hijackers, their safety was all but guaranteed.

Yet another video screen showed the way in which a good portion of the crew had been detained. Dozens of ship's officers, stewards, and other members of the QE2's staff had been locked up in the Library. A rifle-toting sentry stood outside, with other terrorists arriving from time to time to escort various crew members to their watch stations.

With a random key strike, Ricky discovered another terrible scene. One of the terrorists was trying to rape a Filipino chambermaid. He hadn't even bothered to drag her into one of the cabins—he was attacking her in an anteroom that directly adjoined a carpeted section of passageway. He pinned her to a wall with his chest and knee, kissed her, and tore open her blouse. As her head shook back and forth, Ricky could imagine her screams of terror.

Then he saw down the adjoining passageway, a pair of uniformed crew members approaching, apparently completely unaware of the rape that was occurring ahead of them.

They looked familiar and when Ricky queried the computer to determine the location of the camera, he realized with a start just who they were. As the words FOUR DECK—STARBOARD AFT PASSAGEWAY flashed up on the screen, Ricky manipulated the mouse, and the screen filled with a close-up of Thomas Kellogg and Tuff. They were about to pass right by the terrorist, and there was absolutely nothing Ricky could do to warn them.

Thomas Kellogg still had trouble comprehending how incredibly lucky he had been up to this point. To have successfully completed the HALO jump, only to bump into Tuff, as he had done, was an amazing streak of good fortune. Their chance encounter with Ricky Patton was proof that Lady Luck was still with them, for now they could proceed to the Engine Room without having to worry about being caught by one of the ship's security cameras.

Eleven o'clock was rapidly approaching, and it appeared that they'd have plenty of time to get into position for the SEALs' midnight arrival. Tuff continued to be an invaluable asset, his thorough knowledge of the ship's interior layout allowing them to proceed to their goal on the most direct route.

The passageway they were presently transiting would take them to the after tunnel escape trunk. Here a ladder would convey them straight down to Eight Deck, and the aftmost section of the Engine Room. This was where the dual propeller shafts penetrated the hull. It was also where they'd find the two emergency pitch levers.

Thomas had to hurry to keep up with Tuff's brisk stride, and he noted that the passenger cabins they were passing were sealed with tape. Tuff explained that this was all part of their original security plan. Yet before Thomas could learn more about it, the sound of a woman moaning caught their attention.

They found her in the anteroom to the very next cabin on their right, just as her attacker, hearing them approach, wheeled around to face the two ship's officers. He snatched up his machine gun and demanded, "What in the hell are you doing here?"

Stonily, Tuff replied. "Obviously not having as much fun as you are, my friend. We're just on our way to our watch stations."

Sunny examined the tall, dark-haired crew member who stood beside the stocky security officer, and commented curiously, "If that's the case, where's your escort? No officers are allowed to transit the ship without one of us present."

"It seems that your staff was spread a bit thin, and the chap guarding the Library trusted us to go to work on our own. After all," added Tuff in his most accommodating tone. "It's not like we've got anywhere to escape to."

A skeptical grunt passed Sunny's lips, and he disgustedly shook his head. "That lazy fool," he muttered. "Come on, you two. It's back to the Library, until I hear otherwise."

Sunny raised the stubby barrel of his weapon. Yet before getting on with the job of escorting his prisoners back to confinement in the Library, he readdressed his victim, who had slumped to the floor, weeping.

"And you, my lovely, wait right here. We've got unfinished business to attend to!"

Ricky Patton watched this entire capture on a video screen. Stunned, he was able to isolate a succession of cameras in order to follow the gun-toting terrorist as he led Tuff and Thomas forward to the E Stairwell where they climbed up to the Quarter Deck.

Ricky allowed himself a breath of relief only when one of the monitors showed the two cool-headed captives being directed into the ship's Library. There they discreetly disappeared into the ranks of the other prisoners.

The terrorist who had captured them didn't tarry. He returned below deck with all due haste, and Ricky had no doubt where he was headed.

A quick check of the bulkhead-mounted clock showed that a little more than an hour remained until the SEALs were scheduled to arrive. Ricky cursed their misfortune, and knew that the key ingredients in the retaking of the ship were Thomas Kellogg and Tuff. Somehow, they had to be released from confinement before midnight.

Ricky pondered his limited options. He could sit here, do nothing, and watch their only chance for rescue go down the drain. Or he could risk his life and that of his father, by using the key that Tuff had provided to head for the Library himself.

Kristin feared that her father might have a stroke, so intense was his outrage as they arrived in the Security Room and found the open handcuffs dangling from the console and Ricky nowhere to be seen. Kristin tried her best to control her father's ever rising anger by suggesting that one of their associates could be merely escorting Ricky to the restroom.

Several tense minutes passed, and as the wall clock neared eleven with no Ricky in sight, Dennis Liu's constrained rage exploded.

"Damn that brat! I should have never left him without supervision. Kristin, get to work on that console, and track down that young friend of yours. Then personally retrieve him, and join me in the Radio Room. If the fates are with us, there's still a chance that we'll be able to make good the uplink with Red Star. And only after we've passed on the codes to the admiral will I personally make good my previous threats to young Comrade Patton."

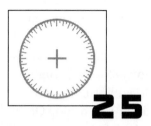

25

Benjamin Kram watched 2300 hours arrive as he paced the red-lit confines of the USS *Polk*'s control room. It was frustrating knowing there was a hostile submarine somewhere in the surrounding seas that their sonar was unable to detect. Kram had only just come from yet another visit with Brad Bodzin and his team, and had seen their waterfall displays firsthand. Except for the signature of the *QE2*, there wasn't another vessel on their screens, which meant that the HMS *Talent* was also not being picked up by their sensors.

"An hour to go until showtime, Skipper," observed COB, who was seated between the two helmsmen. "Are we still good to go?"

Kram answered while studying the dozens of softly glowing dials and gauges of the diving-control panel. "We've still got sixty minutes to tag that *Han*. And until that time is expired, I want to use every second to our best advantage, including getting our SEALs prepped and ready to deploy."

"It's a damn shame about the *Baikal* and the *Casabianca*, Skipper," COB remarked.

"At least the end was quick. Both hulls imploded almost instantaneously, and the crews were dead before they even knew what hit them." Setting his hands on COB's shoulders, Kram added. "Do me a favor, and let me know the instant Bodzin's ready for the next sprint-and-drift sequence. I'll be next door with Commander Gilbert."

"Aye, aye, Skipper," said COB as he turned his attention back to the helm.

Kram's next stop took him to the compartment situated immediately aft of the control room. This area was reserved for SEAL Team Two's operations center.

Seated at the long, rectangular console lining the op center's starboard side were three members of the SEAL team. These individuals were responsible for monitoring the *Polk*'s dry-deck shelter, or DDS. The shelter itself was mounted on the sub's outer deck abaft the sail. It was comprised of a central hangar, where the SDV was stored, and an emergency dive chamber, for treatment of the bends. Another instrumental part of the DDS was the access trunk that penetrated the *Polk*'s hull and was entered at the base of missile-tube number six.

Before the SDV could be launched, both the trunk and the hangar would have to be flooded to equalize sea pressure. This was a complicated, dangerous process, coordinated by the three SEALs currently seated at the DDS console.

This console was unique to the *Polk*. At the aftmost position sat the tender. His all-important job was to monitor the pressure gauges belonging to the main hangar, and log the time that the divers were kept submerged, while keeping track of all personnel. Seated to his right was the DDS dive supervisor. The gauges that he was responsible for watching included the trunk and chamber readings. At the far right-hand position was the shelter officer. This individual was in charge of all communications with the dive team. He was wearing compact headphones, with a microphone around his neck.

A series of three video screens were mounted into the bulkhead above the opposite console. They displayed several underwater views of the dry-deck shelter, as well as the image visible through the *Polk*'s periscope. Commander Gilbert was seated beneath these monitors, watching his men make their initial preparations on the DDS console. Lt. Col. Lawrence Laycob sat at his side, calmly sipping a cup of tea, with an open notebook on his lap.

"Gentlemen," greeted Kram, sitting down on the edge of the console and listening as the shelter officer began a mike check. "I gather that your preparations remain on schedule?"

Gilbert nodded affirmatively. "My laddies are jocked up and ready to party, Captain."

Kram looked at the Englishman and noted that he had yet to change into his assault gear. "Don't tell me that you're planning to take that SDV ride without a wet suit?"

"I should say not, Captain," replied Laycob between sips of tea. "My gear's waiting for me in the missile compartment."

"I understand that you made good use of that virtual-reality program," Kram continued. "My crew was quite impressed."

Laycob grinned. "There are a few high-tech gadgets that SBS has found to be extremely useful, and virtual reality certainly appears to show great promise. Once we complete our operation and retake the *Queen,* you must give it a look, Captain. I've got it set up to display an aft assault that will take you right up the caving ladders by way of her Three-Deck fantail. From there, you have a variety of interactive paths to choose from, including one that shows the most direct route to the ship's Bridge."

Any response on Kram's part was cut short by the arrival of the SEAL team's meteorologist. Petty Officer Murray held a clipboard, and directed his comments to Doug Gilbert.

"Commander, I've got the results of the latest weather-satellite update."

"No sunspot interference this time?" quizzed Gilbert.

"Sir, right now sunspots are the least of our worries," returned Murray. "Hurricane Marti continues bearing down on us. The outer fringe of the storm is already making itself felt topside, with wind gusts up to forty miles per hour, and twenty-foot seas."

"I thought that tropical storms usually weakened once they reached the cold waters of these northern climes?" offered Laycob.

The curly-haired meteorologist was quick with a reply. "I don't anticipate any further strengthening of Marti, sir. Yet the low-pressure system at her heart is tightly organized, and could take several days to dissipate."

"And meanwhile, we have to cope with the winds and heavy seas," said Kram, who looked at SEAL Team Two's commanding officer and added, "Forty-mile-per-hour wind gusts and twenty-foot seas don't bode well for a safe SDV launch, Doug. Those environmentals are way beyond all official safety margins."

"To hell with official safety margins," retorted Gilbert. "All you need to do is get us in a position to reach the *QE2,* and my laddies will do the rest. Shit, this team's ready to drive that SDV right through the gates of Hell, if that's where our op orders are sending us, and no little storm is going to get in our way. That's for damn sure."

Laycob winced. "Sounds like I'd better track down some seasick pills. I don't suppose that the *Polk*'s heard from Command, regarding the manner in which they plan to slow the *Queen* so we can reach her?"

"I'm afraid not," answered Kram. "We'll just have to take it on faith that they've done it for us. Though right now that's not my main concern, nor is it the weather topside. Because if we don't tag that *Han* within the next sixty minutes, and eliminate it as a threat, there's going to be no midnight SDV launch. I'm not about to go opening up my submarine for attack, knowing there's a hostile warship out there, just waiting for a chance to give us the deep six."

"What are you doing about tracking them down?" asked Gilbert with a hint of impatience.

Kram suddenly found himself in the awkward position of having to defend his command decision, and he answered with direct firmness. "You can rest assured, Commander, that the *Polk* is using every means available to locate that *Han*. My top sonar team's got the watch, and they're doing everything short of going active, to scour these seas. As the untimely loss of the *Baikal* and the *Casabianca* so tragically demonstrates, our crafty opponent is an extremely dangerous one. I'm not about to take them for granted, and I won't rest until that *Han* has paid the ultimate price for its criminal actions."

"I do hope Commander Eastbrook and the crew of the *Talent* can be helpful in giving you a hand ridding the seas of this *Han*," said Laycob after finishing his tea. "If it's indeed a rogue sub that we're after, then there's no better pirate to have on your side than Mark Eastbrook. He can be the one to flush out the vermin, leaving the *Polk* free to exterminate them."

Comdr. Mark Eastbrook paced the crowded confines of the *Talent*'s control room like a man possessed. He had personally made the choice to take up a tactical position far in the *Queen*'s baffles. The *Polk* was well ahead of them, and Eastbrook didn't want to join them until he was absolutely certain of what they were up against.

One reality that he couldn't question was that the brave crews of the *Baikal* and the *Casabianca* were no more. Eastbrook was positive it had been an intentional act of subterfuge that was responsible for their demise. Any sonic evidence of the mysterious submarine that had carried out this clever ploy had long since dropped off their sonar screens.

For the past half hour, Eastbrook had confined himself to the sonar room, where he played the tape of this engagement over and over. In each instance, the suspected *Han*-class vessel made its abrupt presence known with an outburst of noise, as it sprinted forward at flank speed. It continued generating this unmistakable sonic signature for as long as it took to gain the attention of the formation's two point-submarines. No sooner did the *Baikal* and the *Casabianca* turn inward to engage this phantom contact than it went inexplicably silent, seemingly swallowed by a black hole of noise-absorbent seawater.

What had happened to it? Try as he could, Eastbrook could find no trace of it, no matter how many times he listened to the cursed recording.

The only sound that remained constant throughout the tape was the incessant, pounding roar of the *QE2*'s nine-diesel engines. It was from this deafening racket that the bogey had emerged. Present throughout the torpedo engagement, the *Queen*'s sonorous signature prevailed to the tape's very end, clearly emanating long after the last crackling report of the two imploding submarines faded to eternity.

Eastbrook stopped at the navigation plot. He picked up a red grease pencil to initiate a cursory sketch on the chart's clear-plastic overlay. He plotted the position and course of the *QE2* during the time of the bogey's initial appearance, and the positions of her two submarine escorts off her port and starboard bows. The unwary ocean liner had continued right over that portion of the Atlantic where the two doomed submarines' tragic destinies had already been written. And the phantom warship that had instigated this havoc? In which direction could it have fled, and why was there no audio evidence of this escape effort?

It was as he circled the large X he had drawn to represent the *QE2* that a sudden thought dawned in his consciousness. It was fragmented at first, but the more he thought about it, the more it began to make sense.

"That bloody Red bastard!" he reflected, oblivious to the curious stares of his shipmates. "I'll bet anything, that's how he did it."

"Sir?" queried the nearby navigator, who didn't know if this spontaneous comment had been meant for him.

Mark Eastbrook met his navigator's confused stare with a smile, followed up with a spirited explanation. "The *Han,* lad! Don't you see, my good man? It was hiding beneath the *Queen* all that time, using the sound of her engines to mask its presence from our sonar. When it finally made its move, it did so with firm intention, sprinting forward into the formation's slot, then scramming its reactor once the deed had been done. After that, all they had to do was wait for the *Queen* to steam overhead before restarting their engines and following her out of the engagement zone, with all of us none the wiser!"

"That does sound like an interesting theory, sir," said the navigator carefully.

"It's way beyond theory, lad," countered Eastbrook. "It's fact, pure and simple. And I'm willing to bet the lives of all aboard the *Queen* that a circumspect approach into the liner's baffles will result in the detection of an unwanted underwater trespasser lurking below her hull. If we hurry, we can even eliminate it in time to let our Yank friends aboard the *Polk* get on with the task of retaking the *Queen.* So chart me the most efficient approach to the big lady, lad. It's time for *Talent* to earn her keep!"

To show his support of the *Lijiang*'s captain, Guan could think of no better gesture than to don one of the white robes himself. It was shortly after Lee's clever maneuver resulted in the sinking of the two enemy subs that Guan excused himself from the control room to track down the quartermaster. Guan found him in the supply office, and the commissar was very fortunate to get the last available robe in stock.

The robe proved to be several sizes too small, but this didn't stop Guan from wearing it. With a white cotton sash tied around his bulging waist, he returned to the control room, anxious to see what the captain's next move would be.

Their sensors showed that one more submarine had to be eliminated before they'd have these depths all to themselves. Guan had personally heard that vessel's unique sonic signature during a stop in sonar. The sonar officer in charge had explained that the barely audible whistling sounds Guan's headphones were conveying were the results of seawater streaming through the contact's numerous free-flood holes. The existence of these holes indicated that the submarine had some type of protrusion on its deck. This was most likely an external dry-deck shelter, meaning that the warship was probably the USS *James K. Polk,* a U.S. Navy submarine designed specifically for special operations. The *Polk,* and the SEAL team it carried, would be the perfect warship to send along on an escort mission of this sort.

With the identity of their opponent all but assured, they were well on their way to formulating a plan to sink it. To hear this strategy firsthand, Guan entered the control room with hurried steps. The candle was still flickering alive on the periscope pedestal where Captain Lee stood bathed in the compartment's muted red light.

"So Comrade Commissar, you've decided to become at one with the Way," observed Lee, as he watched the newcomer take up his usual position beside the fire-control console.

Guan could see that with his donning of the robe, every single sailor inside the control room was now similarly attired, and he responded with pride. "It's an honor to be part of this remarkable team, comrade."

"It's much more than a team," explained Lee. "It's a way of life that has been a part of China since her earliest days. For too many years, our ancestors neglected its call, and the motherland floundered, soulless, and without inner direction. It took the ascension of the Chairman to resurrect the long-dormant spirit, and as a result, our great People's Republic was born. And now it's up to the *Lijiang* to insure that the forces of doubt and greed don't prevail. China has come too far, made too many sacrifices, to give in to temptation, now that our goal is so near."

"Well said, comrade," replied Guan. He looked at the ceiling, as if peering up through the hull to the waters above. "From that distant rumbling roar, it's obvious that the surface vessel holding China's number-one enemy remains close by. Now that the *QE2* is approaching the Hecate Seamount sector, shouldn't we be hearing from Comrade Liu shortly?"

"I have no doubt that Liu has succeeded in his difficult task," said the captain. "He is a fellow student of the Way, and my own blood cousin. But before we can even think about our operation's next phase, one vital obstacle needs to be attended to—the elimination of the special-forces submarine, USS *James K. Polk.*

"The *Polk* remains off our starboard bow. The *Lijiang* continues to be masked by the *QE2*'s signature. We have used this cover well, and now is the time to reinitiate our climb up the twisting mountain path to victory."

Lee lapsed into silence at this point. He turned to face the helm. He shut his eyes, and began breathing in deep, even breaths.

Guan was getting used to this preparatory routine that acted as a type of joint meditation, uniting their wills as one. He was thus quick to follow the examples of his shipmates, as they also shut their eyes and listened to Lee's forceful voice.

"Make one's body like a rock, and ten thousand enemies can't touch you. Prepare yourselves, comrades, to strike yet another blow in the preservation of the motherland!"

Guan's pulse quickened in anticipation of the attack order that would soon be coming. As he struggled to regulate his breath, a hollow pinging sound suddenly filled the control room. The source of this alien noise was revealed by their frantic sonar officer.

"Active sonar scan, emanating from an unidentified submerged contact, bearing two-one-zero and rapidly closing!"

"But that can't be!" retorted Lee, whose eyes snapped open to scan the gauges of the diving-control panel.

Guan also opened his eyes, his heart pounding. He looked on with concerned disbelief as the captain's astounded expression displayed the first hint of rising fear.

"Right full rudder! All ahead flank! Prepare tubes one and two for quick shots, targeting both the *Polk* and the unwelcome stranger in our baffles!"

Guan listened as the diving officer repeated Lee's frantic series of orders. He reached up to grab an overhead handhold as the *Lijiang* canted over hard on her starboard side, with the deep, bass rumble of her engines now overriding that of the *QE2*.

"Tubes one and two ready for firing, Captain," revealed the weapons officer at Guan's side.

"Fire one!" ordered Lee. "Fire two!"

The deck shook twice as the torpedoes shot out of their tubes, pushed out into the sea by a powerful blast of compressed air. All eyes went to the weapons officer as he nervously scanned his console's display screens and excitedly cried out:

"Both torpedoes have gone active—with weapon number one directed to the *Polk*, and number two toward the contact behind us. Time to contact, two minutes and counting."

"We've got them now!" proclaimed Lee, whose eyes widened with a maniacal fury as the amplified voice of the sonar officer broke out from the overhead speakers.

"Torpedo in the water, Captain! I show a single, wire-guided weapon approaching from bearing two-one-zero!"

"Left full rudder!" ordered Lee in response to this warning. "Prepare to launch full spread of countermeasures! And where's that flank speed, Chief? It's time to run like the fox, comrades!"

It all started soon after the *Polk*'s towed array tagged Sierra Four closing in on the *QE2*'s baffles. Jaffers had been the first one to tag the *Talent*, and Brad Bodzin quickly switched the feed of his headphones to focus solely on the sounds being conveyed through the array.

No sooner did he isolate the Royal Navy submarine than the deafening burst of an active sonar pulse filled his headphones with painful sound. Bodzin cursed this unexpected sonic lashing, whose source was definitely the *Talent*.

Bodzin was unable to explain why the Brits had gone active in this manner. Then he heard the hollow ping deflect off an unidentified submerged object lying in the depths almost directly below the *QE2*. This contact, which Bodzin was quick to label Sierra Six, reacted to the ping with a sudden noisy burst of speed. It was surely the long-sought *Han*, thought the Texan, as his wonder turned to sheer terror when his headphones next filled with the buzz-saw whine of an approaching torpedo. Bodzin had previously heard this dreaded sound only during practice exercises, and he wasted no time passing the warning to the control room.

Benjamin Kram was standing beside the navigation plot when Bodzin's frantic warning arrived via the public-address speakers. For the first time in his long career, he found himself the target of an actual hostile-torpedo attack. Kram had no time for fear. His years of training now took over. He rushed to the adjoining helm and positioned himself behind the seated COB.

"All ahead flank! Come around hard on bearing three-two-five, at a depth of eight-hundred-and-fifty feet!" Kram ordered.

As COB repeated these commands to the helmsman, Kram looked to his right, where the boat's fire-control console was situated.

"Weaps," he shouted. "Prepare to launch five-inch evasion device."

As Kram was reaching up to grab the nearest intercom handset, the deck dropped forward and canted hard aport. He balanced himself on the back of COB's chair and addressed the crew over the 1MC.

"Rig ship for collision!"

"Countermeasures ready for launch, Captain," informed Weaps.

"Launch countermeasures!" Kram instructed.

"Countermeasures away!" Weaps revealed, in reference to the grinding decoy that was soon shooting off in the opposite direction.

"Conn, sonar," broke in Bodzin's amplified voice. "Torpedo is at two thousand yards and continuing to close!"

"COB!" directed Kram. "Come around crisply to zero-six-zero. We need to leave the mother of all knuckles in the water behind us."

The *Polk*'s hull shifted hard to the right, and a loose coffee mug crashed to the deck and slipped past the helm. Kram managed to grab it, and as he tightly gripped the ceramic handle, his determined glance locked on the digital-knot gauge.

"Twenty-six knots," revealed COB, whose gaze was also focused on the steadily rising digital display. "Twenty-seven . . . twenty-eight . . . twenty-nine . . ."

"Conn, sonar," interjected Bodzin. "Torpedo is range-gaiting at one thousand yards and closing. It's going to be close, sir!"

"Weaps, launch another decoy!" Kram ordered. "Sound the collision alarm!"

A muted electronic alarm began ringing in the background. As the weapons officer informed them that yet another decoy had been released into the water, Kram dropped the mug he had been holding and tightened his grip on the back of COB's chair.

"Thirty-two knots at seven-eight-zero feet," revealed COB, whose own tone of voice continued to display an unbelievable degree of composure.

"Come on Jimmy K, you can do it," urged the young planesman

seated to COB's left, his steering yoke pushed forward to its full extension.

"Conn, sonar. Torpedo has lost its lock on us. It appears to be going after our last decoy!"

This joyous revelation was punctuated by a gut-wrenching blast, its shockwave arriving seconds later. Tossed to and fro by this powerful concussion, the *Polk*'s hull shuddered violently and the overhead lights flickered.

Kram was thrown to his knees. He struggled to stand. As he regained his footing, a quick survey of the compartment found no apparent injuries, and he addressed the 1MC to determine how the rest of the sub had fared.

"Damage control, I want all parties to report in on the double!"

A tense sixty seconds passed as the calls began arriving from all sections of the *Polk*. Except for a few bruises and cuts, with all stations reporting in as being fully operational, not a single man was seriously injured.

"That was too damn close, COB," whispered Kram with disgust. "Now let's see what we can do about paying our respects to the bastards responsible for this unwarranted attack!"

In the adjoining depths, the HMS *Talent* had also managed to outmaneuver the *Lijiang*'s torpedo. Having ordered the launching of a full spread of countermeasures, Comdr. Mark Eastbrook found himself with no time to refocus the *Talent*'s efforts over to the offensive. For the enemy's acoustic homing torpedo had yet to detonate, being presently on a direct collision course with the *QE2*!

He doubted that they'd be able to eliminate this errant weapon with one of their Spearfish torpedoes. Unable to warn the ocean liner by radio, Eastbrook realized there was only a single option available to them. Though it would take every spare knot they could squeeze out of their propulsion system, he calculated that there was just enough time for the *Talent* to position itself between the oncoming torpedo and its unsuspecting surface target.

Completely oblivious to the suicidal nature of this maneuver, the crew of the *Talent* accepted Eastbrook's difficult decision without question. For the brave, dedicated men of the HMS *Talent*, duty to the Crown prevailed above all else. Individual lives meant absolutely nothing in the defense of this intangible principle, and they willingly put them on the line to preserve the integrity of their beloved *Queen*.

The *Lijiang* had survived its own brush with death by a combination of effective decoys and a daring quick-stop maneuver. The enemy salvo was last heard spiraling down into the cold depths, where the warhead eventually detonated.

Guan had expected that their captain would react to this near miss with a celebration of some sort. Instead of relieved joy, Lee Shao-chi expressed himself with a furious outburst of crude invectives. Gone was his passive, controlled manner, which Guan and the rest of the crew had been so quick to emulate. In its place was a dark side of Lee's personality that they had yet to experience.

His face flushed with anger, his breaths coming in quick, uneven gasps, Lee furiously castigated his sonar officer for failing to pick up the enemy submarine that had sneaked up behind them. Once this verbal punishment was delivered, he stormed back to his command position on the periscope pedestal. Pure madness emanated from his eyes as he monitored the *James K. Polk*'s successful evasion of their attack.

All but forgetting about the American warship at this point, Lee refocused his wrath on the submarine that had taken the potshot at them. It was believed to be a British, *Trafalgar*-class vessel, and Lee had taken it upon himself to personally see to its destruction.

"How could they have managed to evade our sensors, and sneak up on us like that?" mumbled Lee to no one in particular. "Such effrontery is inexcusable!"

"You know how sneaky those Brits can be," offered Guan in a vain attempt to lighten Lee's sour mood. "I still think it's a miracle that we even got them to give up Hong Kong."

"Nobody makes a fool out of me like that," continued Lee, not paying any attention to his commissar's rambling comments. "Nobody, I say!"

Guan didn't like what he saw as Lee's face was momentarily illuminated by the flickering candlelight. His face was drawn and gaunt, his jagged scar giving him an evil appearance.

To make good his revenge, Lee had ordered the *Lijiang* to initiate a tight, high-speed turn that made their sonar all but useless. Seemingly unconcerned by the frothing cavitational wake that they were leaving in their baffles, Lee managed to position the *Lijiang* at the rear of the *Trafalgar*. The Brits were apparently well aware of their presence behind them, for they were in the midst of a frantic, full-speed sprint to the surface.

As the *Lijiang*'s planesman yanked back hard on his steering column, Guan found his body pulled forward as the deck canted upwards. The diving officer began tensely calling out their rapidly decreasing depth, in between constant range-to-target updates from sonar.

Though Guan was far from being an expert in such tactical matters, he knew that the fleeing enemy vessel was well within range of their torpedoes. And when Lee continued to show no sign that such a launch was even imminent, Guan dared to voice his concerns.

"Captain, let's release our torpedoes and be done with this! Don't forget, we still have the *Polk* to eliminate."

Madness flashed from Lee's dark eyes, as he looked downward to meet Guan's fear-filled glance. "This is how a true warrior wreaks vengeance on his enemy, Comrade Commissar! Our attack must be sure; his destruction guaranteed!"

"But what about the Way, sir?" countered Guan.

"The Way be damned!" cursed Lee Shao-chi, with such force that the candle's flickering flame was abruptly snuffed out, causing a veil of crimson red to descend upon the *Lijiang*'s control room.

"Conn, sonar," reported Brad Bodzin into the intercom handset. "Sierra Six has just broken through the thermocline, Captain! We've got a firm lock on them, on bearing two-four-one, range seventy-five hundred yards."

"Snapshot, tubes one and two, fire!" ordered the amplified voice of Benjamin Kram over the sonar room's intercom speakers.

Bodzin and his fellow technicians alertly pushed back their headphones as these torpedoes were released into the sea with two powerful jolts of compressed air. The deck shuddered, and Bodzin reported to the control room that both weapons were running true and headed straight toward their exposed target.

All three of the *Polk*'s sonar operators knew that the *Han*'s life expectancy could be counted off in seconds now—nothing short of a miracle could save them. Jaffers refocused his scan to the dramatic scene taking place in the waters above them.

"I don't believe it, but the *Talent*'s still going for it," Jaffers observed, wonderstruck. "It sounds to me like they really do intend to take that fish right on the chin. Those Limeys are nuts!"

"Or, more likely, incredibly brave," offered Bodzin, who flinched when a succession of three separate explosions sounded from the nearby waters.

As expected, the *Lijiang* was the victim of two of these blasts. The *Han*-class vessel was hit directly amidships and its hull instantly ripped open. Inside the *Polk*'s sonar room, the distinctive crackling sound of an imploding submarine filled their headphones for the third time that day.

There was no time to celebrate, as all attention was now locked on the plight of the HMS *Talent*. Sonar indicated they'd been spared a direct hit, and a rushed underwater telephone conversation soon proved the *Talent* had only been struck a glancing blow that shattered equipment and broke many a bone, but which would enable the pride of the Royal Navy to limp home on its own power. The last the *Polk* heard from them was when Comdr. Mark Eastbrook personally got on the line to wish the men of SEAL Team Two good luck in their midnight endeavor.

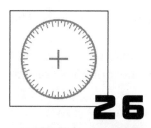

26

Ricky Patton started to have second doubts about his rash decision to leave the relatively safe confines of the Security Room the moment he stepped onto the Quarter Deck from the E Stairway. This put him around the corner from the Library, where the two men he hoped to release were being detained. Barely aware of the pitching deck beneath him, Ricky halted on the landing, and debated whether to return to Two Deck. By instigating this daring plan, he was jeopardizing his life and that of his father. But by doing nothing, and taking the coward's way out, they could very well lose out on their only real chance to retake the ship from the terrorists.

Ricky supposed that it could do no harm to peek around the corner and see exactly what he was up against, and he cautiously inched his way forward. The passageway outside the glass-walled Library was well lit—he could see several dozen members of the crew inside. There didn't appear to be a sentry on duty. As he continued his approach, Ricky spied a key protruding from the Library door's lock. This was all he needed to see to realize that fate had already made his decision for him.

Without hesitation, he made his way to the door and turned the key. The lock opened with a loud click. He pushed open the door and stepped inside. Most of the detainees were Philippine crew members, with both Tuff and Thomas seated at a table, reading.

The ATF agent didn't seem surprised when he saw Ricky and discreetly informed Tuff of his presence. Ricky joined them, and accepted a concerned greeting from Tuff.

"So they decided to put you in detention with the rest of us after all."

"It's nothing like that," informed Ricky. "I saw your capture on one of the security monitors, and used the key you gave me to see if I could help spring you. Would you believe there wasn't a guard at the door, and that I walked right in here?"

Tuff's glance went to the Library's entryway. Upon verifying that the sentry was still absent, he looked at Thomas and winked. "Time's a-wasting, Special Agent. Shall we get on with it?"

Thomas stood alongside Tuff. Before making good his exit, he left Ricky with a single piece of advice. "It's best if you return to security before they miss you. Give us a minute's head start . . . and thanks again for risking your life like this."

Before Ricky could reply, Thomas and Tuff were out the door. Ricky noted the curious stares of the other prisoners, none of whom took advantage of the unlocked doorway to make his own escape. Proud of his newfound courageousness, he decided to take Thomas Kellogg's advice and return to the Security Room. He ducked out the entryway and turned to relock the door before continuing down to Two Deck.

"Going somewhere, comrade?" asked an icy voice from behind.

Ricky felt the hard barrel of a rifle poke into his back. He let go of the key and slowly turned his head. A black-clad, Asian sentry with a disdainful smirk on his pockmarked face shook his head and chastised him as if he were a naughty schoolboy.

"Why don't you be a good boy and go back into the Library where you belong? I'm so seasick right now that I don't even feel like shooting you."

Kristin had been in the midst of a thorough video scan of the ship when she chanced upon the person she was searching for standing outside the Library. It appeared that Ricky had been captured by one of her associates, and she watched as he was escorted at gunpoint into the Library and locked inside.

Her new friend was very fortunate that he hadn't been shot. Kristin wondered how he had gotten free of the cuffs and why he would have risked his father's life by escaping. She supposed that it would do him no harm to remain in detention. This would keep him out of further trouble, and away from the threatening presence of her father.

There was something very disturbing about her father's recent change in temperament. He was getting increasingly irritable and prone to frequent fits of uncontrollable rage. Kristin was well aware of the tremendous pressure he was under. She could only hope that he would be able to center himself before his blind anger caused him to do something that he'd later regret—like killing one of the heads of state.

She had a bird's-eye view of these very individuals, on the center video screen. They remained seated around their table, with several of them slumped over, sleeping. With disheveled tuxedos and beard-stubbled faces, they were beginning to look like the mortals they really were. This lesson alone was worth their effort. Kristin couldn't wait until the first photograph of this motley group was released to the world.

A burst of static on her two-way radio diverted her attention from the console. The gruff voice of her father broke from the speaker and ordered her to report at once to the ship's Radio Room.

She did as directed, and by the time she reached the Boat Deck, she was aware that the seas were becoming increasingly rough. It was a chore to walk in a straight line, and she fought back the first sensation of seasickness.

The Radio Room was located forward of the Queens Grill, its heavy steel door protected by a bank-vault-style lock. Kristin rang the buzzer and stood in front of the door's security peephole. Her wait was a short one, and she was admitted by a very concerned Monica Chang.

Kristin spotted her father seated behind a bank of transmitters. A bald-headed ship's officer in a white uniform was seated beside him, with both of them holding telephone handsets up to their ears. Obviously the officer had been impressed into taking Ricky's place.

"We made the initial uplink with Red Star with no problem at all," informed Monica. "We were even able to broadcast the first half of the code sequence before static interrupted the remainder of the transmission."

Kristin looked at the bulkhead clock. It was only a few minutes to midnight. "How much longer will the satellite be within range?" she asked.

"Another sixty minutes at best," Monica answered. "Yet it makes no difference if this static prevails. If we only had the filter that Max was working on."

Frustration weighed down her father's movements, as he put down the handset and rose to join them. "It's useless," he muttered.

"We still have an hour to reestablish contact," reminded Monica. "All we need is a couple more minutes of clear transmission time, and Admiral Liu will have the complete sequence."

"Dear Monica, always the eternal optimist," said Dennis Liu, who suddenly found himself fighting to keep his balance as the deck began pitching from side to side.

"I had a feeling that this was going to happen," he added while reaching out to steady Kristin. "And I'm afraid that we have no alternative but to go to our secondary plan. It's time to blow up this cursed ship and show the world that we mean business!"

"Patience, Dennis," urged Monica. "I'm not about to give up, and I recommend remaining up here and giving it another try until Red Star is completely out of range."

"I agree with Monica," said Kristin. "And as it so happens, I've succeeded in tracking down Ricky Patton. He's in the Library."

"Why didn't you say so before?" said her father. "Monica, contact the Library watch and have them escort him up here at once."

Liu's train of thought was diverted as he looked up to the ceiling, a peculiar expression on his tired face. "The engines. Don't you hear? They've stopped. No wonder we're wallowing."

As he picked up the two-way radio to call the Bridge, Kristin indeed noticed that the constant low-level background roar of the engines could no longer be heard. The ceaseless pitching motion of the deck further intensified, and it took a supreme effort to remain standing.

"What?" questioned Dennis Liu into his two-way. "What do you mean the captain doesn't know why we've stopped? . . . Don't bother, comrade. I'm on my way up to the Bridge to find out for myself."

"Hangar, conn," said the *Polk*'s dry-deck shelter dive supervisor into his chin microphone from his central position at the DDS console. "Check open Alpha Eleven, Twelve, Thirteen, and Fifteen."

Benjamin Kram listened as the trunkborne SEAL to whom these instructions were directed acknowledged them. Kram had just arrived in the SEAL operations compartment from the control room. He positioned himself beside Commander Gilbert, who was seated at the opposite console, beneath the three monitor screens.

"The *Queen*'s dead in the water, all right," informed Kram. "I don't know how, but Command pulled it off."

A quick glance at the top monitor showed the view from the *Polk*'s periscope. Veiled by the slap of an occasional wave was the rounded aft portion of an immense surface vessel, with the name QUEEN ELIZABETH 2 emblazoned in white letters on the stern.

"All I ask of you is to hold us right here, and I'll have my laddies off in two shakes of a stick," Gilbert whispered.

The *Polk* rolled in the grasp of a passing swell, the keelless submarine at the mercy of the pitching seas.

"We'll keep you here as long as you need, Commander. Just don't blame the *Polk* for this rough ride," said Kram, who listened as the shelter officer spoke into his microphone.

"Hangar, conn. Open Oscar Three. Verify pressure on valve Alpha One."

"Trunk, conn," added the DDS dive supervisor. "Shut November One and verify."

Kram looked on as SEAL Team Two's medical officer joined them from the aft passageway. "Sir," he said to Gilbert. "I'm reading high levels of carbon dioxide in the trunk. Recommend that we take a couple of minutes to thoroughly vent the area before continuing."

"There's no time for that luxury," replied Gilbert. "Get back and watch them closely, and when the first one drops, then we'll ventilate."

"Aye, aye, sir," returned the medical officer, who dared not argue his point further.

"Let's do it, laddies," said Gilbert to his operations team. "Man DDS."

"Trunk, conn," directed the shelter officer. "You have permission to open access hatch."

Kram listened as the intricate process of flooding the shelter to equalize the outside sea pressure began. Throughout this sequence, the 1MC continued to broadcast the latest reports from the *Polk*'s sonar room, with an occasional operational comment from the sub's XO, who was the current OOD.

"Seven feet draft in hangar," reported the voice of one of the divers over the intercom.

They would be able to pressurize the hangar shortly. Kram excused himself to head aft and say his goodbyes to the SEAL team. As he entered the missile compartment, he found the commandos in the last stages of preparation, or "jocking up," as they called it. Each of the divers was in his own private space, putting the finishing touches to his gear. For the most part, the SEALs wore aviator-style flight suits over their rubber wet suits. A few were outfitted in camouflage fatigues, with all wearing combat boots.

The equipment they were carrying was as varied as their uniforms. This gear included an eclectic mix of diving paraphernalia: knives, pistols, handcuffs, flash grenades, cranial radio headsets, and laser-guided submachine guns.

A familiar blond-haired figure stood outside tube six, where the DDS access hatch was located. He had no outer garment over his wet suit. Kram made his way over to him.

"Looks like it's finally showtime, Lieutenant Colonel Laycob," he greeted.

The British commando was making the final adjustments to the waterproof canister holding his two-way radio, and he matter-of-factly replied, "No offense, Captain, but I'm more than ready to get on a vessel where I can properly stretch these old legs and get a decent drink as well."

"No offense taken," replied Kram, who had to reach out to steady himself against the edge of the missile tube's open hatch when the *Polk* rolled hard on its side.

"I suppose that you're anxious to get us off and return to the calm depths," reflected Laycob as he braced himself on an overhead handhold.

"Mount 'em up, gents!" instructed a gruff voice from inside the trunk.

"Ah, it looks like you won't have to wait much longer," added the Englishman as he checked the waterproof integrity of his holstered pistol.

"Good luck," offered Kram.

Laycob accepted his handshake and casually replied, "Please be so good as to thank your crew for their hospitality. I suppose I shan't be seeing them again to convey my regards personally."

"Will do, and bon voyage," said Kram, who stood back and watched as the jocked-up SEALs lined up in front of the open trunk. One by one they climbed into the accessway's darkened recesses, with Kram issuing each of them a crisp salute along the way.

By the time he returned to the DDS operations console, the final deployment sequence was already in progress. As he settled in beside Doug Gilbert, he studied the trio of monitor screens. The top one continued to display a periscope view of the *QE2*'s fantail. Barely visible on the other two screens were the brightly glowing chemlite light sticks of the five-man dive team working on the *Polk*'s outer deck. They would be responsible for actually deploying the SDV from its hangar.

"Flood trunk," ordered the DDS dive supervisor.

"Two . . . three . . . four feet draft in the trunk," revealed the shelter officer.

"You have permission to open hangar door and engage track and cradle," informed the dive sup.

"Hangar door is open," replied a garbled voice over the intercom. "Track and cradle are being rigged out."

The Swimmer Delivery Vehicle was mounted inside the shelter on a cradle. In order for it to be launched, a steel-cable safety tether was attached to the SDV's stubby nose, with the cradle pulled out of the shelter on a telescoping track.

The SDV wasn't a minisub, but a free-flooding, windowless craft, with its pilot, navigator, and six passengers seated side by side in pairs. Because the vessel was completely open to the elements, hypothermia was a constant concern, especially in the cold waters of the North Atlantic.

The SDV's closed-circuit Mark 15 underwater breathing system had a six-hour capacity. Its masks had microphones built into them, with each one connected to the craft's intercom. Communications with the *Polk* were via UHF radio. And since the SDV had no windows, it relied solely on instruments and a high-frequency active-sonar unit to provide navigation.

Kram hoped that in this instance, their voyage would be but a short one. Once free from the *Polk*, the SDV only had to travel a bare 300 feet to be in a position directly behind the *QE2*. As long as the ocean liner remained dead in the water, it would take a few minutes at most to ascend to the surface, slide back the canopy, and board the ship. They would do so with the assistance of air-compressed grappling hooks and caving ladders. The rough seas and high winds topside would make this part of the operation extremely hazardous, as the boarding of another surface ship on the high seas was difficult enough in perfect weather.

"Request permission to launch SDV," said a voice from the intercom.

Before responding to this request, the DDS dive sup turned around and queried Gilbert. "Sir, request permission to launch."

"Permission granted," returned the grizzled SEAL firmly.

"Launch SDV!" ordered the dive sup into his chin microphone.

"What the hell is going on aboard this ship?" demanded a furious Dennis Liu as he stormed into the QE2's Bridge. "I didn't give anyone an all-stop order."

The ship's navigator was the senior watch officer present, and he answered from the navigation plot, a telephone nestled up to his ear. "Believe me, sir, I had nothing to do with it. You can check the combinator yourself. It's still set for eighteen and one-half knots."

"Then how do you account for this loss of speed?" questioned Liu, his face reddened with frustrated rage.

"I've got the Engine Control Room on the line, and they're doing their best to figure out what's occurred," explained the navigator. "Because their controls are also set for eighteen and one-half knots."

"I don't believe any of this crap!" cursed Liu, disgustedly scanning the dimly lit room before storming over to the helm.

A frightened Filipino bosun's mate stood behind the ship's wheel. Liu grabbed him from behind, put a pistol to the back of the young sailor's skull, and violently jerked him around to face the navigator.

"I'm warning you, comrade. On the count of three I'll blow this man's head off unless you give me a satisfactory answer. So quit the bullshit and tell me why we've stopped like this!"

From the serious tone of this threat, the navigator could tell it wasn't to be taken lightly. Yet, because in all honesty, he couldn't answer the terrorist's question, he could only stand there and listen as Liu began counting.

"One . . . two . . ."

"Hold it!" cried the navigator, who offered the only possible answer that made any sense. "You've got to believe me when I tell you that the slowdown wasn't directed from either the Bridge or the Engine Control Room. That leaves the emergency pitch-control levers on Eight Deck, as the only other place where this process could have been effected."

"Emergency pitch-control levers?" repeated Liu, as he lowered the pistol and relaxed his grip on the terrified Filipino.

"The QE2's direction and speed are determined by influencing the pitch of the ship's twin propellers," the navigator explained. "For example, a ninety percent pitch roughly produces twenty-seven knots, while one of . . ."

"I don't give a damn about the details," interrupted Liu. "Just tell me who has access to these emergency pitch levers?"

"Almost anyone can reach them, at the extreme aft end of the Engine Room on Eight Deck," revealed the navigator. "They're clearly marked and located on each of the propeller shafts."

"Somebody's playing with me, and they're going to be awfully sorry when I catch them," threatened Liu, tossing the bosun's mate aside and rushing out of the Bridge.

Ricky expected the worst when a sentry stormed into the Library and angrily shouted out his name. His limbs were trembling as he meekly stood to acknowledge this summons. Without explanation, he was led at gunpoint to the Radio Room.

Both Kristin and Monica were waiting for him there. It was the redheaded actress who ordered him to have a seat at the central transmitter, beside the ship's radio officer. "You're very fortunate that your little act of insubordination didn't earn you a bullet," she remarked while aiming her pistol at the back of Ricky's head. "Help us with our transmission, and perhaps you and your father will be allowed to live."

The radio officer explained the suspected atmospheric problems that had interrupted their transmission, and Kristin handed Ricky a dogeared notebook.

"It belonged to Max," she revealed. "And contains the method he planned to utilize to filter the interference."

Ricky glanced at the notebook's hand-scrawled contents, and listened as the radio officer added, "It looks to me like it's a formula of some sort. The only familiar portion are those numbers that appear to be individual frequency bands."

"It's a computer-programming code," surmised Ricky after flipping through the first couple pages. "Law enforcement agencies use similar frequency-hopping programs to establish secure communications."

Monica glanced at the digital wall clock and asked impatiently, "How long will it take to input the program and get it operational?"

Ricky glanced at the remaining pages. "I'll need at least a quarter of an hour."

"I'll give you ten minutes," returned Monica as she snapped a live round into the pistol's chamber and signaled him to begin.

"What do you think, Tuff, have our SEALs arrived topside yet?" asked Thomas Kellogg from his perch beside the port propeller shaft.

Tuff was leaning against the cowling that protected the starboard shaft. He looked at his watch before replying. "If your lads have managed to keep their schedule, they should be getting ready to set the first grappling hook over the fantail railing on Three Deck. But, of course, in an operation as complex as this one, there are ever so many obstacles that could have popped up to delay them."

"For our sakes, I sure hope those obstacles are few and far between," said Thomas, glancing down at his own watch.

The deck wallowed in the grasp of yet another heavy swell. Thomas expressed himself with sincerity. "All of this wouldn't have been possible without your help, Tuff. Your presence here is a godsend."

"You're the one who deserves all the accolades, Special Agent. It took an awfully brave man to attempt that HALO jump."

There was a sudden concerned look on Tuff's face as he abruptly put his right index finger up to his lips and signaled toward the forward part of the compartment that they were no longer alone. Thomas alertly crouched down, just in time to see a single Asian male break from the shadows. Their most efficient escape route was now cut off, yet Thomas realized that they couldn't run away regardless of this new threat. It was absolutely imperative that they remain here, beside the dual pitch-control levers, to keep the ship in place for the imminent arrival of the SEALs.

"It's no use trying to conceal yourself," said Dennis Liu as he cautiously transited the narrow catwalk, a Sterling submachine gun slung over his shoulder. "I know all about your little game to stop the ship, and now it's time for you to pay the price for this futile gesture."

Still hidden in the shadows, Thomas looked over at a crouching Tuff, and returned his concerned nod. Both of them knew that stalling for as much additional time as possible was their primary goal. Thomas pulled out his 9mm Glock in anticipation of the inevitable confrontation.

"Show yourself now, before I spray this whole compartment with lead," warned Liu, a mere fifty feet away from his hidden adversaries.

As the terrorist brought his Sterling up, Tuff glanced over at Thomas and nodded once more. They proceeded to stand simultaneously, Thomas quick to aim his pistol at the terrorist's broad chest.

"So there's two of you," observed Liu, showing not the least hint of concern or surprise. "And ship's officers to boot. I should have expected as much."

Liu aimed the long black barrel of his weapon at Thomas and took a tentative step forward. "I don't suppose you're going to tell me the reason for this foolhardy act of insubordination? I mean, it's not like this slowdown is affecting my schedule."

Liu was unable to coax a word out of them. He resolutely shook his head. "You're the brave, silent type. I like that in an opponent. I'll tell you what. You put down that pistol, and I'll do the same with my weapon. Then we can settle this like men, with bare fists. And because I'm feeling extra generous this evening, I'll even let you take me on, two against one. Well, comrades, how do these terms grab you?"

"And if we don't accept them?" returned Thomas, trying his best to feel this character out.

Liu grinned. "Don't tell me, I bet you want me to tie one of my arms behind my back as well. No, comrade, I won't give you that much of a handicap, as I won't accept any less than a complete resolution of this act of insubordination. If you won't fight me, then I'm willing to bet that I can cut down you and your friend, before you can take me out with your Glock."

Thomas had no doubt that he could. In these close quarters,

even a single ricocheting bullet could prove fatal. He accepted an affirmative nod from Tuff before conceding.

"Terms accepted," he stated, slowly lowering his weapon.

Liu did likewise, and both of them deposited their armaments out of reach on the steel latticed decking. Continuing to prolong this entire confrontation to use up as much precious time as possible, Thomas looked at Tuff and asked.

"Well, partner, how are your hand-to-hand skills?"

"I learned a trick or two during my time with SBS," admitted Tuff with confidence. "How about you?"

"I can handle myself," Thomas answered, unwilling to reveal the black belt in karate that he had earned while in Air Force Special Operations.

Tuff spit into his open right palm and rubbed his hands together. "Let's give the bloke a decent chance. If you don't mind, I'd like to do the honors."

Thomas knew that such an arrangement would serve to use up more time, and he graciously beckoned for Tuff to proceed. Tuff stepped forward to a small, open landing, where he took up a basic fighting stance, with feet spread and fists cocked before his face.

Dennis Liu casually approached him, hands loosely at his side. To the unwary opponent, the terrorist didn't appear to know the first thing about protecting himself. He merely stood there, a foot or so away from Tuff, his expression one of contrived innocence.

"Ah, SBS," Liu teased in his best taunting manner. "I understand that you really showed those big bad Argentineans something down in the Malvinas. You Brits make me sick; imperialists to the core, always picking on the poor exploited masses. It's too bad Herr Hitler didn't make good his threatened invasion across the channel, so he could have thrown that feebleminded royal family of yours into the ovens, where they belonged."

"Shut your filthy mouth, Chinaman!" returned Tuff, his ire provoked. "You can insult me all you want, but when you include the royal family, that's where I draw the line."

Tuff cocked back his right fist and threw a powerful punch toward his opponent's jaw. Without raising his own fists in defense, Liu jumped aside and the punch met only air.

"You're a quick little Chink, aren't you?" said Tuff. He tested Liu with a probing left jab before letting loose with a wild combination of punches. Not a single blow landed, his opponent escaping this barrage with a series of quick, catlike moves that still didn't necessitate the raising of his fists in self-defense.

"So, you want to play it cute, huh, Chinaman?" managed Tuff between gasps of air.

"Take your time and catch your breath first, Tuff," advised Thomas from his position beside the port cowling.

The frustrated Englishman nodded in acknowledgment, yet moved in for another attack all the same. This time he started his flurry with a short left jab that was meant as a feint. Shifting his body's center of gravity forward, he quickly cross-stepped his rear leg before raising his front foot for a roundhouse kick aimed at his opponent's exposed groin.

Liu saw this sequence coming from the very first feint, and he displayed the degree of his martial-arts expertise by stepping aside and grabbing Tuff's front foot with his right hand. All he had to do now was yank violently upwards to send Tuff crashing to the deck.

"Come on, SBS. Show me your stuff, you limey bastard," taunted Liu.

Tuff took the bait. As he got to his knees, he lunged forward like a defensive tackle on an American football team. To escape this charge, Liu sprang upward into the air. As Tuff passed beneath him, he planted a firm elbow smack into the security officer's forehead. The crack of this wicked blow clearly reverberated throughout the compartment, and Tuff crumpled to the deck for the ten count and much more.

"Bruce Lee was a pussy. Next," said Liu.

Thomas sized up his opponent as adept in San Shou kung fu. A martial-arts form that was extremely popular with the Red Chinese Army, San Shou was a hybrid of kick boxing, grappling, joint locking and wrestling. The name itself meant the free application of all individual hand-to-hand combat skills, and Thomas knew that he'd have his hands full dealing with him.

A quick check of his watch showed that it was 12:30 A.M. If the SEALs had made good their midnight rendezvous, surely they'd be aboard the QE2 by now. Unable to forget about the numerous obstacles that could have popped up to delay them, Thomas slowly stepped onto the small landing, determined to put forth the best effort possible.

*　　*　　*

"Lieutenant Colonel Laycob!" screamed the SDV pilot, the smashing, twenty-foot waves and howling winds instantly swallowing his frantic cry.

Only seconds before, the Royal Marine veteran had been on the bottom rung of the caving ladder, on his way out of the SDV and up to the *QE2*'s pitching fantail. No sooner had he taken his first step upward, than a monstrous, thirty-foot swell smacked into them with such force that Laycob was torn from the ladder. He was last seen crashing into the sea below, with the pilot now having to make the decision whether or not to abandon their colleague.

The last of the five SEALs who had gone before Laycob was in the process of climbing over the rail of the ocean liner's Three Deck anchor-windlass station. One who was already standing behind the rail, though, caught the pilot's attention with a series of wild arm gestures. Though the pilot was expecting a signal to abandon his abbreviated search and cast off, the SEAL was instead pointing at a portion of the roiling ocean at the SDV's stern.

The pilot turned to scan this sector, and he immediately spotted the glow of Laycob's chemlite necklace, only a few feet behind the SDV. The SBS commando had somehow managed to grab hold of one of the vessel's retraining lines, and was in the process of slowly pulling his drenched body back into the submersible.

"Do you still want to join them on the *Queen*?" asked the pilot, having to scream to be heard over the gusting wind.

"You bet I do, lad," replied Laycob, who was wet but none the worse for wear. "Just give me a bloody second to catch my breath, and I'll be good to go."

Thomas Kellogg had never faced an adversary who displayed such lightning-quick reflexes and subtle resolve. Always one step ahead of any punch or kick that Thomas might attempt, the terrorist had yet to be touched by any type of offensive blow. Thomas understood how a mouse might feel as a hungry cat toyed with it.

In a vain effort to penetrate his defenses, Thomas tried his best to attack with short, feinting jabs. This was intended to open up his opponent's weak side to a lead hook. In almost every instance, the Chinese blocked his jab with his rear hand, before feinting a counterattack with his own lead fist. Instead of making solid contact on Thomas's exposed jaw or body, these strikes were intentionally pulled back. This frustrating tactic infuriated Thomas, who felt like an inexperienced student once again.

Completely forgetting that he was supposed to be using up as much time as possible, Thomas moved in to take this man down. And the last thing he remembered before hitting the deck unconscious, was a solid foot headed right for his jaw, where a foot had no business being!

"Let's do it, lad!" yelled Laycob to the SDV pilot, as he reached up for the caving ladder.

To help him grab the wildly swaying ladder, the pilot was attempting to snag it with a hooked extension pole. The swells were arriving with such irregularity that it was impossible for him to time his efforts, and he caught nothing but air.

"Let me try," Laycob shouted, well aware that the SEALs aboard the *QE2* would be going crazy with impatience by now.

Since he considered himself to be the key component in any successful takedown of the huge ocean liner, he wasn't about to be denied. He dared to stand up on the wildly pitching side of the SDV, and on the very first try, Laycob snagged the ladder.

"All right!" he yelled in triumph.

Any further celebration on his part was cut short by a frothing expanse of agitated seawater pouring out from beneath the *QE2*'s stern. His grip on the ladder unexpectedly tightened, and he suddenly realized that the ocean liner was moving!

Though he could have easily let go of the ladder, sheer stubborn determination kept him from doing so. Now finding himself dragged through the frigid sea, he struggled to hook his boot into the bottom rung. His first attempt failed. With the palms of his hands stinging from all the weight they were bearing, he lifted his sodden foot for one more attempt, and the sole of his combat boot at long last made solid contact. A Herculean effort followed, as the forty-nine-year-old commando began the extraordinarily dangerous task of climbing up the vessel's stern—a job made all the more difficult as the *QE2* picked up steam to cut its way through the storm-tossed waters.

A simple adjustment of the dual pitch levers was all that was needed to change the angle of the propellers and get the ship moving once more. Curious as to why the two officers would go to all this trouble, Dennis Liu intended to awaken them. A vigorous interrogation would all too soon bear fruit, and after learning their motivation, he'd kill them.

A pained groan from the stocky Englishman showed that he was the first to regain consciousness. Yet before Liu could get on with his plan, his two-way radio activated with a burst of static.

"Dennis!" exploded Monica's voice from the speaker. "We've made contact with Red Star. We need you up in the Radio Room at once to transmit the last of the codes."

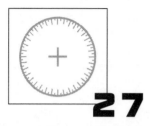

27

"IT'S TIME, LADS," WHISPERED ROBERT HARTWELL TO HIS TWO TABLEMATES. "Take a look at their new watch leader. The guy looks exhausted, as do the rest of them."

Hartwell was referring to Sunny, who had entered the Queens Grill shortly after the ship stopped moving. They were underway once more, making the jolting, rolling motion of the deck a bit more tolerable.

"How do you propose that we do it?" Samuel Morrision questioned. "Just because they're tired doesn't mean their bullets won't prove just as deadly."

"Check out the pantry accessway behind us," instructed the ship's security director. "They've yet to replace the sentry who had been stationed there previously, and I know for certain that there's no locking mechanism of any type on that door."

"Where does it lead?" asked Vince who discreetly glanced over his shoulder to the doorway, located a bare twenty feet distant.

"Straight into the Kitchen," Hartwell answered. "From there, it's a chip shot to the Radio Room or Bridge."

"You've got my blessings," said Vince. "Sitting around like this is driving me stir-crazy."

"I'm game," added Morrison.

"Splendid," Hartwell replied in a conspirational whisper. "A sim-

338

ple diversion that takes place beside the Grill's aft entrance should give you the opportunity to slip out the pantry unnoticed. I did a bit of Shakespeare in my time, and should be able to pull off a sham fainting spell."

"You're much too important to be wasted on the diversion, Robert," offered Morrison. "Your knowledge of the ship will be better put to use if you're one of the escapees and I do the acting. Besides, the way I'm feeling, it won't take much of a dramatic performance on my part to play sick."

Robert Hartwell nodded. "Very well, lads. Let's do it, and may the Lord be with us."

"What in the hell hit me?" muttered Thomas after regaining consciousness and finding himself sprawled out on the Engine Room's cold, latticed-steel deck.

Tuff kneeled close behind him, rubbing his throbbing jaw and thinking the very same thing. "We were properly whipped, pure and simple, Special Agent. By *the* Dennis Liu himself. Looks like those Hollywood choreographers taught him a thing or two about fighting."

"His skills are way beyond that," said Thomas, recognition of their adversary flooding his face as he painfully sat upright and rubbed his own swollen jaw.

The rumble of the *QE2*'s engines filled the background with a wall of sound, and Thomas realized that they were underway once more. "I sure hope the SEALs made it."

"And if they didn't?" Tuff asked.

Thomas answered while reaching up to grab the shaft cowling and standing. "Then we're going to have to take this ship ourselves. Stopping again won't do us any good. It would take them hours to ready themselves again, then it would be too light out to be safe. Where did our movie star go?"

"Though I was still in never-never land, seeing visions of sugar plums dancing before my eyes, I heard his two-way activate. It was a woman's voice, saying something or other about the broadcasting of some bloody codes in the Radio Room."

"The Chinese nuclear-weapons release codes!" exclaimed Thomas, his return to the land of the living now complete. "Tuff, we've got to get up to Radio and stop him from transmitting, or millions could die!"

"Alpha team, you're clear to proceed," directed the SEAL platoon leader into the miniature transmitter of his cranial headset.

Lawrence Laycob was kneeling close beside the individual responsible for this order. From the cover of a recessed anteroom, located outside one of the food lockers, Laycob peered down Six Deck's working alleyway. He watched as the four SEALs comprising Alpha team emerged from their hiding places. With a smooth balletlike movement, they leapfrogged forward, from doorway to doorway, finally joining Laycob beside the closed steel locker.

"Lieutenant Colonel," said the SEAL leader. "It looks like the crew has been pulled from this section of the ship. How should we proceed?"

"I suggest continuing forward to the Hospital," said Laycob. "Then we can take the C Stairwell to Five Deck, where we can access the A Stairwell. This will provide a direct route to the Boat Deck, where the Bridge is only a short climb away."

"Then let's do it," returned the SEAL team leader, glancing at his SBS associate and flashing him a supportive thumbs-up.

"I don't understand it, Dennis. We had Red Star locked in clear as a bell," revealed a very distraught and frustrated Monica Chang.

Dennis Liu stormed over to the radio console, where Ricky and the ship's radio officer sat behind the transmitter. "This better not be caused by another one of your foolish games," he threatened. "Because if it is, you'll die right here."

Ricky looked up and replied sheepishly. "In my hurry to input the frequency-hopping program, I must have hit the wrong key."

"Then correct it!" ordered Liu while glancing up at the clock. "And rest assured that this time, a mistake will cost you your lives."

To support this threat, he raised his gun, and when Ricky reached for Max's notebook his hands were shaking.

"Would you mind lowering your weapon?" asked the radio officer. "The lad's under enough pressure as it is."

Liu's reaction to this simple request was sure and swift. He cocked back his empty hand and hit the radio officer with a chop to the throat. The force of this unexpected blow was enough to crush the officer's trachea. He collapsed on the deck, vainly clutching at his neck and gasping for air.

Sheer horror filled Ricky's expression as the officer's face turned a brilliant blue. For a sickening second their glances met. The doomed Englishman struggled to breathe. With bloody spittle dripping from his purple lips, his oxygen-starved body convulsed in a series of seizures before death claimed him after a final mad spasm.

Ricky dared to look up at Liu, and was startled to find the terrorist smiling. There could be no missing the expression of shocked revulsion that filled Kristin's drawn face behind him.

"You'll be next if you don't fine-tune that transmitter," warned Liu.

Ricky fought back the sudden urge to retch. He closed his eyes to regather his composure before turning his attention back to the keyboard. Slowly at first, then with gathering speed, he began the tedious task of reprogramming the complicated Cobol sequence.

His persistence paid off when a constant, high-pitched tone sounded from the transmitter's speaker. Liu wasted little time in grabbing the nearest handset. As he hit the transmit button, he began reading from the red leather notebook that Monica handed him.

"Delta . . . Delta . . . Sierra . . . Bravo . . . Zulu . . . Tango."

He halted a moment to turn the page—during this brief pause the door to the Radio Room burst open. Liu looked up in startled disbelief as the two men he had confronted in the Engine Room stormed in. The stocky ship's officer who had been so proud of his former SBS service went directly to the compartment's circuit breaker, while his associate covered him with his pistol. Undeterred, Liu hit the transmit button and spoke urgently into the transmitter.

"Bravo . . . Sierra . . . Zulu . . . Tango . . . Alpha . . ."

One tantalizing code word short of completing the final sequence, Thomas fired two rounds into the transmitter, killing the line. Then he drew a bead on Monica before she could get her weapon up.

"No!" Liu bellowed. He threw down the handset, grabbed the Sterling out of Monica's hands, and taking little time to aim, pulled the trigger.

Thomas and Tuff dove for cover behind the telex console. The exploding 9mm rounds tore into the laminated counter. Before they could put their own weapons into play, Liu's voice rang out.

"Drop your guns and stand with your hands up. Or your young friend out here will pay the ultimate price for your spineless act of treachery."

Thomas had caught a brief glimpse of Ricky as he took aim at the transmitter, and he knew this threat was a very real one. They thus had no choice but to obey.

"So it's you two fools again," Liu managed between heaving breaths. "How I'll delight in watching all of you die."

Liu grabbed Ricky by the collar, pulled him to his feet, and shoved him across the room. Thomas caught him, and together with Tuff, watched Liu ram a fresh clip into the submachine gun.

At the same time, Kristin pulled her own pistol from the folds of her coveralls. She disengaged the safety and pointed the barrel at her unsuspecting parent.

"Father!" she cried. "We've seen enough killing. Now that we're unable to contact Red Star, it's time to admit failure and surrender."

"Whatever are you talking about?" countered Liu. "Lower your weapon this instant and come to your senses, girl."

Kristin resolutely shook her head. "I *have* come to my senses, Father. And that's why I'm ordering you and Monica to drop your weapons."

"I knew all along that the little brat didn't have the stomach," said Monica from her position at Liu's side. "And now she's gone and turned traitor."

"Put down the gun, Kristin," said Liu firmly.

Again she shook her head. This time Monica challenged her commitment by taking a threatening step forward. Kristin gripped the pistol with both hands and pulled the trigger. There was a deafening explosion, as a round whizzed by Monica's head and embedded itself in the aft bulkhead.

"How could you betray us like this?" asked Liu, displaying no outward fear himself. "Put down the gun, before you go and do something that you'll later regret."

"My only regret is that I didn't act earlier," Kristin replied. "Too many innocent lives have already been lost. Ricky's right, this isn't the direction that China should take. It's time to quit looking for salvation in the past, and focus instead on the great possibilities that the upcoming century promise."

"Daughter, dear misguided daughter of mine," mumbled Liu while taking a tentative step toward her.

Kristin shifted the aim of the pistol to her father, and Liu pleaded his case with total calm. "Do you really think you could shoot your own flesh and blood? Hand over the gun, and we'll discuss this misunderstanding. Like adults."

"It's too late for talk," Kristin countered, trying with both hands to keep the heavy pistol steady.

Liu took another step and reached out for the gun, now barely an arm's length away. "I admire the strength of your convictions, dear daughter, distorted though they might be. In so many ways, you remind me of your grandmother. So brave; to leave the beloved country of her birth, only to take up the motherland's cause on a distant shore, a world away from all that she cherished. How head-strong and stubborn she was!"

From the other side of the room, Thomas saw how Kristin re-acted to this emotional plea. She was obviously being affected by her father's words, and it was only a matter of time before her will would weaken. Knowing full well that Liu intended to kill them once this crisis was resolved, Thomas listened as Kristin shouted:

"Father, I'm warning you. Stop!"

Liu smiled, and when he dared to take another step forward, the blast of another gunshot resounded through the Radio Room. Shocked disbelief filled Liu's face as he staggered back and blood began pouring from a wound in his left shoulder.

Before Monica could get possession of the Sterling, Thomas glanced at Tuff and together they charged across the room. Tuff moved in to subdue Monica, while Thomas jarred the submachine gun out of Liu's grasp with a well-placed kick, and faced the bleed-ing terrorist.

"It's over, Liu!" Thomas shouted.

"Like hell it is," retorted Liu, all but ignoring his blood-soaked wound.

Monica stood at his side. Together they took up martial-arts stances. Tuff moved in to challenge her. She answered with a flurry of sharp, expertly delivered jabs. Thomas concentrated his attack on his opponent's shoulder, yet in each instance his blows were countered.

Tuff was equally frustrated. He held back his initial blows deliberately because of his opponent's gender. A *Queen*'s man, he was ever the gentleman. But when Monica succeeded in landing a pair of painful punches to his jaw and ribcage, any noble sentiments on his part were soon forgotten.

After deflecting a roundhouse kick, Tuff landed a solid right jab into the side of her skull. Though he presumed that the force of this blow was sufficient to stun her, Monica was able to grab his fist in an excruciating wristlock.

At the same time, Thomas found himself fighting off a furious flurry of kicks and punches. As he jumped aside to escape a jab, Liu grabbed his left forearm with enough force to yank Thomas off his feet. Tuff's attention remained focused on escaping the wristlock, and he failed to duck as Liu spun Thomas around by the arm.

They collided head-on, their foreheads smashing together with a distinctive crack. The force of this concussion was enough to knock Thomas out, and he fell to the deck headfirst, sprawled out on his stomach. Tuff folded to his knees at Thomas's side, dazed and near unconsciousness himself.

Liu's upper torso was completely soaked in blood, and in no mood for fear, he walked up to his daughter and yanked the pistol from her shaking grasp. "Why don't you go and join your boyfriend," he instructed with disgust.

As she crossed the compartment to Ricky, gunfire sounded in the distance. Seconds later, Monica's two-way activated. There could be no mistaking the fear that colored the caller's voice.

"We're exchanging gunfire with a large group of well-armed commandos near the Hospital. They appear to be from an outside assault force!"

The resonant boom of an exploding concussion grenade emphasized this warning, and the radio went dead.

"Call Sunny this instant," Liu instructed Monica. "Have him round up the nine heads of state, and escort them down to the Engine Room. We'll make our stand there, beside the fail-safe device."

Monica used her two-way to carry out this order and Liu did his best to plug his shoulder wound with a folded handkerchief. Another background explosion sounded, and Liu snapped a fresh round into the Sterling to finish off Thomas and Tuff.

"Please, Father," pleaded Kristin, tears cascading down her cheeks. "Can't you just leave them be?"

"Shut up!" Liu exclaimed.

As he raised the barrel to first execute Thomas, Vince Kellogg came bursting into the Radio Room. The Secret Service agent instantly sized up the situation and made a beeline for Liu. He reached him in time to divert his aim, and a trio of bullets tore into the deck, only a precious few inches from his brother's exposed back. Vince then knocked the weapon free and began grappling with Liu.

Monica scurried over to grab the Sterling. Ricky finally summoned enough nerve to act. He darted forward and kicked the submachine gun beneath the telex console. Monica, infuriated, turned her wrath on Ricky, but before she could do him serious harm, Kristin joined the melee. Monica now found herself facing an opponent also trained by Dennis Liu.

Behind them, Vince broke out of Liu's bloody grasp and crouched down in a square stance, his legs and arms open. A former collegiate wrestler, Vince displayed not a hint of fear.

"So the special agent is trained in Greco-Roman style," observed Liu while assuming a similar stance.

Vince didn't tarry, and he charged forward. To respond to this enthusiastic attack, Liu turned swiftly, using Vince's own momentum to get him into a headlock. Before Vince could counter, Liu grabbed his left elbow, and with the headlock still in place, used the resulting leverage to take his opponent down.

Vince fell to the deck hard on his back, with enough force to knock the wind out of his lungs. For a terrifying second, he was unable to breathe. He gasped for air, and watched as Liu towered above him, gloating.

"So much for Greco-Roman," quipped Liu.

Yet more gunfire sounded in the distance. Liu watched Kristin selflessly get in the way of a blow by Monica meant for Ricky. As Monica moved in to finish her off, Liu interceded.

"Forget her. Let her die with the rest. We must join Sunny."

Though Monica desired nothing better than to kill Kristin, she reluctantly backed away. Liu grabbed the Sterling, and led her out of the Radio Room, passing his daughter as if she weren't even there. Ricky meanwhile fought the pitching deck to attend to Vince.

"I'm fine, Ricky," managed Vince between heaving breaths. "Why don't you see if you can help out Tuff and his fallen shipmate."

As Ricky was in the process of crossing the room to help, Tuff's voice echoed forth with concern. "Special Agent Kellogg, are you okay? Special Agent Kellogg?"

"I'll be fine, Tuff," returned Vince, while struggling to sit up. "Just had the damned wind knocked out of me."

Seemingly ignoring this update on Vince's part, Tuff persisted. "Come on, Special Agent Kellogg, snap out of it!"

Vince failed to understand what Tuff was referring to. As he turned around, he found the security officer huddled over the prone body of a fellow officer. Ricky arrived at Tuff's side. Together they turned the man over on his back and began slapping his cheeks. Something about this fellow's appearance was disturbingly familiar to Vince, and he waited for Kristin's assistance before attempting to stand.

He stood upright, fighting off a brief wave of dizziness, then got his first good look at the fallen officer's face.

"It can't be," muttered Vince, who looked on in shocked amazement as the man's eyes snapped open, met his glance and spoke.

"Don't just stand there gawking, big brother, give me a hand."

Tuff and Ricky helped him stand, and Vince wasted no time greeting his brother with a warm hug. "I always knew that you wanted to go along on this crossing, but I never thought you'd stoop to being a stowaway."

Thomas laughed. "Stowaway? No, let's just say I dropped in without a proper ticket."

"Gentlemen," interrupted Kristin, her voice heavy with concern. "I hate to interrupt what seems to be a family reunion. But unless we get down to the Engine Room and stop my father, this ship's going right to the bottom of the Atlantic, with us in it!"

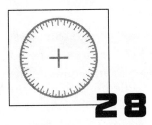

28

"WE'VE LOST COLLINS, SIR!"

This somber radio report arrived via Laycob's cranial headset, and the Royal Marine commando took it upon himself to shoulder the blame.

"It's all my bloody fault," he admitted, from the cover of the anteroom outside the vacant Print Shop.

The platoon's senior SEAL was huddled at his side, and both of them were forced to hit the deck when a submachine-gun round ricocheted overhead.

"It was Collins's impatience that got him killed," managed the SEAL while reloading his sidearm. "As point man, he should have waited for the rest of the assault train to catch up, before continuing up the passageway."

The deep, booming report of a .45 caliber pistol sounded in the background, and Laycob flinched when a concussion grenade detonated nearby.

"It's ironic that they picked the Hospital's anteroom in which to set up their ambush," remarked the Englishman. "By positioning an armed sentry on each side of the working alleyway there, they've pretty well blocked our access to points forward."

"We can always try to storm them," offered the SEAL.

"That would be too costly," Laycob cautioned.

"We can't just sit here," the SEAL returned. "Ammo's getting low and we're losing our momentum."

Yet another bullet whined overhead. Laycob offered the only tactical advice that made any sense: "We can bypass this passageway by returning aft, and then work our way forward through the Engine Room. The only problem is getting back down this corridor in one piece."

"It's nothing that a protective curtain of tear gas, smoke canisters, and stun grenades can't take care of," said the SEAL, who addressed the miniature transmitter of his cranial headset to implement this strategic retreat.

"This is as far as we're going, comrades!" shouted Sunny at the top of his voice. Even then, it was hard for his nine, tuxedo-clad prisoners to hear him over the roaring whine of the engines.

Together with Ping, the QE2's former head laundryman, Sunny had herded the heads of state through the adjoining compartment, where the massive diesel engines were incessantly grinding away. Their prisoners looked strangely out of place in this unglamorous, grease-stained environment. This was the working-man's world, a place of raw machinery, twisting pipe, and snaking insulated conduit. The scent that permeated the steamy air here wasn't that of fancy cologne or French perfume. It was rather that of diesel fuel and sweat. It filled Sunny's nostrils with memories of his early childhood in the oil fields of Hunan.

If his hard-working, peasant family could only see him now, thought Sunny, as he signaled his prisoners to halt beside the grimy bulkhead. He merely had to wave the stubby barrel of his MP-5K submachine gun, to get the chancellor of Germany to tighten his ranks with the rest of this group. Sunny Chu, the son of a Hunanese peasant, currently herding the nine most powerful men in the world as if they were a bunch of frightened sheep! Who would have thought that such an incredible day would ever come?

Proud of his achievements like never before, Sunny took up a position against the opposite bulkhead. Beside him were a collection of oddly shaped, sealed vats, with thick, grease-stained pipes snaking in and out of them. He knew this was the place where the fuel oil was heated. And on the far side of the vat nearest to him was where they had planted the explosive device.

It was a simple mechanism, formed out of a fist-sized lump of plastic explosives, a blasting cap, a nine-volt battery, and a digital timer. A small amount of colored wire connected the components that their leader had placed here on the night of the takeover—the heavy scent of oil masking it from bomb-sniffing dogs.

Dennis Liu had called it their insurance policy, and Sunny assumed that he was preparing to make good his threat to use it. This meant that the submarine they were supposed to rendezvous with was close by. They'd be surely transferring into the hold of this vessel any minute now, with a submerged trip back to the motherland to follow.

Such heroes they'd be, thought Sunny, who knew he'd soon have his pick of China's most beautiful women. The trick now was to stay healthy, so that he could enjoy each and every one of them!

Sunny licked his dry lips in anticipation when Dennis Liu and Monica Chang stepped over the edge of the watertight door leading from the compartment where the engines were noisily grinding away. Their leader looked pale, and there could be no missing the bright red blood that stained the upper half of his coveralls.

"Whatever happened?" asked Sunny. "Are you hurt?"

"It's nothing but a scratch," replied Liu, who was more concerned with the nine men standing before him. "Any problems getting them down here?"

"We were forced to shoot several of the security agents when we began escorting them out of the Dining Room," revealed Sunny. "But other than that, they were as docile as lambs."

"Good," replied Liu while continuing to the vat on which their bomb was placed.

Sunny followed him, watching as Liu bent over and manipulated the bomb's digital timer. After a minor adjustment, he clicked the timer's stem and the electronic display briefly registered seven minutes before beginning a rapid second-by-second countdown.

"Comrade Liu, I believe that you've made a mistake here," remarked Sunny. "We'll never get aboard that submarine in a mere seven minutes."

"Sunny," said Liu with a disgusted shake of his head. "Get over there by Ping and keep your mouth shut. I've got the situation under control as always."

As he crossed over the deck, Sunny realized what Liu must be attempting. It was a scare tactic, designed to put fear into the hearts of the cowardly statesmen. Renewed confidence guided Sunny's steps as he took up a position alongside Ping and directed the barrel of his weapon at the pathetic group of men standing in front of them.

Dennis Liu also approached this group, and he made it a point to isolate the lanky politician standing on the far right. President Li Chen acknowledged Liu's glance with a defiant smirk. Liu reacted to this insulting sneer by reaching forward and grabbing the Chinese leader by the scruff of his neck. He then positioned himself behind Li, all the while planting the barrel of his Sterling firmly against the president's sweating temple.

"This is the spineless coward who's responsible for my presence amongst you!" shouted Liu to the other leaders. "Fifty years ago, it was Li Chen's grandfather who executed my own beloved parent, and left his body to be devoured by dogs. And now Li Chen with his murderous blood has stolen away the leadership of the People's Republic. I know what he was doing here. He was selling out our nation, in the tradition of the weak-willed Russians. China shall not take the Soviet Union's path, and go overnight from a superpower to a nation of beggars. All of you share in the blame. Your greed is limitless, and now you shall pay the ultimate price for your despicable crimes!"

Sunny wasn't certain what was going on when a group of four former prisoners rushed through the watertight door. Several of them carried weapons, and Sunny prepared himself for the worst.

"Do come right in," greeted Dennis Liu, completely unconcerned by their presence.

Kristin and Ricky hovered at the group's rear. She seemed to be in their midst by choice, and Sunny got the distinct impression that something was seriously wrong. Then he suddenly remembered the bomb ticking away on the opposite bulkhead.

"Comrade Liu, the bomb!" reminded Sunny, pointing to the vat where the soft glow of the digital timer was barely visible.

The SEAL team accessed the aft portion of the Engine Room by way of the after tunnel escape ladder. Lawrence Laycob led them down the steep, narrow shaft, with the assault train reforming beside the shaft's dual pitch-control levers.

As they worked their way forward, it was Laycob who noted first that their intended route was blocked. "Damn!" he cursed. "They've closed the bloody watertight doors leading into the Engine Room."

The team assembled in front of the massive steel doors that extended all the way to the ceiling.

"Looks like we have no choice but to return topside and access the Bridge via the exterior passageways," offered the senior SEAL.

"We've got no time for that," Laycob replied. "Besides, now that they're aware of our presence, an exterior approach is much too risky."

The SEAL pounded on the solid-steel door with his fist. "Then we're going to need an acetylene torch to cut through all of this metal."

"There's supposed to be an emergency circuit panel built into each of the watertight doors," offered Laycob, his flashlight sweeping the door. "If we can find it, and trip the circuit, we should be able to open the door manually."

Thomas Kellogg's reaction to the warning of a bomb was motivated by pure instinct. Without considering the dangers involved, he sprinted past the collection of weapons pointed his way, his concerns focused on the explosive device that was soon before him.

Thomas studied the IED. The digital timer had just passed five minutes. It was a relatively simple affair, whose potential destructive power didn't necessarily correspond to its lump-sized piece of plastic explosive. If this bomb were to indeed detonate, it would surely ignite the tons of volatile fuel oil that lay in the bunkers below, and whose presence Thomas couldn't miss smelling.

"Go ahead, comrade. Try to defuse it," dared Liu, his voice barely heard over the engines. "If you fail, we shall die. If you succeed, we will all fall, including the leaders, in the battle that I assure you will ensue. Either way, my friend, I win."

Thomas was unable to get a good look at the manner in which the wires were connected to the detonator and its nine-volt battery. Pulling out a wire at random was tantamount to suicide, and he listened as Dennis Liu declared:

"If only I had a camera to record this scene for posterity." Then with a demented laugh, "And to think that this great ship shall serve as our tomb for all eternity!"

"I wouldn't be so quick to bank on that, lad," shouted Lt. Col. Lawrence Laycob from the dark recesses of the compartment.

From out of this same veil of blackness, an eerie collection of needle-thin red beams projected. As they moved forward, sweeping the room, Thomas saw they originated from the laser sights of SEAL Team Two's weapons, which finally locked on the foreheads of Sunny, Ping, Monica, and Dennis Liu.

Of the foursome, only Liu displayed the reflexes needed to leap away in time, as a deafening volley of shots rang out. In a bare millisecond, three of Liu's closest associates were dead.

Like a cornered animal, Liu's pained voice cried out in rage, and he charged into Thomas's stunned group, wielding his Sterling like a bo stick, his hands and feet whirling. With the intensity of a buzz saw, he cut down Tuff, knocked out Robert Hartwell, and sent Vince sprawling, leaving Thomas alone to face his fury.

Thomas oddly enough found himself more concerned with the ticking time bomb than the enraged terrorist who now stood before him. Barely aware of the odd gutteral sounds emanating from Liu's throat, the blood that gushed from his shoulder wound, and the constant windmill motion of his arms and legs, Thomas lowered his head and blindly charged.

This attack coincided with the arrival of a massive seawave, and Dennis Liu was thrown off balance as the ship rolled hard on its side. His momentary loss of equilibrium allowed Thomas, to whom the pitch leant momentum, to hit Liu full in the gut with his head and shoulder. The force of this blow was enough to drive Liu's body over the protective curved-steel cowling set up against the outer edge of the bulkhead. An anguished wail sounded, followed by a horrible crunching sound, and Thomas fought his way over the pitching deck to see what had happened to his adversary.

Halfway across the compartment, Thomas remembered what this cowling was designed to protect. Peeking over its lip, he saw the bloody remains of Liu, torn to bits by the *QE2*'s spinning propeller shaft.

Thomas fought back the urge to vomit, his thoughts redirected by the concerned voice of his brother.

"Thomas," he shouted. "The bomb!"

Desperation guided his steps. He crossed the deck and returned to the explosive device. Vince was at his side as the digital display dropped below one minute.

"You're the fucking bomb expert, little brother. For God's sake, do something!"

Tuff offered Thomas his pocket knife, saying, "Will this help?"

Thomas waved away the knife. "They only cut wires in the movies, Tuff. One wrong slice, and we're history."

"Then what other choice do we have?" Vince asked as the timer passed forty-five seconds.

As Ricky, Kristin, and the emerging SEALs led the nine statesmen forward through the airtight door, Thomas cocked back his head to determine his alternatives. He briefly shut his eyes to aid his concentration. As he opened them again, he spotted the metallic spigot of what appeared to be a fire-extinguisher nozzle, protruding from the ceiling above them.

"What's that?" he queried while pointing upward.

"It's part of the compartment's halon fire-extinguisher system," revealed Tuff, who was more concerned by the digital timer's breaking of the thirty-second mark.

In a flash of sudden awareness, Thomas shouted, "Trigger the fire extinguisher, Tuff! Activate the damn system!"

Spurred on by the utter intensity of the ATF agent's command, Tuff sprinted across the deck and smashed the glass window of the nearest fire alarm. The automated system was designed for nearly instantaneous activation, and before Thomas could get out of the way, a torrent of thick, white foam poured out of the overhead spigot.

The halon that dropped onto the bare skin of his neck burned with a fiery intensity, and he felt as if he had been struck by a hot poker. Yet what Thomas initially mistook for heat, turned out to be produced by a frigid temperature of well below minus-one-hundred-degrees Fahrenheit.

Oblivious to his frostbitten skin, Thomas shielded his eyes to get a look at the bomb's digital display. Although halon wasn't as cold as Danny Lane's liquid nitrogen, the freon derivative hopefully would do the trick. For a terrifying second, he saw only the single figure 1 glowing from the frosted display window. Thomas instinctively held his breath in anticipation of the upcoming blast, when he saw that the 1 appeared to be frozen in place. This joyous realization was confirmed as the soft light of the display abruptly blinked off, its power source deadened by the enveloping foam.

EPILOGUE

BENJAMIN KRAM STOOD HUNCHED OVER THE USS *POLK*'S TYPE 18 SEARCH PERI-scope. The lens was set for low-light mode, the brightly lit object of his scan appearing to fill the entire northern horizon.

The *QE2* was barely 2,000 yards distant, and regardless of the dangers of collision in these storm-tossed seas, this was the distance of separation that Kram had ordered. As the last surviving sub of the escort formation, the *Polk* wasn't about to let the ocean liner out of its protective sights.

It wasn't long after the SDV returned safely to the dry-deck shelter, minus its SEAL assault force, that the first high-frequency radio message was received from the *QE2*. The dispatch was short and to the point, and after Kram read it to the crew over the 1MC, a chorus of relieved cheers filled the *Polk*. As of an hour before, the ship had been successfully retaken, the terrorist threat eliminated, with the President of the United States and the eight other leaders now under the protective arm of the brave men of SEAL Team Two.

No one was more excited by this news than the *Polk*'s captain. One of the greatest catastrophes in modern history had been averted, and regardless of the fact that hundreds of brave young men had died along the way, the outcome was cause for celebration.

Scuttlebutt had it that Petty Officer Mallott and his boys in Jimmy's Buffet were abandoning turkey and serving a real steak dinner that evening. Of course, they still had two days of escort duty to go, with the *QE2* already back on course for Southampton.

Kram's main concern was that the weather topside would worsen. Hurricane Marti had continued her relentless push to the north, and the *Polk*'s constantly pitching deck was proof of her gathering fury. Even at periscope depth, the churning seas made submerged travel uncomfortable.

Winds were already gusting to well over fifty knots on the surface, with thirty- to forty-foot waves present. This was impressive, considering that the eye of the storm was more than 140 miles distant.

To safely ride out this tempest, the *QE2* had cut its speed to under ten knots. The view from the periscope dramatically displayed the manner in which the giant ocean liner was handling the rough seas. Bobbing from side to side like a bathtub toy, the massive vessel was taking a beating, and Kram felt sorry for its poor passengers.

His view of the ship was veiled momentarily by a wave splashing up against the periscope lens, and Kram began a slow, 360-degree scan of the surrounding seas. Towering swells raged all around them, with jagged streaks of lightning coloring the gray, cloud-filled skies.

"Skipper," barked the gruff voice of the boat's COB. "I've got the latest TACAMO update. I think you're going to want to hear it."

Without bothering to look away from the rubberized lens coupling, Kram replied. "Fire away, COB."

The COB ducked through the heavy black curtain that separated the periscope pedestal from the rest of the control room. With his glance locked on the overhead monitor screen that displayed a view of Kram's periscope scan, COB reported.

"The Priority-One transmission originated in the CNO's Pentagon op center. It informed us that as of 0110 hours, American strategic forces have stood down from a DEFCON Two alert status. This alert was precipitated by threatening moves on the part of outlaw elements inside Red China's military. Shortly after midnight, our time, the ringleaders of this right-wing, extremist faction were rounded up and arrested. Included in this group was Adm. Liu Huang-tzu, who was reported to have committed suicide before being incarcerated."

"So the last of the surviving Maoists is finally dead," reflected Kram, who used his right thumb to amplify the lens to its maximum magnification for a closer study of the wind-carved seas. "If I remember correctly, Admiral Liu was a Long March survivor, and Mao's most cherished naval advisor. We all know him as the father of the modern PLA Navy. It's a shame that he had to end his long career under such a black cloud."

"Speaking of black clouds, Skipper," interrupted COB, his eyes still locked on the monitor screen. "That sky to our east doesn't look very promising. Is that a low-lying cloud bank of some sort, visible on the horizon?"

Benjamin Kram had also spotted this alien, dark gray formation that extended the entire length of the eastern horizon. A quick range-check showed it a good 10,000-yards distant. As Kram rechecked this figure, he realized that the mysterious formation was on the move, headed right for them.

"Those aren't clouds, COB," observed Kram, his pulse quickening. "It's a giant wave. That's got to be over a hundred feet above sea level to be seen from this distance! Get on the radio to warn the QE2. Then we're taking the Polk down to escape this monster ourselves."

Trying their best to ignore the wildly pitching deck, a joyous reunion of sorts was taking place inside the QE2's Bridge. Assembled in one corner were the Kellogg brothers, a bandaged Thomas finally able to tell Vince the exacting details of the events that had led up to his airborne arrival on the ocean liner.

Gathered behind the navigation plot, Lawrence Laycob and Robert Hartwell were discussing old times with Captain Prestwick. It was in 1972 that the three first met on this very same Bridge, on an adjoining portion of the Atlantic. Both men had been SBS commandos at the time, who had parachuted aboard to look for a bomb.

It was shortly after a thorough search of the ocean liner determined that the bomb scare was a hoax that Laycob ceremoniously reached into the folds of his wet suit and pulled out the latest edition of the Times of London for the QE2's captain. Never in their wildest dreams did they ever think that twenty-five years later, they would be reunited on the QE2's Bridge once again.

Ronald Prestwick was in the process of accepting Laycob's apology for having no Times to give him in this instance when the Polk's warning arrived via radio. Prestwick himself acknowledged receipt of this urgent dispatch, and after signing off, joined the Bridge's other occupants at the rain-soaked observation window.

In the middle of this concerned group was Thomas Kellogg, who had to tightly grip the edge of the instrument console to keep from tumbling over. He did his best to peer out the window and spot the giant wave the *Polk* had just warned them about.

It was a struggle for the exterior, rubber-bladed wipers to clear the rain-soaked window. In those rare instances when Thomas was afforded a clear view, what he saw was far from reassuring. The night was pitch black, with visibility poor. The sea was a roiling mass of white foam, the driving spray constantly lashing the ship in blinding torrents. Wave after wave smashed over the bow, leaving the foredeck almost permanently awash.

With the assistance of binoculars, it was the ship's bearded master who was the first to spot the wave. By the time Thomas saw it, Prestwick had already issued the course change needed to point the QE2's bow directly into the approaching wall of water.

"By Jove, if I didn't know any better, I'd say that we were headed straight for the white cliffs of Dover," observed Lawrence Laycob, his clipped British accent delivered with cool aplomb.

Thomas wasn't nearly as composed as the SBS commando, the terrifying sight he was viewing causing goosebumps to form on his skin. "Oh my God, that thing is huge!" he exclaimed.

The immense wave appeared to fill the entire eastern horizon with its malevolent presence.

"Sweet Jesus," Vince muttered. "All this, only to be taken down by a damn rogue wave."

"Concerned, Special Agent?" the ship's captain said. "You forget, sir, that you're sailing aboard the greatest ocean liner ever designed by the hand of man."

"Yeah, and that's what the builders of the *Titanic* said when they labeled her unsinkable," Vince muttered, so that only his brother could hear.

"I would, however, suggest," the captain continued, "that we all hold on."

The company on the Bridge needed little more encouragement as word of the wave went out to the rest of the ship.

What seemed to take an eternity, in reality took less than a minute. In the seconds before the monstrous wave finally arrived,

Thomas remembered the way it appeared to fill the entire night sky. This frightening realization was wiped from his mind the moment the wave broke with a tremendous force over the QE2's bow. A powerful jolt shook the deck, as hundreds of tons of frothing seawater crashed over the Bridge with a resounding roar. Again the deck shuddered wildly, and Thomas got the distinct impression that they had somehow submerged, when the wheelhouse windows failed to clear.

He grasped Vince by the arm, and a surge of panic-induced adrenaline coursed through his body, as one of the windshield wipers materialized. Incredibly enough, it was still working, and as the onrushing water finally cleared, he was at long last able to see the extent of the damages. Except for a portion of bent railing and buckled deck plating, the Foredeck appeared none the worse for wear, with the superstructure itself completely untouched.

"Bit of a wave that," observed the captain coolly.

An understatement if he ever heard one, Thomas let loose his death grip on Vince's arm. He watched as the ship's angled bow bit smoothly into the next thirty-foot swell that followed, and found himself with a newfound respect for the great ship on which they sailed. Though any lesser vessel would have been crushed by the giant wave, this wasn't the case with the *Queen Elizabeth 2*. It had suffered attacks by both man and nature, and once again prevailed in the end.

Acknowledgments

This novel would not have been possible without the invaluable assistance of the following:

The A-team: the late Brandon Tartikoff, Robert Gottlieb, Matt Bialer, and Steven H. Kram, who generated the creative spark that got this project sailing;

Lou Aronica and Stephen S. Power of Avon Books;

Antti Pankakoski, Peter Bates, Bill Spears, Eilleen Daily, Julie Davis, and my many new friends at Cunard;

The crew of the *Queen Elizabeth 2*, including Capt. Ronald Warwick, Capt. John Burton-Hall, Alan Parker, Dr. Andrew Eardley, Martin Stenzel, Dan Robinson, Gerry Ellis, John Duffy, and Brian Price;

Jean Cartier Sauleau and Monika Dysart of Cartier Travel;

The Royal Navy and especially Capt. A. J. Lyall, Comdr. Steve Ramm, Comdr. Geoffrey McCready, Comdr. Mark Chichester, Comdr. Jonathan Westbrook, and the crew of the HMS *Talent*;

Lt. Col. M. H. Arndt and the aircrew members of Canadian Air Force Maritime Patrol Squadron 404;

Dianne Coles and John Money of Ocean Books;

Rear Adm. Kendall Pease and Comdr. Gary Shrout of the U.S. Navy;

Brig. Gen. Ron Sconyers, Col. Napoleon Byars, Maj. Les Kodlick and Chuck Davis of the U.S. Air Force;

Maj. Gen. James Hobson, Maj. Matt Durham, Shirley Sikes, Lt. Col. Stu Pugh, Maj. Dave Horowitz, and the great folks at Air Force Special Operations Command, Hurlburt Field, Florida;

Comdr. Jim Pillsbury, Lt. Comdr. Rory Calhoun, and the crew of the USS *James K. Polk*;

The men of SEAL Delivery Vehicle Team Two, along with Comdr. Doug Lowe, Lt. Comdr. Jim Fallon, and Lt. Don Sewell of the Navy Special Warfare Command;

Director John McGaw, Patrick Hynes, Daniel Hoggatt, John Limbach of the Bureau of Alcohol, Tobacco and Firearms;

Bruce Blair, senior fellow, the Brookings Institution;

Special Agent Mike Tarr and Special Agent Arnette F. Heintze Jr. of the U.S. Secret Service;

Carleigh Prane, research assistant extraordinaire;

and last, but definitely not least, Capt. Jim Patton (USN, Ret.), friend, confidant, and consummate war-gamer.

To all of you, my heartfelt thanks for sharing your fascinating worlds with me and my readers!

Queen Elizabeth 2

GENERAL INFORMATION

Keel Laid:	5th July 1965.
Launched:	20th September 1967 by Her Majesty Queen Elizabeth II.
Maiden Voyage:	2nd May 1969; Southampton to New York.
Built by:	John Brown and Co. (Clydebank) Ltd, Clydebank, Scotland; later Upper Clyde Shipbuilders, at a cost of £29,091,000.
Re-engined:	October 1986–April 1987, by Lloyd Werft. Bremerhaven GmbH, Bremerhaven, Germany.
Port of Registry:	Southampton, England.
Signal Letters:	G.B.T.T.
Official Number:	336703
Satellite Telephone:	00 871 1440412 (Eastern Atlantic & Mediterranean) [prefix 872 for Pacific, 873 for Indian or 874 for Western Atlantic]
Satellite Facsimile:	00 871 1441331 (prefixes as for telephone)
Telex:	Telephone number, prefixed by 581 (Atlantic), 582 (Pacific) and 583 (Indian)
Classification:	Lloyd's A.1.

VITAL STATISTICS

Gross Tonnage:	70,327 GRT
Net Tonnage:	30,038 n.t.

Length:	963 feet (293.53 metres)
Breadth:	105 feet 2.5 inches (32.06 metres)
Draught:	32 feet, 7.5 inches (9.94 metres)
Height:-Mast head above Keel:	200 feet 1.5 inches (61 metres)
Funnel above Keel:	204 feet 1.5 inches (62.2 metres)
Masthead above Sea Level:	167 feet 1 inch (51.054 metres)
Passenger Capacity:	1500.
Approx. total number of passengers carried at 20th September 1997, the 30th anniversary of QE2's launch:	1,875,000
Nautical miles travelled at 20th September 1997, the 30th anniversary of QE2's launch:	4,266,500. This is more than the total distances travelled by the Queen Elizabeth and Queen Mary together.
Deck Space:	4,500 square feet
Decks:	13
Passenger Decks:	10
Electric Current in Cabins:	110/115 volts and 240 volts AC
Lifts:	14 Passenger; 2 Car; 8 Store; 1 Engine Room
Car Facilities:	Room for 16 drive-on, drive-off

TECHNICAL DATA

Engines: Nine 9-cylinder L58/64 (580 mm bore/640 mm stroke) medium speed turbo-charged diesels, running at 400rpm and connected to individual alternators generating 10.5 megawatts each at 10,000 volts. Built by MAN B & W Diesel GmbH, Angsburg, Germany, each engine weighs 120 tons. Alternators built by GEC, Stafford, England.

Motors: Two electric motors, one on each propeller shaft, rated at a maximum of 44 megawatts each at 144 rpm. Built by GEC, Rugby, England, the motors each weigh over 400 tons and are over 9 metres in diameter. They are the largest marine motors ever built. The diesel electric system produces 130,000hp, which is the most powerful propulsion plant of any merchant ship in the world. The 95 MW total power output is enough to light a city the size of Southampton. QE2 is thus the fastest merchant ship in operation.

Boilers: Nine waste heat recovery exhaust gas boilers mounted on the engine exhaust uptakes,

Boilers (cont'd):	and two oil fired boilers. These produce steam for fuel heating, domestic fresh water heating, heating of swimming pools and steam for the laundry equipment and kitchens. Built by Sunrod, Sweden.
Propellers:	Two outward-turning controllable pitch. Diameter 19 feet 8 inches (6.0 metres). The propeller shafts are both 262.5ft (80m) long and 23.2 in (590mm) in diameter. Built by Lips, Drunen, Netherlands.
Bow Thrusters:	Two stone KaMeWa of 1,000 hp per unit.
Stabilisers:	Four Denny Brown, each fin projects from the ship's side by 12 ft (3.65m)(and is 6ft (1.85m) wide. They reduce rolling by 60%.
Speed:	Maximum 32.5 knots, service 28.5 knots. Service speed is achievable using eight of the nine engines.
Tank Capacities:	Fresh Water–1,852.0 tonnes Laundry Water–489.0 tonnes Diesel Oil–206.8 tonnes Fuel Oil–4,381.4 tonnes Lubricating Oil–335.7 tonnes Ballast–4,533.0 tonnes Feed Water–113.8 tonnes
Water Production:	Four Serck vacuum evaporators, producing 240 tonnes each per day, and one reverse osmosis plant producing 400 tonnes. Total production is 1,360 tonnes per day, and consumption about 850 tonnes per day, equivalent to 12 of the ship's swimming pools.
Fire Fighting System:	Housed within the machinery spaces, pressure tanks for the accommodation sprinkler system and continuously running fire pumps ensure that water is always available at sprinkler heads and fire hydrants. Virtually every fire fighting aid is available, ranging from foam and CO_2 to the Halon injection system.
Sanitation System:	The sewage disposal plants, completely self-contained and sealed, are located on eight deck.
Anchors:	Forward–two of 12.5 tons each, on 3 15/16 in. diameter cable 2,200 feet long. Aft– one of 7.5 tonnes, on 3 in. diameter cable 720 feet long
Rudder Weight:	80 tonnes.
Fuel Consumption:	16 tonnes per hour, or 380 tonnes per day. This is equal to six of the ship's swim-

Fuel Consumption (cont'd):	ming pools. The ship's fuel oil tank capacity of 4,381.4 tonnes is sufficient for 11 days sailing at 28.5 knots, equalling 7,500 miles. One gallon of fuel will move the ship 49.5 feet; with the previous steam turbine engines, one gallon of fuel moved the ship 36 feet.
Stopping Capability:	The ship can reduce speed from 32.5 knots full ahead to standstill in 3 minutes 39 seconds, in a distance of 0.75 nautical miles (1.39km). The ship can go from standstill to full speed astern (19 knots) in one minute.

NAVIGATION EQUIPMENT

Radar:	Three Kelvin Hughes Nucleus ARPA radars, 3cm and 10 cm, fully inter switched. Two NINAS navigation works stations complete with an electronic chart display utilising ARCS disks. Two Kelvin Hughes Qubit Master Yeoman plotting tables.
Logs:	Raytheon DSL 250 Doppler Speed Log; Raytheon EML 201 Electromagnetic Log.
Satellite navigator:	Racal MK 90 GPS Satellite Navigator, Magnavox MX 200 GPS Receiver.
Hyperbolic Navigational Aids:	Decca Navigator; Loran C.
Autopilot:	Sperry U.G.P. Autopilot.
Compasses:	Two Sperry MK.37 Gyro Compasses; Lilley and Gillie Magnetic.
Whistles:	Three Tyfon Whistles, audible for up to 2 miles.
Navigational charts:	The chartroom has approximately 1,500 charts, covering most of the world. They are updated weekly.

SAFETY INFORMATION

Lifeboats:	20; total capacity 2,244 persons
Liferafts:	56; total capacity 1,400 persons
Buoyant Apparatus;	12; total capacity 200 persons
Lifejackets:	3,474
Lifebuoys:	42

USS James K. Polk (SSN 645)

The keel for the Navy's 35th Fleet Ballistic Missile submarine and the third ship of the fleet to be named in honor of James K. Polk was laid at General Dynamics Corporation's Electric Boat Division at Groton, Connecticut, on 23 November 1963. A year and a half later, this submarine began her waterborne career after being christened USS JAMES K. POLK (SSBN 645) by Mrs. Horacio Rivero, Jr., on 22 May 1965. For the next 10 months, she underwent fitting-out and on 13 March 1966, she conducted her first sea trials. USS JAMES K. POLK was commissioned as a ship of the U.S. Navy on 16 April 1966.

The POLK combined the almost unlimited endurance of nuclear power with the deterrent might of 16 thermonuclear missiles capable of wreaking more havoc than all the bombs of World War II. These missiles had a range of 2,500 nautical miles and were housed in 16 launching tubes located aft of the sail.

USS JAMES K. POLK sailed to Charleston, South Carolina, in September 1966 to load-out Polaris missiles for her initial deterrent patrol. After completion of the shakedown period, the POLK operated in the Atlantic Ocean and completed 19 highly successful deterrent patrols from September 1966 until May 1971.

USS JAMES K. POLK conducted her first overhaul at Newport News Shipbuilding and Dry Dock Company in Virginia for nuclear refueling and conversion of the weapons system to the Poseidon missile system in July 1971. POLK completed her conversion in late 1972 and commenced a rigorous schedule of sea trials and exercises. These events culminated in the Demonstration and Shakedown Operation (DASO) of the Poseidon missile system. The DASO afforded the opportunity to test the ship's system, train the crew and launch a Poseidon C-3 missile from the submarine.

USS JAMES K. POLK commenced Poseidon deterrent patrols in the Atlantic Ocean in May 1973 and conducted 31 more highly successful deterrent patrols. The POLK conducted her second overhaul at Portsmouth Naval Shipyard after completing her 50th deterrent patrol in September 1981. The ship completed overhaul in 1983 and conducted 7 more highly successful deterrent patrols.

USS JAMES K. POLK returned to Portsmouth Naval Shipyard in January 1986 for a third overhaul after completing her 58th deterrent patrol. POLK departed Portsmouth Naval Shipyard in November 1988 and sailed south for commencement of her Demonstration and Shakedown Operations (DASO). May 1989 marked the beginning of the final series of Poseidon strategic deterrent patrols for the POLK.

USS JAMES K. POLK celebrated her 25th year of commissioned service in April 1991. The POLK completed her 66th and final strategic deterrent patrol in August 1991. The POLK completed a nineteen-month shipyard conversion availability which removed her 16 Poseidon missiles and became a Dual Dry Deck Shelter Special Warfare submarine in March 1994. The POLK will conduct both special warfare operations and general submarine operations.

Keel Laid:	23 November 1963
Launched:	22 May 1965
Commissioned:	16 April 1966
Length:	425 Feet
Beam:	33 Feet
Displacement Surfaced:	About 7000 Tons
Displacement Submerged:	About 8200 Tons
Speed Submerged:	Over 20 Knots
Diving Depth:	Over 400 Feet
Built By:	Electric Boat Division of General Dynamics
Conversion from Polaris to Poseidon:	Newport News Shipbuilding
Conversion to Dry Deck Shelter–special Operations Platform:	Norfolk Naval Shipyard March 1994

HMS Talent

Length, Overall:	85.4 metres
Breadth, Moulded:	9.83 metres
Displacement (Standard):	5208.3 Tonnes
Complement:	14 Officers and 97 men
Builders:	Vickers Shipbuilding & Engineering Ltd. Barrow-in-Furness
Launched:	April, 1988 by HRH The Princess Royal
Armament:	Torpedoes and Missiles
Machinery:	Pressurised water nuclear reactor generating steam for geared turbines